PRAISE FOR ANDREA CATALANO

The First Witch of Boston

"Catalano's character and world-building ably bring to life an era fueled by superstition, repression, and intolerance . . . I can see this book appealing to the many fans of Ariel Lawhon's *The Frozen River* and Chris Bohjalian's *Hour of the Witch*, and eagerly look forward to reading whatever Catalano writes next."

—*Historical Novels Review*

"Fans of *The Frozen River* will love *The First Witch of Boston*! Fiery, outspoken Margaret Jones and her husband, Thomas, find themselves outliers in straitlaced Puritan Boston, but trouble back in England leaves them no choice but to make a home in Massachusetts. When Thomas draws the spite of a local widow and Margaret's skill with healing herbs rouses suspicion of black magic, both will find themselves battling witch-hunters in a court case destined to make history. Andrea Catalano draws a tender, intimate portrait of a marriage and a bold defense of an independent woman ahead of her time."

—Kate Quinn, *New York Times* bestselling author of *The Rose Code*

"Far and away the best novel I have ever read on this shocking chapter of our nation's history. It began decades before Salem, when the first woman to be targeted and executed for witchcraft in Massachusetts was Margaret Jones in 1648. In this story of Margaret Jones's tragedy, the settings, the characters, and the inexorable end are brought stunningly to life in a lyrically written tale of both love and betrayal."

—Margaret George, *New York Times* bestselling author of *The Memoirs of Cleopatra*

"A sumptuous and heartrending tale of the dark power of fear, loss, and love against all odds, *The First Witch of Boston* is a moving and accomplished debut."

—Heather Webb, *USA Today* bestselling author of *Queens of London*

"I knew I was going to love this novel from the first page, where Andrea Catalano immerses you in the world of seventeenth-century Boston. Her research is impeccable but never gets in the way of a gripping, emotional story. Thomas Jones's love for his outspoken, opinionated wife, Maggie, and hers for him, are beautifully described, and their tragedy is almost Shakespearean. This is a story that will stay with me for a long time."

—Gill Paul, internationally bestselling author of *Scandalous Women*

"Andrea Catalano's *The First Witch of Boston* conjures the treacherous history of witches, women, and injustice in America. Her research is ambitious and beyond impeccable. But it is the exquisite portrayal of a marriage that is the star at the beating heart of this novel, and the best I've read in years."

—Kimberly Brock, bestselling author of *The Fabled Earth* and *The Lost Book of Eleanor Dare*

"Catalano's timely and heart-wrenching treatise about the injustices against women in early America will leave traces etched in the reader's soul. Sensory, sensual, and evocative, *The First Witch of Boston* is the not-to-be-missed historical fiction debut of the season."

—Aimie K. Runyan, bestselling author of *The School for German Brides* and *Mademoiselle Eiffel*

"What a wonderful, moving novel. Catalano's debut is great historical fiction that brings the past alive in an exquisitely human, truly emotional way. I absolutely loved it."

—Megan Chance, bestselling author of *Glamorous Notions*

"A brilliant debut, full of passion, peril, and heartbreak. Between her gorgeous prose and her endearing characters, Andrea Catalano has established herself as one of the most exciting new authors in historical fiction."

—Olivia Hawker, bestselling author of *One for the Blackbird, One for the Crow*

"A rare and powerful debut—one that will hold you in thrall from beginning to end. Catalano gives voice to all the passion, anguish, and injustice surrounding the life and death of a woman who deserved a better fate than the one history dealt her. Lyrically written and impeccably researched, *The First Witch of Boston* settles into the deepest places in your soul, and remains there long after finishing. An artful, important masterpiece of historical fiction."

—Paulette Kennedy, bestselling author of *The Witch of Tin Mountain*

The LACEMAKER'S FORTUNE

The LACEMAKER'S FORTUNE

A Novel

ANDREA CATALANO

LAKE UNION
PUBLISHING

This is a work of fiction. Names, characters, organizations, places, events, and incidents are either products of the author's imagination or are used fictitiously.

Published by Lake Union Publishing, Seattle

www.apub.com

EU product safety contact: Amazon Media EU S. à r.l.
38, avenue John F. Kennedy, L-1855 Luxembourg
amazonpublishing-gpsr@amazon.com

ISBN-13: 9781662526015 (paperback)
ISBN-13: 9781662526022 (digital)

Cover design by Lisa Amoroso
Cover image: © Malgorzata Maj / ArcAngel Images; © Africa Studio, © Ajuga lace / Shutterstock; © Katsumi Murouchi / Getty

Printed in the United States of America

In loving memory of Shirley, my godmother, aunt, and friend, who taught me about good music, but more importantly, showed me how to bravely dance to my own beat

PART ONE

NEW YORK, MARCH 1879

CHAPTER ONE

Eileen Maguire shivered as she stepped off the Broadway train and into the frigid night. Her teeth audibly clattered, her spine convulsed in protest, her fingers curled and clamped tight within the thin-knit mittens, her eyes watered, and her legs and feet silently moaned and ached. She was pushed along by the evening rush hour of workers eager to be out of the cold and within the relative comfort of sanctuaries they called home: tenement room, boardinghouse, pub, tavern, shanty under the elevated tracks.

Head held down, chin burrowed within the coat collar she clutched tight against the elements, Eileen quickly descended the stairs with the throngs of others and reached the street below. She noted through bleary eyes how the workers and commuters scattered in every possible direction, much like cockroaches do when you discover their clandestine hiding place beneath some piece of furniture or crockery.

The bitter, biting wind found Eileen before she could evade its teeth; it gnawed its way through her thin wool coat and laid siege to her skin. Though she endeavored not to utter such words, Eileen found that she swore under her breath, "Damn old coat!"

The coat was, indeed, old. It had been secondhand when she was fifteen and still in County Limerick, where her mother had given it to her. Two years later it was far too small. But it was all she had, and Lord knew she wasn't able to afford any better here in New York City.

She thought of supper in Shay's Pub—hopefully mutton stew. And, on such a snowy, ghastly cold night, she would not be so averse to the whiskey that she knew her sister, Mary, would offer her when she sat down to sup.

It was not far now to Shay's. Eileen very seldom took the elevated train from the milliner's where she worked, on Broadway and Twenty-Eighth; train fare meant less money for her to put away in the rusty can, which she hid behind a loose brick in the wall of her bedroom. Today was different only because, early that morning, as Eileen was heading off to earn her wages and Mary was finishing up with her night's work, Mary had pressed a coin into her mittened hand on the steps of the boardinghouse.

"Take the damn train, Eileen. It's too cold, and feels like snow."

"Mary—"

"Hush up! Besides, I had a good night. More eager fellas than usual . . ."

Eileen had tried to ignore the weariness that showed in the droop of Mary's eyelids, the irritated swelling of her lips. As she kissed her sister's forehead in gratitude and brushed past her, Eileen's nose had been filled with the familiar scent of cheap lavender perfume, whiskey, musky male perspiration, and tobacco smoke—Mary's fragrance since their arrival in America. *She's beginning to look older than her nineteen years.*

Now, as she continued in the darkness, Eileen sucked in her lips. One of Mary's coworkers had once told her to always protect her lips from the cold, "for you've got a pretty, pouty pair, and the cold will dry them out and ruin them!" As she walked on toward the pub, she drew up her collar around her mouth; she relaxed her lips, and in doing so, the sharp taste of powder and sweat filled her mouth—a lingering piece of the kiss given to her sister that morning.

Morning seemed a lifetime ago; it always did at the end of the day. Ten hours of lacemaking had an odd way of doing that. As she crossed beneath the elevated train tracks and headed to Shay's, she saw Harry in his usual spot, sitting beside the skeletal metal framework that supported the tracks above. She waved to the war veteran in his wheelchair; his legs and one arm had been reduced to stumps some years back at a place called Antietam. She knew this because, two years ago, she had worked up the courage to ask him how it had happened. He did not seem to begrudge telling her; it was as though she had asked him his middle name.

"Helloooo, Eileen!" Harry called over the deafening screech and beastly huff and puff of the train above. He waved his stump of an arm, and the inhuman look of it seemed to fit in well with the macabre surroundings of the tracks' angular, sharp support structure.

When Eileen and Mary had first arrived in New York City in 1877, the sight of so many men disabled in frightening manners similar to Harry's had perturbed her. Mary had scolded her many times for "gawking," as she had put it. But Eileen had never seen such morbidly curious sights back in Ireland; she could not help but stare until, feeling her own appendages tingle and flinch with the thought, she had looked away, terrified. But the sight of maimed veterans no longer disturbed her, for to see a curious thing so frequently eventually removes its intrigue, its dreadfulness, until, to some degree—though it made Eileen feel guilty to admit it to herself—the thing becomes more commonplace and less jarring.

Quickly, Eileen whispered beseechingly to the Lord that he forgive her, and that he watch over the likes of Harry. "Blessed are the meek . . ."

Finally, Eileen made it to Shay's. She ran inside to be out of the cold night, pushing on the door with all her might and tumbling within the belly of warmth, food, and alcohol-induced cheer. She spotted Mary at her usual table with her usual group of friends; it was difficult for the eye to miss the various heads with artfully arranged henna- and peroxide-dyed locks, the brightly colored dresses and mouths, the high-pitched, carefree, cynical, daring-confrontation laughter.

"Eileen! How's about something to warm you up?" Mary stood up, a glass of amber-colored liquid in her hand. Her naturally lovely, blond locks bobbed with her movement. Eileen's, in sharp contrast, were dark auburn, but equally as curly and unruly.

Eileen noted how Mary's words somewhat slurred, how her cheeks were reddened beneath the layer of rouge.

"Be a sport, Eileen, it's Saturday!" yelled Claire from beside Mary.

Indeed, it was Saturday! Eileen had forgotten; she often lost track of the dreary days. A sudden sensation of freedom and relief came over her—*no work tomorrow, Sunday!* She took the seat beside her sister and soon found herself hungrily finishing off a plate of Shay's mutton stew. And when Mary put a glass of whiskey before her, Eileen readily accepted it, hoping it would be the final step in returning feeling to her fingers and toes.

The night progressed, and though she was exhausted from the week's work, Eileen felt giddy from the whiskey and reluctant to leave the warmth of Shay's. The storm outside howled; the chilling confines of her tiny room on the top floor of Mrs. Brown's boardinghouse were reason enough to make her linger in the packed pub. She watched as a few of Mary's friends took up with clients, or "fellas," and headed outside, some returning in a matter of minutes, some after an hour. And though Mary and Claire and their friends grew more inebriated as the night progressed, and though they laughed gaily, Eileen noted the lack of sparkle in their eyes. Another Saturday night, another night of work, another night of strangers taking one more piece of each girl away with them. Eileen thought of old Miss Annie back at the boardinghouse, who had lost her vision as well as her mind to the French pox she had earned from her years working the same trade. It was of utmost urgency that Mary move on from her current line of work, and as quickly as possible.

"Sure, I'll have another," she said to her sister, who seemed glad of her answer.

It had broken Eileen's heart at first, what Mary was doing to earn money after she lost her job in the milliner's factory for calling their boss a "stupid, fat cow" in Gaelic. Another factory girl, eager to rise up in the world, had promptly translated the insult to the boss, who then, without hesitation, terminated Mary on the spot. It had happened not long after their arrival in New York City. In all honesty, Eileen would admit that life in America was not what they had hoped it would be. There were no streets paved with gold (not that Eileen was ever so gullible that she had actually believed that), and for two young Irish girls, it was no land of boundless opportunity. How many times had Eileen been called "Irish scum" when she applied for work? But she would not think on that tonight, not when she was feeling warm and relatively happy.

"Warming up, eh?" Mary laughed as she noticed Eileen unbuttoning her dress's collar.

"That whiskey does the trick, sister," Eileen replied.

Ma had sent the two of them off to America in hopes of their beginning anew. Da had died from fever when Eileen was eight years old. He had been a solemn man who mostly kept to himself, and Eileen had never felt any fatherly warmth from him. With his passing, the three of them had to downsize to a quarter-acre holding, the working of which barely paid their rent and barely kept them fed. Ma had thought her girls would find a better life in America than in County Limerick, with its emptying crofts and failing soil. She had especially high hopes for Eileen, who had been taught by Sister Theresa, a nun from the local parish, to do fine lacework.

Sister Theresa, a bespectacled, tiny wisp of a woman who seemed overwhelmed by the black habit she wore every day of her life as a nun, was soft spoken and kindly. She had made it her life's work—second after being a bride to Christ—to teach the art of lacemaking to the young girls of Ireland. The church had sent her to the west of County Limerick for this sole purpose during the worst of the Great Famine, so as to give relief to the poor and starving by providing them a trade, and had continued to share her skills ever since. Despite the continuing exodus of young Irish to places that could offer more of a future—Liverpool, Glasgow, Halifax, Boston, New York City—Sister Theresa prevailed in her task. When she had invited Eileen and Mary to become her students, they were two of only twelve young girls in the parish to do so.

Mary had lasted only four weeks under her tutorage. She lacked the patient disposition and attention to detail required for the art of lacemaking. The girls would sit in a circle around one candle, and each girl would have before her a glass pitcher of water, which helped to magnify the candlelight onto her lacemaking. Mary claimed it was never enough light, but really the problem was that Mary was farsighted and could not focus her eyes on the intricate work. She soon returned to help Ma on the croft. But Eileen had not only the required patience and demeanor but also the talent for detail, and the passion for it. When Sister Theresa presented her with her own set of bone bobbins, made from the boiled bones of a gray bog heron, it was as though she had been given a treasure. Sister Theresa lavished praise upon her, and Eilen loved her for it. In fact, she was so enamored with the nun's kindness, softly spoken words, and ethereal piety, Eileen fancied that perhaps she, too, should be a bride of Christ.

When she had confessed this to Mary, her sister doubled over in laughter until she shed tears. She went and told Ma, who only smiled and shook her head. "Nay, my wee one, there is more to life than that way."

"And what might that *more* be?" Eileen demanded. "Being a crofter's wife and toiling away for a pittance, watching your husband die and winding up a lonely widow?"

Eileen had regretted the words as soon as they had left her mouth. Mary's laughter had ceased, and she shook her head ruefully with an accusatory look. "Oh, Eileen, no."

Ma had approached Eileen and raised a hand to strike her, but when Eileen shrank from her, she stopped. After composing herself, Ma said, "Aye, and I'll not have you two end up like me. You'll go away from here to America, if it's the last thing this lonely widow does."

And so with money they had saved from the sale of Eileen's finest bobbin lace, needle lace, crochet lace, and knit lace—because Sister Theresa had taught her eager, talented pupil all the lacemaking techniques—Mary and Eileen had left for America with Ma's urging. They promised to send money home for Ma to join them there.

But six months after bidding her daughters farewell, Ma had died from consumption.

Angry with herself for giving in to such dismal recollections, irate that her glass was empty, Eileen slammed it down upon the table and muttered an oath under her breath.

So, when Eileen and Mary landed in New York City, they struggled to find work. Eventually they were both hired in the milliner's shop. Two years later, Eileen still toiled there, though she had been promoted to strictly lacework. Even her boss was amazed with her talents. Eileen knew that she was far more qualified to work in a proper millinery shop, but the day that a millinery shop took on an Irish girl was the day that Jesus would return from the heavens, Eileen thought with a chuckle.

Two years had come and gone, two years in which Eileen grew from a naive, pious fifteen-year-old to a wise, fairly shrewd, still somewhat pious seventeen-year-old. She and Mary had a pact of sorts: Mary would continue in her current line of work, for there was no denying that it paid handsomely, and the deal that she had struck up with Mrs. Brown, the boardinghouse mistress, was a fair one, as far as how much she paid for use of her room. Eileen had once proposed that she, too, enter the trade, though she was secretly horrified at the prospect, but Mary adamantly dismissed this, insisting that Eileen keep up her work at the milliner's. Eileen's measly wage managed to pay the rent on her tiny closet of a room on the top floor of Mrs. Brown's, which was reserved for boarders who were not prostitutes. The frugal lodgings left enough to save some coin in the rusty can behind the brick.

The two both hid away portions of their earnings in the rusty can, along with a printed advertisement encouraging settlers to move to San Francisco. The Maguire sisters had their hearts set on San Francisco to open their own millinery shop. Eileen, of course, would do the lacemaking, design, and fitting, and Mary would be the accountant, manager, and advertiser. Mary was a shrewd businesswoman and good with money despite her drinking habit.

No matter how grim the days seemed, Eileen would take solace in their dream, and remind Mary of it, so that she might see her sister's tired, powdered, and rouged face alight with hope.

Just one more year of this, and we'll leave this nasty place, and head for San Francisco.

Eileen glanced at the clock hanging on the wall behind the bar. *Ten o'clock, two hours before Sunday.*

Shay's was packed at this point. Weary yet raucous workers squeezed up against enterprising whores. Wide-eyed children searched for family amid the chaos, and the elderly lounged against the wall, drinks in hands, toothless, simple grins on their faces.

Eileen watched as Danny O'Connell made his way to the battered, beer-stained piano, which was situated to the left of the bar, on a makeshift stage of sorts. Tall, skinny, gawky Danny waved bashfully as the bar erupted in cheers. He sat his bony frame on the worn stool, pausing for a moment to catch his breath; Danny had just come from work—hard labor at the gasworks—and wore a grime stain upon his forehead that no one had pointed out to him. A barman quickly brought him a double whiskey and nodded, his eyes eager and encouraging, longing for proper entertainment to distract from the cacophony of drunken oaths and solicitations, much like the rest of the bar's patrons.

The loud din softened and all focused on Danny. His little, dark eyes nervously darted over the crowd as he quickly turned toward the piano, hunching his lanky frame over the keys as he downed the double whiskey in the blink of an eye. He sighed, flexing his weary fingers above the keys, and began to play some sort of jig.

It was a ritual; Danny always began this way. Eileen, Mary, and the other girls sat at the table nearest the stage. As Eileen let the happy tune wash over her, she considered Danny's thin, mouselike, pale face fringed with greasy, dark hair, just beginning to gray at the temples. "Mary, how is it that such a laborer can play the piano so well?"

"Don't you know?" Mary asked. "They say he was a priest in Galway, and that's how he learned to play the piano, for he played the organ at the monastery."

"A *priest*?"

"Aye! And they say that he was discovered to have taken up with one of the nuns, and he was to be defrocked! But he left for America during the night because he dreaded that his folly would shame his mother."

"No!"

"Eileen, I couldn't make that sort of thing up even if I tried!"

As Eileen looked up at Danny and tried to picture him in a priest's frock, he glanced down at her and flashed her a grin missing two teeth. Eileen smiled back and turned away quickly, mortified that a man who was once a priest might try to flirt with her.

"I think Danny fancies you," Mary said, letting out a harsh giggle.

The thought repulsed Eileen. Danny had to be more than old enough to be her father, never mind the fact that he could have been her priest! "Yuck!" she replied, scrunching up her face to shoot her sister a nasty glance.

"Don't you fancy anyone here tonight, Eileen?" asked Mary as she took another gulp of whiskey, hiccuped loudly, and looked about the packed bar.

Eileen followed her sister's glance. Most of the bar's male patrons were Irish, of course. Eileen's eyes fell upon the fine form of a young man she had often seen in Shay's. He was loud and obviously drunk, stripped down to his too-tight undershirt beneath brown leather suspenders. His hair was blond, curly, and cropped short, his blond beard kept neat. He was not very tall yet quite broad, and when he glanced with his mates toward the table of colorful, lively prostitutes, Eileen's heart fluttered. His green eyes flashed, his fine skin glowed with perspiration, and the bar's gas lighting discovered his teeth, which seemed to shine.

"Oh my." Eileen sighed before she could stop herself.

Mary sighed, too. "Oh, so Rory Murphy has caught your eye, eh? No good, that one!"

"Who are you talking about?" asked Claire, whose words were beginning to slur together.

"Rory Murphy, that's who," Mary shot back.

"Ugh! Bad news, he is! He'll break your heart and forget he ever knew you," said Claire with a cold glance at Rory.

Eileen allowed her gaze to linger on Rory. He was all vitality and vigor—every aspect of his handsomeness exuded health and virility. Eileen imagined herself surrounded by his manly warmth, in his arms, his lips searching for hers . . . "Well, he's nice to look at, nonetheless," said Eileen as she tried to dismiss Rory from her mind.

"True, to be sure, sister. Just look at how tight his shirt is over that big, strong chest . . ."

Eileen giggled along with Mary, and they caught Rory's attention. He tried to act casual as he grinned at the two of them and flexed his brawny biceps. The sisters' titters grew to hysterical laughter, for they could not help themselves. But someone else soon caught Rory's focus, and Eileen looked to see who it was.

It was Lucia, the new girl working out of Mrs. Brown's. Petite in stature, yet fashionably voluptuous, Lucia was, indeed, breathtaking: dark hair, pale skin, and sparkling blue eyes. Eileen had never seen such a beautiful Italian before Lucia.

The girls at Mrs. Brown's—mostly Irish and Scottish—had ostracized Lucia since her arrival one month before, claiming it was because she was a "filthy Italian." Even Mrs. Brown treated Lucia with disdain and put her in one of the worst rooms in the house, despite the fact that Lucia was the most successful girl there. But Eileen suspected that it was just plain jealousy that caused the girls to spurn Lucia.

With a determined step, Lucia marched past Rory and his mates, and headed straight toward the stage. She stepped up and bent over to whisper in Danny's ear, who listened as he played. He nodded, and Lucia straightened and faced the audience, a bold smile upon her lips, colored the same scarlet as her suggestive dress.

Eventually, the bar's patrons directed their attention to her.

"Damn tart," said Mary under her breath.

Danny began the introduction of a song familiar to any Catholic's ear, "Ave Maria."

"What a brazen whore," muttered Claire, and Eileen had to stifle the laugh that came to her lips as she eyed Claire's attire, which by no means labeled her a wallflower.

Lucia began to sing, and instantly, the bar was silent, rapt. When she finished, Shay's erupted with thunderous applause. Lucia beamed, curtsied most graciously, and headed directly toward Rory Murphy, who looked as though he'd seen an angel.

Danny O'Connell wept at the piano; he often wept after drinking a few whiskeys and playing a ballad to which a girl sang along. But Eileen wondered, for a moment, if perhaps it was because this particular song conjured up memories of his monastery in Galway.

"There goes your Rory Murphy," said Mary as they watched the handsome Irishman and Italian beauty leave Shay's.

Certainly there were no two better-looking people in Shay's, no two people more worthy of each other in their beauty, than Rory and Lucia. Eileen sighed and turned away, suddenly aware that the whiskey's giddiness was wearing off. To Mary's shock, she ordered up another round.

"Say, how's about a song from you, Mary?" bellowed Claire.

"I don't know that I can top that last act," replied Mary, though she looked up at the stage excitedly. Mary must have known that her fine voice would be sure to drum up business for the rest of her night.

"Go on, then!" called another one of the girls.

"Well, maybe," Mary said as she headed straight to the stage and to Danny, who was getting over his good cry.

Eileen laughed; Mary never shied away from attention. Two years ago, the whole scene in Shay's—the spectacle of watching her sister ply her trade—had been deeply disturbing for Eileen. But one cannot remain appalled for long—the more you witness an appalling thing, the less appalling it seems, and the more mundane it becomes. And when she and Mary excitedly counted the money in the rusty can each week,

Eileen found that she could grow to accept her sister's trade temporarily if it meant they could be completely rid of it someday.

Mary sang a gay tune from a play that had been running on Broadway last year. The audience sang along and cheered for Mary, who paraded this way and that as she smiled and sang, flaunting her assets. Eileen envied her sister's curves. Surely, if she ate and drank as much as her sister, then her own figure would be just as full and fashionable. But there was not enough money for the both of them to eat like wealthy women. It was more important for Mary to eat more, as she made a living from her fine form.

Mary finished her performance with a flourish; the patrons of Shay's applauded her talents, and soon enough she was heading out the door in the company of an eager customer. Eileen watched this transpire; she took another gulp of her drink and reluctantly turned to Claire for conversation.

"So, have you heard the news?" Claire shouted to her over the noise of the pub.

"What news?"

"You've got a new neighbor at Mrs. Brown's."

"Who? When?"

"A young fellow, moved into the room between yours and Mr. Goldman's this afternoon."

"What do you know about him?" asked Eileen. Her eyebrows drew together, her eyes probed Claire's.

"Calm down, dearie! If you're so nervous about a stranger living in the room next to yours, then you shouldn't be living in a boardinghouse in New York City!"

Eileen tried to relax a bit, for Claire spoke sense, for once.

Claire continued, all the while searching the pub for prospective business. "I hear he's quite good-looking; I've not seen him yet for myself."

"Who says so?"

"Your sister, for one, as well as Maggie and Beth."

"My sister finds every young man good-looking," Eileen said with a cynical laugh into her glass.

"Perhaps that's for the best, don't you think?" Claire shot her a steady stare that Eileen thought she could not be capable of after such quantities of drink.

"How old is this fellow?"

"Oh, don't know, perhaps twenty."

"What does he do?"

"Christ, Eileen, I know as much about him as you!"

"Well, there's Beth coming in. Let's ask her." The plump, heavily rouged brunette made her way through the crowd toward their table. She looked as though she was ready for the night to be over, knowing full well it wasn't.

"Beth," Claire called as Beth plopped on the bench across the table from them, "what do you know about the new boarder at Mrs. Brown's?"

Beth rubbed her hands together vigorously before taking hold of the whiskey glass before her. "Oh, yes, the new fellow! Wait till you two see him!"

"That handsome, eh?" asked Eileen, doubtful.

"Oh, aye! He's got the room next to yours, you lucky girl!" She and Claire howled in laughter. Eileen waited for them to finish the laugh at her expense, drumming her calloused fingers on the table.

"Right," Beth continued after she caught her breath and read Eileen's expression. "So he's quite a handsome thing: very tall, solid-looking. The sort that can carry a gal and knock her at the same time, you know?"

"Oh, *now* you're talking! That's the best sort!" Claire shouted, and again the two burst into laughter.

"Anyhow," Beth continued, "he's very pale and blond, fine blue eyes, lovely face, all that sort of thing. But that being said, he's a queer sort."

"How so?" asked Eileen and Claire simultaneously.

"Well, he dresses very somber, black wool. And he carries himself like a gent. We girls gave him a hearty greeting, of course"—she paused to chuckle and nudge Claire with her elbow—"but he seemed quite cold, sort of snobbish, like church folk."

"Well, he's certainly picked the wrong boardinghouse then, eh?" asked Claire as she looked into her glass with disdain.

"What does he do?" asked Eileen.

"Do? Well, he didn't have many belongings, but he did have a number of boxes filled with books."

"Books?" shouted Claire.

"Yeah, books. And I overheard Mrs. Brown say to Maggie that he was a tutor or translator or something."

"Interesting . . ." trailed off Eileen, now deeply intrigued.

"What's his name, do you know that much?" asked Claire, winking at a fellow who happened to catch her eye.

"Mrs. Brown says he's Stanley Jones."

"There's a common name if I ever heard one," said Eileen with a sniff. "So, is he Welsh?"

"Doooon't look it," answered Beth, exaggerating her Irish brogue. "Not one bit. In fact, I would say he's quite foreign-looking."

"So, do you think he's got money?" asked a hopeful Claire.

"Claire, you stupid cow, what on earth would he be doing in Mrs. Brown's if that were the case?" shot Beth, and Eileen couldn't help but giggle.

"Fine, be that way. I'm going to fetch that ugly son of a bitch by the bar," said Claire as she stormed off. Eileen and Beth didn't look to see who the ugly son of a bitch might be.

"Stanley Jones, eh?" asked Eileen as she watched Mary heading back into the pub, toward their table.

"Aye," replied Beth after finishing off the whiskey. "Probably the handsomest man I've ever seen . . ." She drifted off, her sad brown eyes trailing over the pub, looking guilty, as though she had admitted to something most reproachful.

"Hand me the rest of that bottle, will you?" asked Mary as she sat beside Beth, smelling of cold air and booze.

Eileen took note of her sister's irritated lips. "That was a quick one."

"And thank God, on a night so damned cold as this!" Mary declared as she poured out the last of the whiskey into her glass.

"Couldn't talk him into something more?" asked Beth.

"Fellas don't want to walk far on a night like this. They just want a quick suck in the alley." Mary must have sensed Eileen's inner cringe at her blunt words, for she smiled and said, "Eileen, go on up there beside Danny and give us a song!"

"Yes, Eileen, go on then!" encouraged Beth.

Eileen knew that she had a fine voice, but her courage always slacked at the thought of singing in front of the whole of Shay's. But with plenty of whiskey in her belly, Eileen suddenly felt bold enough to grant her sister's request.

"What should I sing?" she asked, unable to restrain the eager grin that came to her face.

"Oh, any old thing," said Mary, going to Eileen's side and pulling her off the bench.

"Oh, Eileen, do sing 'Marble Halls'!" shouted Beth as Mary brought Eileen up to the stage.

Eileen felt herself turn crimson as the crowd's hopeful eyes fixed upon her.

"'Marble Halls,' all right, Danny?" said Mary before jumping down from the stage.

Danny, his skin shining with perspiration, glanced over at Eileen as he finished the ditty he was playing. He smiled his goofy grin and nodded.

Eileen, for one brief moment, thought she might run from the stage or perhaps forget to breathe. She suddenly realized that she needed to piss, and worried that perhaps she would not be able to hold it. She glanced nervously at Shay's patrons, noted how tired and weary they all collectively looked. Yet she held them captive—they were expecting something pleasing and delicious—and for a brief moment, Eileen fancied that she was capable of magic.

Danny charmed the familiar tune from the worn piano keys. The melody filled Eileen, took hold of her, slipped fingers beneath her ribs and underarms and lifted her.

"I dreamt I dwelt in marble halls,
with vassals and serfs at my side . . ."

CHAPTER TWO

Lawrence "Laurie" Barnard donned his hat of buffalo fur, which matched his fashionably regal wool coat lined and trimmed in the same. He slid his long-fingered hands into black leather gloves, which had been custom-made by the best haberdasher in London. One of those fine, gloved hands reached for a crystal glass of brandy. The glass rested upon a buffet, which a Dutch ancestor had brought to America in 1652, though the buffet was thought to date to somewhere around 1550.

Laurie downed the brandy. He longed to be out in the night. He swore under his breath at his friend James for being late once again. Should he take another brandy? He sighed, bored with his evening before it had even begun.

He peered at his reflection in an immense gilded mirror. His skin was growing moist with perspiration; had he known that James would be so late, he would not have donned all his layers so soon. He pulled a handkerchief from an inner pocket of his coat and lightly dabbed at his forehead. When he was finished with this task, his expression changed to one of satisfaction. He was fond of his fair skin and his contrasting dark brows and hair; he thought his green eyes expressive yet not so emotive as to be considered effete. His mouth was wide and hard-set until he smiled.

Laurie endeavored not to smile, for he found it transformed his face into a rather boyish countenance. Everything about his grin—the wide spread of it, the rise of his cheeks—struck him as looking decidedly childish.

"Where are you off to?"

He glanced up, startled by the appearance of his mother in the foyer.

Mrs. Barnard walked toward him, scrutinizing his attire, and reached out with thin, pale hands to adjust his coat collar. He acquiesced to her, though he knew his mother's preoccupation with such details was purely out of concern for appearances rather than his well-being.

"Tell me, Laurie, where are you off to on such a bitter night?" Her gray eyes focused on his. She would not be denied the truth.

"Going out with friends is all," he replied, ending with a nonchalant sigh. He looked down at her as she fussed with his scarf, tucking it within his coat.

"Which ones?"

"One, Mother. James Whitcomb. Do you approve?"

Her pinched face relaxed into a hint of a smile. She nodded. "Yes, I do. Why, I just yesterday had tea with his mother. Such a respectable man, destined for great things."

Laurie could only think of the James he knew, who once paid for a street whore to accompany him on the coach journey to Yale so that she could pleasure him whenever he so desired.

He cleared his throat. "Quite right, I should think."

She laid a cold, dry hand upon his cheek. This sudden touch, this rare physical display, took Laurie by surprise.

"As are you, my dear. You are destined for greatness—even more so than your father, God rest his soul."

His gaze faltered. He could not seem to drum up the proper words to respond.

She removed her hand from his face, turned quickly upon her heel, and made her way out of the foyer and back to the drawing room.

The doorbell sounded; Seamus, the butler, appeared in the foyer to open the door.

There stood James, resplendent in gray wool and buffalo fur, much like Laurie. He removed his hat, revealing a thick mane of strawberry-blond hair coaxed into submission with a profuse amount of Macassar oil. Without a glance, he handed his hat to Seamus and strode toward Laurie with arms spread open. Clasping Laurie roughly on the shoulders, he asked, "Have you recovered from last night's festivities? Are you ready for the opera? There's a masquerade following, but you know that's just a polite term for a parade of the finest—"

"Ahem!" Laurie interrupted James with a loud clearing of the throat as his eyes gestured toward the doorway, where his mother had just exited.

James peered in that direction, then nodded that he understood, a conspiratorial smirk upon his lips.

"Let's not linger. I've been waiting a damnably long time for you."

James gave a joking salute. "Aye aye, my captain." He retrieved his hat from the waiting Seamus, and he and Laurie made their way into the startlingly cold, snowy night, avoiding icy patches as they alighted into James's coach.

Laurie settled in against fine Spanish leather upholstery, shivering as he did so.

"Have some of this to warm you up," said James as he passed an engraved sterling flask to Laurie.

Laurie took a hearty swig—Highland Park scotch. James always managed to have it shipped directly to him from the Orkneys, at God knew what cost.

"You know, on a night like this, the whores retreat off the street like rats! I tried to find a couple so that we might warm up before the opera . . ." James trailed off into chuckles as he glanced out the window.

The thought of such a thing bored Laurie, so he changed the subject. "Which opera house are we off to? Academy of Music?"

"Of course," answered James with a nod. "My, it's good to have you back here in New York!" he exclaimed as he reached over and slapped

Laurie's knee. "Don't know why you had to go all the way over to England for your studies, really."

"A change of scenery, that's all," said Laurie as he reflected on his years at Cambridge. He could recollect only dismal days spent in the stuffy confines of the King's College library, dusks crossing the old bridges of the River Cam, nights in the brothels on the west side of town. He smiled at the thought of the girls leaning out the windows of the half-timbered whorehouses teetering on the edges of the Cam; those same houses had serviced the scholars of Cambridge for over five hundred years. Each time he entered those dingy, ancient walls and fucked to exhaustion, he felt that he was in some way leaving his mark for posterity in the records of Cambridge vice. In his mind, he likened it to the day of his matriculation, when he signed the university's record of scholars, formally entering his name in an honored history with the likes of Marlowe, Cromwell, and Newton. Laurie still derived a thrill from the memory of that moment. He thought to himself that he must somehow live up to this honor, through some act of brilliance, artistic triumph, or perhaps a violent, yet worthy, end.

"Have more," said James with another pass of the shining flask. "You're growing pensive on me, and we'll not have that this evening, my friend."

Laurie made a silent toast to himself, his pursuits—both intellectual and carnal—at Cambridge, and the night ahead. He swallowed the whisky, savoring its hot trail down to his stomach, and thought how sweet it was to be in New York again. Cambridge had been a good romp, but New York beckoned like one of Odysseus's sirens, guiding him to some orgy beyond his wildest imagination.

James led the way from the private seating area to the opera box that his family had owned since the opera house's founding. He held aside the heavy, cigar-scented red-velvet drape for Laurie.

From below, the orchestra bellowed a myriad of sounds in preparation for the evening's performance. As Laurie took his seat, a feeling of pleasant anticipation came over him. The odd tunings of the instruments breathed an excitement into his ears. *Perhaps,* he thought to himself, *just perhaps, tonight my senses will be awakened, and this damn apathy of mine will be banished.*

This sense of apathy, as he liked to term it, had plagued Laurie like a lingering malaise since the spring of his final year of study at Cambridge. He could mark it to the April day when, while deep in reading, he found that Voltaire's cynical humor had been lost on him.

"Why can I no longer laugh at *Candide*?" he had muttered to himself. He thumbed through the novella's pages while sitting in the King's College library.

Things seemed to compound from there. When he crossed the ancient bridge toward King's grazing fields, the sight of the plump cows did not stir within him that secret, boyish delight that it always had. Later, in the pub, his drinking seemed a chore, rather than a respite. And when he headed to the brothels and paid Molly for her pleasures, he found that his culmination, though temporarily satisfying and pleasing, did not deliver that oddly peaceful-yet-triumphant sense of gratification that it once had.

This aspect of his "apathy" troubled him the most, for Laurie always had a voracious appetite for the opposite sex, had found his hungers quite satisfied within the thighs of a willing wench. Though his appetite had not lessened, it had become increasingly difficult to find complete satisfaction beyond the initial physical sort. As Laurie had confessed to James upon his return home to New York, "It's not enough to fuck; it does not satisfy my inner curiosities and desires."

James, much to Laurie's expectations, had looked both dumbfounded and utterly confused at this. Soon, his face had relaxed and he'd chuckled, slapping Laurie's shoulder and declaring: "Laurie, you just need to *diversify* your diversions!"

Since his confession to James, his best friend had launched them both down an almost nightly path of debauched revelries. Laurie's contemplations of deeds done the night before would cause him much amazement, as well as perhaps a twinge of guilt. He would never, of course, admit this to James.

And so, upon hearing the musing sounds of the orchestra's warm-up, he felt a sense of hope that perhaps he might find his boredom lifted, his spirits stirred, by the sound of some beautiful song.

"What's on the program for this evening?" he asked James, who was busy downing a glass of brandy.

After a satisfied sigh, James replied, "Mr. Mozart's *Don Giovanni*. Do you approve?"

Laurie smiled as a sense of eagerness took hold. He recalled the last time he had seen *Don Giovanni* performed: He had been a first-year student at Cambridge and had joined classmates on a sojourn to London in order to see Mozart's opera. The sentiments that had stirred within him as he'd witnessed that opera were so overwhelming that he had wept, for the sound was so beautiful, and he had to quickly dash the tears from his cheeks before his friends might glimpse and mock him.

"It's my favorite," he replied to James, and he secretly hoped that his expectations would be met once again, and that his ears would be filled with a sound just as beautiful as three years prior.

But his expectations had been set too lofty for mortals to reach, especially the mortals who comprised the orchestra and cast of the Academy of Music's production of *Don Giovanni*.

He considered the sound flat; the orchestra never seemed to find its wings and soar. The cast of performers was, he thought, crude and rough, struggling to do justice to the opera's lyrics. Disdainful, he appraised the whole production as amateur, and imparted this to James, who readily agreed, for he was no connoisseur of opera. Gone was Laurie's hope for musical transcendence; he and James began to find amusement in the performers' gestures, their missteps, their feeble attempts at conveying true drama and emotion. They turned their attentions to the audience and gossiped like their own mothers when they spotted spectators whom they knew, which were many. They drank the decanter of brandy dry, called for another.

But none of this eased Laurie's feeling of anxiety over his ennui. What could he do to awaken his senses and curiosity once again?

So, later that evening, when both were exceedingly drunk, Laurie did not decline when James suggested they try something new at Hattie McFee's brothel, their whorehouse of choice.

How foolish, how regretfully foolish.

After collapsing onto the plush settee, removing his condom, fastening his pants, and catching his breath, Laurie began to rue his decision to partake in James's idea.

Yes, it had been interesting, and yes, he had come fairly quickly, for Josie was a skilled whore, knew just how to move when one took her from behind. But the whole act didn't sit well with him, and rather than stirring his curiosity, it had convinced him never to engage in this sort of thing again.

Laurie contemplated all this as he lackadaisically looked on; Josie was still performing fellatio on James, who seemed to be having a difficult time reaching his climax. Laurie leaned his heavy forehead against his hand, rubbing to hopefully encourage sobriety. He noted absently that James's cock was rather small—not that he had seen many cocks, he reasoned with himself, but it was certainly smaller than his own.

"You got off quite quickly," said James, somewhat breathless.

"Perhaps you take too long," Laurie replied in a bored tone.

James blushed a bright red, giving the appearance of a virgin schoolboy.

"Maybe this just isn't your thing, this . . ." Laurie tried to think of how best to label this particular sex act, but eventually gave up.

"Perhaps you're right. Just thought it would be something different," replied James as his gaze fixed on Josie's efforts.

"Tell you what," said Laurie, after tidying his collar, "I'll go downstairs and leave you two alone to finish things up." He scooped up his hat and overcoat before making his way to the bedchamber's door, not caring to look back at the room's activity.

"Why don't you fetch yourself another gal? I plan on spending the night here. No reason you shouldn't have more fun."

The thought of fucking again was as mundane, as commonplace, as the thought of taking a stroll in the park. He ran a hand over his hair as he stared at the brass doorknob, noticing his warped reflection upon its polished surface. *What can be done? What might remedy this numbness? There must be something, something waiting for me out in the darkness.*

"Don't worry about me, James. I'll make my own way home." And with that he left the bedchamber.

Despite his expensive, plush layers of wool and buffalo fur, Laurie shivered mightily as he strode south on Broadway. He swore at himself under his breath for leaving the brothel and therefore forgoing what would have been a relatively warm, comfortable ride home in James's coach.

On his swift departure from Hattie McFee's, the doorman had asked Laurie if he needed a hired coach. In his pensive state, Laurie had declined, heading out into the bitter night with no particular destination. He knew this was folly, that he should simply return home on such an inclement night, but some inner curiosity drove him in the opposite direction, toward the old Bowery.

He thought that perhaps the brisk walk would do him good, allow him to get his thoughts back in order. Soon he had the fancy of walking the whole length of Broadway, to its southernmost point, and then hiring a coach to bring him home. But at about the half-way point to his destination, Laurie had grown bored and decidedly chilled.

Perhaps I should make an adventure of this, find the roughest pub I can and warm up with a drink. Laurie glanced at the various establishments lining Broadway, but none struck his fancy. He decided to head off Broadway, and turned west onto a side street. Beneath the elevated tracks, he warily squinted into the darkness to be sure that no thief or criminal lurked to make a move for his pockets or his throat.

"Good evening to you, gentleman!" a voice bellowed from beside a support beam.

Startled, Laurie stopped short and looked to see a cripple in a chair, bundled beneath a ragtag bunch of blankets. The vagrant waved his stump of an arm in greeting. Laurie walked on, feeling awkward and annoyed in his present situation. "Hello," he responded gruffly as he averted his eyes. His wallet was well within the confines of his jacket, and he was certainly not about to stop, unfasten his layers, and fish for a bit of coin. Had the cash been readily available in his coat pocket, he would certainly have given some. This acknowledgment somewhat appeased his sense of guilt.

He walked on and spotted what looked to be a rowdy, crowded pub on the next corner. Glancing above the door, he was able to make out a sign that read **SHAY'S**.

"This will suit me fine," he declared to himself in a quiet mutter, so that he might hearten himself for the unfamiliar and quite foreign establishment.

Swinging the door open, he was met with a blast of heat and the sharp odor of sweating bodies and booze. Conspicuous in his fine dress, it was only a moment before the pub's patrons took note of Laurie and stared as though he were naked rather than properly attired. He tried to make his way through the throngs without bringing any more attention to himself.

Finally, he made it to the bar and found an empty stool. Though he was growing hot beneath his layers, he dared not remove any of them, lest they be stolen. The balding barman eyed him curiously as he approached; Laurie ordered up a brandy, trying to act as casual and relaxed as possible. The barman produced the brandy and smiled most unnaturally. *He hopes for a fine tip.*

Once settled upon his stool, Laurie felt comfortable enough to remove his fur hat and set it before him on the bar. He held it between his arms. *Surely no one will try to grab it if I hold it such.* He began to scan the surroundings, studying the odd mix of patrons, trying to pick up on conversations being shouted and slurred around him. *Irish and Scottish, the whole damned lot.* He chuckled to himself, proud to have found what he considered a very lowly drinking hole.

A piano played, he realized, and his eyes found the source of the sound, upon a stage of sorts to the left of the bar. He turned on his stool to get a better look; he was amazed at how skilled and talented the skinny pianist was. His attention was then averted to a table of brightly colored prostitutes howling in laughter. *Of course; every pub must have its whores.* He studied them as they chatted and drank and laughed, as a buxom blonde jumped up and began to pull on the arm of a young girl; she was not attired like the rest of the girls with whom she socialized. He watched as the two got up on the stage; the blonde whispered into the pianist's ear and was quickly gone. Looking very shy and uncomfortable, the young girl in a worn wool dress glanced about the room. Laurie noted how the crowd quieted, focused its whole attention upon her.

The melody began and it was unfamiliar to Laurie. He was more taken with studying the audience than he was by the young girl. That was, until she began to sing.

"I dreamt that I dwelt in marble halls,
With vassals and serfs by my side . . ."

Laurie's eyes immediately found her again, and the sound of her voice held him rapt. His breath seemed to stop before her every note. He watched as her face became less anxious and more relaxed, happy. To him, she was no longer some random pub patron; she became beautiful and bloomed right before his eyes. He fancied her some magical maiden from the Arthurian legends he'd so adored as a boy. He noted the fine paleness of her skin and the pretty mouth forming these most delicious notes. Her auburn curls, somewhat wild in their attempted escape from her bun, shone in the gaslight. And when her green eyes fell upon him, he felt as though they pulled on strings attached to his insides.

This was what I longed for at the Academy of Music! I feel alive, once again.

Her gaze held him for what seemed like an endless, magical inhalation and exhalation of breath, then fell to the stage floor before her.

Is everyone as rapt as me? He quickly glanced around at the patrons as the pianist played the end of the tune; grown men were silently weeping into their cups, others self-consciously dashing the tears away. Women had been singing along, smiling. When the pianist finished, the crowd erupted into fervent cheers, many of which were in a growling, gruff language he could only assume was Gaelic.

She bobbed a quick, awkward curtsy, smiling in true happiness. Her eyes went to him again, and his heart raced. But suddenly he felt a gentle hand on his shoulder, and his nose was filled with an earthy, exotic, smoky perfume. He turned to see to whom the hand belonged, and he saw a woman: young, olive-skinned, foreign, intriguing.

And she whispered into his ear, "I can show you something beyond your wildest dreams, beyond this pub and its music." Her breath was warm, fragrant with the same scent, and her voice was tinged with an accent unknown to him.

"I'm not interested in your body," he said dismissively, trying to shrug her hand away, looking back toward the stage for the beautiful girl, who was no longer there.

"It isn't my body I offer, but a glimpse of heaven, from the Orient."

He turned and stared into her dark eyes. She smiled seductively. Without a word, she lifted her hand from his arm and gestured for him to follow her. And without a thought, as though in a trance, he followed her out of the pub, forgetting his buffalo hat upon the bar.

CHAPTER THREE

Danny predictably wept as he played the final notes of the tune. He then brought his long, calloused fingers to his eyes, pressing them upon his reddened eyelids as the pub erupted into drunken, rambunctious cheers. His bony shoulders hunched forward, and his torso curved into the letter *C*.

Eileen bobbed a self-conscious curtsy and longed to depart the stage. But she could feel her involuntary grin; her cheeks ached and her eyes watered in that pleasing way that kept her lingering on the stage beside Danny. And there had been that brief, delicious moment when she spotted the young man at the bar. She searched for him again, but Shay's raucous crowd had swelled and blocked her view.

Eileen was brought out of the blissful moment of limelight by the sound of Danny's voice.

"Oh, beautiful! 'Twas just perfect, lass," he uttered between sobs.

She giggled slightly, giving his shoulder a gentle squeeze. Startled by its skeletal feel, Eileen quickly drew her hand away and left the stage.

"Fine, fine performance, dear sister," bellowed Mary as she gave Eileen a hearty embrace.

"Perhaps she could fix something up with Shay, get a regular job singing for a bit of pay, huh?" suggested Claire.

Eileen ignored Claire's comment as she strained her neck to catch a glimpse of the bar. "Did you see that gentleman, Mary?"

Mary followed her sister's gaze. "Oh dear, she's spotted a besotted audience member," she teased with a chuckle. "Who, Eileen?"

Finally a group of gasworks laborers sat down at a table, revealing the patrons seated at the bar, including the young man in regal winter attire.

"There!" Eileen shouted, her heart quickening again at the sight of him.

"I see him—quite the gentleman! Perhaps I should try him up for some business—"

Mary halted in her speech. She and Eileen watched as a woman approached the gentleman and whispered into his ear.

Eileen then witnessed how this unfamiliar, olive-skinned woman appeared to charm him with her words, watched as the woman led him out of the pub as though she had cast a spell over him. Endeavoring to understand what had just transpired, she waged a futile fight against the sense of disappointment that filled her as the beautiful gentleman walked out the door.

"Oh damn, so that's what he's about, eh?" Mary posed her question to no one in particular.

"What do you mean?" Eileen asked as she turned to Mary.

"Do you know who that woman is?"

Eileen shook her head.

"She's the den mistress."

"Den mistress?"

Mary rolled her eyes, looking exasperated with her sister. "I always forget that you know *nothing*!"

"That's not so!"

"Oh, right, Eileen, *so learned* in the ways of the world."

"Tell me, who is the den mistress?"

"Where's the den mistress?" Claire chimed in.

"She's just left with a fine gentleman," answered Mary.

"Not so fine a gentleman, then!" Claire scoffed.

"Mary, for the love of God, are you going to tell me—"

"She's mistress of the opium den, at the back of the alley behind Shay's."

Eileen tried to make sense of her sister's words. "That's a bad thing, is it?"

"You know how we make sport of Lily on the second floor of Mrs. Brown's, because she's always in a stupor?"

"Lily and the green fairy?" Claire asked with a giggle.

"That's the absinthe that does that, isn't it?" asked Eileen, unsure.

"That's right, the absinthe. Well, opium does far worse things than that," Mary said with an authoritarian nod.

"Oh . . . right," said Eileen as she learned one more aspect of the anatomy of city life.

"Poor chap," said Claire, slumping back onto the bench.

There was a sudden jarring of the table as a group of men surged toward Eileen and Mary.

"There's the songbird, Paddy! Go on, then!" someone shouted as they thrust a ruddy-faced man forward, toward Eileen.

The man, who Eileen assumed was Paddy, looked at her, his mouth slightly agape as though he was in awe. He was somewhere in his mid-life and stank of beer and coal ash. Removing his hat and revealing a disheveled, black mat of hair, he held the hat before his heart, dropping clumsily to one knee before Eileen.

"Dear Miss . . . Miss?" he asked.

"Eileen," offered Mary, watching the spectacle from Eileen's side.

"Dear Miss Eileen, you sing like an angel. You've broken my heart with your sweet voice . . ." He paused, as though searching for the rest of his speech.

Eileen tried to turn away, as she was terribly embarrassed and bewildered by the stranger's behavior. But Claire, from behind, placed both hands on her shoulders, bracing her and preventing any escape.

"Go on and ask her!" shouted a companion from behind Paddy.

"Right!" Paddy seemed to gather up his courage. "Will you, that is, might you do me the honor, and marry me?"

The entire table of whores stopped mid-conversation, gripped by the marriage proposal that hung in the air, mesmerizing and somewhat garish, like a gaslit chandelier.

Eileen sensed that all eyes were upon her, awaiting her reply. She looked down at the pitiful stranger before her; she couldn't begin to articulate what struck her as a completely unreal moment. She tried to find something to say; her mouth formed soundless words. Finally, she gave up, succumbing to her nervousness and the absurdity of the proposal, falling victim to a fit of hysterical laughter. Soon Mary joined in, as did the table of whores. Paddy's head slumped down in dejection, and soon his mates were laughing as well. Paddy slowly got off his knee, replaced his hat, and joined in the laughter before falling in a drunken stupor into the lap of a large man at the table behind him.

Eileen, Mary, and Claire were no fools; they quickly moved away from the scene, which was devolving into an imminent pub brawl. Still laughing, they moved toward the bar, where Claire ordered up yet another drink for herself.

"Oh, look here!" exclaimed Eileen, noticing the buffalo fur hat that lay on the bar, beside her elbow.

"There's a fine-looking hat," said Mary, running her fingers over the wavy, black fur.

"The gentleman was wearing it—I remember seeing it on him when he sat at the bar, when I began my song."

"Try it on, then!" shouted Mary as she placed the hat atop Eileen's head.

The hat was too large for Eileen. It slipped down her forehead, grazing her eyebrows. The two sisters giggled.

"That hat will fetch you a pretty penny," said Mary as she watched Eileen remove it.

Eileen held it gingerly between her hands. She turned it over and peered inside at the elegant black satin lining and delicate, silver embroidery.

"Comes from London, this hat," she said.

"Like I said, you should try selling it," reiterated Mary.

"Perhaps," said Eileen, pensive.

"Of course you should! You're daft if you don't!" Suddenly Mary eyed Eileen and broke into a grin. "Wait, *I know*, you're going to keep it as a memento of the dashing gentleman!"

Eileen felt herself blush slightly. "Leave me be. I found the hat, and I'll do with it as I wish!"

Mary shook her head, giggling. "Well, you can wear it tonight on your way back home, eh?"

"Want to go?" asked Eileen, somewhat surprised at the time on the clock above the bar.

"I'll walk you back," said Mary, taking the buffalo hat from Eileen's hands and placing it atop her sister's head before locking arms with her.

Eileen and Mary walked arm in arm toward Mrs. Brown's. They made their way on the side of the street, trying to remain in the streetlamps' light. Dodging the occasional drunkard and coach, they hummed a melody together, stopping to snicker over Eileen's marriage proposal. Their laughter materialized from their mouths, turning into a vapor that slowly danced in the frigid night.

When they were about a block from Mrs. Brown's, Eileen noticed someone leaving the tenement, headed in their direction. She watched as the figure approached; it was a man, dressed in black. She observed his imposing stature and build. He wore a black top hat, somewhat tattered and many years out of fashion—Eileen was keenly aware of hat fashion from her work at the milliner's. She and Mary remained silent as the man drew closer. She felt a slight pang of guilt when she realized that she was not unnerved by this man's approach—a woman should always be on guard at night.

"Mr. Jones," Mary said with a bob of her head and a smile.

The new boarder at Mrs. Brown's. Eileen stared up into the man's face when he was but a few paces away.

"Evening," he said, touching the brim of his top hat, tipping his head slightly.

In that one word, his deep and melodious voice was made manifest. For a brief moment, he made eye contact with Eileen; the flickering streetlight revealed eyes of piercing, illuminated, otherworldly blue. He averted his gaze quickly, turning his face toward the street ahead. The gas lighting lovingly traced the contours of his startlingly pale face, sliding over and caressing the sharp angles, the strong nose, kissing the fine yet firmly set lips.

He is a man with purpose. This observation came to Eileen not from within, but without, as though someone, or something, else—perhaps the streetlights—had whispered it into her ear beneath the oversize buffalo hat.

Eileen, entranced, turned her head to watch Mr. Jones pass. He wore his hair long—*very old-fashioned*—and tied neatly with a black ribbon, whose darkness stood in stark contrast to the gold tresses. She watched his form move away from them; there was determination yet great grace in his gait. Instantly she became aware of the oddly pleasing, throbbing sensation beneath the hollow of her neck, behind her navel, within the palms of her hands. She turned her gaze to the street ahead, closing her eyes for a moment so that she might memorize the hauntingly beautiful figure she had just witnessed.

"What do you think? You certainly stared long enough," said Mary, bursting into giggles again.

Eileen was silent for a moment, then looked at Mary and joined in her laughter. "Mary, this has, indeed, been one of the most amusing nights in all of my life." She sighed, as though she had just finished a dear novel, placed it on the bedside table, snuffed out the candle's flame, slid beneath the blankets and into the arms of sleep.

CHAPTER FOUR

She led him to the alleyway beside Shay's Pub and plunged into the darkness. Laurie hesitated for a moment at the alley's entrance, wondering if it were a wise decision to follow her into the blackness.

"Come!" she coaxed as she emerged from the shadows, her hand outstretched.

He looked down at her palm, which was rough and somewhat grimy.

"Treasure from the Orient, yours for the taking, if you follow me," she purred in an eastern Mediterranean accent.

He had heard stories of it, had read about it, this very mysterious pleasure. At Cambridge it was not so common a thing, although, with a brief sojourn southwest to London, one could procure it quite easily in the Limehouse district. Why had he not done so before? Perhaps because his social circle—a mix of future financiers and entrepreneurs, rugby and polo athletes, engineers, mathematicians, lords and dukes—had scoffed at the mere idea of it. They had labeled it "the downfall of poets, painters, bohemian artists," seeming to forget that Laurie was a student of literature. He would remind them, with quotes from the ever-popular *Rime of the Ancient Mariner*, that Coleridge had created some of his most enduring verses whilst under its spell.

And this recollection, along with an imaginary vision of Coleridge in fits of rapture while scribbling away at poetic masterpieces, was what convinced Laurie to take the foreigner's outstretched hand, and follow her into the depths of the alley.

How she was able to see her way to the little, recessed doorway in the blackness, Laurie could not fathom. She scratched at the door with long fingernails just as a rat scurried over his shoes. A cold shiver snaked up his spine as he watched the door open slightly, liberating a smoky exotica into the frigid night. He heard an exchange of words in a language unfamiliar; he guessed it was perhaps Turkish. The door opened wide, and he obediently followed as the woman beckoned him inside. His eyes adjusted for a moment to the hazy, dimly lit confines of the room as the door slammed shut behind him. She still held his hand, and her eyes studied his face as he observed his surroundings.

There were maybe a dozen people within the tiny chamber, all lying prone upon what looked to be straw mats. There was an eerie silence, but for the sucking, deep inhalations of those on the mats and the soft chatter of the three or four attendants who worked the room. Despite the deep, mysterious aroma of the smoke, Laurie found it could not mask the pungent odor of dirty bodies, unwashed feet, and mildew. His eyes watered, and through their blurriness, the little lanterns beside the smokers looked like candles floating on dark waters. His attention was averted to a diminutive East Asian man who chuckled, perhaps at him. Laurie grew hot, for the room was surprisingly well heated.

"Ah, perhaps I take you to the special room," said the woman as she led him to another doorway, draped in a dark material. She held the curtain aside for him to enter.

The ensconced space was very small and housed a bed carved in Oriental fashion, festooned with fine silks in a profusion of colors. A small table was beside the bed, on which was set an elaborate glass lantern and various foreign-looking utensils. The scent in this alcove was far more pleasant; gone was the odor of filth and grime, in its place only the mysterious incense.

The woman helped remove his coat and placed it at the foot of the bed. She smoothed out the silk cushions, patting them lightly, and he sat down. She gave a low, throaty chuckle and took hold of his legs, coaxing him to lie prone. Laurie, confused and bewildered, followed her every suggestion. She loosened his tie and collar, the sensation of her fingernails' slight scratching at his neck somewhat arousing.

She smiled down at him. "Now, I'll teach you how it's done. If you don't remember, it's fine. I will always be here to help, yes?"

He nodded in response.

"I have a clean pipe, just for you, made of bamboo, the best kind for the opium."

He watched, deeply engrossed with the whole process of preparation. He did not take his eyes from her hands as he moved closer to the lantern, watching as she skillfully warmed and stretched the gummy resin with a long needle. She held the resin above the lantern flame, threading it back and forth from the edge of the pipe's bowl, stretching it and manipulating it until the gum began to glow and smoke. Then, with a rapid movement of the needle, she balled the resin up and forced it into the tiny hole atop the pipe's bowl with a quick flick.

"There you are, go ahead, breathe as deeply as you can." She patted his knee reassuringly, eagerly awaiting his first inhalation.

He reasoned that it must be quite the same as smoking tobacco from a pipe. He placed his mouth upon the carved bamboo and inhaled as deeply as he could. The exotic aroma filled his mouth, his lungs, his nose; it smelled of dark earth after a rainstorm, of softest leather, of burning sandalwood, of delicious, slippery sex, of some Oriental flower, in shades of blue and yellow, unfurling over and over and over again until, deep within, a beautiful, golden fairy awoke, spread her gossamer wings, and blew him a kiss.

"For a little more money, you can have me," purred the Turkish voice as she ran her fingernails over the front of his trousers.

He said "please," for she appeared almost—but not quite—as beautiful as the fairy, in shades of ruby rather than the gray she had worn earlier. He blinked slowly—an eternity of eyelids closing and opening. He fancied that he was within the unfurled blue-and-yellow flower, the petals so soft and dewy, the golden fairy watching from above, happy that he had freed her from the flower.

Later, as he was coming off his high, he watched her smooth her skirts and adjust her bodice. She went to the doorway, slightly opening the curtain and calling out orders to someone in a sharp whisper. She closed the curtain, turned, and quickly began to prepare another ball of chandu, the dark-brown opium paste.

"Hurry," ordered Laurie tersely, for he was growing disgusted with himself, with her.

She nodded, focused on her preparations. "The more you smoke, the longer your ecstasy lasts."

He inhaled three times and searched the ceiling for the golden fairy. On the fifth inhalation, he cared not whether he ever saw the fairy again, for he felt so warm and safe, so contented, unlike any other contentment. He lay on a bed of fragrant blue flowers, and the soft petals began to engulf him, swallow him up. His body felt lithe, no longer enslaved to gravity. He noticed his hands, cradling the bamboo pipe, and they appeared to glisten and glow, golden and sparkling, and he thought that perhaps he was becoming the golden fairy. And he could only smile, and shed three diamond tears of utter joy.

An angel came to him. The angel pushed aside the mounds of blue and yellow flowers, lotus blossoms, jasmine vines, tuberose petals, and lifted him out. The angel spoke to him in a deep, melodious voice, wiping Laurie's sweating face with cool, rough, large, pale hands. The angel gently pulled up Laurie's eyelids and looked deep into his eyes, and Laurie gasped, for never had he seen such illuminated, blue eyes. And as the angel placed his head upon Laurie's chest and listened to his breathing, Laurie whispered, "Angel," and stroked the wavy, silky, pale-gold locks on the angel's head.

For a brief moment, the angel seemed to succumb to the sensation of Laurie's caress, his lids closing, his fine lips slightly parting as he let out a shuddering exhalation. But soon the angel's eyes opened again, his fine lips hardened, and he moved away from Laurie's chest.

"Indeed, I am an angel, sent to you by the Lord and his only son, Jesus Christ. I will raise you from this den of sin and restore you to health, as the Savior did unto us when he died for our sins."

Laurie became aware of the silk pillows beneath him, the dingy surroundings. He heard muffled voices in the next room. He focused on the angel's eyes and once again forgot to breathe for a moment.

"But who are you, really?" Laurie asked feebly.

"We've no time for questions now. We must get you back to your home, for I fear both your soul and your body are gravely ill."

Laurie marveled at how beautifully deep this man's voice was. He allowed the man to help him up to a seated position, and suddenly Laurie found himself exceedingly cold, shivering violently, a metallic taste in his mouth, his body feeling bruised and worn.

"Oh, Lord help us, you are feverish," said the man, shaking his head as he gathered up Laurie's coat from the edge of the bed. "Here, try to stand up so that I can help you into your coat."

Laurie stood, and an aching traveled like a cramp from his feet up his legs, much like the sensation he once had when he waded in the icy ocean at Newport. He allowed the man to dress him in his coat, then fell back upon the bed. The man immediately hoisted Laurie up to his feet again, supporting him beneath his left shoulder with his large, strong frame.

"Where is your hat?" the man asked as he placed his own, very passé, top hat upon his head.

Laurie scanned the room drowsily. "I think I forgot it somewhere this evening. Oh yes, at the saloon round the corner. My hat, it's made of buffalo fur."

"Then I'm certain it's long gone now."

"You cannot leave with him!" exclaimed the foreign woman as the man helped Laurie into the next room. "He owes still for his night here!"

"Don't come near us, you damned Jezebel," he warned. "Do you know how much you will have to pay in hell for your sins?"

She laughed aloud, and the small East Asian man in the corner joined her.

"My wallet is here," whispered Laurie, pulling it from within his coat. "How much do I owe?" he asked her.

She named the price, and Laurie pushed the wallet into the man's hand. "Pay her what she asks, please."

The man seemed reluctant to hand over any money to the woman, but eventually took the wallet and opened it. He paused for a moment, and Laurie noticed how the man's eyes widened at the sight of the large sum within the wallet's folds. Tentatively, as though he were touching shards of glass, the man pulled out the bills, then violently threw them at the woman, who quickly got to her hands and knees to gather them up.

"My address, it's on one of the calling cards in the second fold," said Laurie faintly. "Please, I'll pay you handsomely if you get me home." He leaned more heavily against the man's sturdy frame, his strength seeping away from his legs as his body shuddered.

The man took the ivory, printed calling card from the wallet. He then reached inside Laurie's coat and replaced the wallet in the breast pocket. Laurie, despite his chills, felt his skin thrill beneath his waistcoat and shirt at the proximity of the man's hand to his heart.

They headed out of the den, into the bitter night. As they emerged from the alley, Laurie noticed that the first light of dawn was touching the east sky. He leaned against the man, who was as steady and forthright as a large tree. The man finally found a coach for hire and flagged it down. He practically lifted Laurie into it, and did so with the least appearance of effort on his part. He gave the calling card to the driver and stepped into the coach, sitting across from Laurie.

"You've been very kind, sir. I fear I'm dreadfully ill, and I don't know if I could have made it out of the den myself," said Laurie.

The man did not respond, just nodded in agreement. He only stared into Laurie's eyes with such a penetrating, fiercely beautiful gaze.

Laurie found himself both mesmerized and unnerved. "Will you tell me your name?"

"I am Stanley Jones, your servant," he replied with a tip of his top hat, his probing stare uninterrupted.

The sun was rising, and it cast its harsh light through the fingerprint-smeared coach window. Laurie watched as dawn discovered Stanley Jones, instinctively bestowing its favor upon his remarkably handsome face. The worn black satin of the decidedly outdated top hat stood in stark contrast to the paleness of his skin. Dawn's light lovingly traced the sharp angles of Stanley's cheekbones and nose. After much effort, Laurie was able move his gaze from the mesmerizing blue eyes to the fine, firm mouth graced with lips that were slightly chapped.

"I am indebted to you, Mr. Jones." Laurie watched with sudden delight as Stanley's mouth broke into a dazzling smile. He was like a knight from Arthurian legend come to life.

"Mr. Barnard, I am the Lord's servant. He saw fit to place you in my care, and I shall do my best to get you to your home and under the supervision of a doctor. You owe me no debt." Stanley seemed to consider his words, then spoke again. "Well, you owe me just one thing."

"What is it?"

"A vow," Stanley replied with an even more handsome smile.

"Name it," said Laurie, unable to take his eyes off Stanley.

"You must swear never to go to the den again," ordered Stanley in a slow, low, commanding voice that captivated Laurie further.

"I swear it—never again, Mr. Jones."

Stanley looked pleased with Laurie's response. He regarded Laurie, his gaze tracing the contours of his face, his coat. "Please, call me Stanley," he said softly.

"And you must call me Laurie," he replied, suddenly aware of how much his throat ached. "Where are you from, Stanley?" He thought he detected a hint of an unfamiliar accent in Stanley's words.

"I'm from New York!" he replied with a low, throaty laugh that filled Laurie's insides and carried a feeling of contentment almost equal to the perfumed, smoky resin in the bamboo pipe.

But quickly the sense of contentment was usurped by a greater feeling of embarrassment. *I shouldn't feel this way about a man.* His gaze fell to his knees, then out the window. He found that, despite his self-chastisement, it was a difficult task to keep his eyes averted from Stanley.

The coach slowed down.

"Is this your home, Laurie?" asked Stanley, peering out the window, studying the large brownstone before him.

"It is," replied Laurie as the driver opened the coach door for the two of them.

Without a word, Stanley bounded out of the coach first so that he might assist Laurie, who felt somewhat ashamed at his helpless state, yet he readily accepted Stanley's help. Laurie allowed him to place his hands beneath his arms, lift him, and place him down upon the sidewalk, much like a child. Laurie became aware of how much his legs ached and his body shivered in the crisp early-morning air. He glanced up the flight of steps leading to the front door of his home. The coach driver had taken the liberty of approaching the door and turning the bell, most likely in hopes of a fair gratuity.

Seamus, the butler, opened the door—a look of relief upon his round, ruddy, white-whiskered face. Laurie, in his ailing state, became aware of just how happy he was to be home after his night crawl. As Stanley helped him up the stairs, Laurie noticed that his mother had come to the door as well.

"Oh, thank goodness!" She stepped outside, looking somewhat bewildered and annoyed as Laurie and Stanley made their way up the stairs. "I was absolutely *distraught* with anxiety, wondering where you were all night. I mean, honestly, Lawrence, you *know* how fragile my nerves are. It was most unkind of you to give me such a fright. I was about to notify the police—"

"I'm fine, Mother," Laurie interrupted, already tired of her chatter.

The party entered the home's grand foyer and Seamus bustled about, removing Laurie's coat and scarf, paying the coach driver and seeing him out.

"Did you tip him well?" Laurie asked Seamus in a quiet voice, as though the driver were still present.

"Of course, sir," Seamus answered in the accent he used whilst in the presence of Mrs. Barnard—an accent that revealed an Irishman unsuccessfully feigning his identity as a gentleman from Kent. "Worry not, sir."

"Madame," said Stanley in his low, melodious voice, "may I suggest that Mr. Barnard go straight to his bedchamber for much-needed rest? I would also suggest that you summon a doctor, as Mr. Barnard is quite feverish."

Mother, son, and butler both paused in their doings, arrested by Stanley's presence.

"And you are?" asked Mrs. Barnard, her eyebrows raised, her critical gaze traveling down her nose before resting upon the humble yet striking young man before her.

Laurie longed to wipe the imperious look off her face.

Stanley removed his unfashionable top hat, held it to his heart, and bowed. "Stanley Jones, Madame."

Mrs. Barnard's stance and expression remained unchanged. "I thank you for your assistance this morning, Mr. Jones. Seamus," she called to the butler, snapping her fingers impatiently in that way that Laurie so despised, "fetch Mr. Jones some gratuity."

Laurie felt himself seething, and were it not for his being sick, he would surely have reproached his mother for such disrespect.

But Stanley appeared completely unbothered by the slight. He smiled radiantly and replied, "Indeed, Madame, you are most kind, but I require no pecuniary reward for my services."

"Indeed," she replied, not hiding her longing to be rid of Stanley.

"I would only request that I might have the pleasure of calling on your son in the near future, once he is recovered from his illness," he added, unwaveringly awaiting her reply.

Mrs. Barnard must have been unnerved by those remarkable blue eyes, for Laurie was shocked to notice that for a woman who was never at a loss for words, his mother was silent.

"Yes," Laurie answered for her, "you may call in the future, Mr. Jones. I look forward to it."

He was rewarded with a most breathtaking smile, and Laurie felt his insides flutter again before he damned himself for having such irrational sentiments for another man.

But, as he watched Stanley Jones leave his home, he could not fight the overriding sense of sudden loss, as though all the daylight were suddenly eclipsed, leaving him in eerie shadow. As though he had turned the last page of Malory's Arthurian masterpiece.

CHAPTER FIVE

"*This* is why I seldom drink in excess," moaned Eileen to no one but herself, as she was alone in her tiny room, perched on the fifth floor of Mrs. Brown's boardinghouse.

When she had awoken and sat up in her bed, her head ached most dreadfully, and she immediately formed a picture in her mind's eye of a hammer striking an anvil over and over. She removed her nightcap, shaking out her mass of unruly auburn curls, pressing her chilly, calloused fingers against her scalp, and rubbing to and fro. It was a futile attempt to massage away the nasty headache, but most successful in creating even unrulier locks.

"Dear me, if only I didn't have to go to mass," she muttered, watching as her words became vapor in the chill of her room. Quickly, she made the sign of the cross, for she felt somewhat guilty for what she had said.

When she got to her feet, the hammer came down upon the anvil with a hearty whack and she moaned aloud. She made her way to the filthy little coal hearth, where she took three pieces from the coal bucket and set to kindling them. *All for naught,* she thought. *By the time they warm the room, I'll be on my way to mass.*

She peered into the pitcher in her washbasin, moaned aloud again. She shook her head before reluctantly punching her fist down into it, breaking the layer of ice that had formed in it during the night. After she tipped the pitcher, watching the ice chunk plop into the basin followed by water, and scrubbed her face and arms as quickly as she could, she wrapped herself in a blanket from her bed. Dropping down on the floor before the hearth, she removed the last piece of bread from her grocery basket, telling herself she must eat something to calm the feeling of unease in her stomach.

As she tried to take a bite out of the stale bread, she realized she was wasting her time without water, and got up again and poured herself a cup from the icy pitcher. Sitting down once more, she dipped pieces of the hard bread into the water and ate them, despite her lack of appetite.

On Sunday mornings, before church, Eileen thought of her ma. The local priest back in Limerick had sent a letter about six months after she and Mary arrived in New York City, informing them that Ma had passed away from consumption. Because she had not witnessed her passing herself, it was easy for Eileen to forget this, and think wistfully of what her mother might be doing at just that same exact moment in Ireland. But then she would remember, with a pang of both sadness and guilt that she could not have held her ma's hand at the end. Eileen would quickly turn her thoughts to how proud she was of herself for being so self-sufficient in such a big city as this, and how proud her mother would be of her. And then her thoughts would, of course, stray to what her mother would think of Mary and her profession. That was when Eileen would rise from the floor and dress herself in her corset and Sunday dress. It was a dark-green wool affair that Eileen knew was out of fashion and very ill-fitting around the bust and along the arms.

At least I have two dresses, she thought, always mindful to count her blessings rather than her misfortunes.

She put on her stockings and boots and hurried out of her room and down the stairs to the main foyer, where the one mirror in the whole boardinghouse resided proudly, with a dark crack running along its upper-left-hand corner. On a Sunday morning she did not have to wait her turn to peer and preen at her reflection, as the whole house still slept after a long Saturday night.

After she had waged battle with her thick curls and coaxed them into something of a reasonably acceptable look, she affixed her bonnet—a secondhand black hat that she had adorned with gray lace of her own making as well as new gray ribbons that were remnants from the milliner's—and tied the ribbons in a pretty bow beneath her chin. She quietly closed the front door of the boardinghouse as she left. It was always remarkable how very still and quiet the boardinghouse was on a Sunday morning.

Once outside, she was met with a blast of cold air and startling sunshine. She squinted against the wind and the brightness of the sun reflecting off the white snowdrifts on the sides of the street. Soon her vision grew accustomed to the light, and she made her way toward Saint Patrick's on Mott. As she walked, she saw some familiar faces heading in the same direction: Mr. and Mrs. O'Heir and their brood of six children; old Mrs. Donnel, huddled beneath her worn, plaid blanket she used as a winter coat; Danny O'Connell, the piano man, making his way in long-legged strides, looking like a man on a mission to be united with the Lord as soon as physically possible.

But there was a figure striding in the opposite direction of the churchgoers, straight toward her. At first, she squinted to see who it might be, for she wasn't sure. But then as he came closer, she was certain—Stanley Jones, the new lodger, the remarkably handsome man she had passed last night on her way home. *Well, he's no gentleman, that is for certain, if he's only coming home at this hour of the morning!* When he was a block away, she felt sure that those fine blue eyes were upon her, and she noticed that he slowed down his stride.

She grew nervous. *Do I look well enough? What will he think of me in the daylight?* She chastised herself for being so silly: *Stupid Eileen, like he'd ever take notice of you!* She pinched her lips with her teeth, feeling the tingling sensation as they swelled. She thought to herself that she might at least make an attempt to look pretty. *But why do I bother? He's obviously up to no good if he returns from his night out at nine in the morning. Though he certainly looks as bright and fresh as though he slept the whole night through.*

When he was but a few paces away, he paused and removed his hat, bowing to her. She knew she must stop and be polite, though she was growing increasingly shy and bashful at the thought of having to engage in conversation with this handsome man. She managed to muster a smile as she stopped.

"Good morning to you, Miss Maguire." His melodious voice seemed to be made of fur, caressing her.

"Mr. Jones, good morning to you also," she replied, looking up into his eyes, feeling suddenly as though all the brightness of this day emanated from their blue depths rather than the morning sun. *Good God, he knows my name!*

"And where are you off to in such a hurry this morning?" he asked, holding her gaze.

She thought that he must know that those eyes of his were like weapons, able to break a heart within seconds. "Why, off to Saint Patrick's for Sunday mass, of course," she replied, with a little hint of reproach to see his reaction.

"How foolish of me—of course! You know, I would like to attend mass also. Might I accompany you?"

Eileen was speechless for a second as she tried to make sense of the many thoughts swimming around in her head. *He wants to accompany* me *to church! Oh, what will the parishioners think? Is it not proper? What do I care!*

"Yes, you may accompany me, if you'd like," Eileen replied, and the bold response came as a surprise even to herself.

"You're very kind, miss," he replied with a smile that could have killed her right there, three blocks from Saint Patrick's.

"You may call me Eileen, Mr. Jones." Eileen grew anxious as soon as she uttered this to him, for was she being too familiar too soon?

"Then you must call me Stanley," he responded.

The bells of Saint Patrick's chimed out, and the two of them exclaimed "Oh!" simultaneously, giggled a little, then proceeded to run the last three blocks to the massive, carved doors of the church. Eileen was breathless, yet Stanley looked as collected as though he had been standing by the church doors all morning. She did not want to enter the church in such a state. Stanley seemed to understand this without her saying a word, as he stood right beside her, patiently waiting for her to catch her breath.

"Ready?" she asked.

"When you are," he replied with that stunning smile.

He held the door for her as she entered the dim, hushed church. Eileen's heart raced, despite the calming ritual of dipping her fingers in the holy water by the last pew and touching them gently to her forehead.

She selected a pew about one-third of the way within the church, as it was one of the few left with room for two worshippers. Just as her knee touched the genuflect, the organ began to play. She rose and joined in the hymn as the priest approached the altar. But soon her attention was focused solely on the beautiful baritone voice coming from the man by her side. She was most disappointed when the hymn was over, and eagerly awaited the Psalm Response, when she might hear Stanley's voice again.

When the congregation was seated, Eileen had to shift to accommodate the large buttocks of the woman to the right of her. She thrilled as her skirts and left arm pressed against Stanley, and soon realized that her hammer-and-anvil headache was completely gone.

But is he truly a Catholic? About halfway through the mass, Eileen concluded that Stanley was, indeed, a true Catholic, as he not only recited the Latin prayers verbatim, but he had passed the ultimate test: He knew exactly when to stand, sit, and kneel. Her imagination wandered as she allowed herself, for the briefest of moments, to contemplate what life would be like as this man's wife, by his side, attending Sunday mass. Her palms grew moist as she clasped them in prayer. She asked for forgiveness, knowing that the Lord saw all her thoughts, especially now that she was in His presence, witnessing bread transformed into His only son's flesh.

But will he accept communion? This, Eileen thought, was her final test, for if he accepted the body of Christ, then he was free from sin, was he not? She considered Stanley's all-night outing and prepared herself for a letdown, for most likely, after a debauched night crawl, Stanley would not—could not—receive the body of Christ.

Yet, as those accepting communion rose from their knees, Eileen was startled to find Stanley rising with them, stepping out of the pew, allowing her to proceed before him in the aisle. She tried to contain the smile that warmed her lips, as she was mightily glad that Stanley seemed perfect in every way. She endeavored to focus her thoughts on the communion she was about to receive, attempting to recite a prayer to herself.

Hail Holy Queen, mother of all holiness, our life, our sweetness, our hope.

But it was difficult to remember the words when, just one stride behind her, she could feel Stanley's presence—like a roaring hearth, singeing the back of her wool dress, turning her skin flush.

To you do we cry—poor, banished children of Eve. To you do we send up our sighs.

And just then Eileen let out a sigh, and gave up on reciting the rest of the prayer to herself, as she was but three people away from the priest. She received communion, closing her eyes, making the sign of the cross while the wafer on her tongue quickly dissolved. Eileen made her way back to the pew, and once kneeling and bowing her head over clasped hands, she gave her usual thanks to the Lord that she hadn't choked on the wafer. On the day of her first communion, a nun had told her the story of how a parishioner once choked on the wafer, coughed it up upon the altar, and was banned from ever receiving communion again in that church. Eileen was always a trifle scared that the same misfortune might befall her. So she was always certain to give thanks to the Lord that she did not suffer the same fate, especially today, with Stanley right behind her in line.

Eileen removed her rosary—made of polished alderwood beads and given to her by her grandmother, who didn't trust Mary with it—from her pocket and dutifully began to recite it to herself as she knelt. Eileen's fingers, though quite calloused from lacework, knew well the beads made smooth by countless recitations by many ancestors in her maternal line. With her eyes closed, she moved from one bead to the next, one Hail Mary to another, until she was thrown off in her prayers once again by the presence of Stanley Jones kneeling by her side.

She resumed her rosary, only to feel a change in the weight of the beads. Stanley, without a word, had taken up the opposite end of the rosary hanging from her hands, and begun to recite the fifth decade. Eileen's thoughts scattered. Head still bowed, she glanced over to her left at her rosary beads in Stanley's large, pale hand. How tiny the beads appeared when in the clutches of his forefinger and thumb! She considered whether these rosary beads had ever been touched by a man before. A sudden sense of guilt and shame came over her as she remembered her grandmother's aged, vein-knotted hands placing the beloved rosary into her own tiny, seven-year-old hands. *Grandma is watching all of this, I'm sure of it.*

But the moment was over, and the congregation rose from their knees and seated themselves as the organ's communion hymn ended. Eileen placed the rosary beads in her pocket, squeezing them tight to somehow assure her grandmother that she still had them safe.

Embarrassment flooded her when Stanley helped her out of her coat, hanging it on the hook adjacent to their booth in Café Nouveau. She feared he might notice how old, ill fitting, and decidedly worn her coat was, and perhaps think less of her. *But why such thoughts? He knows I'm not a wealthy woman, of course.* As she slid into the worn, leather booth, he removed his own coat and hung it over hers. She noticed that his suit was of simple, black wool, and that the elbows were worn and faded.

Despite his somber dress, his presence attracted many stares from the café's other patrons, especially the females.

It had been Stanley's suggestion that they go for tea and pastry after mass. Eileen had accepted his invitation eagerly, though she instantly grew nervous and worried that perhaps she was not showing enough propriety. But by the time they had reached Café Nouveau—a renowned rendezvous spot for working-class lovers, bohemian artists, and enterprising prostitutes—Eileen had reasoned with herself that propriety had perhaps become a thing of the past. Maybe it was a vestige of Ireland that had no place in New York, in her new life, where she had no mother to scold her and a sister who sold herself daily. Indeed, this last thought somewhat emboldened her, eased her anxiety, and happily, soothed her unsettled stomach.

A young waitress, wearing as much rouge and lip color as a streetwalker, approached their table. She nodded curtly at Eileen, then turned all her attention to Stanley, offering him a sultry smile. "And what might I get you?" she almost purred.

Stanley seemed to take little notice of the special attention he elicited from the waitress. "Yes, ma'am, we'd like two pots of breakfast tea and, please, what sort of cake do you have today?"

Eileen noticed that the waitress paused before answering, pencil held aloft over pad, as though captivated, as she looked into Stanley's eyes.

He looked at her questioningly. "Do you have any cake left at all? Or has the Sunday church crowd already cleared you out?" he asked, and then looked to Eileen, chuckling.

"Honey cake," the waitress blurted out, finally coming back to her senses. "And we've got almond cake, raspberry torte, Boston cream pie."

"Eileen, what sounds good to you?" he asked.

She felt herself blushing yet again. "The almond cake would be just fine, thank you," she replied in a soft voice. Eileen wasn't used to being in a proper café with waiters and waitresses.

"That does sound just fine. Make that two," he said to the waitress with a nod.

As the waitress left the table, Stanley turned his full attention to Eileen, his smile filling her with an unfamiliar sense of euphoria, quite similar to the sensation she'd had when she had ridden a tree swing as a small child. But this sensation was deeper, warmer, and lingered in the depths of her.

Eileen racked her mind, wondering what she could possibly bring up for a conversation topic, and decided upon asking Stanley his opinion of the Sunday service at Saint Patrick's. She was opening her mouth to ask, when he began to speak.

"That was a lovely service this morning, didn't you think? Oh, I'm sorry—were you about to say something, Eileen?" His eyes widened in question.

"Oh, I was only going to ask your opinion on the service," she said, and couldn't control the nervous giggle that escaped her. *Oh, stupid, silly Eileen!*

"Now, how's that for a coincidence, eh?" Stanley said with a laugh, and Eileen noticed for the first time not only how fine a laugh he had, but also that he spoke with the slightest, yet unfamiliar, accent.

"Where are you from?" she asked.

"I'm from New York," he answered.

"But were you born here?"

"Yes indeed," he answered proudly. "I'm an American citizen."

"But where is your family from?"

"New York City—why do you ask?"

"Oh, it's just that I thought I detected something of an accent in you," she said, looking down at her hands, fearing that she was too bold in her questioning.

"My father was a schoolteacher," he said, "always making sure that we spoke properly, with the right sort of inflection. Maybe that's what your ears detect?" he offered, his fine brow rising.

"Perhaps," she replied, still unconvinced, but willing to drop the subject.

"I'm an American, just like you are now, Eileen," he said with a smile.

She giggled again. "Sometimes I don't feel very American."

"And why's that?"

Eileen pondered how she might answer. Could he be so naive that he didn't know how much discrimination the Irish faced? Should she tell him how many times she'd been called "Irish scum" in her search for a job, a wage? "It seems that my accent, my name, make it difficult for me to feel American," she offered, studying his expression to see if he understood.

His expression offered encouragement. "How so?"

"Well," she replied, sighing, her fingers fidgeting with the wrinkled cotton napkin on the table before her, "I had a difficult time finding work when I first got here."

"And what is it that you do now, Eileen?"

He delighted her each time he said her name aloud. "I do lacework for a milliner."

"Well now, that's a fine skill to have, and one I'm sure your employer values, yes?"

"I suppose," she replied, thinking of the stern, stonelike face of her supervisor, trying to recall if she had ever witnessed the woman smile. "And, might I ask, what's your work, Stanley?"

Just then the waitress came with the pots of tea and huge slices of cake. Eileen stared at the dessert before her, thinking of how it could possibly feed a family of four.

"I translate books, write correspondence for people, that sort of thing," he replied, offering her the milk first for her tea.

Her fingers brushed his as she took the little pitcher from his hand. She thrilled. "How many languages do you speak?"

"Oh, a few: French, German, Italian, Greek, and Latin, of course," he said as though it were no great accomplishment.

"How did you learn so many?" Eileen asked as she handed him the milk, watching him pour it into his cup.

"My father taught me," he replied before taking a sip of tea. "Ah, now that's a good cup of tea!"

Their conversation paused while they drank their tea and tasted their cake. Eileen tried to eat as daintily as possible, noticing how Stanley devoured his with huge, quick bites from his fork, as though he hadn't eaten in days. When he was finished, he wiped his mouth with his napkin, sipped his tea again, and sighed contentedly, focusing on her again. Her eyes went to her cake—only a fourth of it finished, because it was so very sweet and rich—and she rested her fork on the plate, uneasy to eat under his gaze.

"May I ask you a question?" he asked, his low voice becoming somewhat lower, quieter.

"You may," she replied.

His gaze seemed to penetrate into hers. "Why does your sister work as a prostitute?"

The question caught Eileen by surprise. Her fingers wrapped around the napkin. "I don't see why that's any of your concern, now."

He did not answer, waiting for her to continue.

"I mean, what I'm trying to say is," she stammered, "what's that got to do with you? Is it causing you offense in some way?" Eileen's tone rose slightly, and she noticed that a woman at a neighboring table looked over. *Calm yourself, Eileen, you're becoming too defensive.*

"Indeed," he replied, after a pause, his gaze unwavering from hers, "I do find it offensive. I find it offensive that any woman might resort to selling her body into sin for the sake of profit."

Eileen was stunned. Her tongue was paralyzed in her mouth until she found what she deemed the proper response. "And what about the men who pay for their pleasures? What of them? What about the men who fire the women from their hard-earned jobs, so that the women have no other option to feed and house themselves but to sell their bodies? What of them, eh? Or do they not count?" Eileen felt her face growing hot with anger, and realized her lips quivered slightly.

And to think, up until now this had been such a perfect day.

She raised her eyebrows, awaiting his response, but he just sat there, looking somewhat blank, and this provoked her anger further.

"By the way, Stanley, what were *you* doing all night last night? You were just beginning your night as mine was ending, and you were only returning home this morning, isn't that so?" But she felt deeply ashamed as soon as the accusation had left her lips. *Oh, now you've gone and ruined everything. You couldn't just keep your mouth shut and bite your wild tongue, could you, Eileen!*

"I'm sorry," she whispered, directing her gaze down to her teacup.

"Don't be," he replied softly.

Eileen looked up from her cup, surprised.

Stanley smiled reassuringly. "You've every right to be suspicious of me. I'm sure, by the looks of it, I might have been cavorting all night long. But I assure you, I wasn't. In fact, I was at my other job."

"What's that?"

"On Friday and Saturday evenings, I do charity work."

"What sort of charity work? For the church?"

"Well, not any church in particular," he replied, his large fingertip absently circling his teacup rim. "I go out, looking for people who are suffering from vice, and I try to help them, pick them up, get them back on their feet, get them to see the err of their ways. I try to bring people back to the Lord." He paused, his finger still moving along the cup's rim, his eyes intent upon her. "And you're right, Eileen, about the men who use prostitutes, the men who fire unmarried women from their jobs. They're the ones who spread sin, they're the ones who tempt women into sinful employment."

Eileen felt her insides lurch into tumult. Any lingering doubt she had about the character of this man had been vanquished, and she felt mightily upset with herself for suspecting the worst of him. "Why do you do this, this charity work?"

He shrugged, looking out the window. The day's sunshine caught in his eyes, illuminating them, and Eileen found herself transfixed to their depths once again.

"We are all the Lord's servants, but do we take up our tasks? Or do we shirk them? I try my best to do what is right by the Lord."

"Oh," Eileen replied, dazed.

They said nothing more, finishing their tea, until the waitress returned with the bill.

"Ma'am, could you possibly wrap the rest of the lady's cake, so that she can take it with her?" he asked most politely.

Eileen was charmed; she never had been referred to as a lady before, and it sat very well with her. She could not contain her smile while the waitress took the cake away, returning moments later with a little box.

"Please, allow me to pay for this," said Stanley, pulling out his wallet.

"Oh, no," replied Eileen, putting out her hand to stop him. "Really, it wouldn't be right."

"And why wouldn't it? I suggested that we come here, didn't I?" he asked with a chuckle. "I'll hear nothing more about it. It was my pleasure."

Eileen nodded, blushing like a schoolgirl once again.

CHAPTER SIX

Laurie woke from a nasty dream, all shivers, aching limbs, enflamed throat, watery eyes, anxiety. His breath came from him in a shudder as he burrowed within the layers of bedsheets and blankets. Why could he not get warm?

His bedroom door opened, and he hoped that it was one of the servants with more blankets or, better yet, a hot brandy. He peered out from beneath the bedcovers to see his family's trusted physician, Dr. Prescott.

The doctor, through a pair of pince-nez perched precariously on the bridge of a bulbous nose, studied Laurie. A wrinkle of concern etched its way along his forehead, and he sighed through pursed lips embedded in prodigious white whiskers. Laurie knew that exact expression well; Dr. Prescott had been the family's physician for as long as he could recall.

"Why can I not get warm?" Laurie asked, trying to mask his anxiety with mock annoyance.

Dr. Prescott placed a hand upon Laurie's forehead, seeming to ponder the question. "Well, Lawrence, I fear that you show signs of influenza." He opened up his black leather satchel, rummaging through its medicinal contents.

"I never should have gone out last night," said Laurie, more to himself than to anyone else. He scanned the ceiling as images from the previous night's events flickered within his mind. Well, perhaps it would have been fairer to say that he regretted only some aspects of the prior evening. The thought of the opium-induced magic, the remembrance of a lovely girl singing in the Bowery pub, the image of Stanley Jones, sitting across from him in a coach at dawn . . . regret certainly was not attached to these.

"Lawrence, be frank with me." The aged doctor pulled a chair close to the bedside and sat down with a weary sigh. "Now, where were you last evening?"

Laurie started somewhat at the question. "Why do you ask?"

"It's important that I know so that I can warn my patients to stay away from whatever establishment it was that you frequented last night. Influenza is a most dangerous illness, as you know."

Laurie's anxiety must have shown, for Dr. Prescott patted him lightly on the arm. "Worry not, you'll make it through because you're young and strong. But those who do not have such a robust constitution—the very young, the old, and the fairer sex, for example—well, we need to worry about them."

Laurie thought of what he might tell Dr. Prescott of his prior evening's activities. After considering each deed, Laurie concluded that he could share only the first part of his evening's activities, and then concocted an alternative ending.

"I went with friends to dinner at Delmonico's, and then we attended the Academy of Music—they're staging *Don Giovanni* presently."

"Are they, now?" Dr. Prescott pulled his watch from his vest pocket and checked the time.

Laurie knew he had sufficiently bored the man. "Yes, and then we went to James Whitcomb's for a nightcap. And that was the extent of it, really."

"Dear me, I do hope that everyone is healthy at the Whitcomb house," said Dr. Prescott, the crease of concern running across his forehead again.

"Oh, I'm certain they are," said Laurie, trying to cover his lie. "I didn't stay there very long. Perhaps this is an illness I caught on the steamship back from England?"

"Possibly," said Dr. Prescott absently as he fetched a small bottle from within his satchel. "Here, take five drops of this in the morning and evening, but no more, you hear?" he asked Laurie, white eyebrows raised well above the wire frame of his pince-nez.

"Of course, sir."

"And stay in bed until the fever subsides. Take plenty of broth, cold compresses to the forehead. Of course I'll leave these instructions with your servants as well."

"How long do you think it will be until I'm recovered?"

"Oh, I would say less than a week, if you're fortunate. I'll be by tomorrow evening to check on your progress, my boy."

"Many thanks, Doctor Prescott." Laurie watched as the doctor left a small bottle filled with an amber liquid on the bedside table, closed up his case, and rose from the chair. "By the way, Doctor, what is this medicine?"

"Five drops, twice daily, no more."

"Yes, sir, but I asked what *is* this medicine?"

"It's laudanum, my boy."

When he awoke again, shivering and aching, he realized that the sun had set some time before. He heard Seamus humming a tune as he gently laid a cold compress upon Laurie's forehead, and he clenched his teeth together, fighting the convulsion that came over him.

"Oh damn, that's awfully cold, Seamus!" he exclaimed before he could stop himself.

"I'm sorry, Mr. Barnard, but the doctor says it's what we should do."

"When did Mother leave?"

"Well, I believe you came home around seven o'clock this morning, and we summoned Doctor Prescott, who came around eight. When he told us that it was influenza, your mother had her trunks packed and a telegram sent to her cousin in Newport by ten, and was headed to the station by eleven."

Laurie shook his head. His mother's selfish behavior was something that he had learned long ago he must abide. Though he was always civil and polite, as a good son should be, he secretly knew that he housed no love for this woman who, though titled "mother," was by no means motherly in any fashion.

"Typical, really," he said to Seamus.

A wry smile spread over Seamus's lips. "Was your father just as selfish?"

Though Laurie knew he ought to be offended by Seamus's familiarity, he found he was not. "Well, I don't remember much about him, but no, I don't recall feeling a cold wind when he was present in a room . . ." Laurie tried to collect all the memories he had of his father, who had passed away when Laurie was only seven years old, leaving him the sole heir to an immense estate and even greater legacy. It felt, at times, a painful burden, to live up to the name and fortune of a man he really never knew.

"I think it's time for your medicine now," said Seamus as he counted five drops from the bottle to a spoon.

Laurie obediently took the medicine, which was bitter and harsh down the throat. He grimaced at the unpleasant taste, and Seamus laughed, removed the compress from his forehead, and left the room.

Perhaps it was only a moment later, perhaps it was an eternity. A ray of sunshine-like warmth had crept beneath the bedcovers and wound itself around his feet. Like a snake, it slithered up his legs, relieving them of the aching, the shivering. Soothing and comforting, the warmth ran itself along his hips, his torso, bathing his chest in a pleasant heat. His fingers were no longer icy, his head no longer shrouded in a cold dampness. A sun-kissed contentment had discovered the whole of his body and eased him so completely.

Once he had visited Florence in summer, had stayed at the villa of an aging aristocrat. It was situated in the hills north of the city, overlooking it and the lazy, fat Arno River. Between two stalwart cypress trees he had discovered a hammock, a thing he had never, until then, had the pleasure of experiencing. Such a simple thing, really, yet when he had tentatively placed himself within its supporting, cradling embrace, he was captivated. As he lay there, the hot Tuscan sun had lovingly caressed and licked his exposed skin until he felt as though he glowed golden pink, like the sandstone villa looming behind him. Gently, to and fro, he rocked, undisturbed, suspended between two trees and within a moment. The wind was soothing; it carried the heady aroma of wild jasmine vines, combined with the stringent scent of the cypress tree sap and the smell of sunbaked earth.

And now, his sickbed was no longer that, but rather that very same hammock, between two cypress trees, above the languid, sluggish Arno. And oh, it was such a pleasant thing, to be back in that hammock again! But wait, perhaps he was not in a hammock, but rather a bed. And no, the sun was no longer bathing him. Perhaps he had been mistaken, or had he dreamed this? But he had been so certain that it was real, and oh, he was growing cold very quickly, and there, just then, when he swallowed, the scratchy, inflamed feeling was within his throat again.

Laurie opened his eyes to his bedroom, acutely disappointed. He sat up in bed, staring across the room at the smoldering coals in the hearth. He was very much within his sick body again. But there had been something familiar in the warmth that had engulfed him earlier, and it was not just the memory of the hammock at the villa above Florence.

"My word, it was the laudanum," he muttered aloud to no one but himself. Though it had not been nearly as intense as the dreamy comfort he had experienced in the opium den, it was certainly akin.

Laurie turned his gaze to his bedside table; with the glow from the coal hearth, he saw the glass bottle filled with an amber liquid, winking at him in the faint light.

"Five drops, twice daily, no more," he heard Dr. Prescott's voice say within his head.

Laurie reached for the bottle, uncorked the top. Within this bottle was perhaps the cure to not only his present ailment, but also his long affliction of apathy. This liquid had magic in it, he was certain. He brought the bottle to his lips, telling himself he would indulge in only two sips. But how would he explain it to Dr. Prescott? Perhaps he could say that he clumsily knocked the bottle over, spilling all the contents. Yes, that was a good plan.

One. Two. Laurie winced again at the nasty taste of the stuff. He carefully placed the cork in the bottle, set it back on the table, and slid down between the bedcovers, thinking of the smell of warm earth, cypress sap, and wild jasmine vines.

CHAPTER SEVEN

"Tell me, Eileen, who is your favorite saint?"

Eileen watched as Stanley halted his pacing and leaned his graceful, strong frame against the bedroom wall. The setting sun's rays filtered through the small, dingy attic window beside him and drew patterns along the wooden floorboards. The tiny room was not unlike her adjacent one, yet it seemed much smaller with both her seated self, before the little coal hearth, and his mesmerizing presence.

Cradled in his pale hands was a worn, thick volume of Caxton's translation of *The Golden Legend.* Eileen knew this only because it was the reason she had agreed, when invited, to enter Stanley's room, as well as his agreement to leave the door open, upon her insistence, for propriety's sake.

He had boasted with pride that he owned a complete set of *The Golden Legend*, which, after noting what was most likely her quizzical expression, he explained was a very old compendium of the lives of all the saints. Of course, Eileen did not require any specific reason to enter the realm of Stanley's living quarters other than that it was his.

"I suppose my favorite saint would have to be Patrick," she answered, "as he brought the Word of God to Ireland." She awaited his reaction.

A smile slowly unfolded upon his face. He looked up from the tome in his hands, his eyes locking with hers, and Eileen believed that even if she had wanted to look away, she could not. And then the butterflies fluttered about within her insides again and she stifled a giggle.

"Yes, Saint Patrick, it makes sense that he would be your favorite, being from Ireland." He closed the tome, emitting a little plume of dancing dust in the sunlight.

As he carefully placed the book back in its place upon a makeshift bookshelf, Eileen took note of a framed photograph nearby. Although she could not study it from such a distance, she was able to decipher two little girls, one holding a third, a baby, upon her lap.

"Who are those girls? In the photograph?" she asked, gesturing to it.

He froze, seeming startled by her question. He looked at her, then to the photograph, and then back at her, appearing to consider his words before speaking. "They are my nieces."

"How sweet!" Eileen thought it very charming that he was such a doting uncle that he would display this photograph with pride. "Are they the children of your brother? Sister?" She longed to learn more about his family, his life.

He busied himself with reorganizing some of the books upon the shelf. "Yes . . . my brother's children." He brushed his hands together as he turned to face her. "They reside in Hoboken."

He returned to his spot next to the window, crossing his arms in front of his plain, fitted, double-breasted, black waistcoat. Eileen considered how well suited Stanley would be in one of the loud, colorful plaid waistcoats one often saw on the gents in the Bowery.

"And who is *your* favorite saint?" Eileen asked, wanting to break the uncomfortable silence in the room.

"Saint Francis of Assisi," he responded.

"And why?"

Stanley fidgeted a bit, glanced down at his worn shoes. Just then a beam of setting sunlight washed over his face, and Eileen noticed how thick and dark the lashes were on his downcast countenance. She did not realize that she held her breath, awaiting his response, for she was beginning to feel that she was in the presence of an angel.

"I suppose it's because I have much in common with him."

"How so?" She began to worry that she was asking too many questions, but then she told herself that she didn't care.

He raised his head and met her gaze, and the copper sunbeam illuminated his eyes, affirming Eileen's belief that he might be a heavenly seraph.

"I . . . well . . ." He stroked his chin with the backs of his fingers—a pensive gesture becoming more familiar to Eileen after having spent most of the day in conversation with him.

"Do you love animals?" she offered, smiling.

He grinned. "Yes, I suppose I do love all of God's creatures, but that isn't the only reason that I feel akin to Saint Francis."

"Then what? You're not from Italy." Eileen laughed at her little joke, but he did not.

The room grew silent again, and Stanley took four strides toward her, seating himself at her feet. Eileen pulled her own feet and skirts more closely toward the old wooden chair she sat upon, startled and overwhelmed by Stanley's sudden proximity. The blood rose to her neck, her cheeks, and the silence in the room was much like a third person, watching.

Stanley clasped his hands in front of his bended knees and looked up at her. His face held some sense of tragedy, of longing. She was reminded of a picture she had once seen in a prayer book, of Jesus in the garden of Gethsemane, his hands outstretched to heaven, his face beseeching, asking God why, why he must suffer so. Her heart had ached when she glimpsed the picture, just as it did now, as she looked upon Stanley.

"I must confess something to you, Eileen."

She was certain that he could hear her heart thumping. She thought that perhaps she should leave, for she was unsure of what his words might be, of whether they would ruin what had been a most perfect Sunday. "Yes?" came her whisper.

"Like Saint Francis, I have much sin within me."

She had never met a young man so demonstrative of his piety as Stanley, and his comment struck her as odd. And again, she felt like the room's silence was watching and waiting. "But Saint Francis acted upon his sinful nature when he was young, and that was why he went into the woods, to do penance for his bad deeds."

She tried to consider her words, to better express her thoughts. She looked to the dingy window, then over to the blanket-covered bed in which he slept, and she felt the blood rush to her cheeks. "We are all imperfect, and though we might have sinful thoughts, it's more sinful to act upon them than to only house them in your mind, no? If you go to the confessional box and confess that you lied, the penance is far more severe than if you only confess to *thinking* about lying, isn't it so?"

"But Eileen, you don't understand the *depth* of my sinful nature." He reached his hand out before him, almost fingering her skirts, but then moved it away as though the skirts were made of flames. "Such wretched, evil thoughts . . ."

She was unnerved by his words and gestures, and felt she must lighten the mood of the conversation. "Come now! You exaggerate! You're very pious—have you never considered the priesthood? Perhaps taking the Holy Orders would set your mind and conscience at ease."

He shook his head, casting his gaze to his knees.

"Honestly," Eileen continued, "if I were a man, I would become a priest. Sometimes I wonder if I should have become a nun . . ." She trailed off, thinking fondly of her time making lace with Sister Theresa. "But I never received any direct sign from God—isn't that how they say it happens? I don't know . . . but there is nothing more honorable in God's eyes, in the eyes of people . . ."

"But a man like me," he said, "with such a sinful nature . . . no, it isn't possible, Eileen." Once again, he moved his hand slowly to her hem, lightly fingering it.

Eileen's heart raced as though he had kissed her full on the mouth.

"*What's* going on here?" shouted Mary from the doorway.

Eileen jumped up from the chair, mightily startled, and Stanley got to his feet, brushing off the back of his trousers. Eileen hoped he would say something, anything, to make her visit appear as innocent as it was, but again, the silence was pacing the room, waiting.

"Mary, we were only—"

"Only *what*!" she railed, entering the little attic room, the heels of her boots stomping along the floorboards like a call to arms. She walked straight up to Stanley, who stood his ground. Looking him up and down, she demanded, "And just what the hell do you think you're doing with my little sister?"

His face was grave. "You've nothing to worry about, Mary. Your sister is far safer whilst with me than you are whilst walking the street."

Smack! The sound of Mary's hand meeting Stanley's face seemed to echo off the walls and scare away the silence. Eileen gasped, her hand over her mouth.

Stanley turned his face away, his hand touching his cheek where Mary had struck him.

"Mary!" Eileen cried.

"You!" Mary turned, pointing her finger at Eileen. "Get out of this room and leave this to me!"

"I will not!"

Mary ignored Eileen, as there was a better fight to be had with Stanley. "Are you messing about with my sister?" She took a deep gulp of breath. "So help me God, if you even lay a finger on her, I will disfigure that handsome face of yours and cut your prick off with a dull knife, I will, I swear it!"

The raucousness had caught the attention of some of the girls from the floor below, who now congregated at the door to Stanley's room, witnessing the scene.

"You set him right, Mary!" shouted Claire.

"Everyone, just shut your mouths!" yelled Eileen as loud as she could, which was much louder than she had intended, and everyone obeyed.

She turned her attention back to her sister. "*Nothing* happened, Mary. Nothing! We went to Saint Patrick's together"—she considered it was best to leave out the part about Café Nouveau—"then went for a long stroll in the park, then returned here to talk about the mass and his . . . his old saint books." Eileen fumbled here, forgetting the formal title of the books. "That's all, Mary! Now calm yourself!"

"Oh, now! That's a fine way of going about it, laddie!" said Mary, leaning closer in toward Stanley. "Let the innocent girl think you're a pious one, then make your move, cat and mouse–like, eh?"

"Mary," came Stanley's low, melodic voice, "I had no ill intentions toward your sister, I swear it."

"Well, your oaths mean nothing to me. You're a man with a cock, and unless you show me otherwise, I'll lump you in with the rest of the lot, who are after only *one thing*."

The audience of whores in the doorway muttered their approval, and Eileen shook her head, mortified.

Stanley uttered not a word, for he must have known it was a losing battle with the likes of Mary.

Mary was very much aware that she had a captive audience, and she would not let the chance slip away of putting on a fine performance. She paced around Stanley, hands on hips, head held high. "My Eileen is a good girl, she is. She's a good, innocent Catholic girl, and I'll not let some fine and handsome gent try to get his hands up her skirts—"

"He *wasn't* putting his hands up my skirts!" Eileen interrupted, although she was unsure of whether Stanley's fingers upon her hem had been a precursor to something more.

"I'm not finished, Eileen!" Mary's leer was upon Stanley again. "Eileen is not like the rest of the girls here. She's not up for the taking. She's going to get married someday and be a proper lady, do you hear me?"

The audience had gone silent. Eileen noted Mary's expression, how her eyes grew wider with something that wasn't anger. Mary had touched upon a sore spot within herself and her audience.

"That's right," Mary continued. "She's going to marry a proper Irishman, who will take care of her and give her a home and chubby babies who will call me 'Auntie Mary.'"

The silence was in the room again, its presence filling it, making it difficult to breathe. Two tears escaped from Mary's blue eyes, and she dashed them away just before again pointing her finger in Stanley's face.

"Did you hear all that, Mr. Jones?"

Despite her accosting gesture, Stanley remained composed, nodding slowly. "I understand, and I think it most brave of you to look after your sister so. From now on, I will think of you with utmost respect."

By the sudden loss of words and her odd expression, Eileen gathered that Mary had not expected such a response from Stanley. But soon her brow and mouth smoothed, her shoulders relaxed, and with a lift of her chin, Mary cast Stanley a look of condescending assessment.

"And we shall keep things that way, Mr. Jones, or else." With a flourish of her skirts, Mary walked toward Eileen, grabbed her by the elbow as though she were a child, escorted her to the doorway, where the audience made way, and tossed over her shoulder, "Good day to you, Mr. Jones."

Eileen could feel her face burning red with indignation, her hands trembling, as Mary roughly pulled her by the arm back to her room.

Once inside, Mary spun around, her skirts swishing with the abrupt movement, and faced Eileen. "And what the bloody hell did you think you were doing in there, with *him*?" Mary nodded her head toward the wall that separated Eileen's room from Stanley's.

Eileen sucked in her breath; she longed to strike her sister's face. Never had she been made to feel both so embarrassed and affronted. "It's none of your bloody business!" she railed, much louder than she had intended.

"Oh, now, isn't it?" responded Mary, who quickly raised her hand to strike her younger sister.

But Eileen was sharp and fast; she pushed Mary's arm away, then shoved her backward. Mary temporarily lost her footing, but quickly regained it and pounced upon Eileen, attempting to slap her. Eileen fought off each blow with her own, and the two grunted and exclaimed in their fighting, until they locked arms and wrestled each other to the floor. With the hard fall, Mary was briefly stunned, until she halted in her attack and began to laugh heartily, clutching at her sides.

But Eileen was not equally amused. She shrieked with anger after falling, then shoved Mary with all her might, which was feeble, as she was on her behind, tangled in her skirts. She stared at Mary, startled by her laughter.

"What's so bloody funny?" she demanded.

Mary responded only with howls of laughter, falling to her side so that she was now lying down fully on the floor.

"Damn you!" shouted Eileen through gasps of breath. Her anger was now receding after all the physical activity.

Through fits of hilarity, Mary was finally able to catch her breath to speak. "Oh, Eileen, *what* a fury you have in you! You wild thing! You should consider boxing—we'd be sure to make our money for San Francisco in no time!"

"Shut it, Mary!" she said as she wiped the perspiration from her forehead with the back of her hand.

"Oh, but I'm glad of it, Eileen. I sometimes worry that you don't have enough of the fighting spirit in you."

"I wasn't doing anything wrong," said Eileen, abruptly changing the subject and looking straight into her prone sister's eyes.

There was silence for a moment, but for their labored breathing.

"Honestly, Mary!"

"It's not *you* I'm worried about doing something wrong—it's *him*! Don't you know what their game is? What they're—"

"Yes, Mary, I know!" Eileen interrupted. "I'm not an imbecile!"

"I never said you were, I just worry—"

"I don't need your worrying, Mary. I'm a grown woman, I can take care of myself. You worry about taking care of your own self."

Silence again. "Right," Mary replied, sounding tired and resigned. She sighed, and then a mischievous look took over her face. "My, Eileen, he's a fine-looking fella! But he seems a bit queer, no?"

In a whisper, Eileen replied, "He's very pious, that's all." She had suddenly remembered Stanley's close proximity.

"Well then, why ain't he a priest?"

"Says he's not good enough."

"Hmm, that's odd. Well, maybe for the best, eh? Would be a shame to see the likes of him frocked up, wouldn't it?"

The two laughed. Mary rose up to a seated position, trying to keep her voice low so that she wouldn't be overheard. "Can you just imagine?" She paused to giggle again. "All the girls lining up for the confessional box, pretending to faint in their devotion and piety, in hopes that he'd carry them out!"

Eileen couldn't control her giggling, either, and the thought of Stanley as a priest made her blush, for it was beautiful yet somehow shameful all at once.

Mary was now taken with her image of Stanley the priest, as she laughed uncontrollably. "And then, oh, how hard it would be, to see him up there on the altar, all splendid-like with the candles lit around him, the censers spewing frankincense—how could a gal *not* think impure thoughts, eh?"

"All right, Mary, that's enough of your musings," said Eileen, shaking her head and laughing at her sister.

"So, then, does he fancy you, Eileen?" Mary had grown very serious quite suddenly.

Eileen paused, looking down at her calloused fingers resting on her skirts. "I don't think so, really," she answered with both uncertainty and sadness in her tone. She felt Mary's gaze upon her, awaiting more. "I think he considers me a friend, that's all."

"Well, I don't know about that," said Mary in a cheery voice, as though attempting to lift her sister's spirits. "You know you are a pretty thing, Eileen."

"Come on then, off with you!" said Eileen, rising to her feet, brushing off the back of her skirts.

Mary smiled as she got up off the floor, still watching Eileen. But Eileen noted that there was something more in her sister's shining, wide eyes than just mischief. Mary was frightened.

"I've more money," Mary said in a whisper.

Then Eileen understood; Mary was afraid that Eileen might be whisked away by love before they made it to San Francisco, before Mary was freed from her present employment. And presently Eileen felt very sorry indeed, for how would it feel to have worked so diligently at so wretched a trade to make one's dream come true, only to have it stolen away by a force beyond your control?

Eileen went across the room toward the brick and mortar wall and deftly removed what looked to be an otherwise inconspicuous brick. From within the hole, she removed a rusty can and placed it upon her bed. She looked at Mary and smiled.

Mary returned the smile, appearing relieved. She fished in her skirt pockets and produced a roll of bills and some change. The two sat on the bed and pooled this and the contents of the can together. In barely an audible whisper, they counted their small fortune simultaneously.

"Six hundred thirty-four dollars and thirty cents," said Eileen, looking into her sister's eager, yet tired face.

"We're getting there, we are!" whispered Mary.

"Mary, you don't need to worry. I'm not going anywhere. You and I are going to San Francisco, and nothing will change that."

Mary rose from the bed and headed toward the door. When she turned to look at Eileen, her face had transformed to a hardened mask of an expression, one that Eileen was most familiar with. "Damn right it is, you're not going anywhere! I'll beat you senseless to keep you here if I have to!"

With that, Mary left Eileen's room with a slam of the door.

Eileen carefully placed the coins and bills back into the can, within the folds of the San Francisco flyer. After she had secured their savings within the brick wall, she walked over to the dingy attic window, looking out at the now-dusky sky. She reflected on her day with Stanley and felt her heart race with the remembrance of his eyes upon her.

Just then there came a light knock upon her door, causing her to start from her dreamy contemplations.

"Who's there?" she called out.

"Eileen, it's Stanley. Would you like to join me?" came Stanley's voice, muffled by the barrier of the door. "I'm attending an evening Bible reading about six blocks from here."

There was a pause as Eileen stood by the window, considering the odd invitation.

"There will be supper following the meeting. I'll pay for the group," he added.

At the mention of food, Eileen's stomach growled. She advanced to the door and opened it, finding her eyes level with the breast pocket of his black wool overcoat. Her gaze went to his hands, which held a worn, leather-bound Bible and his trusty stovepipe hat. She then glanced up shyly into his face; his eyes met hers, then faltered, as though he were trying to hide his thoughts from her.

"Let me just fetch my coat," she said, going to the nail on the wall where her coat hung.

"I'm glad you're going!" he called, now sounding cheerful. "It's going to be a cold one out there, tonight. Be sure to bring your scarf and mittens."

As Eileen fetched these items, she grew somewhat giddy—he had invited her out again! Then her eyes alighted upon the buffalo fur hat, resting atop her dresser. On a whim, she grabbed it, placing it atop her head. "This should keep me warm, don't you think?" she asked, giggling.

Stanley smiled in surprise, but as his attention rested upon her, he turned somber. "Where did you get that?" he asked, and his tone sounded accusatory to Eileen's ears.

"Why, I found it in Shay's Pub," she responded, looking him squarely in the face.

"When?"

Eileen was taken aback by his questioning. "Just last night. Why do you ask?"

"I believe I know the owner of it."

There was silence.

"How can you be certain that you know its owner?" Eileen asked, incredulous.

"Did it once belong to a young gentleman, pale complexioned, dark hair, green eyes?"

Eileen was thoroughly startled. She recalled the fine young gentleman who had caught her eye as she sang on the stage in Shay's. *I can simply tell him that I don't know who it belonged to*. She was about to utter this falsehood, but Stanley's penetrating stare seemed to have a mysterious, magical power, as though he could read her thoughts, as though he were a priest. And when she thought of his piety, she faltered, unable to respond.

"Have I correctly described the owner?" he asked, seeming to know the answer just by studying her face.

Eileen found her boldness. "But he carelessly left it behind!"

"Eileen! Do not covet thy neighbor's possessions, remember?"

"Fine!" she said, feeling defeated and embarrassed. She traded the hat for her bonnet, and walked toward Stanley, the buffalo-fur hat in her hand, held out to him. "Give it back to its careless owner, then." But Eileen could not deny that she had become intrigued that Stanley somehow knew the hat's mysterious owner.

"We'll return the hat to him within a week," he said with a tone of finality.

"We?" asked Eileen.

"Yes. You found the hat, so you should return it."

She placed the hat back atop the dresser, wondering why on earth she must accompany the hat back to its owner. The thought made her quite unsettled, for indeed the young gentleman who owned the hat surely came from the upper class. What if he should accuse her of theft?

"There's no need to worry, Eileen. He is a friend of mine, that's all."

Perhaps he can read my thoughts.

Stanley's face relaxed into a smile. "Now, let's be on our way. Wouldn't want to miss the free supper, would we, now?"

CHAPTER EIGHT

He didn't want to wake up, for if he did, he would only be back in his bedchamber, with the aches and the chills, his throat on fire, his head throbbing in pain. Why must he awaken? Earlier, he had dreamed the sweetest of dreams, resplendent with airy clouds and soft sunlight; there had played pleasing music, and he watched as a beautiful girl sang to him and only him in the most melodious voice. She was clad in white, her head adorned with a mass of long, cascading, auburn ringlets like an Arthurian maiden; her green eyes flashed excitement, devotion, and something like shy anticipation. Was she his bride?

And then he felt a hand, gentle, yet with purpose, upon his shoulder, turning him around. The large figure was dressed in black, wearing a stovepipe hat. And Laurie knew that his own eyes, much like those of the beautiful girl, could not hide his undying affection and happiness that he was in this man's presence.

And he said to the man, "You were the one who saved me."

To which the man replied, "I am but the Lord's servant. I do his bidding."

"Mr. Jones," said Laurie as gratitude filled his heart, his mouth, his every breath, "do not speak of the Lord anymore. Only speak to me, speak of your heart."

Laurie did not want to be stirred away from his dream. He did not want to leave Mr. Jones's presence. He did not want to feel within his earthly body so soon again.

"Mr. Barnard . . . Mr. Barnard?"

Laurie's eyes opened and spied Dr. Prescott.

"Dear God, Mr. Barnard, how much laudanum *did* you consume?"

Dr. Prescott appeared blurry; Laurie could not find the man's eyes so that he might meet them with his own. "Doctor Prescott, please," he whispered, "I was just speaking with Mr. Jones . . ."

Nothing could have prepared Laurie for the brisk slap on the face that Dr. Prescott administered to him. Quickly his vision focused, and he was able to find Dr. Prescott's eyes, stern and disgusted, looking down at him. There was silence as Laurie, both surprised and increasingly indignant, managed to raise himself to a seated position in bed.

"Honestly, young man," scolded Dr. Prescott in barely more than a whisper. "You should know better than not to heed my instructions on taking the medicine."

Laurie did not feel compelled to respond. He only noted that his fingers felt numb and tingly.

"You, Mr. Barnard, of all people. You are a bright young man, Cambridge educated. I would expect better from you than to indulge in laudanum—"

"Doctor Prescott," Laurie interrupted as he brought his tingling fingers to his temples and endeavored to massage away his nasty headache, "I beg you to stop in your lecture. I merely spilled some of the medicine in my clumsiness."

"Indeed," came the doctor's quick reply.

Laurie dropped his hands from his temples and studied the doctor, annoyed that the old man had spoken to him in such a tone. "I would like to remind you, sir, who is the head of this estate, who rewards you most generously for your services to this family."

"Of course, Mr. Barnard," said the doctor with a slight bow of his head, but certainly no trace of deference in his tone. When he looked up, he wore a knowing and chagrined look.

"And in the future, if I should require more medicine, I trust that my request will go unquestioned, for I'll pay you handsomely for it." Laurie felt as though his words were coming from another source, for he was still quite groggy. After uttering his demand, he felt somewhat ashamed, as though he had admitted to Dr. Prescott's brazen insinuation of indulgence.

"As you wish, sir." The doctor's disgruntled expression remained unchanged as he placed his wrist upon Laurie's forehead. He then pressed his fingers to Laurie's wrist, checking the pulse against the time of his pocket watch.

Laurie wished him out of the room. He wanted to be alone again, away from this judging man.

"It seems as though your fever has subsided, Mr. Barnard."

"Then when, pray tell, will this headache and damn sore throat be gone?"

Dr. Prescott closed up his leather bag of instruments and tinctures. "You must be sure to rest; do not leave the house for a week. Take brandy, plenty of broth, and *no more* than ten drops of the laudanum a day. Do I make myself clear, sir?"

"Indeed," replied Laurie, impatient for the doctor to leave his presence.

As the door closed behind Dr. Prescott, Laurie noticed a piece of correspondence awaiting him on his bedside table. He opened it and noted that it was on James Whitcomb's personal stationery.

Dear Old Chap,
I have word that you are ill.
Get well soon, so that we can get back on the prowl!
—Best, James

It was becoming most lucid now, indeed. If James was not ill, then certainly Laurie must have caught the illness in the filthy opium den. He rose from his bed, donned his robe and slippers, and rang for Seamus. As he awaited the butler, he paced back and forth before the vibrant hearth. Each step seemed to rattle his spine and increase his headache, but he did not cease.

A light knock sounded at the door. "Sir?" came Seamus's voice.

"Come in," Laurie responded.

The redheaded butler entered, awaiting Laurie's bidding.

"Please, Seamus, sit with me by the fire."

The addition of Seamus to the Barnard serving staff had been Laurie's doing. Certainly Mrs. Barnard never would have made such a decision, to hire an Irishman for such an important position as butler. When the position had been vacated shortly before Laurie's departure for Cambridge, four different butlers of Mrs. Barnard's choosing had been tried in the position, and each had been dismissed by Laurie, much to his mother's annoyance. He had his reasons for disliking each, rest assured.

But one day, while in his coach and passing one of the graveyards south of Canal Street, Laurie had noticed one man, dressed in black mourning, standing beside a freshly filled grave. The man held his tattered hat against his chest, and sobbed aloud, unconcerned and oblivious to the world around him, solitary in his grief. Laurie had the coach stop, for, being young and having recently read some of Lord Byron's more mournful poetry, he was deeply moved by the scene. Laurie disembarked from the coach and slowly made his way into the Catholic graveyard, until he was standing beside the mourning man. Laurie had removed his own hat, paying respect.

Finally, the man had spoken in a melodious Irish brogue: "She was my everything, my life, my heart, my only reason."

Laurie had been stirred by the man's words. "Your reason for . . ." He encouraged the man to finish his thoughts.

The man had turned his reddened, tear-streaked face to Laurie. "My reason for existing. And now I've nothing left, no joy, no sunlight, no love. My dearest friend and wife is gone, and I've nothing left."

Laurie searched for words to assuage the sadness. "Do you not have any children?"

"No, sir," came the man's reply.

"Do you not have some livelihood you might take solace in?" offered the very young and naive Laurie.

The man shook his head. "I lost my job at the gasworks when I stayed home to care for her in her final days." He broke into a torrent of sobs again, and naturally, without any thought, Laurie put his arm around the man's shoulders.

"Will you consider an opportunity?" Laurie tentatively asked.

And so Seamus was hired, and so Laurie had a loyal friend in him.

"Sir, what troubles you so?"

"I must confide in you, Seamus."

"But of course, sir."

"I fear I'm quite responsible for my own sickness."

There was a pause. Seamus's gaze went to the hearth, his hands, the corner of the room, then back to Laurie as he seemed to try to find something to say. "Sir, perhaps you brought an illness into the house, but these things are beyond our control."

"But Seamus, you don't understand just *how* I came to have this illness."

Silence again. "Sir, you cannot blame—"

"Just listen, Seamus," Laurie interrupted. "I visited a most unsavory establishment two nights ago."

Seamus smiled and nervously chuckled. "Oh, now, sir, don't be telling me about your escapades."

"Seamus, I believe I caught the illness in an opium den."

Seamus's mouth dropped somewhat, and his big eyes grew larger. He looked to the hearth again and then shook his head. "Oh, sir, that's a bad business, that."

"I'm aware of that."

"Then why?"

"Curiosity?"

Seamus shook his head again. "You should know better, a fine, educated gentleman like yourself."

Laurie laughed a bit at this. "Indeed, but it seems I don't."

The two watched the coals glowing in the hearth.

"I have become something quite brutal, Seamus. I fear I'm being punished for my deeds now."

Seamus didn't respond.

Laurie continued, "Isn't that what you Catholics believe?"

"Yes, sir, in a way."

"I believe now I must change my ways, Seamus. But I don't know how."

"So, then, it was that big blond fellow who got you out of the opium den?"

Laurie thought of Stanley Jones, both the image in reality and in his dream, and his insides lifted. "Yes, Stanley Jones is his name."

"Thank the Lord for him, then."

"Yes . . ." Laurie contemplated Stanley Jones further.

"Didn't the man say that he'd call on you again?"

"Why, yes . . . yes, he did."

"Perhaps the Lord has put him in your path for a reason? Perhaps he's the sort who can help you to change your ways?"

Laurie roused somewhat with the thought of meeting Stanley Jones again. "Yes, perhaps you're right, Seamus."

"He seemed like a very kindly sort."

"Indeed."

The two sat in silence, again studying the contents of the hearth.

"You may go now, Seamus."

"Of course, sir," Seamus responded, rising from the chair and making his way to the door, where he paused. "But sir, I have faith in you. There is much goodness in you, of this I truly know." And with that he exited the room.

CHAPTER NINE

"Do you realize the enormity of His gift? Do you?"

His only answers were hushed silence and wide-eyed nods. Finally, someone shouted out, "Yes, indeed!" This was followed by murmurs of approval.

"He gave us His only son—sacrificed him—so that we might find eternal life in His love and glory!"

"Amen," voices called out around the room.

"Amen," Eileen declared, and it sounded breathless and eager to her own ears, as though she were telling Stanley that she believed in him more than the actual words he uttered.

She noted the other young women among the Bible study gathering—they, too, appeared as though they beheld their one true love. Their lips glistened, their skin glowed, their breath came quick and short, as though they awaited their wedding nights rather than the Word of God.

The men, too, seemed stirred; their gazes were unwavering, penetrating, like they were watching a Thoroughbred race upon whose outcome the whole of their earthly fortunes rested.

"Yes, it is true," Stanley said from the podium, which was set at the front of the church's parish hall. The crowd hushed again as he held out his hand, as though he displayed something delicate and rare. "His only son, so that we might live forever!" His fevered gaze washed over the parishioners.

Eileen thought it akin to sunlight, for when it touched each member, they seemed to lean forward, as though basking in some sort of honey warmth. And when his gaze finally fell upon her, she understood. Her heart soared, her skin tingled, as though he had wrapped her and her alone in his great embrace.

"How can we return such love?" he asked the crowd in little more than a whisper.

"How can we?" asked a woman in a breathless voice as she caressed her worn Bible with languid strokes of her calloused fingertips. "What can we do for His glory?"

His eyes softened, his fine lips spread into a warm, inviting smile. He slowly nodded and a hush descended over the hall. "We are His disciples, chosen by Him to spread His word and His love and His glory!"

A collective "Ah" rose from the members.

"We live in a most momentous time in history. Each day, this great nation of ours grows and flourishes." His arms made a large, circular gesture. "We are His disciples of a new era. We must fulfill our destiny—our one, collective destiny—to spread *His* destiny to all corners of our nation!"

Affirmative mutters filled the hall.

"Now," he said, his steady gaze washing over his captive audience, "will you fulfill his desire?" He extended his arm toward the members, his palm upward, his fingers reaching out to enfold someone's—anyone's—hand.

The congregation surrounding Eileen disappeared. The hall that housed her crumbled and turned to dust. The calluses on her hands were made smooth. She was no longer a lacemaker, she was no longer a laborer, no longer a sister who shared a dream with her sister—a dream housed in a rusty can behind a loose brick in her bedroom wall. She was no longer Eileen.

"Yes," she sighed, for she wanted so dearly to do nothing but fulfill his desire, be nothing but the fulfillment of his desire. And it had nothing to do with Jesus or the Holy Ghost and everything to do with him.

And his gaze fell upon her and she knew he must be an angel, for how could such a being not be?

"Then come," he said. "Come and follow me."

And at that moment, with no thought and all fever and sentiment, she became his disciple.

Through the darkness of the bitter cold night, the prophet and disciple forged homeward to Mrs. Brown's. Their unity and fervent discussion were interrupted only by the steady rhythm of gaslight every ten, eleven, twelve, thirteen paces, and by the tumult of her heart each time he would grasp her mittened hand in his own in some moment of utter agreement.

Words, thoughts, ambitious plans were exchanged. He said such grandiose things as "our great mission," and Eileen would focus on the "our" and "great" and could think of nothing else.

Finally, Eileen asked those questions she'd been longing to ask. "When, Stanley? When will we begin this great mission? And where will we go?"

He halted beneath a gas lamp and quickly took hold of her mittened hand between his two, clad in worn black leather. As he looked down into her upturned face, a smile spread over his lips. He placed her hand upon his chest, over his heart, as though about to solemnly swear a vow. Eileen quivered, and not from the cold. She was spellbound, awaiting his answer.

"I promise you, my Eileen—"

My Eileen! She could not help but gasp ever so softly.

"—that we will embark upon our great mission very soon, and we shall head to the West, to where the word of God shall be like a candle burning bright in the great void of darkness."

"Yes, the West," Eileen agreed, until a sudden doubt took hold. Her gaze drifted to her hand upon his heart as she puzzled over her new dilemma.

His gloved fingers gently touched beneath her chin and lifted her face to his again—a gesture that thoroughly befuddled her. This was something, indeed, a lover would do. Was he about to profess some devotion to her? Was this all a dream?

"What troubles you, my Eileen?"

She remembered her concern once he removed his fingers from her chin. "How can we possibly go in one week's time? And with what money?" She thought of the rusty can and the valuable contents safely tucked within. But Eileen, though subject to such powerful persuasion, was not fool enough to offer her own money to this cause, no matter how great and honorable it might be. She was not born yesterday. Some things were untouchable. Two years of toil and her sister's sin and suffering would never go to any charity—her and Mary's future was a worthy enough charitable cause, in her opinion. And then the thought of Mary brought further doubt to her mind. She drew her brows together.

"And what else troubles you, besides logistics and money? Are you fearful of this Great Mission?" The heat of his breath caressed her face.

How could she be so foolish? Mary would never agree to such a wild whim! She laughed a little, shaking her head, looking away from him. "My sister will never agree to go, and I will not go without her."

He pressed her hand tighter against his chest with his own. "Eileen, look at me."

She did so, of course.

"I'll speak with your sister. I will convince her of how important this Great Mission is. I will make her understand." He nodded, his mouth setting hard, and there was determination in his stare.

Eileen laughed again. "Then I wish you the best of luck, because Mary is a stubborn girl."

"I don't need luck, my Eileen. I am most capable of creating my own destiny."

She looked up again; his fierce gaze had not changed. Indeed, it was very easy to believe that a man—an angel—such as Stanley could very well create his own destiny.

"Do you understand, Eileen?"

She nodded solemnly. Her hand slid free of his as he let go to head toward Mrs. Brown's. She followed behind, trying her best to keep up with his quickened pace.

~

"And where the hell have you two been?"

Mary stood before them, blocking the way to the stairs that led to the fifth floor. She was clad in a worn burgundy-velvet dressing gown. It tightly clung to her corseted form, making ample display of her fine cleavage. The sleeves cascaded open at the elbows, revealing her white forearms as she grasped the stair rail with one hand and pressed against the wall with the other. Her hair was in disarray, with blond curls a riot around her face and head and down her back. She wore no rouge or paint, and Eileen was struck by just how beautiful her sister was.

Mary glared up at Stanley, plainly not swayed in the least by his powerful presence or handsome features. At that moment Eileen feared that Mary could never be convinced to go west on his Great Mission.

"We attended a Bible study, Mary," Eileen finally stuttered.

Girls walking past in the hallway heard this and guffawed.

"Oh, aye? Bible study?" Mary mocked. "Was that all, Mr. Jones? For we have an agreement, you and I, don't we, now?"

Eileen looked to Stanley, awaiting his response.

"Yes, we do, Mary," he replied, taking a step closer to her sister as he spoke, his gaze upon her. "And unless discussing the message of our Lord and Savior is somehow in violation of our agreement, I have kept my word."

Eileen noted how Mary's breathing quickened, her bust rising and falling above her stays. Mary's expression of contempt softened for a moment into something else that Eileen did not recognize, but her gaze was as unwavering as his.

"Don't get smart with me, Mr. Jones. I'm warning you." Mary, without letting go of the stair rail or the wall, leaned in closer to Stanley, giving him a haughty appraisal.

Stanley quickly unbuttoned his overcoat, removed it, and tossed it over his arm before placing his hands on his hips. "Eileen," he said, glancing over at her, "I think perhaps you should retire for the night."

Eileen did not want to be dismissed. "But—"

"Aye, Eileen," Mary said. "You've got to get up for work in the mornin', don't you?" She let go of the stair rail and gestured with her thumb up the stairs. "Go on, then. I need to have a word with Mr. Jones in private."

Eileen was speechless, a sudden dread filling her. What on earth would Mary say now to humiliate her? How would she scare Stanley away?

"*Go*, Eileen!" scolded Mary, gesturing up the stairway once again.

Eileen wanted to alternately stand her ground and run away and keep running. She opted for the latter, dashing up the stairs past the two of them, unlocking her door and slamming it shut behind her, before the two of them could glimpse her tears of frustration.

Once she had removed her coat and hat, sat down upon her bed, and wiped her tears away, Eileen resolved to leave New York and join his Great Mission. She was no longer a little girl. She could make her own decisions and do as she pleased. Mary could stay or join her; if she would not go, then Eileen would split the money they had saved and give half to her sister.

"The millinery shop," she whispered aloud, as though suddenly remembering the plan—the dream—she and her sister had shared for some two years. How many times had she envisioned the store in her mind? A red door with a brass knocker, a room filled with . . .

What was it filled with? She had seen it a thousand times in her mind. As she readied herself for bed and burrowed beneath her blankets, she found she could not remember how she had envisioned it. Each time she struggled to recall, she saw only Stanley's determined stare. As she drifted to sleep, she no longer tried to picture her millinery shop, for her hand still tingled from being held between his hands, pressed against his chest.

CHAPTER TEN

Before reading the morning papers, Laurie added a sizable drizzle of honey to his tea and stirred. His headache had subsided, and all that lingered from his bout of illness was a slightly stuffy nose.

Seamus entered the breakfast room. "Dr. Prescott to see you, sir."

"Ah, show him in, Seamus."

Dr. Prescott wore a kindly expression, though it did not seem to reach his eyes. "Mr. Barnard, how do you fare this morning?"

"Much better, Doctor Prescott. Just a bit of a head cold, that's all."

"Very good, very good. I'll return this afternoon, Mr. Barnard, unless you should show sign of worsening, yes?"

"Indeed, very good."

"And is there anything else I might provide you with, Mr. Barnard?"

Laurie took note of the doctor's slightly accusatory tone. Looking directly at him, he replied, "No. Nothing at all, Doctor Prescott."

The doctor lifted his chin, his expression softened. "Very good, sir. I am glad to hear it." With a slight bow, he left the breakfast room.

"Bastard," Laurie muttered as he returned to his morning papers.

Midday light streamed into the immense library through the stained-glass windows, in which the family crest was detailed. Dust particles danced in the light. Laurie's mood lifted when he found that, after taking a deep breath, he could detect the scent of thousands of tomes, novels, books, atlases—*his* books—some of his own acquisition, of course, and most handed down by generations of Barnards. He thought that, indeed, he was just about recovered from influenza if he could smell that ever-pleasing library scent.

Seamus, as usual, had left the morning mail, as well as more newspapers and periodicals, upon the great mahogany desk in the center of the library. Laurie eased himself into the desk chair and lazily flipped through the correspondence. He sighed and pushed it away—nothing of interest to him presently. He then came upon a letter from his investment firm. *What ridiculous scheme could they be proposing now?* There was talk of the rising price of silver, and opportunity in the West, in silver mining. *Where in the West?* A place nicknamed "Cloud City," the town of Leadville, Colorado, approximate elevation of some ten thousand feet.

Suddenly, Laurie's attention was grabbed; the whole idea of an infinite, vast West had always given him pause, caused his heart to skip a couple of beats, and taken fast hold of his imagination. What would it be like to ride, ride, ride into the sunset and not see another white face for days, not reach the Pacific for months? Why, the concept was enough to set the roots of his hair tingling.

Though he would not readily admit it in polite company, Laurie was a subscriber to many of the so-called dime novels detailing the escapades of various characters of the West. As he leaned back in the plush leather chair with yet another heroic tale of Buffalo Bill in his hands, he was ready to escape to this West of his imagination: a place of golden prairie, majestic mountains, red-rocked desert. He liked to picture himself stepping out of a rough-hewn log cabin, stretching his arms wide to herald the sunset as it caressed the surrounding, breathtaking rock formations . . .

A knock sounded upon the library's door.

"Yes?"

"Sir," Seamus said as he opened the door, "Mr. Jones is here to call."

Laurie's mind's eye picture of a western homestead melted away with the recollection of Stanley Jones.

"You know, sir, the kind gentleman who—"

"Yes, yes, Seamus, I remember."

"Shall I send him in, sir?"

"Yes, of course, Seamus." Laurie rose, laying the dime novel upon the desk. He smoothed his hair. "And bring some coffee and scotch, would you, Seamus."

"Of course, right away, sir." Seamus gave an enthusiastic nod before leaving.

He returned a few moments later, showing Stanley Jones into the library.

"Mr. Barnard, so good of you to accept my call," said Stanley as he approached Laurie, hand outstretched, a warm smile upon his lips.

Laurie, once again, was awestruck by Stanley's commanding, handsome presence. As he took Stanley's large, rough hand in his, he found his voice. "Why, it's a pleasure, Mr. Jones." Gesturing to one of the great chairs by the hearth, he said, "Please, do make yourself comfortable."

"Thank you, Mr. Barnard."

As Stanley sat, Laurie noted his companion's slightly outdated, black wool suit, somewhat worn and shiny at the elbows and knees. But when Stanley looked intently into his eyes, Laurie once again found that he could think of nothing but the beauty before him. Luckily, Seamus soon arrived with the tray of coffee and scotch, which he placed on the table between them, thereby allowing Laurie the chance to recollect his thoughts while coffee was served.

"Would you care for a touch of scotch in your coffee, Mr. Jones?" Laurie asked.

"Well, I don't usually indulge in spirits—"

"Nonsense, sir," Seamus interrupted, "on such a cold day as this, you ought to enjoy what comforts there are, aye?"

Laurie chuckled at Seamus's forwardness, knowing full well that most other employers—his mother most certainly included—would never abide such boldness in a manservant.

Stanley seemed surprised by Seamus's frank words of encouragement. He smiled, eyes wide, and chuckled, too. "Well, then, right you are! Yes, I will take a spot of spirits."

Seamus nodded, looking quite pleased with himself, and measured out a quick shot of scotch before pouring the steaming coffee from the porcelain pot. When both men had been served, he made his swift exit.

"Mr. Barnard, what a wonderfully personable manservant you have."

"Please," Laurie said between sips of coffee, "remember our agreement? You must call me Laurie."

Stanley smiled at him over his coffee cup. "That's right. And you must call me Stanley."

The two sat in silence for a moment, Laurie savoring the peat smoke of the scotch mixing with bitter, aromatic coffee.

"I see that you are feeling better?" asked Stanley.

"Yes, much better," replied Laurie, placing his cup down on the table. "And I should thank you, again, for coming to my assistance."

"And will you keep the promise you made to me, Laurie?"

Stanley's gaze was most intent, and his low, serious tone caused Laurie's heart to skip. He felt himself blush. "Yes, yes, of course. No need to trouble yourself over that," he dismissed with a wave of his hand. He looked down at his coffee cup, remembering the little glass bottle of amber liquid in his bedroom. He cleared his throat.

"I am glad to hear it," Stanley said. "You see, very soon I will be leaving New York, so I won't be able to check up on you to make certain you've kept your promise."

Laurie started. "Leaving? Why, wherever are you off to, Stanley? Have you found employment elsewhere?"

"I am heading to the West, Laurie. As the Lord's servant, I feel—no, I know—that I've been called to spread His word on this nation's great frontier."

Laurie was awestruck by the coincidence that Stanley mentioned the West after his prior musings. The news that this captivating man would be exiting his life so soon after entering was a disappointment. He straightened in his great chair.

"This comes as a surprise, I must say. We've only just begun to know each other." Laurie silently damned himself for sounding like an indulged child who did not get his way. Certainly, that was not his intention.

Stanley took another sip from his steaming cup, his eyes never leaving Laurie's.

Laurie tried to find a way to break the uncomfortable silence. "It's coincidental that you mention the West."

"How so?"

"I say, I was just reading about a possible investment opportunity. Silver mining in Colorado."

"Really? Where in Colorado?"

"A place called Leadville, I believe. Ten thousand feet above sea level, high up in the Rocky Mountains." Laurie again thrilled at the thought of such a remote, exotic destination. "Can you imagine that?" he asked, unable to contain his enthusiasm.

Stanley suddenly rose from his chair, glancing about his surroundings. "This truly is an amazing library, I must say!" He smiled, shaking his head as if in amazement. "Do you mind if I take a look at your collection?"

Laurie was jarred by Stanley's sudden shift in conversation. "Well, no, not at all. Please, let me show you around."

Slowly Laurie led Stanley around the numerous book stacks, indicating those collections added by himself, his father, various ancestors. He pointed out the seventeenth-century Dutch collection, which Stanley seemed to gaze at in reverence. Laurie then led Stanley up to the second-level balcony, which housed further books. All the while, Stanley followed close behind, his full attention on Laurie, his every word. Laurie's heart beat faster the closer Stanley drew.

"And here is the poetry collection," said Laurie, about to gesture to books on the upper shelves. His hand accidentally touched Stanley's; there was an instant, shocking heat that reached his core. He stopped his tour, unable to think of anything but Stanley's presence.

Stanley smiled down at him knowingly. "Laurie," he said in barely more than a whisper.

"Yes?" Laurie asked, hopeful—for what?

"Have you a good, up-to-date atlas depicting the West?"

Laurie paused. *Atlas, what is an atlas? Ah, yes.* "Indeed, I do, back downstairs in the maps area." He led the way back down the narrow spiral staircase, over to the corner that housed an impressive array of atlases and maps. Laurie then produced his most recent atlas of the United States and Territories, printed just months ago, in August 1878.

"Let's take a look at where this Leadville is, yes?" asked Stanley, as though he were about to open a Christmas gift.

Laurie spread the atlas out upon one of the many walnut tables waxed to a fine gloss. He flipped to a map of the Centennial State. "It must lie somewhere within the Rocky Mountains, if it is of such high elevation," he muttered, his index finger tracing along the illustrated ridge from south to north.

Stanley then bent close, placing his hand over Laurie's. Laurie's hand felt so small beneath his. His breathing stopped for a moment while Stanley slowly guided his hand and index finger farther north, to the center of the mountain range.

"There it is, do you see? Leadville, right there, just a little ways southwest of Breckenridge," Stanley said, speaking softly in Laurie's ear.

Finally, Laurie remembered how to form words. "Yes, I see." His gaze was intent upon Stanley's hand wrapped around his. He was overwhelmed; he had never felt this sort of instant, consuming emotion for anyone ever before. Yes, there had been girls and women he would fixate on and think of for days on end, but never did they have this power over him, over his mind, his heart, his every breath. He knew this must be wrong—it *was* wrong—but quite honestly, he didn't care. This was the melding of two things—his desire to go west and his desire to be possessed by something and someone from some idyllic, almost Arthurian realm and time—and this melding had completely obliterated the horrid apathy that had hung round his neck like an albatross, it had seemed, for so very long.

Stanley removed his hand from Laurie's and stood tall. Laurie followed suit, waiting to hear what Stanley might say next. He looked up into Stanley's countenance and saw knowledge there—a melancholy, resigned knowledge.

"You should go west, Laurie. Join me and my family—"

"Your family? You will be taking your parents and siblings with you?" Laurie asked, in dread that he might learn that Stanley was married with a bevy of children. *Does he wear a wedding band?*

"When I say 'family,' I refer to my fellow flock, who aspire to spread His great word into the unknown."

"Ah . . . so none are your actual family?"

Stanley shook his head. "No, my family all passed away years ago. I've been alone for some time now."

"I see."

"I sense in you a restlessness that makes you unhappy, Laurie. I do hope that I am not being too presumptuous or forward in saying so."

Laurie could do nothing but nod slightly, returning Stanley's gaze. Maybe Stanley was correct, perhaps that was what he had suffered from all along.

"Join me, Laurie. Go west with me. Perhaps you will find your *own* fortune there, be a Barnard in your own right. And maybe you will find great satisfaction for your soul in helping to spread the Word of God."

"I have always wanted to see the West—"

Stanley chuckled, and the sound so pleased Laurie. "I had a notion that the frontier called to you."

"Did you? How?"

Stanley shrugged, then placed his hands on both Laurie's shoulders, giving a small caress. He let his hands linger there. "Will you go? Say you will. I feel that we were destined to meet, don't you?"

"Yes," came his immediate response.

"So will you go?"

"When do you leave?"

"In a week or so."

"So soon!"

"Hush, Laurie," Stanley said, drawing closer to Laurie, strengthening his grip on his shoulders. "Hush now, just say yes . . ." And then he placed his hands upon Laurie's face and laid his lips upon his. He lingered there, not demanding anything more, but asking, asking for something, hopeful yet secretive.

It was as though every inch of Laurie's physical self, every ounce of his blood, had been created to experience this one fleeting moment. If he could have shattered into a thousand stars, he would have, just then.

And when Stanley drew away, looking down into his eyes with possession, Laurie gave the only answer he was capable of giving, the only answer that could possibly exist: "Yes."

CHAPTER ELEVEN

Eileen hurried home with the usual crowds of other workers, all intent on reaching their final destinations for the evening. She tried, in futility, to dodge the piles of slush that dotted the city landscape. *Squish, squish, squish* went her worn boots. If her feet weren't so cold, she would have taken some childish satisfaction in how the slush undulated with her every step.

When she was about three blocks from Mrs. Brown's, she saw Mary heading toward her, waving enthusiastically. Sudden dread crept over Eileen; she still had no idea what had transpired between her sister and Stanley the prior evening.

"Turn round, dearie," said Mary. "We'll sup at Shay's."

"How come?" Shay's on a Monday night seemed a reckless indulgence.

Mary hooked her arm through Eileen's and led her back toward Shay's. "We're meeting Stanley Jones there. It's his *treat*," she said with a delighted giggle.

"Why?"

"Oy, stop with all your damn questions, Eileen. He told me that it was on him this evening. He wants to talk about *the West*," Mary said, making a sweeping gesture with her free, mittened hand.

"Does he? What did he tell you about the West?" Eileen asked, wary of her sister's intentions.

"Oh, he told me a great many things last night," said Mary.

Eileen scrutinized her sister's face. Mary only looked thoughtful—pleasantly pensive. What *had* transpired the night before? "Are you going to tell me what you two talked about last night, already?"

"Oh, don't fret, Eileen. Stanley simply told me about his plan to head west, spread 'the Lord's word,' as he likes to say."

"Aye? And I hope you didn't make fun of him too much."

"Well, of course I could not help but laugh at first. Asked him why he hadn't become a priest if he were so devout-like, you know?" Mary raised her brows, awaiting Eileen's response.

Eileen pushed open Shay's door. "Aye, I asked him the same myself."

They made their way to the end of one of the long wooden tables. Compared to the prior Saturday evening, Shay's was only about half filled to capacity. The two removed their mittens and ordered two ales from the barmaid.

"And what did he say to you?" asked Mary.

"Said something about having 'too much sin' or some such nonsense." Eileen scoffed, shaking her head. "Can't see how that's true. Seems like a very pious one to me, don't he to you?"

Mary looked down at her hands upon the table before her and smiled a bit. "Aye, seems a good man."

Eileen was puzzled by how quiet her sister had grown. "So, go on, what else did you discuss?"

"Well, he asked if I would join him, said that you had already made up your mind to go west. Is that so, Eileen?"

Eileen worried that her sister was trying to trick her into telling the truth. Then Mary could lay into her with a diatribe involving a mention of honesty, sisterhood, promises, and so on.

"I told him that it sounded like a fine idea, but that I would not go without you, that I did say, and you can ask him yourself, you can," was Eileen's nervous, fast-paced response.

Mary smiled at her, reached out, and put her hand upon Eileen's cheek. Her hand was soft and warm, despite the winter weather outside. "I knew you'd never break your promise to me, Eileen. Never doubted it for a second."

Eileen put her hand over her sister's, upon her cheek. "Good, because you know it's the truth."

Their ales arrived, and Mary removed her hand from Eileen to raise the mug. "To sisters," she offered, awaiting Eileen's mug.

Eileen smiled, clinked mugs with Mary, and they both sipped.

"Stanley told me you said you wouldn't go without me. It made me glad to hear that."

"Listen, Mary," said Eileen, taking hold of her sister's hands upon the table. "I figure that maybe the sooner we can get to San Francisco, the better off we'll be, yes? Who knows, maybe things cost much less there. Maybe we could rent a shop with a little room out back where we could set up house, don't you think?" She had just come up with this idea right on the spot, to further encourage her sister. Certainly she couldn't say to her sister that the effect Stanley had upon her heart had something to do with it. "So what do you say to it?"

"Well, I'll tell you what," her sister replied, "I know we wanted to save up some more before we headed out west, but honestly"—Mary lowered her voice to a whisper—"I can't take much more of this work, Eileen."

"No! Of course you can't, Mary!" It was the thing never spoken aloud, but always there like a specter, looming. "I know this, I do."

"Besides," Mary said, perking up, "Stanley tells me that he has a wealthy benefactor who will pay our train fares to Colorado. Why, we'd be daft to turn that down, wouldn't we?"

Eileen was surprised by this news. "Did he say that? Who is it?"

"Don't know, he didn't say. Doesn't matter, does it?"

"Well, I suppose, then, we *would* be daft to turn down such an offer. Isn't Colorado right next to California?"

"Don't know, but I think so," replied Mary. She looked around the tavern until she lit up with recognition. "Say, Danny, do you know how close Colorado is to California?"

Danny the piano man had just fetched a drink from the bar and still wore the smears of the gasworks upon his face and hands. He looked surprised to be directly spoken to by a woman—and an attractive one at that—but then his expression changed to one of pride that he'd been singled out as a possible man of knowledge. He came over to the table, stroking his mustache. "May I?" he asked, gesturing to the bench beside Eileen.

"Yeah, go on," said Mary.

"Well, to answer your question," he said, placing his mug down upon the table and leaning toward the two of them in a conspiring manner, "not so much."

"Damnit!" shouted Mary, most chagrined by his answer.

"Well, now, let me explain before you get your pantaloons all twisted up."

Mary playfully smacked his hand, laughing. "Fresh one!"

He smiled, looking well pleased with himself. "So, let me explain to you how America is laid out." He took his mug and placed one to the right of him on the table. "That's New York." He then took Mary's mug, placed it about two feet left of his mug. "That's Colorado." He moved Eileen's mug about one foot to the left of Mary's mug. "And that's California." He leaned back, surveying his makeshift map. He looked across at Mary. "You're in Canada right now, and Eileen is—"

"In the Pacific?" she asked.

He chuckled. "That's right."

"So where are you, then, Mr. Know-It-All?" asked Mary.

Danny rubbed a grimy hand over his chin. "Well, I suppose I'm in Texas?"

The three of them laughed.

"But look, Mary, do you see?" asked Eileen, gesturing to Danny's map. "Colorado is two-thirds of the way to California, it seems. That's much closer than New York is!"

"Aye, that's true, it is," Mary replied, studying the three mugs.

"What have you two got planned?" Danny asked, then checked himself. "That is, if you don't mind my asking."

Just then Stanley arrived and made his way to the table, sitting down beside Mary. "Good evening, ladies," he said cheerfully, removing his black leather gloves and placing his worn top hat over them upon the table. "I hope I haven't kept you waiting too long, have I?" He then noticed Danny. "Hello there, Danny! How are you this evening?"

Eileen noted how Danny seemed to look up at Stanley as though he were beholding a high-ranking member of the clergy. "I'm well, thank you, Stanley. And you?"

"Oh, very well, thank you. Say, what are all of you drinking?"

"Ale," the three of them readily answered.

"Well, then I'll have the same," he said to the barmaid, who had appeared by Stanley's side the instant he sat down.

Eileen watched, bemused, when the barmaid hurried straight over to the bar, barked the order to barman, got the ale, and brought it directly over to Stanley, ignoring the other patrons hailing her.

"Shall we have some supper, too?" Stanley asked the table.

Danny held his long-fingered, grimy hands before him in protest. "Well, I couldn't—"

"Nonsense, Danny, I won't hear it. I insist you do, my treat." Stanley turned to the captivated barmaid. "Miss, the four of us will have whatever is being served for supper."

"Smoked shoulder and cabbage," she readily answered.

"Sounds just fine, thank you," he said, giving her his beautiful smile.

The barmaid turned a shade of red as she bobbed an awkward curtsy and quickly made her way to the kitchen. Mary laughed, and Eileen bit her lip to stifle her own chuckle.

"What's so funny?" Stanley asked, turning to Mary beside him. His smile had spread to his sparkling, blue eyes as he looked kindly at her, like a dear friend might.

Mary smiled back at him, looking him square in the eyes.

Eileen then noticed how Mary was the only person she knew who could look at Stanley directly and not seem swayed by his supremely handsome features. In fact, Mary looked back at Stanley as though he were her equal, her old friend. Her regard was very familiar—all too familiar—as though she knew every aspect of Stanley. Eileen felt a sudden, hot flare of jealousy run through her, but then tempered herself. Surely, she was being ridiculous; Stanley was pious and frowned on prostitution and vice, and Mary was a prostitute who never gave it away for free. There was clearly no reason to assume something lewd had transpired between the two of them.

"Eileen?" Stanley asked. "Did you hear me?"

"Sorry, what?"

"I asked how your day at work was."

"Oh," she said, trying to recall her day. "Well, it was the usual, except that my boss called me lazy because I didn't complete the new lace pattern as fast as she would have liked."

"That cow!" Mary said, looking disdainful at the mention of her former boss.

"Well, not to worry," said Stanley. "Soon you can make your own way and create your own destiny in the West, and help to spread the Word of God."

The three sat in silence, not knowing how to respond to Stanley's declaration.

"Are . . . are you two going west with Stanley, too?" Danny asked, pointing at Stanley, his mouth slightly agape.

Mary looked to Eileen and nodded. "I believe my sister and I are. We are ready to move on to bigger and better things, right?"

Eileen was flooded with relief and excitement. "Yes!"

"And also to do the Lord's bidding, yes?" Stanley asked, his glance moving from Eileen to Mary.

Eileen could not help but note how Stanley transformed slightly when looking at Mary. He was no longer the commanding presence, the impressive, pious orator, but almost one of the lads. *Why?*

"Yes, of course," Mary replied, patting his hand as though reassuring a child.

"Well, so am I!" declared Danny.

"Are you?" Mary and Eileen asked in unison.

"Yes, I am. No more gasworks for me, lassies," the pianist said, straightening up and puffing out his scrawny chest. "I'm off to the West, to make my own life."

"Then we'll be sure to have good music, at least," declared Mary.

Danny nodded effusively, blushing.

"Who else will be going with us?" asked Eileen.

"Do you know Mr. And Mrs. Ahern?" asked Stanley. "They and their daughter, Ruth, will be traveling with us as well. They were at the Bible study last night, Eileen."

Eileen shook her head, not recognizing the name.

"Well, I believe they're coming right now to join us for supper." Stanley stood to hail a middle-aged couple and their daughter, who trailed behind.

Once they sat at the table, Eileen did, indeed, recognize the family, specifically Ruth, the daughter. She had been one of the enraptured female members of Stanley's audience the night before. Wan, pale, with brown hair and thin lips, today she looked like a candidate for the convent. That was, until her gaze fell upon Stanley. Her skin took on a rosy hue, her dark eyes became animated. Eileen felt empathy; what woman—aside from her dear sister—could resist Stanley's beauty?

After Stanley had made introductions and supper had been served, Eileen noticed that, though they were polite to her, the Aherns would not converse with Mary. *So, they are that high-and-mighty sort, eh? Word of God, indeed.* Eileen glanced over at her sister to see if she was bothered by the Aherns' slight. Clearly not; she ate her supper with a hearty appetite, stopping every now and then to chat with numerous acquaintances who happened to pass by in the tavern. Eileen was glad; she could not abide if someone's slight should upset or hurt her sister.

"So, my brothers and sisters," Stanley said, pausing to drink his ale, "we will be leaving New York City on this Friday morning, on the 8:00 a.m. train to Philadelphia, and then we'll head to the West from there."

"So soon?" asked Mrs. Ahern, her mouth slightly quivering.

Eileen noted that Mrs. Ahern was one of those women who always looked like she might cry at any moment.

"Yes, Mrs. Ahern—the sooner we can leave here and go out and spread the Word of God, the better!" Stanley declared. "We shall head to Leadville, Colorado, though I am not exactly sure how long this journey will take. But not to worry, we'll find out soon enough. Perhaps our benefactor and friend will know. I will ask him when I see him again this Wednesday."

"Will we need guns?" Danny asked.

Mrs. Ahern gasped. Ruth looked down at her hands.

"Good question!" shouted Mary. "I wager I'd be quite handy with a pistol, don't you think, Stanley?" she asked, elbowing him before taking aim with an imaginary gun at an innocent patron across the tavern.

"Well, hmm." Stanley stroked his chin. "Do you have a gun, Danny?"

"Why, no, sir," replied Danny, looking taken aback. "Never had the money for that sort of thing."

"Mr. Ahern?" Stanley turned to him.

The old man looked just as skeptical as Danny, shaking his head.

"Well, then perhaps I can ask our benefactor if he might have some rifles. I suppose we will be needing them once we get to Colorado," Stanley said.

"Aye, it's Indian country, ain't it?" asked Mary, smiling with a sort of delight at the thought.

Eileen could not help but laugh at her sister. Though some might be frightened to the bone by the mere idea of seeing an Indian, she had to confess that she, too, was intrigued. Besides, after what she had witnessed on the streets of the Bowery the past two years, she didn't much think that Indians could scare her.

"And what will we do once we get to Colorado, brother?" asked Ruth.

Eileen had to stifle her laugh, for Ruth sounded like a good little schoolgirl, rather than a young woman of about twenty.

"I'm very glad you asked, sister," Stanley said, bestowing one of his angelic smiles upon her, which made her visibly thrill. "We will build ourselves a church house and welcome all to it, and spread His Word to all that will listen."

Mary took a loud gulp of her ale.

"Oh, Eileen, might I have a word with you?" asked Stanley.

Eileen had just stepped out of Shay's after bidding her sister good night; Mary wanted to stay in the pub and chat with friends.

"Well, we are walking in the same direction, yes?" Eileen joked. She was glad to realize that she was becoming more at ease in Stanley's presence, though he still unnerved her quite a bit.

"Well, yes, I suppose we are," he replied with a chuckle. "I wanted to talk to you about that buffalo-fur hat."

Eileen stopped in her tracks; she had completely forgotten about the hat and Stanley's scolding the prior day. "What about it?"

"As I told you, I know the owner of the hat."

"Oh, really," Eileen challenged, still skeptical of this claim.

"Yes, indeed. He is our benefactor."

Eileen's jaw dropped. "He is? But isn't he very young?"

"Well, yes, he is, about my age, I would guess?"

Eileen just stared up at Stanley. *Could it really be? The handsome young man with the dark hair who left Shay's with the den mistress?* "Honestly?"

"Yes!" Stanley laughed a little. "Why are you so skeptical, Eileen? Do you not believe me?" The two began to walk again.

"But he left Shay's with the den mistress," she blurted out, regretting her words as soon as she uttered them.

Stanley's eyes searched hers. "He has since changed his ways, Eileen. Come, you cannot judge someone by their mistakes or transgressions. For example, some folks might say that your sister—"

"You can leave my sister out of this conversation, please, Mr. Jones."

He nodded slowly. "You know your sister's heart—that is why you so vigilantly defend her. She is lucky to have such a sister as you."

His words made her heart glad. They walked on in silence for a moment.

"Just as you know your sister to be a good soul, I know the same of my friend and our benefactor."

Eileen found she could not argue this point with him.

"But getting back to the business of the hat," Stanley said, "I would like you to come with me on Wednesday to meet our benefactor and return his hat."

Eileen again stopped walking. "I can't go. I must work."

Stanley smiled at her. "Eileen, you'll be leaving your job for good on Friday. Why not do so two days earlier?"

"Because that's two days' wages I need!" she declared.

"I believe our benefactor will reimburse you for your troubles, Eileen."

She opened her mouth to respond but closed it. She was utterly petrified of meeting this "benefactor" and bringing him the hat. He could still very easily accuse her of theft! "What if I just give you the hat to give to him?"

Stanley shook his head. "No, that will not do. Besides, don't you want to meet the man who is so generously funding our journey to Colorado?"

Once she got past her initial anxiety, Eileen had to admit to herself that was she interested to learn more about this mysterious, darkly handsome "benefactor."

They had reached Mrs. Brown's and headed up the stairs to the fifth floor, passing by a couple in a heated embrace on the third landing. Stanley loudly said, "Pardon us." Neither took note, as their lips were locked. Eileen snickered, shook her head.

"Now Eileen, you really ought not worry about this," Stanley said when they reached the door to her room. "Mr. Barnard is a very kind, amiable young man. I'm certain you will become fast friends. I mean it!"

"Well, I do hope you're right," she muttered before turning to unlock her door.

"Wait," Stanley said. "I need to properly bid you good night, sister."

"Huh?" Eileen looked up at him with wide eyes as he moved closer to her. *What is he about to do? Certainly not—*

He placed one strong hand on her left shoulder. She could feel its heat through the wool of her coat and dress. She shook slightly, looking up at him with a mixture of utter fear and elation surging within her. He bent forward, his lips touching her forehead. They lingered for a moment, just warm, reassuring, like a brother to a sister, or was this something more? She did not know, couldn't know. She stopped breathing. He pulled away. She exhaled in a shudder.

"Sleep well, sister," he said in little more than a whisper before going down the hall to his room and disappearing inside.

Still standing in her doorway, Eileen pressed her fingers to where his lips had been, wishing that he hadn't called her "sister."

"And what happened yesterday, when you quit your employment?" Stanley asked Eileen as the two disembarked from the Broadway train.

Eileen fussed with the chin bow of her bonnet. My, but she was terribly nervous about meeting this wealthy young man and returning his hat, which Stanley held for now. "How much farther must we go?" she asked, wondering just how far uptown this benefactor might live.

She had heard it said once of New York City, "the farther uptown you travel, the richer the residents."

Stanley had led her across the elevated platform and down the staircase to the street below.

"We will need to take the streetcar now," he said, readily producing the fare before she could, again, protest that she did not have it.

As they waited for the streetcar, a portly, mustached man across the street stopped, started at the sight of Stanley, and smiled. He began to wave ecstatically. Eileen turned to Stanley, whose jaw was sternly set.

"Do you know that man? I believe he knows you."

Stanley shook his head. "Indeed I do not."

The portly man was now crossing the street, heading toward them. He laughed, and began chattering away in a foreign language that Eileen did not recognize. He laughed again, giving Stanley's back a hearty pat.

Stanley stepped away, staring at the man, seeming affronted by his familiarity. "Pardon me, sir, but you must have me mistaken for someone else."

The man raised his brows, looking thoroughly surprised. "Stanislav?"

Just then, the streetcar pulled up before them.

"Come, then, Eileen," Stanley said, taking firm hold of her elbow and leading her onto the streetcar.

Eileen glanced out the window at the portly man, whose face appeared stricken, like an abandoned child's. He stared after the car as it pulled away and moved onward up the street.

"Are you sure you didn't know him?" Eileen asked.

Stanley laughed a little. "Surely I don't! He must be mad or drunk."

Eileen knew that the man was no drunkard. Was Stanley hiding something? She felt sudden suspicion.

They found enough room for themselves on the bench, about halfway down the length of the car. When Eileen sat and smoothed her worn wool coat, she glanced up, only to notice the critical stares she garnered from the swells on their way uptown. Her suspicion of

Stanley was forgotten, for she was then painfully reminded of how poorly her attire was, despite it being the best she owned. She was ashamed, yet angry. Were these people, really, any better than her?

Her irritation soon shifted to amusement, though, when she noticed how the swells were mesmerized by Stanley's handsome, powerful presence. Men seemed intimidated, women seemed spellbound. Eileen smiled to herself; it was always the same, and she had best get used to this. A young, attractive woman seated across from them let her eyes run all over Stanley, without shame. *Lady, indeed!* The woman tried her best to make eye contact with Stanley, but he was looking at Eileen.

"So, tell me how it all happened yesterday with your employer."

"Oh!" Eileen was reminded of his original question. "Well, to be quite honest, she seemed very surprised." She giggled a little in delight. "In fact, she then asked me how much I wanted to make per hour!" It had been shocking, indeed, to hear her sullen employer ask *her* to name her price. Eileen had almost been tempted to name an exorbitant amount, but she remained true to her original intent. "But I told her that I was headed west with family. She actually wished me luck and then told me to stay out of trouble."

"Well, then, it seems as though your employer truly valued your skills, Eileen. No employer wants to lose an honest, diligent, skilled worker."

Eileen shrugged. "Was a surprise to me, really. Never knew she thought so highly of me."

"Many people are not demonstrative of their feelings, especially when they are in positions of power."

Eileen nodded, considering his words. She glanced around again, realizing with sudden embarrassment that everyone around them had been listening keenly to their conversation. She decided to remain silent the rest of the journey. Strangers did not need to know her business.

Eileen stood, awestruck, staring up at the grand facade before her.

"Well, come on then, up the stairs," Stanley encouraged from the top landing, smiling at her.

For the hundredth time, she adjusted her hat and chin bow, then made her way up the stairs. Once she reached the top, she could feel her heart racing with nervousness.

Stanley lifted the brass knocker. Within moments, a manservant or butler answered the door. *What is the difference between them? Oh dear.* Eileen felt herself sorely lacking in the requisite manners and etiquette.

"Please, do come in, Mr. Jones," said the servant, an elder man with fuzzy white whiskers.

"Thank you, Seamus. And how are you today?" asked Stanley.

Seamus? Eileen quickly followed behind Stanley into the foyer. *Could the butler actually be an Irishman? Certainly looks it.*

"I am very well, thank you, sir," answered the butler, who seemed to be trying his best to temper his Irish accent. "And who should I announce as your companion?" he asked, giving Eileen a kindly look.

"Eileen Maguire, sir," she readily answered.

Seamus smiled at her. "Very good, Miss Maguire. I shall announce your arrival to Mr. Barnard."

Eileen watched Seamus hurry away, up the largest staircase she had ever seen in her life.

"Eileen," Stanley whispered, "come look at this table here." He led her over to a very solid-looking wooden piece. "Take a guess at how old this might be."

She studied the legs, the handles and knobs on the drawers, the gleaming finish. Was he trying to trick her? She had no idea how old the piece might be. Certainly it could not be so old if it was so shiny and unscratched. "I don't think it is very old," she said, unsure.

"Ah, but you are wrong," Stanley said, smiling down at her. "I'd wager it is early 1600s."

Eileen's jaw dropped. "Really? I don't believe you."

Seamus's footsteps approached down the stairway.

"We'll ask Mr. Barnard later," Stanley quickly whispered.

"Let me take your coats and things," Seamus said, helping the two of them out of their coats, placing them in an adjacent room. "Please, follow me into the sitting room. Mr. Barnard will be down momentarily." He led them into a great room, walls covered with numerous portraits, landscape paintings, a huge stone hearth with a roaring fire. "Do make yourselves comfortable. Would you like some tea or coffee?"

Eileen looked over at Stanley, deferring to him.

"What would you prefer, Eileen?" he asked.

"Tea, please," she answered in little more than a whisper.

"Same for me, Seamus," Stanley said.

"Very good," the butler said, then exited.

Eileen sank down onto a plush burgundy-leather great chair. The leather moaned as she sat, which made her terribly self-conscious.

"Beautiful home, yes?" Stanley asked, sitting in adjacent great chair.

"Indeed."

Just then the door opened and the dark-haired young man entered. "Welcome!" he said jovially.

Stanley stood first, and then Eileen remembered to follow suit. Just then, the young man noticed her. His eyes grew wide, as though he had pleasantly stumbled upon some exotic flower while on a walk. His pace slowed.

Stanley cleared his throat in the silence. "Laurie, allow me to introduce my friend Miss Eileen Maguire."

He was shorter than Stanley, and not nearly as physically impressive, that was for certain. But Eileen found him just as attractive as she had when she had spied him in Shay's. Stanley was angelic, a marble statue or ancient artwork come to life, but this young man was very earthly, real, dark-haired like some of the more mysterious men who lived near her village in Limerick. There was something of home about him, and she couldn't shake the eerie feeling of it, despite the fact that she knew he was so opposite of anyone from her home in Ireland.

Eileen remembered to extend her hand amid this onslaught of feelings and ideas.

"I've seen you before," he said as he took her hand in his. "I believe I heard you sing in a pub near the Bowery?"

Eileen could not help but smile, not only because he so quickly recalled her but also because his very wide, boyish smile was so endearing. "Yes, it was at Shay's."

"Yes? Was that the name of the establishment? I fear I don't recall," he said, laughing a little at himself. "I'm Lawrence Barnard, by the way, but my friends call me Laurie."

Eileen giggled, too, for she was both nervous of and delighted by him.

Stanley came closer to Laurie and placed his hand upon his shoulder. The moment he did so, he had Laurie's full, undivided attention. The young man looked up into Stanley's eyes with admiration, as though he existed to serve Stanley only. Eileen was amazed by the transformation, but then reminded herself that Stanley did have this effect on everyone, it seemed.

"Eileen has found something of yours," Stanley said, gesturing over to the table on which he had placed the buffalo-fur hat.

It took Laurie a brief moment to take his gaze away from Stanley's eyes, but when he looked upon the hat, he exclaimed, "My buffalo hat!" and took it in his hands, looking both pleased and relieved. "I thought this hat was long gone. How did you find it?" he asked Eileen.

"Oh, you left it behind at Shay's, right on top of the bar."

"Did I? How careless of me," he said, placing it down on a chair across the room. "That hat is very dear to me. I used to wear it on my trips down to London from Cambridge."

Eileen had been wondering why something so simple as a fur hat held such value to a man wealthy enough to perhaps buy a new one for each day of the year.

"Thank you, Miss Maguire, for bringing it back to me. I cannot tell you how glad it makes me to have my hat back. You were very, very kind to retrieve it for me."

"It was nothing," Eileen said, not knowing how else to respond.

Seamus entered with the tea tray, placing it down upon a table before them. The three sat down while Seamus served them.

"Seamus, Miss Maguire has found my dear buffalo hat and returned it to me," Laurie said.

Seamus looked over at Eileen. "Well, now, that was very good of her, sir. You will have to find a way to express your gratitude, I'm sure," he said, giving Eileen a sly wink as he handed her a plate with a piece of lemon cake upon it.

"Yes, yes, of course," Laurie said. "Seamus, do bring me my checkbook when you have a moment."

Eileen was not exactly sure what a checkbook was.

"Well, sir," the butler said after he had finished serving Stanley, then Laurie, "not everyone has a bank account in which to deposit a banknote."

"Ah, how foolish of me," Laurie said, laughing at himself, and also seeming slightly embarrassed. "I'll trust you to fetch some appropriate payment, then."

"Of course, sir," Seamus said before leaving the room.

The three sat in silence, enjoying the tea and cake. Eileen never had held such beautiful china in her hands.

"So I am happy to report that we have six others joining us on our journey to Colorado, Laurie," said Stanley after finishing his cake.

"Well, now, that's good to hear," replied Laurie.

"Miss Maguire and her elder sister are two of them."

"Really? You are to join us, too?" Laurie asked Eileen, looking pleasantly surprised.

"Yes, my sister and I have always dreamed of moving west."

"And so have I, I must confess," he replied. "I wish we were leaving right now, though I still have so much to pack and so many last-minute matters to take care of before Friday morning. Have you and you sister finished your packing, Miss Maguire?"

Eileen swallowed her bite of cake. "No, but we've not much to pack, Mr. Barnard."

"Ah," he replied, and Eileen could not help but notice the slight blush that spread over his cheeks. She felt sorry for having made him feel uncomfortable.

"Well," he said, smiling, "I'll at least have my buffalo hat, now, for our journey!"

"I am reminded of a concern voiced by one of our party," said Stanley. "Laurie, would you happen to own any rifles that you would not mind sharing with the other men of the party?"

Eileen was surprised at Stanley's familiarity with Mr. Barnard, and also at the forwardness of his query.

"Worry not," Laurie said with a wave of his hand. "I've already arranged to have a number of firearms shipped with my belongings. One simply cannot go west of Missouri without firearms. Why, we wouldn't be able to go elk hunting!"

"Right you are, Laurie," Stanley replied.

"Mr. Barnard, might you know how long the journey will take to Colorado?" Eileen asked.

"That's a very good question, Eileen," said Stanley.

She knew it was a good question, and didn't enjoy Stanley's telling her so as though she were a schoolgirl.

Laurie stroked his clean-shaven chin. "Oh, it's rather difficult to say, Miss Maguire, but my estimate would be slightly less than a week to Colorado, if the weather cooperates. Then, of course, getting to Leadville from Denver will be no easy task."

"How so?" Eileen asked, for she wanted to know everything she could so that she could tell Mary later on.

"My agents in Denver inform me that there is no direct rail service to Leadville as of yet, though the construction of such a line is underway. We will have to take a narrow-gauge train from Denver to a town called Webster. From there we will have to hire a stagecoach and travel over a high mountain pass, then down into Leadville. I'm told that, for the right price, some intrepid coach drivers will boldly take the most direct route, over Mosquito Pass."

"Is it dangerous?" Eileen asked, growing worried with the idea of a treacherous mountain pass.

"Well, there is some risk, yes, especially with the mercurial nature of mountain weather," Laurie replied, "but hundreds of people have been making the journey successfully every day, I am told, so I don't think we need to worry." He looked at her kindly, like an elder brother would. "Besides, it will be a great adventure!"

The pleasant moment was loudly interrupted by Stanley's clearing his throat. He turned to face Laurie, who then immediately seemed to forget about Eileen.

"Now, Laurie, have you worked out all the final details of your mine stake in Leadville?"

"Oh, yes, of course," Laurie replied. "I have the title and deed in my possession. The area is east of town, toward the Mosquito Mountain Range."

"Very good, very good," said Stanley.

Eileen sat in silence while Laurie detailed his plans on how to proceed with his mine claim. Though most of the talk was quite technical, Eileen was able to understand that Laurie had already begun the process of hiring workers to dig a mine shaft and build a pull house. She did wonder, though, how all these entrepreneurial plans fit in with Stanley's desire to spread the Word of God. She longed to ask him how he would be involved, but then decided that it might be much too forward a question to ask. She would learn soon enough, she was sure.

Soon the visit came to a close, and Laurie escorted the two of them out to the foyer, where Seamus awaited with their coats and hats. After assisting them, he then quickly handed Laurie an envelope.

"Ah, and I would like to express my gratitude to you again, Miss Maguire, for returning my dear hat to me." Laurie handed her the envelope. "I suppose I am a sentimental fellow, to be so attached to a silly hat!" He laughed at himself.

Eileen giggled. "It's a fine hat, to be sure, Mr. Barnard."

"Well, I will see you very soon, Friday morning."

Eileen looked to Stanley, and noticed that his expression appeared somewhat annoyed, though she could not understand why. Had she said something wrong?

"Until Friday, then," he said, giving Laurie's shoulder a squeeze.

Laurie looked up at him with that captivated expression Eileen was becoming familiar with. "It seems a long way off, doesn't it?" he asked in a soft voice.

His question pulled at Eileen's heart, much like witnessing a child who must part with something very precious to him.

"So?"

They sat side by side again on the streetcar.

"So, what?" Eileen asked Stanley.

"Have you looked to see how much Mr. Barnard gave you?"

The envelope was clutched tight in her mittened hand, within her coat pocket. "No, I haven't. I'll not count money in public in front of strangers," Eileen whispered. "Do you take me for a fool?"

Stanley looked surprised to hear her speak so, then turned his gaze away from her. "No, you are right not to do so."

It felt as though the sunshine had gone from her day, to have him look away from her so when she'd had his full attention. *Silly Eileen!*

CHAPTER TWELVE

The Irish girl. Laurie contemplated her while sitting at his desk in the library. She was lovely. And there was something so very real about her. He couldn't find any other way to describe her—real. Like dear old Seamus, she had come from the poorest of poor, risking everything to cross an ocean and try to make a life in a land very inhospitable to her people. Yet she obviously thrived, for she looked healthy, very healthy. And she was lively and bright; no, she was not educated, that was for certain, but her curiosity and eagerness to learn were something to behold. He liked her very much, and hoped to befriend her on their journey, get closer to that realness he felt he sorely lacked.

The journey! How he thrilled each time he thought of the great move he was undertaking. To see the West, to create his own destiny away from the trappings of his inherited legacy—why, he could barely contain himself. He was restless and could not sit for long in one place because he was so filled with excitement. And it was all because of Stanley Jones, who had precipitated this great change, this momentous turn of events. Thinking of Stanley, he absently touched his lips, remembering the kiss—the sweetest of kisses. He trembled, closing his eyes tight, reliving the moment with Stanley. He grew hot, from both the intensity of the memory and his shameful, shameful secret. No one must ever know except himself and Stanley. His lips spread to a smile beneath his fingertips—this shameful secret was so very thrilling, too.

There was a knock on the library's door.

"Yes?"

Seamus entered. "Sir, might I have a word with you for a moment?"

"Yes, of course, Seamus. I was just finishing a message to my mother."

"I'll have it sent out directly, sir."

"Oh, no, no rush on this, just whenever it can be done. Now, what is it, Seamus?"

The manservant stood about six feet before Laurie's desk. He opened his mouth to begin speaking, then seemed to think the better of it, looking perplexed.

Laurie sensed his unease. "Have a seat, Seamus."

He sat across from Laurie. "Sir, I have come to a decision about my future."

"Well, that's a serious matter. And what might that be?"

"I would—that is to say—I was wondering if you were planning on taking me as your manservant to the West?" He looked up from his shoes, his pale-blue eyes meeting Laurie's.

Laurie had been puzzling over this same question. At first he thought that perhaps he should head to the West with as few trappings of his privileged, East Coast life as possible. But then he thought that he would not be able to do without Seamus and his good company. And certainly he could not just leave him here, to be at the mercy of his mother. That would be a cruel fate for such a faithful manservant. "Would you like to go to Colorado, Seamus?"

"Oh, yes, indeed, sir. I would very much like to go out west. And sir, if I might be so bold, if you will not have me with you, then I shall have to find new employment, for I'll not remain here."

Laurie nodded. "No, of course not. I assumed as much already." He leaned forward, clasping his hands before him on the desk. "I would very much like to have you in my employ in Colorado, Seamus. But

I should tell you that this will be a different life, lacking much of the comforts and amenities we have presently."

"Do pardon me, sir, but I'm aware of this. You need not worry about me. I came from very humble beginnings in Cork."

"Yes, then of course you understand better than most."

"Sir, it would make me very happy to journey to Colorado in your employ."

"Well, then it's settled." Laurie rose from the desk, went to the brandy decanter on the side table, and poured Seamus a glass. Handing it to the older man, he toasted, "To the West."

Seamus, a relieved smile upon his ruddy face, touched his glass to Laurie's. "To the West!"

CHAPTER THIRTEEN

Mary flopped down upon Eileen's bed. "Oh, but I can't even begin to tell you how very carefree I feel, Eileen!" She ran her fingers through her blond curls, cascading them all around her head upon the mattress.

Eileen sat beside her, admiring how her sister appeared like an angel with a golden halo. She watched a genuine smile spread over her sister's lips.

"I'll never sell it again, you know," Mary said, sounding very serious. "I'll only give it to those who deserve it."

"Aye, well, I believe that's how it was intended to be, right?" Eileen responded.

Mary playfully whacked Eileen's arm, laughing. "You know what I mean. I'm serious, you know."

"Oh, I do know. And I'm glad." Eileen caressed her sister's cheek. "Now, I've something to show you," she said as she removed a folded envelope from her skirt pocket.

"What's that?" Mary rolled to her side and propped her head up on her hand.

"This is payment from our benefactor for my returning his buffalo hat today."

Mary gasped. "You met him? How old is he? Oh, wait—the buffalo hat? Didn't that belong to that young dandy we saw in Shay's who left with the den mistress?"

Eileen nodded.

"Our benefactor is a no-good opium eater?"

"Stanley tells me that he has changed his ways."

"Well, that was very quick. He was only hitting a pipe just last weekend." Mary rolled her eyes.

"Everyone makes mistakes, Mary."

Mary considered for a moment and then nodded. "Aye, true. So what was he like?"

"Do you want to know what he's like or do you want to know how much is in this envelope?"

"Oh, the envelope, please!"

Eileen opened the envelope, counting out thirty dollars.

"Thirty dollars! For returning a hat! Is he daft?"

"Whether he is or not doesn't matter to me so long as he's willing to give me thirty dollars," Eileen said, going to the wall and pulling out the brick that hid their savings account tin can. She brought the can over to the bed, placed it between them. "We've now got $695 saved up, Mary."

Mary smiled. "And we're leaving this godforsaken place and heading to San Francisco, where we'll be proper shopkeepers."

"Mary, how long should we stay in Leadville before moving on to California?" Eileen had been struggling with this matter ever since they had agreed to accompany Stanley on his Great Mission. Would it be deceitful of them to accompany him and then make their own way not long after?

Mary shrugged. "Don't know. I was thinking, though, that if we have this benefactor and he is willing to pay for our room and board while we're there, do you think we can make some more money up there?"

"How?" Eileen raised her brows, wondering in what manner Mary thought they might be able to make money in Leadville, aside from the most obvious.

"Well, I ain't married. If I wanted to date a rich miner for a little while, what would be the harm in that?"

"But you just said a moment ago—"

"Aye, I know what I said, Eileen, and I'm sticking to it. But you never know, there might be a dashing, young, rich mining man who has a liking for a bossy Irish lass. And besides, maybe Stanley fancies you, Eileen. Maybe he wants you to be his *bride*."

Eileen's heart raced at the thought, but she tempered herself. "Stanley doesn't fancy me. Stop saying such things."

Mary giggled. "Oh, why can't I? You're a pretty one, Eileen, and a good girl. And I see you blushing! You'd be his blushing bride!"

Eileen laughed in embarrassment. "Stop, Mary!"

"You fancy him," she sang. "You fancy him, indeed!"

"Everyone fancies Stanley, you cow."

Mary shook her head. "Not me, dearie." She rolled to her back, running her fingers through her hair again. "Not me," she said wistfully, her gaze drifting to the cracked, water-stained ceiling.

Eileen couldn't make any sense of Mary's attitude toward Stanley—could she not see how beautiful he was? She shook her head, getting back to the original matter. "But I'm being serious, here, Mary. We don't want to stay for too long in Leadville or else we'll lose sight of our original plan."

"You're right, Eileen. And I suppose that we'll have to play along with Stanley's *Great Mission* for a little while to satisfy this benefactor. Say, by the way, what was the opium-eating benefactor like, eh?"

"Well, you saw him for yourself," Eileen said, cursing herself for the grin she could not hide.

Mary studied her, smiling. "He was a looker, that one."

"Certainly not as handsome as Stanley, though." She waited for her sister's reaction.

"My dear sister, men come in all sorts of varieties. He's just another variety."

"Well, he's the wealthy variety, that's for certain."

"Aye, obviously. Did you go to his home?"

"With Stanley, this afternoon. It was the largest home I've ever laid eyes upon!"

"That grand, eh?"

"Oh yes. He's very rich, indeed."

"Well, now, maybe you can fetch yourself a rich husband, then, Eileen. He could certainly set you up in a first-class millinery shop in San Francisco."

Eileen grew tired of her sister's teasing, shoving her. "Will you quit with all this marriage talk? It's ridiculous."

"Nothing is ridiculous in this life, dearie!"

Eileen rose from the bed. "Have you packed your things?"

"Oh yes, all packed. And you?" she asked, sitting up on the bed.

"Well, no, though I don't have much to pack, really. Might I put my two spare dresses in your trunk?"

"Eileen, you are *not* taking your two shabby work dresses with you, nor are you traveling without your own trunk! Sister, you'll look like a lowly immigrant traveling west!"

"Isn't that what I am?"

"Indeed, no. You're an American now, just like me."

"Too bad others don't see us that way."

"Listen," Mary said, rising from the bed. "Tomorrow you and I are going to go and get you a proper trunk and some new clothes. I can't be seen traveling with such nice things when my sister looks like a street urchin."

"No I don't!"

"Well," Mary said, giving Eileen's best Sunday dress a once-over, "if that's the best you've got, then we're in trouble."

"But I don't want to use any of the money we saved," Eileen protested.

"We won't need but five dollars, I know how to bargain. Things might not be brand new, but no one will ever suspect it." She kissed Eileen. "Now, go to bed and we'll set out in the morning to shop."

"Mary, have you told anyone that we're leaving?" Eileen had not said a word to anyone in the house, hoping to sneak out without being noticed and without having to pay Mrs. Brown for the week's board. She felt no guilt about this when she considered the exorbitant cost for such lowly dwellings.

"No, of course not! Don't want to pay old Brownie if I don't have to. And I haven't told any of the girls."

"Not even Claire?"

"No, certainly not Claire. Why, she'll make such a fuss about it all, start drinking, and then she'll want to have a wake for us as though we're crossing back over the Atlantic again."

Eileen laughed a little. "Aye, you're right about her."

"We'll pack our things and have Stanley help carry the trunks out early Friday morning. He says that there will be a coach to take us to the train station, can you believe it?"

Eileen thought of the kindly, lively face of Mr. Barnard, warming inside. "Aye, I can believe it. We've had a turn of luck, Mary."

CHAPTER FOURTEEN

"I don't know how I can begin to tell you this," Stanley said as he stood before Laurie in his sitting room, one day before they were to embark upon their adventure to the West.

Laurie could not help but note how Stanley's alabaster skin appeared even paler. "Stanley, please, do have a seat."

Stanley seated himself opposite Laurie, before the hearth.

"Pray tell, what is it? You're not having second thoughts, are you?" asked Laurie with a nervous chuckle.

Stanley's eyes widened in surprise. "No, certainly not."

"Then what is the matter?"

"Do you remember how I mentioned that there was a wealthy older gentleman who was to be the benefactor for our friends heading west with us?"

Laurie nodded. "Yes, I recall."

"Well, it seems that he has rescinded his offer at the last moment." Stanley shook his head, looking down at his knees before continuing. "I cannot say what sort of evil design would make a good man do such a thing, but I have just learned of it today. I'm afraid it puts our Great Mission in jeopardy."

"Do not some of these friends have their own money saved for such a journey?"

Stanley looked up at him. "Laurie, these people are the very poorest. You met Miss Maguire just yesterday—"

Laurie suddenly felt ashamed of his question. "Yes, how very foolish of me."

"Laurie, I do believe that—if you were to be so generous—all that would be required from you is the cost of the journey to Colorado, and perhaps part of the cost of building a church once we arrive in Leadville."

Laurie held his hands up in protest. "This is not a problem, Stanley. I am certainly willing to pay for the journey of these well-intentioned friends, as well as help you to build your church."

"Oh, but you are very kind, Laurie." Stanley rose from his seat, his hands held over his heart. "I cannot express—"

"But please, I must place a stipulation on this generosity," Laurie interrupted.

Stanley cocked his head slightly to the side as he sat back down.

Laurie had suddenly formed an image in his mind of poor families clinging to him, constantly nagging him for money for food, for housing, for this and that. One must help the poor, but not let them become dependent. He did fully believe in the adage "give an inch . . ."

"Yes? What is the stipulation?" Stanley asked.

Laurie could not help but notice how Stanley grew rigid in his posture, his mouth setting in a stern expression.

"I will not pay to have these friends fed and clothed and housed once we have settled in at Leadville. People must learn to be responsible for themselves, Stanley. Don't you agree?"

"But what of the Maguire sisters?" Stanley posed, intent on Laurie.

A good question, Laurie realized. Women could not just go and make a living for themselves—especially in the wild frontier—in any respectable way, other than to become teachers. He knew this wasn't a realistic option for two uneducated Irish women.

"What do they do presently for employment?"

"Well," Stanley said, taking a breath, his gaze going to the hearth, "they both work in a millinery factory."

The image of Miss Eileen Maguire working twelve hours a day in a poorly lit factory, bent over lacework, was disturbing for Laurie. He did not like to think of such a bright, pretty thing doing such menial labor.

"There will be no opportunity for that in Leadville, I am certain," Laurie said. What were the other options for a working-class woman: maid, cook, waitress, dancer, whore . . . "I will provide for the sisters until they are able to find some employment suitable for respectable women."

Stanley's brows rose. "This is very kind of you, Laurie."

"It isn't kindness, but the responsible thing."

"True. But not every man would do this."

"But you would, Stanley, wouldn't you?"

"Oh, but of course I would."

The two young men contemplated the hearth. Stanley drummed his long fingers in a staccato rhythm upon the chair's arm. Laurie found the silence and tension within the room uncomfortable.

"So the coach will arrive at your residence at six o'clock in the morning," Laurie said.

"Yes, and I've arranged for the rest of the party to meet there, to make for a speedier trip to the station."

"Are you excited, Stanley?" Laurie asked suddenly, tired of all this talk of practicalities and logistics and such. He did not want to think about these things. He wanted to escape into his ideal: wide open plains, towering mountains, herds of buffalo, a secret kiss from Stanley . . .

Stanley's eyes met his. "Yes, Laurie, very excited."

Laurie felt a rush of heat, as though he were already in a desert surrounded by red rocks.

"But I just can't wait to be away from here, Stanley," he said. "How greatly I look forward to a new life out west."

Stanley rose from his seat. "Laurie, your new life has already begun."

Laurie rose, longing to touch Stanley, not wanting him to leave so soon. He took an awkward step forward, holding his hand out. He could not bring himself to be the initiator of something more.

Stanley took his hand in his, then pulled, coaxing him closer.

When Laurie was but inches from Stanley, he looked up into those illuminated blue eyes. "I—I just cannot wait," he whispered. He was completely at Stanley's mercy.

Stanley's gaze went from his eyes to his lips. He wrapped one arm around Laurie's back, took hold of his chin, descending for what seemed like forever to Laurie, until his lips claimed Laurie's mouth. He lingered, then boldly kissed, urging Laurie to part his lips.

This was the laudanum and the opium and the finest scotch and Miss Maguire's sweet face and the Tuscan hammock and the dozens of Cambridge whores and the pleasures of Voltaire, Coleridge, Poe, and the jagged mountains and a thousand buffalo and a red-painted desert below an endless sky. Endless, endless.

His breathing heavy, he tasted Stanley's breath, so delicious. This was their shameful, wonderful secret. He wanted to go wherever Stanley might lead him. Oh yes, he would. This was an undiscovered frontier and he would. He would a thousand times over.

Stanley pulled away. "Laurie," he whispered, breathless, "this is between you and me. This is our secret."

Laurie bit his lip to stifle his grin, his joyous laugh.

CHAPTER FIFTEEN

By the light of one cheap tallow candle, Eileen and Mary held the two little sacks that Eileen had made from a torn edge of the worn bedsheet. They filled them with the tightly rolled wads of bills and the coins from the rusty metal can. Eileen took the crumpled advert for San Francisco and stuck it in her skirt pocket. She held the empty can and contemplated it. There was no more need for it, but she found she could not let it go, as it had been the trusty vessel of their hard work and dream. So she quickly went to her trunk, unlatched it, and shoved the old can down into the bottom corner, being sure not to let Mary see, for she would have ridiculed her for her sentimentality.

In silence, the two then unbuttoned their jackets and blouses, shoving the money sacks between their breasts, just above their stays. Quickly they buttoned up again, just as Stanley lightly rapped upon Eileen's door.

"All ready?" Stanley asked, worn top hat in hand.

The two nodded.

Stanley went to Eileen's secondhand-but-new-to-her trunk, bent down, and grabbed the handles at either end.

"Stanley, you can't get it yourself," Mary scolded in a whisper, going to his side.

He rose without effort, gripping the trunk as though it were a parcel of papers. "Of course I can, Mary," he said.

Eileen could have sworn she noticed him wink at Mary. *Could he have?* But then she pushed the idea out of her head; she couldn't see much of anything by the light of one measly candle.

He made his way out of the room and down the stairs. Mary followed, stopping at the doorway.

"Well, come on, then," she said to Eileen.

"Let me just look around to make sure that I haven't forgotten anything," she said absently, holding the candle in her hand, taking a tour of the small, dingy, freezing room that had been her home for the past two years.

"Eileen, you haven't forgotten anything! Now let's go before the house wakes up!"

A sudden, gasping sob escaped from Eileen. This was all she had known since coming to America. This was her first home that was of *her* making. Ireland would always have some sense of home, or at least she thought it would, having been born and raised there. Though now that she was leaving *this* home, Ireland was someplace very distant—in her mind, anyhow. This was the home most real and most recent. It was the familiar, the sanctuary, despite all its flaws, of which there were plenty, she would readily admit. But even the flaws seemed to have an emotional hold on her of a sort.

"Why on earth are you crying, you daft cow?" asked Mary, coming to her sister's side.

"This has been our home for two years, Mary," she said, wiping the tears from her cheeks that kept spilling involuntarily.

Mary put an arm around Eileen's shoulders. "Aye, it's true. And a shitty one, at that. Now say your goodbyes, you sentimental thing. We're off to a new home now."

In a quivering voice, Eileen whispered, "Goodbye, New York home."

As dawn rose over New York City, Eileen gazed out the window of the coach—she'd never, ever been in a coach before—and watched as they passed by piles of grimy snow. The piles became a blur. She couldn't believe she was saying farewell to New York City. Would she miss it? She already did. *Silly cow, how can anyone miss the Bowery?* Would she ever return? She couldn't even think about next week, never mind years from now. She didn't see herself coming back. At this realization she bit her lip to fend off further tears; certainly she would not cry in front of Stanley, Danny, and the Aherns.

This was all she had known, this city teeming with people. She was scared to leave the familiar. To assuage her sorrow, she concocted an image of herself as a wealthy businesswoman, returning with Mary, standing before Mrs. Brown's and saying, "And this was where it all began." For it *was* where it had all begun. My, but she was falling in love with the city she had to leave. It is said that absence makes the heart grow fonder, but Eileen was not yet absent. Her heart was growing fonder as she said her last goodbyes.

And it was not just New York City that Eileen would say goodbye to over the next week. She would bid farewell to life in a metropolis, a life where one is alone yet surrounded by thousands upon thousands of others working through each day; in a way, there, one is alone yet never alone, and perhaps that is why loneliness in an Eastern city is not true loneliness. There is a difference between a loneliness resulting from lack of companionship and a loneliness resulting from lack of other living, breathing humans. The latter was more cold and chilling than the coldest winter night in New York City.

She would say goodbye to the Atlantic and all its familiar, sulfur-salty smells and the cries of its gulls. Great, large trees only just showing signs of buds would overwhelm her view from the train window, only to slowly and gradually become sparse, soon disappearing and giving way to a flat landscape dotted with farms, random little towns, and eventually nothing but prairie. She grew suspicious of this new, treeless landscape—it was not like the East. It was ugly and desolate, devoid of civilization and life as she had always known it.

Some things she did not mind saying goodbye to. Her sister was no longer a prostitute. She was no longer a factory worker.

The noise of the steam locomotive was unnerving at first. Its hiss and chug, its constant breathing like a great, hulking beast soon began to keep time to her heartbeat, she believed. Ah, but her heart—a whole heart—was yet another vestige of her old life to which she bid farewell. And some farewells are bittersweet. She soothed herself with the two ways she knew best how: silent prayer and lacemaking. She had packed a carpetbag with her collection of crochet hooks and knitting needles, along with numerous skeins of lace-weight wool. She had even splurged on two skeins of precious silk thread, the palest blue shade that shone when held to the light. She had used this to start on some fine lace for Mary. Each day of travel, her fingers worked, by their own volition, with either crochet hook or thin knitting needles, and the repetitious pattern of it, the creation of something from nothing, was an endless source of familiar comfort to her.

By the time the beast locomotive huffed and puffed its way into Denver, Eileen's heart had been taken and split in two. Eileen was not consciously aware of this theft; sometimes a thing is not missed until one finds one needs it once again, and urgently. But she would, unknowingly, search for the two pieces until she was whole again.

It is said that those who live at high altitudes have bigger hearts than those who don't. Those from the East will smart at this, see it as yet another pointed accusation that Easterners are a cold, heartless lot. But anatomically, it is true; the heart must grow when high in the mountains in order to keep a person alive with so little oxygen. And so each piece of Eileen's divided heart would grow.

Her heart had been divided by two men, who each took a piece with them as they disembarked the train in the city at the foot of the Rockies. The Preacher had one half, the Benefactor had the other.

She awoke before Mary, as usual. The timepiece upon the mantel read about seven o'clock—they had two hours to dress and have breakfast down in the hotel restaurant before catching the narrow-gauge Denver, South Park & Pacific Railroad, which had only just begun its run to South Park two months prior. Eileen stretched her arms above her head, yawning, then tiptoed her way over to the washstand. After splashing the cool water on her face and patting dry, she walked to the window.

They had arrived in Denver after dark, so Eileen had not seen much of this Queen City of Mountain and Plain. She pulled the heavy, burgundy-velvet drapes aside, then drew open the elaborate lace sheers. She gasped. Peering out the seventh-floor window, she stood in awe. Facing west, she beheld mountains like ferocious, jagged animal teeth. The rising sun tinged their snowcapped peaks a glowing rose hue.

She had seen mountains on their journey; Laurie had indicated them when they passed through Virginia or West Virginia. What had he called them? Appalachia? Yes, that was it. They had been gentle, heaving, mist-shrouded knolls in comparison to what she now stared at. *Is this what we must travel over? How?* The journey of the past eight days had been arduous at times, but now she could not even fathom this next leg of their adventure.

"Morning, dearie," Mary said in a sleepy voice. She sat up in bed with a hearty yawn.

"Mary, come see this."

"Whatever's wrong?" Mary asked, rising from the bed and making her way to the window. When she looked out, she gasped. "My word," she said as she stared straight ahead.

They did not speak for a moment, each lost in her contemplation of the view.

Eileen felt Mary's hand take hold of hers, by her side. Eileen squeezed hers back.

"So that's where we're headed, isn't it?" Mary said.

"It is."

Mary shivered a little. "Oh, but it looks frightful cold, don't it?"

"Have you seen the mountains yet?" Eileen addressed the whole table, who were just finishing their breakfast.

"No," answered Laurie in between sips of coffee. "My window faces south, so I see only the buildings across the way."

"Yes, I'm on the south side also," said Stanley.

"We see just buildings," replied Mr. Ahern.

Danny nodded as he wiped biscuit crumbs from his mouth. "And me."

"Then you must all come up to our room before we leave," declared Mary, "so that you can see the mountains."

"Are they very majestic?" asked Laurie in his usual, boyish excitement, which Eileen had grown much accustomed to over the past days.

She smiled at him. "You just wait and see."

He rose, downing the last of his coffee. He set his cup on the table and said, "I must see the view this very instant."

Eileen had given up on endeavoring to stifle the giggles that Laurie always charmed out of her. "Come on, then," she said, heading toward the lobby stairway.

The entire party followed Eileen and Mary up the seven flights of stairs, down the hall to their room. The sisters went to the window and held the curtains apart so that everyone could catch a glimpse of the view.

Eileen was very glad, indeed, when she saw the awe written upon both Laurie's and Stanley's faces.

"How stirring, how astounding," Laurie sighed, drinking in the sight before him.

"God's majesty is endless," Stanley said.

Laurie glanced over at Eileen. "It's just as I have always imagined, ever since I was a child."

"Come now," ordered Mary, "let the others have a look."

Stanley and Laurie moved away, allowing the Aherns to step up to the window, with Danny and Seamus standing close behind, peering over their heads. They all exclaimed at the beauty before them.

"How will we ever make our way over them?" Mrs. Ahern fretted in her usual manner.

"With God's grace, Mrs. Ahern," Stanley replied, "we will journey safely through."

Mary glanced at Eileen and rolled her eyes.

CHAPTER SIXTEEN

It had been that nothing held any interest for him; life had lost its delight and wonder.

As the train lurched out of the depot on Sixth and Larimer Streets, headed west, Laurie chuckled to himself, recalling this. How different things were now, little more than a week later. Before he had been a jaded soul, ensnared by his wealth and stature, turning to vice to fill the void within him, to satisfy the only curiosity he had held—a perverse curiosity.

Ah, but now! His chest filled with pride, for he had stepped away from all the trappings of his entitled life in order to take a risk, to seek adventure. His money was now funding a most worthy cause, that of helping his new friends move to the West. He also assisted his dearest friend in his ambition to become a preacher on the frontier. And these new friends—especially the Maguire sisters—were truly among the most underprivileged members of society. Just as when he had saved good old Seamus from a life of poverty and despair, he emphatically believed that he was doing the same now, especially for these two young women.

He enjoyed eavesdropping on the sisters' easy banter whilst traveling by train; it was heartwarming to witness how close they were with one another. But as soon as he would hear Mary utter a nasty oath regarding something or other, Laurie was reminded that these young women were very different from those of his prior social circle.

Laurie thought Mary a peculiar girl, like some odd, new species one might observe at a zoo. She was, of course, very pretty in that popular, coquettish, buxom blonde way. Her worldly view, forward manner, and blunt speech indicated to him that she was not simply the "factory worker" Stanley had said she was. Such aspects could not be attributed simply to her immigrant status and poverty, or else her sister, Eileen, as well as the Ahern women, would share these in common with her. Laurie had spent enough time indulging his vice over the years to know that such traits in a woman bespoke a promiscuous past.

But he could not hold this against Mary; surely poverty begets vice, just as clouds beget rain. And besides, he was not unjust, and considered himself to be a very forward-thinking young man; to judge or spite a woman for the same vice he had so eagerly partaken in himself would most certainly shout of utter hypocrisy. He liked to think that such moral conundrums were a nasty vestige of past, stuffy generations.

The train pulled through what looked to be a small farming village southwest of Denver. As Laurie watched the farmland roll past, his thoughts went to the issue of morality, which he had pondered quite extensively while journeying west. Laurie was not a religious man, never had been. He liked to consider himself an agnostic, like some of the founding fathers of America. There was a godlike being, yes, who was the Great Creator, or Decider, or whatever name one might use to encompass something so beyond human comprehension. Laurie believed, though, that religion was something necessary, something that had its place in social order. But it was something more suited for the poor, the unenlightened, the simple, honest workers and farmers, so that their moral consciences could be shaped and guided.

So, what was he doing, funding a trip west to establish a church? He had asked himself this in his moments of doubt whilst upon this journey—usually before succumbing to sleep. It was the right thing to do, the honorable thing to do, he assured himself. And he had never, ever met anyone as forthright and inspired as Stanley Jones. Why, had the man not rescued him from the dank vice of an opium den? Surely it had been Laurie's lowest point, and this man of God had burst into his life and saved him. Of course, Laurie would be dishonest to himself if he were to say that Stanley had set him on a righteous, religious path. And Laurie would never tell Stanley this, for he feared both hurting him as well as losing his love and devotion.

Yes, love and devotion, for was that not what they shared for one another? And in his mind, was this secret, forbidden love at odds with Stanley's moral and religious righteousness? Absolutely and unequivocally, no: How could such a love, so pure in intent, somehow harm those around them, mar society, threaten the good in the world? Does a man's love and desire for a woman do so? Certainly not, and Laurie, in his conveniently, newly egalitarian mind, did not see how this was any different.

But of course, it must be secret. The world still frowned on such a thing and probably always would, unfortunately. Though Laurie was not a religious man, he viewed Stanley and this shared love as something sacred. He smiled at the thought, in both elation and self-deprecation; perhaps he was spending too much time around these Irish Catholics if he was beginning to think of sentiments in Papist terms.

"Oh, look, Mary," said Eileen, seated behind Laurie. "Do you see the deer out in the field?"

Laurie's gaze drifted out the train window to the small herd perhaps twenty yards away, out in a freshly plowed field.

Eileen—how could he describe his sentiments for her? He had been taken with her the moment he had glimpsed her in the Bowery barroom and heard her sing. To him she was beautiful and exotic, with her auburn curls, pale skin, and bright green eyes.

When he had studied the history of ancient Rome at Cambridge, read the Romans' accounts of their dealings with the *Keltoi*, he would often let his imagination run to a romanticized vision of the Celtic world. Yes, Laurie had always been enamored with Arthurian lore, ever since he was a young boy. His imaginative wanderings would easily create a world of noble warriors—both male and female—fiercely painted, sinewy bodies primed for inhospitable weather and battle against invaders. Sometimes he fancied that he might have passed for a Celt back in Roman times, what with his dark hair and green eyes.

When he had seen Eileen again, in his sitting room, he thought again that she was like an Arthurian or Celtic princess—bright with curiosity, endowed with a natural pride and self-awareness, and capable of standing her ground—a young, modern Boadicea, how utterly thrilling!

And he so enjoyed teaching her; quite often on their journey he had told her anecdotes of American history and imparted geographic knowledge to her. He was charmed by how she absorbed everything he taught her, such a precocious pupil. And so industrious and skilled, her fingers always working with a tiny metal hook or thin knitting needles and thread, creating lace. But he especially delighted in how her gaze met his directly, despite the blush that often crept over her creamy skin, and in her genuinely warm giggles and smiles. In fact, he delighted in her so much that, sometimes, at night, while alone in one of the many nondescript, anonymous hotel or inn rooms in which he stayed along this journey, he would relive his earlier interactions with her and become aroused. And he would imagine teaching her more—so much more—and he would quench his own arousal, come at his mere envisioning of her, wide-eyed with curiosity, wonder, and ecstasy, beneath his wise hands, his knowing mouth, his urgent need.

No, she did not consume him so much that he could forget his desire for Stanley. But Stanley was an elusive love, and Laurie was acutely aware of the fact that he was the prey and Stanley the predator; he clung to each fleeting, shared glance, to each kind word, exchanged smile.

Stanley had barely touched him in these past days of travel. Laurie knew that he must bide his time and wait for Stanley to come to him again, and he was completely unsure of when this might occur. Meanwhile, Eileen was most certainly the hunted and he the hunter; she was a doe in his sights, and really, was there anything so fundamentally basic yet utterly thrilling, delicious?

PART TWO

LEADVILLE, SEPTEMBER 1879

CHAPTER SEVENTEEN

He peered into the scope, the cross marks directly positioned upon the elk, who was some sixty yards away and protectively watching over his harem of cows.

"One, two, three, four, five, *six*." Laurie counted out the points along the bull's crowning rack in a whisper.

"A prize," Eileen whispered back from beside his shoulder.

He became one with the rifle, as he had learned to do in his past five months in the mountains surrounding Leadville. At first, he had hired renowned huntsmen to guide him and impart their skills to him. But Laurie always had been an adept pupil, and he quickly inherited their talents, putting them to good use on his own for the past six weeks. Deer, pheasant, duck, mountain sheep, and even one black bear, of which he was most proud, had fallen before his rifle.

He had taken Eileen along with him on this day so that he might display his talents to her. He greatly enjoyed impressing her. It was an endless source of delight for him.

Eileen's breath was sweet; it was carried by a slightly northerly wind just beginning to tousle their hair. He then tensed when the wind changed direction from north to west and grew in strength.

"Damn," he muttered, for he would not shoot until the moment was perfect, in his mind, and he knew that the elk would soon detect their scent upon the wind.

Sure enough, the bull urged his harem onward, northward along the mountain meadow, which was peppered with the bright-red blooms of Indian paintbrush.

He sighed, relaxing his hold upon the rifle, turning slightly onto his left side to face Eileen, giving her a chagrined smile.

She lay very close beside him, upon her belly, on a soft carpet of fallen yellow aspen leaves. She watched the elk herd in the meadow below their place upon a gentle rise at the edge of the woods. He could detect her rose perfume—a gift he had given her two months prior. He let his gaze drift over her prone form; her tailored, brown riding outfit had been his gift to her as well, and he felt a great sense of satisfaction with himself as he admired the cinch of the riding coat along her lovely waist. The sight of that cinched waist often provoked a longing in him to trace the curve with his tongue.

His first gift to her—and her rambunctious sister, Mary, of course—was to insist that he pay for their lodging in the fine Clarendon Hotel, on Leadville's bustling Harrison Avenue, for an indefinite period. It had been his original intention to do so upon their arrival in the mining city. He could not bear the thought of Eileen taking up lodging in one of the seedy boardinghouses abutting the endless numbers of brothels and cribs. But when Mary had manufactured the tale that Laurie was a close friend of their nonexistent father's and their chaperone in Leadville in order to procure work for both herself and Eileen at May's Dry Goods, well, then Laurie had no choice but to provide for their lodging until a suitable alternative could be found.

Laurie did not care much for Mary and her coarse, forward manner. But Eileen, oh, how he delighted in caring for her. He became glad of Mary's fib, for it allowed him to pretend that he was, indeed, Eileen's protector, chaperone, guardian, mentor. He, at first, objected to the idea of Eileen working in the shop, and when he expressed this to her one morning over breakfast, she was speechless, giving him only a look that said, "Then what, sir, would you have me do in this place?" And indeed, what would he have her do? If he provided for her to become a woman above work, it would put her reputation into question in this strange town so full of every vice imaginable, yet ruled over by the most prudish, proper, judgmental array of bourgeois society he had ever encountered. Besides, there was no denying that Eileen had a most artful talent for lacemaking and millinery design; she enjoyed the work, expressing to him on more than one occasion that it had always been her desire to design and craft women's millinery. And he had spent many an hour on their train journey marveling at how deftly her slender fingers worked away on crochet and knit lace. It almost seemed a compulsion, as though her hands could never be idle.

Through May and June, the days had been long. The sun was a relentless orb just hovering over their heads until, finally, it would set behind the westerly mountains, coloring the sky with the most magical hues of orange, rose, and purple. It was then that he had made up his mind. He despised the thought of Eileen on her feet the whole day through, measuring and placing hat after hat upon the likes of Mrs. Pickering and Mrs. Tabor. They were nothing, nothing at all, compared to his Boadicea. If he delighted so much in caring for Eileen, teaching her, providing for her, making her his and his alone, then why not announce it to the world?

And so he showered her with gifts, the sort of gifts a man might give to his fiancée, his intended. The rose perfume, fine kidskin gloves sent direct from London, and a most generous allowance for her to purchase the finest of fabrics to create for herself a wardrobe fit for a true lady. At first, blushing and flustered, she had quickly uttered declinations—he was "too generous," she "did not deserve" such kindness, it would "not seem right." But oh, she was so easily persuaded! He had to do naught but take her hand in his and gaze soulfully into her emerald eyes—a very easily accomplished feat and one he quite enjoyed all the same—and declare something to the effect of how much he would be wounded if she should not accept, which, really, was not a lie.

"What are you looking at?" Eileen asked, smiling knowingly as she caught Laurie's gaze upon her waist and backside.

"I'm not looking," he replied. "I'm admiring."

Her smile grew, her eyes sparkling.

It had been effortless. The sister had confronted him as to his designs and intentions, and when he declared to her that his motives were pure, she immediately warmed to him. It was not long afterward that word began to spread around town of a possible betrothal. He tried to avoid any discussion upon the matter with feigned embarrassment, but businessmen would still make little passing comments teasingly. Their wives would often express dismay that a man of Laurie's great breeding and wealth (his mine—which, in keeping with his romantic, idealistic spirit, he had named the Avalon—was one of the top silver producers in the town, bested only by Tabor's Matchless) would stoop to marry "an immigrant girl" rather than one of their own prissy, plain, pasty daughters, who could only wish to be as precocious and intellectually curious—never mind as lovely—as his Eileen. Why, he could laugh just considering the idea of having to converse with one of them for longer than five minutes.

"I think they might be moving back this way," Eileen whispered, bringing his binoculars to her eyes, scanning the meadow below.

He took his gaze from her and saw that she was correct. But he quickly returned to contemplating her, noticing how she bit her lower lip with one of her front teeth. He wanted to do the same.

He then heard Stanley's voice in his head. "You ought to find a wife, Laurie, to temper your restless soul. Say, how about Eileen?"

Laurie squinted his eyes shut at the thought. Of course he had considered making Eileen his long before Stanley had suggested it. Ah, Stanley, who had built his little wooden church with his own powerful hands, on the south edge of Leadville, where the small, glistening streams melded together to form the Arkansas River. Stanley had quite a large congregation, despite the location on the town's outskirts. And also despite his insistence to Laurie, about five months prior, that he purchase land for him in town, at ten times the cost, or else he would not be able to spread God's light.

That was the beginning of their drift apart. They moved in entirely different circles. Laurie was the wealthy miner from the East. Stanley was the impassioned preacher winning new converts each day. Laurie, of course, was never the religious sort. Stanley lived to spread the Word, he claimed. The only way Laurie might have been persuaded to attend a service at Stanley's church was if Eileen were to attend, too. But Eileen was born a Catholic, and she faithfully attended Sunday service at the temporary housing for the almost completed Annunciation Church, sometimes with her sister, if Mary had not imbibed too much the prior evening.

But Laurie had, on a few occasions, invited Stanley to supper with him at the Clarendon, and Stanley had accepted perhaps half of these invitations. Laurie had by no means forgotten about Stanley—the mere sight of the tall, golden-haired preacher still stirred him deeply. And Laurie was certain that Stanley had not forgotten about him, for he could see it in the way his gaze met his own, would hold him captive, then falter, as though he were ashamed—or overwhelmed.

When once, while awaiting their supper, Laurie fleetingly touched Stanley's roughened, tanned hand, laying on the table before him, and whispered, "What of us, Stanley?" he had felt like a child deprived of love and affection. Stanley had visibly paled, cleared his throat, and replied softly, in his low voice, "We know what exists between us, but is it right?"

"I don't care," Laurie had replied, immediately worried that he sounded petulant.

Stanley had gently withdrawn his hand from Laurie's. "But you do care, and I care, too." He had replied with a smile, as though teaching Jesus's words to a child. "We know it exists—it does—but there is nothing we can do—nothing we *should* do," he had whispered.

Laurie had felt the wind had been knocked from his lungs, just as he had felt when they had crossed the Mosquito Pass on their way to Leadville some months before. There never seemed to be enough air to breathe in this mountain town.

Stanley must have sensed this. "You ought to find a wife, Laurie, to temper your restless soul. Say, how about Eileen?"

"They are moving closer, I believe," Eileen whispered, awakening him from his brooding contemplations.

Laurie turned his attention away from the herd, focusing again on Eileen. She was intently watching the elk through his binoculars.

"Eileen," he said, his voice sounding low, hoarse.

She lowered the binoculars and returned his gaze. "Aren't you going to take a shot?" she asked in a whisper.

He moved closer to her without making a sound. Surprised, she turned to her side to face him. He gently removed the riding hat he had given her and tossed it to her feet. Her eyes were wide, watching, afraid yet knowing. He knew that she knew; she knew this was inevitable. As he came closer, leaning over her, she rolled to her back, upon a carpet of fallen, golden aspen leaves. He took in the sight of her, and his fancy seized hold as it always did. She was his Celtic queen, resting upon a bed of gold.

"Marry me," he said, not asked.

She let out a little gasp at his words, her green eyes sparkling. "Is this real?"

He kissed her to prove it was. Her lips were unsure and tentative, but soon seemed to melt beneath his. He urged himself to pull away.

"Say you will." He focused on her lips, slightly swollen from the kiss.

They trembled a little, then spread to her beguiling smile. "Yes! I will."

Relief spread over him, though he wasn't sure why, for he'd known she would say yes. He bent to kiss her again, but she pressed her hand against his chest. "Aren't you going to finish the hunt?"

"I thought I had."

She giggled. "No. The elk?"

He nodded. "It will be my gift to you," he said as he gripped his rifle again, positioning himself upon the rise, peering through the scope and delighted to see that the bull was but sixty yards away.

He cocked the rifle, exhaling. Just then the bull raised his great head and crown of antlers, letting out a shrill bugle that sounded throughout the clearing, seeming to take life as it echoed in the woods behind them. The sound was haunting, lonely and heartbreaking, to Laurie. He would never get used to it. It always made him ache inside, to hear that sound.

He fired. Eileen did not flinch beside him. His shot penetrated through the base of the bull's shining, sinewy neck. The creature started, jumped slightly, moved three paces, and then wilted to into the bloodred petals of the Indian paintbrush.

CHAPTER EIGHTEEN

Harrison Avenue was empty, devoid of all people and traffic, but for two lone gunmen. They were perhaps twenty paces apart and stared each other down. Each, hands upon his hip holsters, awaiting the merest flinch from the other.

By the light of the moon, Eileen could see the flash of their pistol hilts, the startling gleam of the bullets dotting their belts. She stood before the entrance of the Clarendon Hotel, unable to move, silent, held captive by disbelief and horror.

Not a sound could be heard. The waxing moon cast everything beneath it in a bluish-white glow.

A wind stirred, whipping up one of the gunmen's coattails. The other, fast as a cat, produced his pistol and fired, lodging a bullet square between the eyes of his opponent, who staggered back and fell to the ground, pistol still in hand and cocked for a shot that never was.

Eileen brought her hands to her mouth to stifle the scream caught in her throat. She watched, unbelieving, as the murderer turned and walked southward, soon fading into the night.

Finally she unfroze and ran to where the victim lay bleeding into the street. When she reached him, she dropped to her knees by his side. She gagged at the sight of the gaping hole in his forehead and the stench of blood, so much blood. Surely he was dead, his lifeless eyes staring skyward, reflecting the waxing moon.

"Eileen," his voice croaked.

"Yes?" she asked, terrified that he could still speak and knew her name.

"Come closer."

Shaking in fear, she bent toward him.

"Leave this place," he said, his voice raspy and dry, like sagebrush rustling in the wind. "There's nothing here for you but misery."

She awoke, gasping for air, sitting up straight as a board. She blinked a few times, trying to catch her breath as she slowly remembered where she was. She was home, home in her room at the finest, newest hotel in Leadville: the Clarendon. The room had been her home for the past five months.

It had happened this way so often, perhaps every other night, sometimes every night. And it had happened this way ever since her first night in Leadville, at the Clarendon. She recalled how she and Mary had stood by their third-story window, peering out at the ever-busy, always-crowded Harrison Avenue below. They had spoken of its rowdiness, not unlike the Bowery, yet so unlike the Bowery. Just then, the crowds and traffic had parted to make way for two men, who faced each other down in the street, right below the sisters' view.

Eileen had begun to say, "What do you think—"

"Certainly not—" Mary had interrupted. "Oh, but maybe—"

She hadn't had a chance to finish her thought. Just then the two sisters became witness to a gunfight. The guns had been drawn so quickly, the deadly shot fired before either could blink. The victim had crumpled to the ground, a pool of blood rapidly spreading from his head.

They had been speechless for a few moments, unable to take their eyes away from a scene that seemed so unreal, like something acted out upon a stage.

"Now that's something I never saw in the Bowery," Mary had finally uttered.

They would come to learn that such violent scenes did occur more often than not in Leadville. But the deadly spectacle of that first night had haunted Eileen ever since. She had been unable to shake herself free of it, as it revisited her in her dreams almost nightly, always the same, always those exact words uttered by the victim. What did he mean? And how could he know her? And should she heed him?

She shuddered, wrapping her arms around herself to try to settle her nerves.

Mary stirred beside her in bed. "Bad dream again?" she asked sleepily.

Eileen only nodded.

Mary sat up beside her, rubbing her hand over Eileen's back in her usual effort to soothe her sister. "Come now, you're all right, my lass."

"But why, why does he tell me the same thing every time?"

Mary shrugged. "Don't think about it. It's just a dream."

"Do you think he knows something I don't know?" Eileen asked, turning to her sister.

Mary shook her head. "But I know something *he* doesn't know, that's for certain."

"What?"

Mary gave her a slight shove. "You stupid cow, you're getting married tomorrow to one of the wealthiest men in Leadville, in New York, in the whole of America! I'm betting that if that sorry chap with the bullet between the eyes knew about *that*, he'd change his tune!"

Eileen laughed a little, the terror from her nightmare transforming to nervous happiness over the following day's events.

"Honestly, dearie," Mary said, "can you even imagine what the gals at Mrs. Brown's would say if they only knew? Or can you even imagine what dear Ma would say? Oh, but she'd be so proud of you, so very proud, God rest her soul. You've done swell for yourself, Eileen, just swell!"

Eileen nodded, smiling. It was true, and she would not hold back her pride; she had done swell for herself. She'd never, ever dreamed she would become the wife of such a wealthy, accomplished, and handsome young man.

"Pinch me, Mary. I still can't believe it's happening."

"Well, believe it," Mary said with a rough pinch of her cheek. "Just don't forget about your poor sister."

"Now *you're* the stupid cow," Eileen teased, giving her a hug.

"Oh, aye, well, we'll see what happens once you're living in his fancy home up there by Fryer Hill."

"Nothing will happen! You're my sister and always will be." Eileen grinned, but noticed that Mary did not return the smile. A sudden feeling of guilt flooded her. "I don't think we will be going to San Francisco, Mary. Does that upset you?"

Mary shook her head and fussed with a tendril of Eileen's hair that had slipped free at the nape of her neck. "Nah! You've done and gone something far greater than open a millinery shop in San Francisco."

Eileen took hold of Mary's hand. "But what about you, Mary?"

"What about me?"

"What are you going to do now?"

Mary's gaze finally met hers. "Eileen, for the Lord's sake, I'm a woman now—I can make my own way in the world. You've no need to fret over me, now, you hear? Besides," she continued, "you'll be fixing me up with a fine gent who owns a silver mine, isn't that so?"

"Oh yes, Mary!" Eileen imagined herself and her sister dining in fancy restaurants, buying dozens of hats and shoes, hosting society tea parties—no, the last one, that was hard for Eileen to picture, admittedly. Mary would never seem "genteel." This thought caused Eileen's heart to sink.

Eileen heard Mary's tired sigh as she settled back into bed. "Get some sleep now, bride-to-be. You don't want to look tired tomorrow when all those rich old cows watch you walk down the aisle."

Eileen lay down beside Mary. "Do you think it's a sin that I'm not getting married in the Catholic Church?"

Mary guffawed. "Lord, Eileen, you're asking the wrong gal what's a sin and what isn't. Really, I don't think it matters. You're getting married in a church where people will bear witness. That's all that matters as far as I'm concerned."

"But is Stanley's church a real church?"

"To most people, a church is a church, Eileen."

Eileen bit her lip, recalling how Stanley had visited her on her last official day of work at May's Dry Goods.

"Eileen," he had said, gently taking hold of her hand. "Nothing would make me happier than to preside over your wedding. Will you allow me to marry you and Laurie?"

His sparkling blue eyes held her captive. He still had a piece of her heart, she knew. She had always known this. Any time she happened to see him in town, her heart raced so she thought it would burst through her chest. It was a very different feeling from when she saw Laurie; when she saw him, she felt warm inside, like one feels after a gulp of whiskey.

"I will have to speak to Laurie about this," she had stammered in reply.

"No need," Stanley had said proudly. "I have already spoken to him and he said the choice was yours. Though, quite frankly, I think he would like nothing more."

Her heart had raced again. "Well then, yes."

He had squeezed her hand before letting it go. "You've made me a very happy man, Eileen. I will be marrying two of my dearest friends!"

"We had best be on our way or else we'll be late," Eileen said as she took one last, hasty look in the dressing table mirror.

The hairdresser—a Frenchwoman with darkly hennaed hair and rouged lips, who Mary had learned also turned tricks on Second Street by night—put the final hairpin in Eileen's elaborate arrangement.

"Eileen, the wedding cannot start without the bride," Mary said, laughing. "Who cares if you're late? You should be late!"

"Listen to your sister," the hairdresser lectured, toying with one of Eileen's auburn ringlets. "You should put on lip rouge. I have some if you like—"

"She's fine just as she is," Mary interrupted. "She doesn't need that sort of thing, her lips are pink and sweet already."

The hairdresser shrugged indifferently as she packed her styling tools into a carpetbag. Mary handed her the payment, which she readily counted. Once she realized that she had been generously tipped, she smiled at Mary, then at Eileen. "You are a beautiful bride, chérie! I wish you much happiness. You know," she continued in her thick accent, "all of the working girls are so proud of you. They see you as a fairy tale, because you are one of us."

Mary quickly opened the door to the hotel hallway. "She's not 'one of you,' Genevieve," she said with a tilt of her head to usher her out of the room.

Genevieve made her way to the doorway. "I meant that she once had to work to pay her way in the world. You mistake my meaning." She gave Mary a haughty appraisal. "Good day, ladies."

Mary closed the door shut. "Good riddance, slut."

"But she did do a lovely job on my hair, don't you think?" Eileen said, rising from the dressing table.

Mary smiled at her. "You look like a princess! Now, get that dressing gown off and let's get you into your bridal gown."

Mary gathered up Eileen's gown and deftly slid it over her, completely avoiding the perfectly coiffed hair. She continued to fuss with the layers of white tissue silk skirts, then got to fastening the buttons along her sister's tightly corseted back, above her elaborate bustle.

"Do you think my gown is too low-cut on the bust?" Eileen fretted, taking in her reflection, noticing how ample her cleavage appeared in the very fashionable V-necked gown. She had made the bone bobbin lace that draped the neckline, which created a somewhat Grecian effect of draping from the very edges of her shoulders down to the low bodice.

"You don't need to be modest on this day, my dear. This is *your* day, remember?" Mary asked as she fastened a pearl choker—a wedding gift from Laurie—around her sister's neck. "Besides, it's the fashion, and your husband will love it."

Eileen stifled a giggle at Mary's reference to her "husband." It still seemed a dream to her.

The two sisters stood side by side, peering at their reflections. They clasped hands. Eileen felt a sudden wave of anxiety rush over her. She was so very nervous to leave the room, to be under the scrutiny of everyone in the Clarendon, everyone on the ever-bustling streets of Leadville. She was nervous to become a wife. And she was especially nervous to leave what had been her home these past five months.

"What is it, dearie?" Mary asked, for she must have noted the change of expression that had come over her sister.

"This is the last time I will be in this room."

Mary glanced around. "So?"

"It has been our home . . ."

Mary rolled her eyes. "Oh, honestly, you are much too sentimental. How could a hotel room have been your home? It's no home, it's just temporary shelter."

Eileen searched for the words to express her feeling. "I know, but it was what we called home—"

"Listen," Mary said as she put a bouquet of white and red roses in Eileen's hands, "this is no home. Home is where you will be going, with your husband. A proper home, at that! Just think of it, six bedrooms, a dining room, and a breakfast room and three water closets! Now *that*, my dear, is a real home!"

Eileen knew her sister was right, of course. And indeed, she was very excited to live in such a grand home as the one that Laurie had ordered built on the very eastern edge of town, on the road to Fryer Hill. But still, this room was what she had known, all she had known.

And for Eileen, there was always a pain involved in leaving the known, no matter how lowly the known had been.

There was a sudden loud knock upon the room's door. "Are y'all ready to go yet or what?"

It was the voice of Beauregard Stinson—or Beau, as he was called. He had been Mary's suitor, of a sort, for perhaps two months now.

"Stop your fussing," Mary shouted as she made her way to the door, yet Eileen noticed her smile.

She opened the door, to be greeted by Beau. He promptly and with great skill spit his tobacco into a spittoon by the doorway before roughly wrapping one arm around Mary's waist and planting a kiss square on her lips.

Finally, she pulled away. "My dress, Beau! You'll ruin my dress before the wedding!" She gave him a slight shove.

"Are you getting fresh with me?" he drawled in his usual manner and grabbed a handful of Mary's bustle.

Eileen tried to ignore Beau's lewdness toward her sister. She did not much care for Beau; everyone in town knew he was nothing more than a gambler and troublemaker who rode with a posse. She disliked how he always wore the same outfit, even on this day, her wedding: tight, fitted buckskin trousers tucked into brown riding boots with shining, jingling silver spurs, a black, collarless shirt of surprisingly fine linen coupled with a red neck stock, and, of course, the ever-present weathered, fitted gray leather, double-breasted jacket with shining gold buttons—a vestige of his self-glorified days as an officer in the Confederate army.

He was swell, to be sure. Perhaps in his late thirties, he was still fairly youthful, tall with tanned skin, gray eyes that matched his jacket, and a sly, sensual grin that revealed fine teeth. His hair was blond but beginning to show signs of gray, as did his goatee, which he religiously kept coiffed into a perfectly shaped, pointing V. Eileen had to admit that, judging solely on appearance, Mary and Beau made a handsome couple. But beyond that the handsomeness ended. She did not like that her sister—already prone to vice—was keeping company with such a "hoodlum," as she had once heard Mrs. Pickering describe Beau. But Mary, of course, was not one to be lectured or warned. Harnessing Mary's desires was an impossibility; this Eileen had known since she could walk and chase after her older sister. Mary always loved a risk. She was the sort who would balance precariously on a saloon railing simply because someone dared her to do so. Beau Stinson was the kind of dangerous, handsome conquest that Mary hoped to win. And the more people warned her, the more she wanted to prove them wrong. Mary was always the moth to the flame.

"Ready, bride-to-be?" he asked Eileen with a wink. She hated when he winked at her, for she felt it hid something more than mere friendliness or flirtation.

In a way Eileen was glad to be distracted by Beau, for then she would not have a chance to get teary-eyed. "Ready," she said as she gathered her skirts with one white-gloved hand and held her bouquet in the other.

Beau let out a loud whistle. "Well, my stars, Eileen, you look like a ripe peach about to be picked!"

Two of his posse members also loitered in the hotel hallway, and they got a good laugh out of Beau's comment. Mary just whacked his arm.

"I don't know, Mary, I might have chosen the wrong sister," he said, letting his eyes linger on Eileen's bustline.

"She's with the rich Yank, Beau, not you," said one of the posse.

Beau scowled at this, spitting more tobacco into the hallway spittoon.

"Miss Maguire? Are you ready to depart?"

Eileen was never so relieved to see the bushy side-whiskered face of Mr. Pickering. He had come up the stairway to escort her to his awaiting carriage, and then onward to Stanley's church on the edge of town. Eileen smiled, happy to be rescued from Beau and his posse.

"I am, Mr. Pickering." She took his offered arm.

"Mr. Stinson, gentlemen," he greeted Beau and the posse with a quick nod.

"Good day to you, Mr. Pickering," Beau replied in kind, a bemused smile playing on his lips.

As Mr. Pickering and Eileen descended the great staircase into the lobby of the Clarendon, a crowd gathered below. But instead of growing nervous, Eileen suddenly felt confident, especially after Mr. Pickering patted her hand on his arm and said, "I'd bet my whole mining fortune that Leadville's never seen such a beautiful bride as you, Miss Maguire."

Eileen noted the approving and admiring glances of the various men gathered in the lobby, along with the curious and sometimes jealous expressions of the many ladies.

"Make way for the bride, ladies and gentlemen!" Mr. Pickering shouted in a jolly manner, causing some of the crowd to applaud, others to wish Eileen much happiness. For once in her life, she felt like the most beautiful woman in a room, and she rather enjoyed that feeling, not wanting it to end.

Once outside on the boardwalk, Mr. Pickering assisted Eileen, and then Mary, into his grand coach before he sat across from them. Mary busied herself with smoothing Eileen's skirts as the driver took his station at the front of the coach.

"See y'all at the church," Beau said, donning his hat.

The coach effortlessly made its way back into the thoroughfare of Harrison Avenue after the Clarendon hotel attendants stopped the traffic with calls of "Make way for the bride!"

"Why, that's a sight I never thought I'd see on Harrison Avenue," said Mary, staring out the coach's back window.

Eileen fussed with her gloves, somewhat overwhelmed to be in such a grand carriage. Mr. Eliot Pickering was, like Laurie, one of the wealthiest men in Leadville, if not the country. The former Philadelphian's mine, the Liberty Bell, was adjacent to Laurie's Avalon, and almost as lucrative. His wife, Constance, was even more portly than he, and not nearly as generous with smiles and niceties.

She had been indifferent to Eileen—a mere Irish shopgirl—until the engagement had been announced. After that, she had invited her to teas and luncheons, much as a wealthy, distant relative might do, for it was what was done, whether one wanted to do it or not. She was not unkind, but neither was she warm. Eileen was certain that any invitations she might receive from Mrs. Pickering were actually from Mr. Pickering, who insisted his wife be on social terms with the future wife of one of the richest men in America, Lawrence Barnard.

"What a beautiful day you have for your wedding," commented Mr. Pickering while he smiled and gazed out the coach window.

It was quite clement for an early November day in Leadville—mild, bright sunshine and a gentle breeze. Eileen had learned early on in her stay in Leadville that the weather could be a fearsome, fickle thing, changing from calm and idyllic to blustery and unforgiving. Just four days ago it had snowed over a foot, and by now there were few vestiges left of the storm but for a few dry, crunchy patches in north-facing locations.

"Old Mr. May told me yesterday that he feels a snowstorm coming in within the next couple of days," commented Mary.

"Old Mr. May is always right about the weather," Mr. Pickering said with a nod.

"It's a pity you can't make it to Denver for your honeymoon until spring," Mary said, adjusting one of her sister's curls.

"Come late September, that Mosquito Pass is always impossible to cross," Mr. Pickering said. "It will be such a blessing when the rail line is finally completed."

"When will that be?" Eileen asked.

"They say spring of this coming year."

"Seems so far away," Eileen replied.

Mr. Pickering chuckled, his puffy side-whiskers seeming to grow more prodigious. "Young folks always think that time goes too slow, they do."

"Oh come, Mr. Pickering," Mary joked. "You're not so very much older than us!"

He blushed a little. "Oh, old enough to be your father, I'd say, Miss Maguire."

"And have you heard from your son lately?" Eileen asked. Eliot Pickering Jr. had, these past four months, been away on a grand tour of Europe, having completed his studies at Yale last spring.

"Oh yes, we received a letter from him, dated about a month ago, from Edinburgh." Mr. Pickering's portly chest visibly grew with pride. "He's having a grand time of it, he is."

Mary began to hum a tune. Eileen glanced at her, surprised by her sister's lack of tact. Eileen had, these past couple of months, been reading much on proper manners and etiquette whilst in polite company. This was the point in the conversation where Mary should insert some agreeable compliment regarding Mr. Pickering and his family, certainly not when she should begin to hum a song.

"You and Mrs. Pickering must be so proud of him," Eileen quickly said, hoping that Mr. Pickering would not consider her sister too rude.

He did not seem to notice, for he only smiled and nodded. "Indeed, Miss Maguire, we most certainly are, thank you."

They passed the remainder of the coach ride in light conversation. Eileen anxiously glanced out the window to see how close they were to the church. Her palms grew damp within her white silk gloves as she finally spotted the small, simple, isolated white church in the distance, beside a great field where the silver streams danced together to eventually join and become a river. What river? Oh yes, Laurie had told her—the Arkansas.

Mary placed a hand on her forearm. "Now don't get nervous, dearie. Why, you're the star of the show!"

Mr. Pickering chuckled, but Mary's comment did nothing to calm Eileen's nerves.

When they approached the front of the church, Eileen noted the many other horses, carriages, and carts, as well as the multitude of guests still filing inside. She also heard the loud, lazy chortle of Beau somewhere from behind their coach. His laugh was a constant irritant to her, which she knew was most irrational on her part. But the sound reminded her of a man up to some mischief. She glanced at her sister, who was smiling to herself.

"That would be Beau," Mary said with a chuckle.

"Aye, I know," Eileen replied, turning her gaze out the window again to the church.

"Now, ladies," Mr. Pickering said as his groom opened the coach door, "I shall pop inside and see if everyone is ready. Then I'll come back out and fetch you, yes?"

Eileen nodded. "That would be most kind of you."

She watched Mr. Pickering go inside the church and the last of the guests follow suit.

"I do wonder how so many will fit in that small church," Mary commented.

The church was small, indeed. Stanley had built most of it with his own hands, along with some help from new parishioners he had quickly wooed on his entrance to Leadville. Eileen recalled hearing young ladies, shopping in May's, commenting on the "fine, handsome, young preacher" who was laboring away on a church on the south edge of town in nothing but his trousers, undershirt, and suspenders. The sight of him had so impressed that word of it had traveled back into town. It wasn't long before Stanley Jones had acquired a sizable number of female parishioners. It also wasn't long before Eileen decided to visit him on one of her free days.

She had gotten a ride with Mr. Ahern (God rest his soul these past four months—both he and his wife had died of pneumonia) down to the church site. She had brought with her freshly baked cornbread from the little bakery behind May's, run by a woman who said she was from Louisiana. And Eileen still thrilled when she recalled the sight of Stanley, laboring in front of the rough frame of his church. It had been an oppressively hot day beneath the relentless mountain sun, to be sure. He had worn his unfashionably long blond locks tied back, and was attired in nothing but his trousers and suspenders—shockingly, no shirt. He had labored at the saw, his powerful arms and torso tanned from the sun, damp with perspiration. Eileen had been rendered speechless by the sight of him, and could only stare. If ever she had pondered the meaning of masculinity and how it differed from femininity, of what might be the essence of a man, she had found her answer on that hot day in late May.

"Eileen!" he had exclaimed as he put the saw aside and wiped his face with a handkerchief produced from his trouser pocket. "How very good it is to see you!"

Eileen's heart raced at the memory.

Mr. Pickering opened the coach door, startling Eileen from her pleasant recollection. He offered his arm to her. "I believe we are ready for you, bride-to-be!"

CHAPTER NINETEEN

"Are you ready?" Stanley asked.

Laurie took another swig of Highland Park whisky from his sterling flask—which he had crafted from the very first silver lode taken from the Avalon—and placed it down on the rough-hewn table, which was in the center of Stanley's one-room living space at the back of his church. Laurie had never been inside the small, barely furnished, rather ascetic room before this day.

Laurie was not the typical, unnerved groom on this, his wedding day. In fact, he had eagerly looked forward to it as a new adventure, the next chapter of his life. But once Stanley had invited him into this most intimate place—the place in which Stanley dwelled, wrote sermons, ate, dressed and undressed, and slept each evening—he had grown inexplicably uncomfortable. Everything in this room was Stanley's, even the unforgettable scent, somehow. Everything about this room reminded Laurie of the erotic, often base dreams of Stanley that still haunted his sleep. The close proximity of Stanley recalled a kiss—*the* kiss—that had changed Laurie, which he longed to forget but could not.

"Laurie?" Stanley came closer to him, put a large, roughened hand upon his shoulder as he peered down into his face.

Laurie nodded, shaking away his disturbing contemplations. "I'm ready."

Stanley did not step away. He tightened his grip upon Laurie's shoulder. Laurie felt warmth run through the whole of him, and it was not from the whisky.

"Again, I cannot tell you how happy I am that you are marrying today, and that you are allowing me to do the honor."

Laurie looked into Stanley's sparkling blue eyes. "But who else?"

Stanley gave him something of a knowing smile. "This will set your life on the right path, my friend. Trust me."

Laurie's brows drew together. What was Stanley implying? "I believe my life has been on the right path since I arrived in Leadville," he stated in his own defense.

Stanley still held his shoulder. "But you will understand, once you are married."

What did he mean? Was he hinting at something between the two of them? The preacher both infatuated and infuriated him. Perhaps he should have married Eileen in the Annunciation Church. Construction of the church would be complete in just a few weeks' time. Perhaps they should have waited for that? But of course, most of his New York circle would certainly have disapproved of such a vulgar, Catholic ceremony. In their opinion, it was bad enough that he was marrying so beneath himself—and an Irish girl, no less! He recalled with joy how he tore his mother's shocked, spiteful telegrams to shreds. Yes, he was doing something very daring, very adventurous. Everyone—including Stanley—be damned.

He took a step away from Stanley, from his hold upon him. "Come, I don't want to keep my bride waiting," he said, as though challenging anyone who might try to hinder him.

Never in his life had Laurie imagined that he would be married in a church with nothing but a Finnish woman singing soprano accompanied by an elderly banjo player for the wedding march. But there it was, and it would have to do, but not before he had to stifle the chuckle that bubbled up inside him.

Later he would not remember the singing and the banjo. But seared in his memory for the rest of his days would be the sight of Eileen making her way up the aisle, escorted by Eliot Pickering, who was giving her away. He never imagined she could look so beautiful, his Irish wife-to-be, his Boadicea in the guise of a blushing bride. She did, indeed, blush all the way to the low, fetching neckline of her sumptuous white gown. Her auburn curls had been so very fashionably arranged, and when she glanced over at him, her green eyes sparkled, then went to the bouquet in her hands as she smiled in—what? Embarrassment, excitement?

Stanley took his place before the simple pulpit, Bible in hand. Eileen looked up from her bouquet to Stanley, and though he could not believe it even possible, Laurie was amazed to see her become even more beautiful right before his eyes.

Soon Eileen's slender, gloved hand was in his, and her bouquet was bestowed upon Mary, who stood to Eileen's left. Stanley's low, melodic voice carried over the packed church, quoting this verse and that verse from the Bible, though Laurie did not care what the words were. He only cared that her hand was in his and she would soon be his. He only cared that Stanley's voice washed over the two of them, sweeter than any blessing could be. Everything was a blur: his vows, her vows, the exchange of rings. He would remember so very little of his wedding day, but for her, his voice, and, finally, the kiss that made her his.

Was it not the same for all grooms? Laurie did not know, but he would assume that, yes, it was. He wanted to be out of the church, past the reception, finished with the dinner, holding her in his arms for dance after dance (oh, yes indeed!), wishing his guests good evening, ushering his bride quickly up the great stairway of the Clarendon, and into his room, their bridal suite.

All this went through his mind as they made their way down the aisle as husband and wife, as they walked beneath a shower of rice and well-wishes from guests, as they stepped up into the awaiting carriage. Finally, they were on their way.

Yet why, why, did he feel as though he had left a piece of himself behind in the church? Why this emptiness in the corner of his heart, cloying at him, nagging him for moving ahead instead of lingering behind?

Despite Laurie's personal vow to become a new man of the West and to leave the trappings of his New York society life behind, he was a man who had never been without, and so it was inherent in him to enjoy the finer things. Thus it only followed suit that his wedding reception be the grandest affair that Leadville had yet witnessed. The guest list was composed of the wealthiest, most prominent, and most powerful citizens of Leadville. The Clarendon's dining room was adorned with fresh, hothouse floral arrangements of rose, lily, and peony, which Laurie had had shipped in the day before via Hartsel and Denver at a cost that would have made many a hardened, driven Leadville miner weep. The menu for the reception was an extravagant eight courses: caviar, salads, poached fish, Cornish hens in crème sauce, prime rib of beef, cheeses, even ice cream to accompany the wedding cake. Champagne flowed the whole of the evening. Members of the orchestra at the newly constructed Tabor Opera House (adjoined to the Clarendon via an enclosed bridge) were on hand to provide the music for the evening. Surely no one could find fault in such an elaborate affair.

Laurie sensed that his bride was overwhelmed, and he was bemused when he beheld her green eyes grow wide as she took in her surroundings. She nervously nibbled at each course, watchful of those around her as to which fork and knife to use. He was glad of this; he wanted to overwhelm his wife and show her things she had never before seen or experienced. At this thought he checked his gold pocket watch, for despite the splendor of the evening, he longed for it to end soon so that he might continue his bride's education. He smiled at the thought as he replaced the watch in his waistcoat pocket.

The orchestra struck up the inaugural waltz of the evening, signaling the bride and groom to dance their first dance as husband and wife. Laurie escorted his bride to the center of the room, aware of the hush that had fallen over the assembly watching the two of them. He took his bride in arm and hand. Her eyes met his and he saw that she was terrified.

"What is it?" he whispered.

"I don't know how . . ." She bit her lip.

"Come now, there's nothing to it. I'll lead, and you follow, yes?"

Laurie had always been most self-assured of his dancing skills. It was one of the few things in his childhood to which his mother was most attentive—she had hired the best dance instructors in New York City to teach her child to dance from just about the time he was walking steadily on two feet. He began slowly with his bride, and as he knew she would be, she was an astute follower of his lead. Soon he guided her around the center of the room, and he laughed a little as he looked down at her and noticed just how intent her gaze was upon his bow tie, her brow furrowed in concentration. Soon enough, the waltz was complete, and the orchestra invited all the guests to join in the next dance.

"That wasn't so bad, now, was it?" he asked her, putting a finger under her chin and lifting her face to his.

She was flushed. Her lashes fluttered. "No, not so much." She gave him a shy smile.

He could not help himself; he wrapped his hand round her waist and clasped it tightly—very tightly. Oh, but it was so small in his grip. God, he longed to feel her waist naked beneath his hands. What time was it, anyhow?

Just then there was a shriek from the dance floor. Laurie turned to see Mary, who had slipped from the very low dip Beau had thrown her into and fallen right on her backside. She proceeded to laugh hysterically; surely an excess of champagne had lessened the impact for her, Laurie thought.

Beau yanked at her arms, trying to pull her up. "Come on, you lazy thing!"

Guests had stopped to stare. Laurie shook his head slightly—his sister-in-law must always make a spectacle of herself. He often found it difficult to fathom how this woman and his bride were even related.

"I'm not lazy! You dropped me!" Mary shouted between fits of laughter.

"Mary," Eileen hissed, her brow now furrowing in distress.

"Oh, but did I, now?" Beau mocked. "Well, then, I'll remedy that directly, ma'am!" He bent low and scooped up Mary in his arms, then threw her over his shoulder like a sack of flour.

Mary squealed in laughter again. "Put me down!"

Beau then nodded his head to Eileen and Laurie before addressing the assembly. "Well, I'll bid everyone good evening now, and we'll be on our way." He gave a knowing wink.

Laurie had no use for a man like Beauregard Stinson. Though he had lived the privileged life of a country squire on his family's South Carolina plantation, Beau was nothing but a lowlife thief and gambler now. And even still, some fifteen years after the war with the South, the man insisted on parading about in his Confederate officer's jacket. If ever there had been a cause that Laurie had vehemently supported, it had been that of the Union (although he was but a young child at the time of the war). Each time he glimpsed that weathered, fitted gray leather jacket, Laurie felt a visceral contempt for every conceit, oppression, hatred, and self-righteous arrogance the gray and gold stood for. And this man had the audacity to wrap himself in all this and consider it some glory. Glory, indeed.

"But wait!" Mary shouted as Beau made his way through the crowds and toward the Clarendon's lobby. "I still have to give my sister the wedding-night talk!"

Laurie heard Eileen gasp beside him. He put his arm protectively around her.

Beau stopped and laughed his typical, raspy laugh. "Indeed, I cannot think of anyone better than you to give that talk!"

Mutters of disapproval flowed through the assembly as the two left the reception in a fit of hysterics.

"Come now, let's have another waltz!" shouted Mr. Pickering, and the orchestra—to everyone's relief—struck up another dance.

Mr. Pickering met Laurie's gaze across the room. Laurie felt a rush of gratitude, and mouthed a silent "thank you" to the gentleman, who gave a quick, knowing nod.

"Oh, how could she, on my wedding day?" Eileen whispered, her lower lip quivering.

Laurie knew to stop what might be a show of tears. "Come now, Bride, let's share another piece of cake, yes?"

Eileen only nodded and blindly followed Laurie back to their table, where he took a plate with a neatly cut piece of vanilla cake and proceeded to give Eileen little forkfuls. She dutifully took each bite, but then held her hands up. "I am so full, Laurie, please."

"Very well." He placed the cake down and checked his watch again.

"Are you tired?" Eileen asked.

"Oh, no, not one bit," he said, giving her a wink.

She immediately transformed, smiling and blushing, glancing away.

"Oh, but don't look away from me," he said, putting his arms around her. "Are you happy, Bride?"

"I couldn't be happier, honestly," she replied.

"Really? You don't think you could be happier?"

She looked up at him, questioningly. "Why, this is the happiest day of my life."

"But it isn't over yet," he said, lightly kissing her forehead. He felt her shiver beneath his lips. This made him glad, in a way.

"I don't know what to say," she said, giggling nervously.

"Lawrence."

Laurie was startled to see Stanley before them, smiling.

"Stanley, are you enjoying yourself?"

Stanley gestured with his arm to the room. "How could any man not? But one thing would make my evening complete."

It was now Laurie who shivered. "What is it?"

"Might I have this dance with the bride?" he asked, smiling down at Eileen.

Within his arms, Laurie felt Eileen's breath come quickly, her carriage straighten. Oh, no. She was his tonight. He would not allow Stanley to put his hands, literally, on this, his very own evening, his wedding night.

"Why, we were just about to dance, weren't we, Bride?" Laurie asked, glancing down at Eileen as he moved her back toward the dance floor.

"Yes, of course," she replied, sounding unsure.

"Very well, then. I see you two cannot be separated this evening," Stanley said with his magnanimous grin. "Well, then, I shall be on my way. I bid you both a very good evening."

When Stanley departed, and when the two began to dance again, Laurie felt as though he had been lifted out of the warmth of the room and deposited outside in the chill of the mountain night. He also thought he sensed distance from Eileen, though he chided himself that this was but a figment of his imagination. He took hold of Eileen's waist again with a fierce grip and she gasped slightly. The warmth returned to Laurie once more as he glanced over at the clock in the room's corner and estimated the time remaining before he would hear her truest gasp.

CHAPTER TWENTY

He lay on his side, one arm beneath his pillow, the other tucked under the covers. She listened to his steady breathing—a soothing sound. His expression was serene, and she found it remarkable how boyish and young he appeared in sleep. She had a strong desire to kiss his forehead, but she thought better of it—he might be cross with her if she woke him. These were things she did not yet know about her husband: what time he awoke, if he would wake quickly or slowly, what his temperament would be as he met the morning.

Eileen, herself, awoke without much hesitation. Her eyes would open and she would meet the day, regardless of whether she really wanted to. It was what was to be done, was it not? Of course, this had been the way of life, the way of things, for Eileen for as long as she could remember. She never had the luxury of lounging about in bed, for there were always tasks to tend to or jobs to arrive at on time. How strange it would be, to have nothing to wake for, no consequences if she should be tardy, and no neighbors to startle her awake at any time of day or night. Mary never hailed the morning. She had always been almost impossible to wake, moaning and muttering indecipherable words and obscenities.

As Eileen considered this aspect of her sister, a dread crept over her. She had just remembered Mary's behavior the prior evening at her wedding reception. *Oh, but how could she?* She scrunched her eyes shut and shook her head when she recalled Mary's drunken shrieks—and oh! Those words, those words she had uttered about "the talk." Her stomach clenched into a ball, for she was mortified by the thought.

She stared up at the ceiling of the hotel suite. And what was this "talk" that Mary had in mind? Would she have imparted some sage advice, some secret passed from woman to woman regarding her first time with a man? Eileen exhaled through her nose, considering that, in such an inebriated state, Mary's words would have been all a jumble, and most likely she would have made a crude joke of the topic. And for Eileen, it was nothing to be joked about. She had been secretly petrified by the whole idea of it. Not that she hadn't known what would happen—she had lived on the fifth floor of a boardinghouse of rather ill repute, and of course there was Mary, always Mary, with her stories and comments that Eileen only partly understood.

But still, Eileen wondered if perhaps there had been a secret she should have known, to make the whole thing easier, not so fumbling, not so rushed. She had known it would hurt and it had, indeed. She had known that she should just lie there beneath him and let him take charge, for she had no prior knowledge of such things. She had delighted in everything that had transpired beforehand: his tender words, his gentle hands as he helped her out of her gown, his soft kisses upon her bare shoulders, neck, and lips. He had carried her like a helpless thing to the bed and laid her down. He had seemed to know that she was frightened and unsure, yet his knowing smile indicated that perhaps he took an odd pleasure in her fright.

She had felt a surge of warmth through the whole of her as he ran his hands over her nakedness in soft strokes, as he whispered avowals of love and devotion, of happiness and contentment, of dreams come true. *Dreams come true—had he said that?* Yes, he had, and Eileen remembered this with a sudden unmistakable clarity, for he had uttered this in a low, strained tone just as the pain and the burn and the panic had taken hold of her and at such an odd moment, when they had become one. Yet she had felt rent in two as he shuddered in release, his breath hard against her skin like the incessant winter wind against the shaking windowpane in her New

York room. Yes, a window had been opened to another world, yet the window was shattered, rimmed with jagged shards.

Would it always hurt? She wished now that she could go to her sister and ask her this, but she closed her eyes—she would not speak to Mary until Mary came to her and apologized for her behavior.

Would it always hurt? She opened her eyes to the ceiling, then turned her head to glance at her sleeping husband. Could she ask him such a question? Or was it not the proper thing to do? Would it wound his pride, would it be an insult? She hated that she was so ignorant. It wasn't fair that she was so confused. Was he confused? No, surely he was not—men were never confused about such things, were they?

He stirred, his dark lashes fluttering before he opened his eyes.

Does he still love me? Is he still glad of this?

"Good morning, Bride." His voice was low and warm.

"Good morning," she whispered back, hearing her voice quake.

His green eyes focused on hers. "Are you well?"

"Oh, yes," she readily answered, reminding herself to give him a smile.

He moved closer to her, putting his arm around her waist, beneath the covers. He smelled pleasantly of his clean, limey cologne and his own musk. A slight grunt of satisfaction came from him as his hand took hold of her hip.

She glanced up at the ceiling, growing nervous beneath his gaze.

"Why is your brow furrowed?"

"Is it?" Her eyes met his.

"Yes," he said. He leaned closer toward her and placed his lips softly between her brows. "Right there," he said as he laid his head back down upon the pillow.

She did not know what to say, or what she should say.

"Come now, Bride, tell me what troubles you."

"Nothing, really."

"There should be no secrets between us now," he said, smiling at her.

"Will it always hurt?" she blurted out in a rush of words, before she could stop herself.

His smile faded. "What?"

She hesitated. "Will it always hurt?"

"What hurts?"

She felt the flush of embarrassment spread over her skin.

His expression changed from confusion to realization. "Oh . . . I take it that you mean—"

"Oh, but do not say it!" she gasped. She could not be any more uncomfortable.

He chuckled a little. "Now, now," he soothed, stroking her hip gently. "You've nothing to be embarrassed about. And no, it will not always hurt, my Bride."

She let out a breath of relief. "You're not cross with me for asking—"

"Heavens, no!" He raised himself on his elbow so that he could look down upon her. "A wife should be able to speak of such things with her husband, I believe. I don't agree with all these silly rules of propriety—"

"Then I shouldn't have asked, should I?"

"Nonsense, Bride." He placed his finger upon her lips. "Hush now, and don't fret. Poor Bride, so frightened by the unknown . . ."

Eileen detected that he spoke to her as though she were a child, and though at any other moment this would not sit well with her, at this moment, in her discomfort, she was not offended.

His hand moved to her waist, then slowly to her breast. She tensed, then relaxed, deciding to enjoy the sensation rather than fight it.

He watched her, smiling as though they conspired together. "I know you will enjoy it. I am sure of it."

His mouth met hers, urging her to return his kiss, and she did, though timidly. His hand caressed her, and she moaned before she could stop herself.

And when he was within her again, there was still the discomfort, the burn and the pain, but there was not the fear. And when he took his pleasure again later that morning, she realized that it was not so terrible a thing. No, it was not so terrible a thing, and perhaps, if he guided her, she might enjoy it, too.

"I have come to a decision about a matter, and I would like to discuss this with you." Laurie said this as they breakfasted in the suite later that morning. He poured her tea for her, then settled back into his chair.

"What is it?" she asked, wary of his serious tone and words.

"Regarding your sister."

Eileen held the teacup suspended before her, not moving to take a sip, waiting for him to finish. "Yes?"

"Please, do not be so fretful, Bride. Drink your tea."

She did as told.

"Though her behavior was most inappropriate last night, and though I do believe she owes us—you, especially—an apology . . ." He paused and scratched his sideburn. "I do believe that the proper thing to do is to continue to pay for her room and board here, at the Clarendon."

Eileen placed her teacup in its saucer. She had not expected such kindness from him. "That is very generous of you, Laurie."

Laurie nodded. "I had considered, after our engagement, that we might have your sister live with us, for certainly we have ample accommodation at our home, and she is your only family. Had you thought this also?"

Guiltily, Eileen realized that she had not considered this scenario because, plainly, she had presumed—and desired—that she would be living a new life with her husband. She had figured that her sister would take care of herself, as she always had, and with a bit of financial help in the form of an allowance from herself—or her husband, more practically speaking.

"Frankly, I had assumed that I might—with your permission, of course—provide Mary with some small allowance to supplement her earnings at May's, so that she might find a suitable living situation. But if you would choose to continue her room and board here at the

Clarendon"—she paused, searching for the right words—"well, that is more than generous, I believe, especially given her behavior last night."

His eyes searched hers. "You must be very upset about the whole incident."

Eileen felt her stomach clench again as she remembered the utter shame and embarrassment of the prior evening. She nodded. "I am quite hurt, yes."

Laurie shook his head, then reached across the table, taking Eileen's hand in his. "It greatly upsets me that my bride was upset on our wedding day. I do not like it one bit."

Eileen smiled at his show of indignation. "It will pass. I am sure she will apologize."

"I do hope so," he said, letting go of her hand. He spread marmalade on a slice of toast, passing it to her. "I must say, Bride, I don't care much for that Mr. Stinson." He proceeded to spread marmalade on another piece of toast as she nibbled on hers. "He is not a suitable companion for your sister, nor any young lady, for that matter, in my opinion."

Eileen thought to herself how little Laurie knew of Mary's past. Good thing, that. She nodded. "I do not like that Mary has taken up with him."

"Then it seems we are like-minded on this matter. This pleases me."

They ate in silence for a few moments.

Laurie continued, "He is the sort of man that I have no use for, quite honestly."

Eileen was surprised that Laurie still spoke about Beau, but was glad of it, for she had no use for Beau, either.

"The things I have heard said about him in town . . ." He paused. "Well, let's just hope that Mary realizes, soon, that there are far better, more suitable men out there for her."

"Perhaps we should think of some suitable men for Mary?" Eileen offered. "If you would help me to do so, maybe we could introduce her to businessmen of better quality here in Leadville. This is my hope for her." Eileen considered her words. "But you know that Mary is most willful. Stubborn, in fact. When she gets an idea in her head, she runs with it, and for some reason she has taken a real shine to Beau." She pursed her lips, regretting her use of slang before Laurie.

He nodded, chuckling. "Yes, it would seem she has taken a *shine* to him, as you say. I like that word."

Relieved, Eileen giggled.

"I'll consider your suggestion, Bride. I'll make inquiries. Perhaps there's an eligible, honest bachelor within my circle of acquaintance," Laurie said. "Has your sister always been so willful?"

"Oh yes," Eileen readily answered after a sip of tea. She nodded emphatically.

Laurie laughed. "And you have always been the prudent one?"

Eileen wasn't certain what, exactly, "prudent" meant, but she assumed it had something to do with quiet and reserve. "I suppose so, unless you count the occasional singing in a Bowery barroom."

Laurie slapped his thigh, laughing again. "And how could I forget, the first time I ever beheld you. What a fateful night . . ." His eyes grew distant in contemplation, his smile fading slightly as he focused on some mental picture that Eileen could only guess at.

"I enjoy singing, then and now," she said, in order to break the silence.

"Yes," he replied, his attention returning to her, in the present. "I shall look into a box at the Tabor Opera House. Would you enjoy that, Bride?"

"Oh, yes, I would." She began to wish he would say her name, instead of "Bride."

"Looks like we'll be getting quite a storm this evening, sir," said Seamus as he lit the oil lamps in the sitting room.

Laurie went to the window and peered out. "There looks to be a few inches of snow already on the ground."

Eileen sat in a large leather chair before the fire, holding a diminutive crystal glass of port in her hand. She took a sip, feeling decidedly uncomfortable in her new surroundings—her new home, their home. Placing her drink down upon the side table, she felt something was missing. Her fingers curled in on each other, not used to being idle. She wished she had her lacework. *Yes, I'll be sure to keep a lace project in this room, perhaps even some bobbin lace.* Never, ever had she imagined that such idleness, such a home, would be hers. She wished she could show Mary—oh, Mary! Daft chit! Eileen took another sip of port, hoping it would help her lessen the pain each time she thought of her sister.

"Will you be needing anything else this evening, sir?" Seamus asked.

"I don't believe so." Laurie turned to Eileen. "Bride, do you require anything else?"

"Oh, oh no. I'm fine, thank you." She glanced over at Seamus, who gave her a kindly smile.

"Very well, then. I'll bid you both good evening." And with a light click of the door closing, Seamus was gone.

Eileen thought it quite amusing and interesting that Seamus's accent had changed from one that sounded decidedly British to one that was most certainly of Cork origin. Perhaps the wilds of the Rocky Mountains and the circus that was Leadville had made him realize that there was no longer any need for pretense. Some of the wealthiest men in Leadville—in the country—came from the most humble of origins. Was not Mr. Tabor a stonemason from Vermont in his former, far less affluent and charmed life?

"Would you like me to read the daily to you?" Laurie asked as he settled into the leather chair across from hers.

"Please do," she replied, glad to have something to break the uncomfortable silence of the room.

Laurie opened the newspaper. "Why, it seems our wedding celebration is one of the headlines."

Eileen had a sudden chill, for she worried that the story might mention her sister's humiliating behavior. And besides, she could not bear to hear a description of herself—it was so unnerving to think that people had viewed her wedding day as a news story. "Oh, Laurie, please, don't read that." Then she worried that she sounded too forceful.

He looked at her, above the newspaper, brows raised. "Whyever not?"

"It . . . it makes me so uncomfortable, the thought of hearing a story about me."

"But it shouldn't, my Bride."

"Oh, Laurie, do read something else, please."

He studied her for a moment, then resumed the newspaper. "Ah, well, it seems that Shay's Saloon was ransacked in a brawl last night."

Again, Eileen started; Shay's, with, oddly enough, the same name as their old haunt in New York City, was one of Mary and Beau's favorite watering holes.

"The owner reports that in the midst of the brawl, some thief or thieves made off with most of the gambling revenues." Laurie paused before he read on. "One witness had come forward to the sheriff but was found dead this morning in Stillborn Alley. Apparently shot in the head."

Eileen was reminded of her recurring nightmare. She moved to take another gulp of the port to steady her nerves, only to realize that her glass was emptied. She rose and went to the sideboard to pour herself another.

"Lovely port, isn't it, Bride?" Laurie asked.

"Indeed. Very. I don't think I've ever had anything like it before," she said, giving him a weak smile. Eileen settled back in her chair again, happy that Laurie had touched on another topic that she might coax him to elaborate on. "Does your mother enjoy port?"

He took a sip of his brandy. "Not particularly."

Eileen felt as though she must help pry the door open further. "What sort of things does your mother enjoy doing?"

"She enjoys drawing—she's quite talented at watercolor sketches," he answered in a bored tone.

Eileen did not know what a watercolor sketch might be. Perhaps drawings of the ocean?

"And she also enjoys embroidery. And birds."

"Birds?"

"Yes, she's always loved birds."

"Oh, I see. Does she keep them as pets?"

Laurie's brows rose as he thought for a moment. "No, Mother was never the sort to keep a pet." He stroked his sideburn with the back of his fingertips as he fixated on some distant memory.

Eileen placed her port down on the table beside her and waited for him to continue, for she realized that Laurie was sharing something very personal with her.

"Mother is a cold sort."

The wind howled outside. Eileen breathed through her nose, detecting the scent of the fire in the hearth, the fresh paint and wallpaper upon the walls, the wood that comprised this stately home, newly built. "Do you not get along very well?" she ventured to ask.

Laurie sighed. "For the sake of civility, we give the appearance of being amicable." His gaze went to the hearth. "Mother is very concerned with appearances, you see."

"Aren't all women?" Eileen asked with a smile.

Laurie smiled back at her. "Indeed, most are, but there are those who are like wild, willful creatures that won't be tamed."

Eileen wondered if Laurie was speaking of someone in particular: A past lover? Someone he knew now?

"And which do you prefer?" Eileen knew her question was bold, but she also knew that she was the sort of person who always sought the truth of a matter, politeness be damned.

"I like a little of both, I believe," he said with a wink.

She wondered if she had a little of both in her, enough to interest him.

He then rose from his chair while he finished the last of his brandy. "Shall we retire for the night, Bride?"

She took his offered hand and stood. "Laurie, do call me Eileen."

He looked quizzical. "Do you not like my pet name for you?"

"Well, yes, I do. But I like to hear you say my name sometimes, too." She knew she was being bold and knew it must be the port.

"Very well, Eileen," he said, patting her hand lightly. "Let us retire."

CHAPTER TWENTY-ONE

For the three days following their wedding, it had snowed. For three days they could not leave their new home. For three days they woke together, shared meals together, even read together. But at the end of three days, once the sunshine finally returned to Leadville, Laurie was eager to be alone.

In the weeks following, he had also made up his mind to hire a tutor to sharpen Eileen's extremely rudimentary reading skills and appallingly paltry vocabulary. Though he had thought it would be diverting to undertake her education himself, after three days he realized he lacked the patience and basic interest to do so. He then thought to teach Eileen something of more interest to himself: the geography and topography of the United States. At first it was pleasing, for the two shared a curiosity in the origins of river systems high in the Rocky Mountains, and how they meandered their ways, like drunk snakes, to the faraway seas. But soon enough, that lost its appeal to him also.

They had now been man and wife for over a month. And it was not only Eileen's vocabulary and geography education that had lost their appeal, but also her education in the bedroom. Part of him felt guilty for admitting this, but he believed himself justified in feeling so. Honestly, how long did he think that such a lack of imagination and curiosity in the ways of lovemaking could sustain his most worldly needs?

Indeed, it had been most intriguing and entertaining at the first. Despite all his dalliances, Laurie had never had a virgin before. It had been thrilling to take her the first time. There was something of the violent, imminent hunt in it that appealed to a primal aspect in him. Never had he been so utterly dominant in the act before. But the succeeding encounters had been far less exciting; she knew what to expect, so it was no longer terrifying or foreign to her anymore. There was no longer the shine of fear in her eyes. She knew when to part her legs for him, how to tilt toward him.

Yes, he knew there was still much education that she needed; one could not expect a person unacquainted with a piano to immediately learn to play Chopin. But the idea of instructing her in what was second nature to him seemed tedious; he could not bear the thought. And he had realized that it would always be so with her when he had coaxed her atop him. She had appeared stricken, insecure, her brow furrowed—and not in that manner so delicious as when a woman ascends to climax, that was for certain. Did she even know what it might be to climax? He rolled his eyes at the thought. My, but he couldn't even begin to explain it and lacked the patience to try. Perhaps some men had the willingness and ambition to take on such a task, and he would gladly lift a glass and toast them. But he was not that sort of man, and though he would humbly admit that this was a shortcoming on his part, he felt no guilt over it.

She was not frigid; she responded to his touch and was not averse to giving herself to him. But she knew nothing, nothing at all. Perhaps it *would* have been beneficial for Mary to have stuck around at the wedding to give her sister "the talk." And she seemed overwhelmed by this role of wife he had bestowed upon her. She was unsure of herself in the bedchamber, unsure of herself during the day, at the dinner table, in the sitting room, around the servants. She seemed to retreat into herself, busying herself with crochet or needle lacework, at which she was quite skilled and adept, he must admit.

Despite this, Laurie was still glad that he had taken her for his wife. He was a pioneer in many respects, for no one in his family or in any of the old New York families had ever done anything so wild, brash, and infamous as marry someone so beneath their station. And he had taken the lowest of the low—an Irish immigrant—and elevated her to a place beyond her dreams. Eileen was a good woman, he knew, and quite beautiful, too, and so he would always be pleased with his choice of wife.

He had thoroughly scandalized his damned mother, never mind the rest of that stuffy, judgmental set in New York—including even his old pal James Whitcomb. James had sent him a most offensive letter, asking him if he had lost his mind, wondering what would have possessed Laurie to stoop so low. "Is she really so special? What tricks does this witch from Hibernia know that have so beguiled you? My, Laurie, you know you have the means to get it from her without making her your wife!" It was this outrage, this spurning of all the social mores of that old world of New York that would continue to be a source of pride and pleasure for Laurie.

And, of course, it had been Stanley Jones who had made the suggestion to begin with. And Laurie knew that it gave Stanley much joy to see him marry Eileen, and nothing gave him more satisfaction than to know that he had pleased Stanley in some way. In his overly idealistic imagination, Laurie hoped that maybe—just maybe—in pleasing Stanley, Stanley would then reward him somehow. What that reward might be, Laurie could not begin to define with words, but he could most certainly imagine.

But, quite simply, Laurie realized, he had idealistically and ridiculously thought himself marrying his Boadicea, but Eileen was by no means a formidable warrior queen. She was, indeed, more like a beautiful yet passive Arthurian maiden. When Eileen had climbed atop him, she had appeared like a wary fox rather than a proud, powerful lioness, and it was then that his illusion of a Celtic queen had been destroyed.

So what was to be done? Reluctantly, he realized that the only thing to do was what most men of his stature and power did: remain married and seek pleasure on the side.

But first, as soon as the blizzard—the third one in the span of a month—was over and as soon as the streets were somewhat navigable for his sleigh, Laurie would pay a visit to Stanley, for no reason other than to see and feel his smile, so much like the relentless sunshine in this nook atop the Rocky Mountains.

His knock upon the rear door of the humble wooden church—the door that led to Stanley's meager living quarters—was quickly answered by Ruth Ahern, now Ruth Denahy. Ruth had become one of Stanley's most loyal and fervent disciples, even after marrying Bill Denahy, a local wheelwright who had come to Leadville via Chicago, Boston, and Cork. Perhaps twenty years his bride's senior, Mr. Denahy, who was missing an eye from some prior, grim accident, had been in need of a wife, and Ruth had, of course, needed a husband after her father's death. Wearing a crisp apron and her perpetually persecuted expression—which had grown in intensity since the passing of her parents months before—she nervously wished Laurie good day, telling him that Stanley was not in.

"That's most unfortunate," Laurie replied, his spirits sinking. "Has he gone to town on business? Perhaps I might catch up with him there."

Ruth shook her head and smoothed her hands over her apron skirt. "No, Mr. Barnard. He's gone fishing."

"Fishing? How can that be?" Laurie asked, imagining that, after these past weeks of arctic cold and snow, there was no body of water near Leadville that would not be frozen over.

"Ice fishing, sir, over yonder," Ruth replied, pointing out toward the great expanse of snow-covered land where various streams danced together before merging to form the Arkansas River.

Sure enough, Laurie spotted a figure far in the distance. "Is there a road that leads over there?"

"No, sir, you've got to walk over if you must."

Laurie glanced down at his fine, polished leather boots, already caked in snow. "Very well, then, I'll leave the sleigh here and walk. Good day, Mrs. Denahy," he said with a tip of his hat.

He sensed Ruth's gaze upon his back as he turned and tenuously made his way over the field of snow, trying his best not to topple over into snow piles and drifts that made his footing awkward. He hoped she had closed the door before witnessing him trip once, his trousers now completely dusted with downy snow.

The snow was different here, in the mountains, than it was in New York. Here it was like an idealized vision of snow, in terms of the fluffy, fine-grained texture of it, the way it sparkled in the sunshine as though dusted with tiny sapphires and diamonds. New York snow was heavy and unmovable, and certainly there was never enough sunshine to notice any hint of sparkle, though he doubted it was in there to begin with.

The wind stung his exposed face, yet when it ceased to blow, the sunshine actually caused him to perspire beneath his hat as he pushed himself farther across the meadow. He traversed iced-over streams about a half dozen times before finally reaching Stanley.

"Good day, Laurie!" Stanley hailed him with a big wave.

There, in the midst of an empty, desolate, snowy plain, the sight of Stanley left Laurie awestruck. Clad in a bulky, intricately patterned wool sweater, oilskin overalls, boots, mittens, and knit hat, Stanley held a rough-hewn wooden spear in his hands. Smiling, skin slightly ruddy from the sun and wind, long blond hair tied back in his usual, decidedly old-fashioned manner, Stanley appeared to Laurie like some proud, powerful Norse warrior, minus the armor, or like King Arthur, without his crown.

"I've had a good day of fishing so far," Stanley cheerily said, glancing down at a hole he must have cut himself, Laurie surmised, in ice about six inches deep. Stanley stood on the edge of the bank, where the stream naturally pooled into a tiny lake of sorts. Beside him was a large metal washing tub, half filled with fish packed in snow.

Laurie stood perhaps four yards from Stanley, on the opposite bank. "How is it done?" He had finally found his voice, after being so undone by the sight of Stanley.

"Oh, quite simply, really. Watch." Stanley held the spear in both hands, pointed edge poised directly over the hole in the ice. He stood, legs akimbo on the bank, and kept his gaze upon the dark water. After a moment, Stanley swiftly plunged the spear into the hole. "Success!" he shouted, looking quite proud of himself as he lifted the spear, displaying a decent-size trout skewered right through. The fish weakly flapped about for a brief moment before going limp and still. Stanley shook the fish off the spear, into the bucket.

"How primitive," Laurie said, and he intended no insult, but, rather, adoration.

"Would you like to give it a try?" Stanley asked, presenting the spear to Laurie.

"No," Laurie said, suddenly feeling embarrassed. "I don't think so."

"Well," Stanley said, glancing down at his wash bucket of fish, "I think I've probably caught plenty for today." He then jammed the spear into the bank with a powerful thrust. He clasped his hands before his chest. "Oh Lord Jesus, I thank you for blessing me today with such a bounty of fish, and I promise to share it with all who are in need. I do so in your name and glory. Amen."

Laurie tried to hide his discomfort at the sudden outburst of prayer by shuffling his feet in the snow, glancing up to the bright-blue sky.

Stanley lifted the large wash bucket, balancing it upon one shoulder, holding it in place with his arm. He plucked his spear from the bank with his free hand and crossed the ice, joining Laurie on the other side. "Shall we head back and have coffee?"

"Ruth, thank you for your help today," Stanley said as he and Laurie settled down at the simple wooden table, pot of coffee between them. "You may head home now to your husband."

Ruth appeared crestfallen. "But what about the fish, Reverend Jones? Shall I gut and clean them?"

"Do not trouble yourself. I'll tend to them later this afternoon," he said with a kindly smile.

A flush came over Ruth's pasty skin. Her plain, pinched face almost appeared pretty for a moment under Stanley's smile. It was as though she lived for such moments, like they were some divine revelation.

She hesitated, transfixed.

"Go now, Ruth, and take some fish with you, to cook for your husband."

She did exactly as told. Laurie watched out of the corner of his eye as she removed her apron and donned her coat. She chewed on her lower lip, much like a child who refuses to allow anyone to spy her tears, lest they ridicule her.

Once she was gone, Stanley poured Laurie's coffee into an enameled tin cup, passing it to him before serving himself. "So, how does married life suit you, my friend?"

Laurie took a tentative sip of the coffee—still much too hot—before sitting back to answer. "Well, I suppose."

Stanley regarded him from across the simple wooden table. The fire in the potbellied stove burned furiously, and the outside wind echoed down the metal chimney pipe.

"You 'suppose'? What sort of answer is that? You've married the loveliest girl in Leadville."

Laurie had never heard Stanley refer to Eileen in such praiseful terms and it took him by surprise. "Do you think her so?"

Stanley scrunched his brows together, as though puzzled. "Of course I do. Don't you?"

Laurie, in his discomfort, took a sip from his cup again, remembering too late that the coffee was still too hot, scalding his tongue.

"Are you all right?" Stanley asked.

"Just burned my tongue."

"Ah. Give it a few minutes to cool."

Laurie wished he had something stronger to drink, to take away his discomfort, being so very close to Stanley.

"But yes," Stanley continued. "I do think Eileen is the prettiest girl in Leadville. Most men do, I would think. She strikes me as lovely as the Queen Guinevere of my imagination."

Laurie was surprised that he and Stanley shared the same Arthurian ideal of Eileen's beauty. "Well, true as that might be," Laurie replied, "a pretty face can only beguile for so long." He regretted his harsh, frank words just as soon as they came from his mouth.

Stanley's brows rose. "What are you implying, Laurie? You are already dissatisfied with her?"

Laurie shifted uncomfortably in his chair. "Well, no, I'm not sure that I would use that word, but maybe . . . I don't know."

"Tell me what you're thinking, friend." Stanley put his elbows on the table, all his attention focused on Laurie.

Laurie was disconcerted by the intensity of Stanley's dark-blue stare, the angles of his face. He felt his heart race. He wished they could cease talking about his marriage, his wife. He didn't want to think about all that when here, here was Stanley, so very beautiful, so perfect . . .

"Where did you get such a sweater?" Laurie asked, acting on his instinct to change the subject.

Stanley, seeming surprised, quickly glanced down at his sweater, beneath his oilskin overalls. "This? One of my parishioners from Finntown made this for me."

"I thought it was rather Nordic-looking."

Stanley's eyes met his, then faltered, before returning. "I'm American."

Laurie thought this response very odd. "I didn't say otherwise. I only said the sweater appeared Nordic. Though, all things said, you look rather Nordic in it as well."

Stanly rose from his seat, which loudly scraped upon the simple floorboards. He went to a little wooden cabinet, opening the door. "Would you like cornbread?"

"No, thank you."

Stanley returned to the table with a small basket. He unfolded the cloth within, took a small piece of bread, and devoured it with one bite. After he brushed his hands upon his overalls, he took a sip of his coffee.

"Ruth makes very good cornbread," he commented.

"Perhaps you should have married her," Laurie said, laughing uncomfortably at his attempt at a joke.

Stanley chuckled, too. "I don't think so. She is a good woman, but not nearly as pretty as your Eileen."

There was silence in the room. Laurie finally ventured to take a sip of his coffee; it was bearable now.

"So, are you going to talk to me about what troubles you with your marriage?"

Laurie sighed. How could he tell Stanley, who so obviously admired Eileen, his sentiments without the man thinking poorly of him?

"I'm bored," he stated loudly, for yes, indeed, he was bored of the topic, of his wife, of this pretense between him and Stanley. All he could think of, in this small room with Stanley's scent all around him, was that day in his study, when there had been a kiss, so sweet a kiss. Good god, it seemed ages ago now.

"Bored? Bored already? You've been married what, all of a month?" Stanley appeared utterly shocked.

"We've been married some six weeks now."

"And you know you are bored already? Your life together has only just begun!"

"You don't understand!" Laurie said, slamming his fist down upon the table, shaking the tin cups and coffeepot.

"Indeed, I don't. Please explain."

"She does not satisfy me."

There was silence. Stanley appeared wary, his eyes narrowing. "How do you mean?"

"Must I spell it out?"

"So you mean in her wifely duties?"

Laurie rolled his eyes at such an ambiguous, biblical expression. "Yes, specifically in the bedroom."

"I don't think I am the right person for you to speak to about such matters," Stanley said, rising again from his seat to return the cornbread basket to the cupboard.

Laurie let out a snide chuckle. "Why not? Have you never been with a woman before?"

Stanley rounded on him, arms crossed in front of his chest. "I believe that's none of your business."

Laurie leaned back in his chair, trying to solve the puzzle before him. Could it be? Could it be that Stanley was so pure, so righteous, that he had never been with a woman? *No, no, it cannot be; he could never have kissed me the way he did that day.*

"Look," Stanley said, uncrossing his arms and taking his chair again. He folded his large hands into a steeple before him, on the table. "I am not very knowledgeable about worldly matters, but this I do know: A man must teach a woman. He cannot expect her to know these things, if she be a virgin when she marries. How could she?"

Laurie knew that Stanley spoke basic truth, which he himself had often considered. But he also knew his nature. "But I don't have the patience to teach her." He ran his hand through his hair, his heart racing with the truth of the moment. "I want what I want, when I want it."

There was an uncomfortable silence that followed Laurie's declaration. The words seemed alive and lingered in the room, pacing about, panting like a hungry dog.

"What do you want?" Stanley asked in little more than a whisper.

"You know what I want. What I've always wanted." Laurie would stop this charade.

"From me?"

"Don't play the fool. You know what lies between us." Laurie's heart pounded like a war drum in his ears and even the roots of his hair.

Stanley began, "I don't know what to say—"

"You can stop pretending that you are unaware of this, of me." Laurie leaned over the table, intent upon Stanley.

"I've had to."

"How do you mean?"

"Look at me, Laurie!" Stanley's voice rose. "I'm a minister, a preacher!" His gaze was penetrating, somewhat wild. He then asked in a whisper, "What would you have me do?"

Laurie understood his meaning, but did not want to hear it, did not want to accept it. "Why did you encourage me to marry?"

Stanley rubbed at his eyes, sighing. "I thought that, perhaps, if you were married, then you would forget about me, and maybe I could forget about you."

Laurie's heart quickened. He reached across the table and took Stanley's rough hand in his. "How could I? You woke me . . . you *woke* me." He could not think of how else to shape his sentiments with words.

"Then why did you marry?" Stanley asked, allowing Laurie to hold his hand.

"She pleased me. She was exciting and foreign, and I felt bold and rebellious—"

"Lord above, don't tell me you married her just to spite your family, Laurie." Stanley began to pull his hand away.

Laurie clasped his hand tighter. "Maybe I did, Stanley, and you'll never understand the motivation for someone like me, of my standing, to do such a thing."

"Indeed, I won't." There was cynicism in his voice, and this angered Laurie.

"And I did it to please you!"

Stanley stared at him. "What?"

"I thought that it would make you happy, and I wanted to make you happy. I *want* to make you happy, don't you see? I thought that maybe if I pleased you enough, you would reward me, somehow."

"My word, Laurie," Stanley said, taking his hand from his. "You speak like a child. *A child!*"

"I don't care if I sound like a child. I'm being completely honest with you."

Stanley did not respond. He only leaned back in his chair, letting his head drop back as he stared at the ceiling and let out a groan.

Laurie drank in the sight of Stanley's sinewy, pale neck above the neckline of his sweater. He saw a deep-blue vein running up the right side. He longed to kiss it. He longed to kiss it and then violently shove his hand down inside Stanley's overalls and please him because it would please him to please him. He might go mad. He was a caged animal. He rose from his chair and grabbed his hat and coat from the hook upon the wall.

"Where are you going?" Stanley asked, sitting forward again in his chair.

"I can't be in here anymore. It's killing me."

Stanley shook his head. "Don't say that. It pains me."

"*You* pain me!" Laurie shouted.

Stanley rose from his chair and walked toward him. "Laurie, please, listen to me." He placed his hands gently upon Laurie's shoulders. "We must be patient."

Laurie could smell the coffee on Stanley's warm breath. He wanted to lick the inside of his mouth, taste how coffee tasted upon Stanley. "For what must we be patient? What? What will you give me? What must I wait for?"

"Hush," Stanley said, then bent his head and placed his lips upon Laurie's.

Laurie melted into something, some shape, some likeness that was a better, a truer, a more beautiful aspect of himself.

Stanley pulled away.

Laurie's heart felt rent in two. He had glimpsed something and now glimpsed it again and he wanted more but the door was closed and he felt himself shiver. "Tell me," he pleaded in a whisper.

"Wait until spring," Stanley whispered back.

"Spring?" Laurie tried to make sense of what he was being told.

"Yes. Let's get through the winter. In spring, when it is warmer, I'll think of something. Or perhaps by then this passion will have waned. Either way, I promise you."

Laurie felt the warmth of the sun again. He could only nod.

"But you must promise me something in the meantime."

"What? Anything!"

"Do not hurt Eileen. She is too good a soul. Be decent."

Laurie was surprised to hear Stanley mention his wife. It jarred him.

"If you must indulge your pleasures elsewhere—though I hope you won't—then do so. But do not let her know, and do not cause her pain. Do you understand?" Stanley squeezed Laurie's shoulder. "I care about Eileen very much. She is very important to me. More important than she'll ever know."

CHAPTER TWENTY-TWO

For the first time in her life, Eileen had hours and days to herself. At first, it made her utterly anxious; she would pace the rooms of her luxurious, well-appointed home, wringing her hands, wondering what on earth she should do with all that she had never had before—both the comfort and time. A clock's ticking became a nuisance, for it reminded her how wasteful, so very wasteful, and unresourceful she was. At times, she even became angry with herself for not being more content. She took a bit of solace from the thing that had always come easy to her and offered her a sense of purpose. To create something from nothing had always given Eileen a sense of satisfaction. She went to her old trunk, beneath the settee in her bedroom, and found her treasured bone bobbins, kept within a linsey-woolsey sack, the same that Sister Theresa had given her many years before. She took one of the damask-covered, decorative pillows from her settee and used that as the base of her pillow lace. With her old set of long tom pins, she began an elaborate pattern of her own design, her fingers weaving the bone bobbins together almost of their own volition, for it came so naturally to her. There was a soothing that came from the soft sound of the bone bobbins dancing together, clicking and thumping, creating their own special rhythm.

While she worked away, she thought to herself, was her life now not the stuff of dreams come true for girls young and old who toiled away in factories, on farms, or in the cribs on State Street? How dare she feel anything but complete happiness and bliss in her new life situation. *Silly, stupid Eileen.*

Laurie had, of course, procured her a personal maid—Florence, the adolescent daughter of a local grocer with too many daughters. But Florence was no companion, for she was even more nervous and uncomfortable in her new position than Eileen was herself. Such like sentiments should have fostered empathy, commiseration, perhaps, but indeed, that would not be decent. A lady must preserve the proper distance from her maids and staff. This Eileen had learned from the tutor Laurie had hired for her instruction soon after their wedding. She had learned this and did her best to uphold it but, in truth, it only added to her awkward discomfort.

The governess was a Mrs. Landry, a widow originally from Baltimore whose late husband, a successful land surveyor, had had the most unfortunate yet fantastical luck to be struck dead by lightning while surveying on Fryer Hill one year before. She was upright and strict like the nuns Eileen recalled back in Limerick. Mrs. Landry, with reading pince-nez perched upon her pinched nose above her pursed expression, encouraged Eileen to constantly practice her newly acquired and expanding reading and writing skills. Eileen did so, that was, until her head and eyes ached something awful after much time spent bent over books and ledgers. These spells, it seemed, worsened directly preceding inclement or stormy weather, which was, of course, a frequent occurrence at Leadville's high altitude. At times, Eileen's eye aches were so fierce that there was no remedy but to recline somewhere with a cool compress over them. *My word,* she would laugh wryly, *I've become quite the proper lady now. Soon I'll be requiring smelling salts.*

Of course there was Seamus—kindly, sweet Seamus—but he usually accompanied Laurie to the Avalon or assisted in whatever business tasks were required of him. There was also Jacob, the boy of fifteen hired to tend to the horses in the stables, run errands, and occasionally act as driver. He was German, or Czech, or something like that—Laurie had told her once—and spoke with a heavy accent, therefore offering little in the way of conversation. A temporary cook—Harry, a Chicagoan who had failed miserably at mining but had a knack for cooking and preferred to ply that trade rather than toil away in a mine shaft for some other man's benefit—had been hired by Laurie. But Harry would be heading back to Chicago as soon as spring arrived. And Harry did not seem much interested in socializing with the lady of the house—whether it be for propriety's sake or because he did not much like women in general, Eileen could not be sure. And so their conversations were limited to talk of the weather and what should be prepared for the evening's meal.

Her husband, she had found, was not much of a companion. Eileen was no fool; she knew when someone feigned false sentiment. The true joy she once beheld in his green eyes was gone, and she was at a loss as to why, or how she might bring it back. She had spied that genuine joy once, fleetingly—had it been on the train journey to Denver, when he had eagerly imparted his knowledge of a great many things, places, people? Had it been when he'd taken her on the hunt, that fateful early-September day months ago?

When she thought of that day, she would go to the study, lined with cases brimming with leather-bound books she might like to read someday, and stand before the marble hearth to gaze up at the great, mounted elk's head. Laurie had said he would give it to her as a gift, but in honesty, it had become both of theirs, not just hers. She would stare up into the lifeless, glassy black pools of eyes, fringed with thick, brown lashes, and silently beseech the bull to offer her some clue, some answer, as to how to please her husband, as the bull had been present that blissful day in September. And the longer she stared, the more she realized that her husband's eyes were almost as lifeless as those of the bull, and soon it seemed that the bull was accusing her of something—what? His early demise in the meadow dotted with Indian paintbrush? Some shortcoming on her part as a wife, as a woman? She soon hated the presence of the elk with his great, powerful rack. He reminded her of happier, seemingly simpler days that no longer were. He reminded her of his death, of her loneliness.

She was lonely but did not like to admit it to herself. Why should she? It would only further frustrate her to admit to something other than contentment—it would smack of self-pity, and how very ridiculous that would be, when she had acquired such comfort and luxury.

She was lonely but endeavored to ignore this, for if she did not, then she would long for Mary. Two months had transpired since her wedding day, and still Mary had not offered any sort of apology for her behavior, nor had she made any effort to contact her sister. This pained Eileen and infuriated her at the same time. Oh, how her heart ached and her blood boiled when she thought of her sister! The passage of time and the absence of her sister had magnified both Eileen's embarrassment and her anger at Mary. Though, in her loneliest hours, she had fleeting moments of clarity when she considered that, just perhaps, she might have made too much of the incident, a mountain out of a molehill, so to speak. But she would quickly chide herself, and the burning fury at her sister would return. Besides, if ever she hoped to please her husband, disobeying his wishes in regards to her sister was the last thing she should do.

Laurie had encouraged her to invite groups of the local ladies who had not gone to Denver for the winter to teas and luncheons at the house, and she had done so. But whenever she hosted such social gatherings, or whenever she herself was invited to one, she always felt as though she were completely detached from her surroundings. She knew the ladies watched her every movement, whenever she served or sipped tea, ate her cake, tasted her soups. In order to cope with her supreme discomfort, she would pretend she was alone and that their eyes no longer were upon her. She was not one of them, and they knew it as well as she. She never would, truly, be one of them, no matter how much money and power her husband might have. And so she would continue to be invited to social gatherings, but she knew it was all show and pretense, just like her husband's contrived contentment when they ate supper and sat together in the study, sipping port or brandy until it became far too exhausting to continue the facade and the two would retire.

The bedroom caused her unending anxiety. She was not nervous of him, of course—she knew what to expect now—and at times she found herself experiencing some small pleasure in his caresses. But when it was over, she found herself wanting something more, something beyond her comprehension. And he would not bother to show it to her, she knew. He was satisfied, yet not, and oh, how she wished she knew something more than this. It was like all those leather-bound books in the study—she knew they offered something far more thrilling than the simple, boring reading lessons she labored at each morning with Mrs. Landry. But when she opened them, the words became indecipherable, a mystery she knew not how to solve.

If only Mary had imparted this knowledge to her.

It was then that Eileen made a decision. For the past two months, she had had Jacob or Florence go to May's Dry Goods to fetch whatever she might require. Eileen would not dare set foot in there and risk confronting her willful sister—just the mere contemplation of such a meeting was too painful and frustrating. But she decided that she must at least see her sister, see how Mary would react to her presence, and then proceed from there. Maybe her sister would plead for forgiveness? Eileen laughed a little at the thought of Mary pleading for anything, yet she remained hopeful that maybe, just maybe . . .

"Mrs. Barnard! What a pleasant surprise!"

Mr. May hurriedly came round the counter to personally greet Eileen as she entered the shop, removing her bonnet.

There were a few other patrons mulling about the store, and all stopped to stare at her.

"How can I be of assistance to you today?" Mr. May asked.

"Have you any ladies' linen handkerchiefs?" She had no need for them, had plenty at home, but while driving down to May's, she'd decided that this would be what she would ask for, as Mary worked in ladies' accessories.

Mr. May extended his arms, leading the way. "But of course! We just received a new shipment a few days ago. Had to come by way of South Park, of course," he said, chuckling in what seemed like nervousness.

Eileen thought it strange that her former boss would now be nervous in her presence. How odd life could be.

When they approached the glass counter displaying an array of kerchiefs, gloves, hatpins, stockings, and the like, Eileen was surprised to notice a shopgirl who was most certainly not Mary smiling at her, curtsying.

"Mr. May, where is my sister today?" Eileen asked suddenly, before she could temper her surprise.

"Oh, but did you not know?" he asked, then quickly blushed, perhaps recalling the scandal between the sisters that, Eileen was certain, everyone in Leadville knew about at this point. "Mary quit her job about four weeks ago."

That was not long after the wedding. "Quit?" Eileen couldn't make sense of it.

"Yes, ma'am."

Eileen felt Mr. May's discomfort at imparting this news to her, for he cleared his throat and fussed with his red bow tie. "But Celia here will assist us, won't you, dear?"

The pretty shopgirl nodded enthusiastically, her curling-ironed brown ringlets bouncing. "Yes, it would be my pleasure, Mrs. Barnard."

"Do you know if she's found work elsewhere?" Eileen asked, not caring if her question seemed too pointed.

Mr. May shook his head. "I'm afraid I can't answer that, Mrs. Barnard. But"—he stepped a little closer to her in a conspiring manner, lowering his voice—"my brother tells me that he saw her singing in Shay's Saloon about a week ago, on Friday night." The red flush deepened upon his cheeks.

Eileen could do nothing but stare at the contents inside the display case. The store had fallen silent. She glanced over at the other shoppers, whose stares were still upon her, but who quickly went back to their shopping after having been caught in the act.

"We have some lovely linen kerchiefs right here, Mrs. Barnard, that you might like," said Celia the shopgirl while she displayed the wares upon the glass counter. "They are edged in very pretty pink satin, you see?"

Eileen absently fingered them as she attempted to calm her racing mind.

"Do you find these suitable, Mrs. Barnard?" asked Mr. May.

"How many do you have?"

"We have twelve in stock, ma'am," replied Celia.

"I'll take them all, please."

Both shopgirl and owner smiled in satisfaction, perhaps, Eileen realized, because she had not bothered to ask the price.

"Is there anything else I might get for you today?" Mr. May asked.

Eileen suddenly found that this deference being shown to her—which had originally caused her odd amusement—was rather satisfying, or soothing in some strange way.

"We just received the most luxurious rabbit fur–lined ladies' slippers. Perfect for chilly Leadville evenings. Would you like to try them?" Mr. May asked.

Mr. May had not built such a successful dry goods business without the valuable skill of being able to read his clients' thoughts, Eileen knew. But she did not care. She allowed herself to be led to the shoe area, where Mr. May ushered away Carl the shoe salesman and personally fitted the sweet little rabbit fur slippers to her feet. She sat for a moment, numb to everything but her bewilderment at her sister's disappearance, which, somehow, seemed lessened only by the comforting feeling of fur around her feet.

"What colors?"

"Pink, blue, white, and lilac."

"I'll take a pair in each color."

"Jacob, drive by Shay's, on State, please."

"Yes, ma'am," he replied with a tip of his hat and a quizzical expression at her request.

With various parcels and packages secured around her in the sleigh and a buffalo fur draped over her lap, Eileen steeled herself for a possible sighting of Mary in the bawdiest part of Leadville. *And what will I say should I see her?* Eileen thought up a great many formal, polite salutations that she might deliver to any stranger who happened to greet her. All seemed contrived, for they were. She puffed her cheeks as she exhaled and began to wonder why on earth she had decided to tempt fate in such a way.

Once on State Street, Eileen was unsurprised to see that there were already large, raucous crowds filing in and out of various bars, saloons, brothels, and cribs despite it being just past noon. Inevitably, they encountered traffic, and Jacob groaned impatiently; the boy was quite adept at driving a sleigh or carriage, despite his youth. As the sleigh slowed down, Eileen glanced up at the second- and third-story windows of the motley, often haphazard wooden buildings.

"Good day, Mrs. Barnard!" hailed a whore from one of the windows.

Eileen was unsure of how she should respond, or how Laurie would want her to respond. Should she ignore the whore? Curtly nod? Or should she return the greeting, as she would have only a year ago, back in the Bowery?

"Good day to you," she called back. Laurie was not with her, after all.

"My, but you've sure done well for yourself," said the whore in a thick Irish lilt. "We girls are awfully happy for you, you know."

Eileen could not help but smile. "That's very kind of you."

"Speak for yourself!" yelled another brothel worker from a window in the adjacent building. "Now that she's gone all high and mighty, she'll have nothing to do with her own sister!"

"No!" said the Irish whore.

"Aye! It's true, isn't it, *Mrs. Barnard*?"

Eileen was beside herself, shocked to hear her worst fear loudly announced by a whore she did not know or care to know. In fact, this made her angry; *who was this woman, and how dare she?*

"Well now," Eileen challenged, "as my good mother always said, there are two sides to every story, are there not?"

"It's true," agreed the Irish brothel worker.

"Well, a sister is a sister, that's all I know," replied the anonymous whore, whose attention was soon distracted by a prospective client hailing her from horseback.

Just then, the traffic broke and Jacob was able to make headway farther up State Street, only to be hindered again, right before Shay's Saloon.

Eileen's cheeks still burned from the exchange. She took a deep breath and glanced over at Shay's. Sure enough, right out front, upon the boardwalk, stood Mary, chatting with Beau Stinson and her friend Dolly McGraw from May's Dry Goods. Dolly, who had been fired from May's for stealing a pair of tortoiseshell hair combs, was a beautiful divorcée of questionable background said to be from Wisconsin by way of Central City, and was rumored to be the object of Mr. Pickering's desire. It couldn't get any worse. The three turned to face her, and Eileen felt as though she were staring down a judge and jury, and a bemused one, at that.

"Well, well, Mary," drawled Beau, "if it ain't your high-and-mighty sister."

Dolly giggled.

Mary stepped forward with her gloved hands upon her hips. She wore more lip rouge than she had since their arrival in Leadville, but not quite as much as she had in the Bowery.

"Aye, that's my high-and-mighty sister," said Mary. "I wonder if she has anything to say to me, since I certainly have nothing to say to her!"

Some patrons milling about in front of Shay's stopped to watch the unfolding scene, but Eileen refused to oblige them, despite all the questions and accusations choking her to be free. *She is horrid. Laurie is right in thinking I should not speak to her until she apologizes.* She turned her head away, reminding herself to breathe as she put forth her best effort to appear unbothered, unruffled. Luckily, the traffic broke once more and Jacob was able to make his way down the rest of State Street unhindered.

Once they were away from the crowds, Eileen allowed herself to shed the angry tears she had been forcing back by biting the inside of her cheek so very tightly that she now bled. Now, despite the fine sleigh, the soft, curly buffalo fur blanket, the numerous packages from May's filled with all sorts of delightful purchases, and the kindly Irish whore's words, Eileen felt very much alone, so very lonely.

"Ma'am, should I head home?" asked Jacob, glancing over his shoulder at her, then abruptly bringing his attention back to the street before him, seeming to pretend that he had not spied her tears.

Why was she so alone? She couldn't bear to return home, the fine home that was a constant reminder of how very lonely she was while also being the source of her guilt for feeling so miserable despite all its comfort and luxury. Should she surprise her husband and visit him at the mine office, up on Fryer Hill? No, he might grow cross with her for disturbing his business, which he never seemed to want to discuss with her, anyhow. So where?

"Jacob, will you take me to the Minister Jones's church, on the south edge of town?"

And with a crack of the whip, they turned southward, to where the streams wove together in the meadow and eventually became that big river—what was it? Oh yes, the Arkansas.

"But this is a most pleasant surprise, I must say!" hailed Stanley as Jacob guided the sleigh before the church house's entrance.

Eileen did not even endeavor to stifle the silly grin that overcame her at the sight of Stanley. Indeed, she was so genuinely happy to see him, to see a familiar, friendly face. "Do you have time for a quick visit?"

"For you? Always," he replied, and he offered his hand to assist her out of the sleigh. "My, my," he said as he eyed the collection of packages and parcels within, "I see someone has been doing a bit of shopping. Did you enjoy yourself?"

Eileen shrugged, feeling Stanley's keen gaze upon her.

"This is fortunate timing. I have the kettle already heating up for some tea." He ushered her through the stark, cold church to his living quarters, which were cozily warmed by a woodstove. Ruth Denahy was removing her apron and hanging it upon a nail. She quickly turned, eyes wide with hope, only to look down at her feet when she noticed that Stanley was not alone.

"Hello, Ruth." Eileen removed her hat and coat, handing them to Stanley.

"Good day, Mrs. Barnard," Ruth replied in little more than a whisper and bobbed an awkward curtsy.

This was the first time Eileen had seen her fellow traveling companion since her wedding. She was struck by Ruth's sudden deference and instinctively rebelled against it. Despite the fact that they were never friendly, these two had traversed the nation together, had shared breakfasts together, had vomited together in their altitude sickness upon Mosquito Pass, at the top of the world.

"Ruth," she said with a little giggle, "you needn't curtsy, and please, call me Eileen."

Ruth blinked a few times as she donned her coat and hat. "Good day," she replied before quickly making her exit, like a mouse.

Eileen was perplexed by Ruth's discomfort. She looked to Stanley, who just smiled and chuckled as he offered her a seat at his table.

"Ruth is just trying to do what is proper, what is right," he said as he checked the kettle upon the stove.

"Stanley, I'm still the same Eileen. Nothing will change that," she said, almost as much to him as to reassure herself, for she often forgot this, too.

"Oh, but you're not," he said with a grin. He set a pot of honey and two tin cups upon the table. "You are something much more now, Mrs. Barnard."

She studied his face, trying to decipher whether he was teasing her. He took the seat across from her, his blue eyes meeting hers. For a moment she forgot to breathe. She giggled to break through the intensity of the moment.

"What?" he asked, smiling.

"You're teasing me, aren't you?"

"Maybe I am and maybe I'm not," he replied with a wink. He rose again to pour the boiling water from the kettle into a chipped ceramic teapot.

She felt herself grow warm in this small room, where his scent lingered everywhere like something palpable.

He poured tea into her tin cup, then his. "Would you like some cornbread?"

"Oh, tea is fine, thank you."

"Now." He settled back into his chair. "Tell me how married life suits you, Mrs. Barnard."

"Married life" conjured up an instant flash of images in her mind's eye: the study lined with tomes, the taste of port, the loneliness inside such a great house, her husband's forced smiles, his hands gently yet impatiently pushing her thighs wider apart. *Oh, how could I?* She chided herself for allowing such an indecent thought into her mind as she sat before Stanley. Could he see? Could he notice?

"You blush," he said, smiling. "I'll take that as a very good sign, indeed."

She noticed for the first time his attire: a sweater with an intricately knit pattern, worn over his collarless, white shirt and black wool trousers. And before she could stop herself, Eileen was thinking about how much she would rather help Stanley out of his trousers than her husband. She thought of what it might feel like to have Stanley's hands parting her thighs. She bit her lip, squinting, and reached for the pot to drizzle honey into her teacup. She never took honey in her tea.

"You are happy, then," he stated, rather than asked.

Eileen's eyes met his again. "I suppose."

He only raised his brows, awaiting more.

Something about him, the room, the honest smell of the wood-burning stove, the rustic furniture she had been accustomed to in her prior life, before arriving in Leadville, coaxed her. It was as though she were in a confessional box, and suddenly she realized just how long it had been since she had last confessed her sins properly. The Church of the Annunciation was almost completed, but there had been no traditional confessional available during the construction. She missed the ritual of it, the relief that came from the unburdening, the shedding of the things that caused dread. She did not stop to think, for she was relieved to finally have a chance to disencumber.

"I am terribly lonely," she said, her voice sounding hoarse to her ears. And after the words had come from her, she felt drained of all energy for pretense. She slumped, placing her forehead upon her hands, folded before her upon the table. She would often do this in church, after receiving communion. But she never cried, as she did now. Sobs escaped her, sobs she had held inside herself that she was not even aware of. Her body shook; she was both relieved and ashamed.

He brought his wooden chair beside hers. She sensed his warmth and presence and quaked, but it was a different shaking than from the sobbing. His hand was gentle between her shoulders.

"Come now, Eileen," he cooed in the softest voice. "Tell me what upsets you, why you feel so lonely."

She raised her head from her hands, felt the tears coursing down her cheeks. Where could she begin? How could she begin to express all this? She could not find the words. The only sound that came from her was a choked sob.

"Come now," he said, pulling her toward him. "Come sit upon my knee and tell me."

She longed to do as he bade, like a child, but she was not a child. She shook her head. "No."

But he had shifted her weight from her chair and onto his adjacent knee. There was nothing indecent to her in his intent as he put his strong arms around her for support. He was so tall that his eyes were level with hers.

"Tell me, Eileen."

"I don't please him."

"Nonsense," he said in a voice that an adult would use to comfort a distraught child.

His compassion undid her again. She wrapped her arms around his neck and rested her head upon his shoulder. Her nose filled with his scent and the scent of the tear-dampened wool of his sweater. His arms pulled her closer to him, upon his thigh. She wanted to stay there forever. *When was the last time someone held me so? Has anyone ever held me so? Da never held me so.*

"Hush, now," he whispered into her hair.

The feeling of his warm breath upon her skin and his hand moving up and down the length of her back caused her to shiver. She was filled with a new warmth. She could not get close enough to him. She pressed her nose against his neck and breathed in. She felt his shudder.

"I don't please him," she said again, for she knew not what else to say.

"It cannot be," he replied, his hand moving from her back to her cinched waist, where it remained, took hold.

Her tears waned. She raised her head from his shoulder to meet his gaze, to get some answer, any answer, from him.

He shook his head slightly as he looked into her eyes. "It cannot be," he said in a low tone. He removed his hand from her waist and brought it to her face.

His touch was hot, his palm tough and dry, and she thought to herself that she preferred such hands—the hands of an honest man—to those fine, soft ones of her husband. She wished he would kiss her. *Kiss me. Oh, but just kiss me.* She did not know if she could live for another moment if he did not kiss her. If he did not kiss her, she would have to return to her lonely world.

And when he kissed her, she could not have enough. She kissed back. He breathed her in, she breathed him in. She moved his hand from her face back down to her waist, placing her hand over his, urging him to take tight hold, which he readily did. She ran her fingers through his hair. He parted his lips and she tasted him. He moaned, shivered slightly, tasted her. His hand moved from her waist, gliding upward, and she gasped, pulling away from his kiss, reveling in the feeling. Why was it not like this with her husband? How could it be so different?

He had lost her lips, so he kissed her neck and she moaned again. She wished she were naked. She wanted nothing more than for him to be naked. She did not care about anything else but that. This feeling was something bigger than them and it was ferocious and she wanted to bite something. She pressed her teeth to his neck as she moved her hand down his sweater, to the front of his trousers. She felt what she knew would be there and was glad, so glad! And as she gripped him through his pants, he gasped, put his hand on her wrist and pulled her away.

The room spun as they drew apart. She saw double. The sound of their breathing filled her ears. Finally, her eyes focused on his. What had happened?

He shook his head woefully.

She placed her hand upon his face. "No, don't, please."

"How could I?" he whispered. "Will you ever forgive me?"

She had no words left inside her. She could only return his gaze.

He gently shifted her away from him, back to her chair. She allowed him to do so, but did not like the growing distance between them. The farther apart they drew, the more reality set in, the more Eileen realized the implications of what had just transpired. She was waking from the dream and now found herself trying to make sense of it.

Stanley rose from his seat, gingerly placing it back at the opposite end of the table. He walked toward the small window that looked out onto the snowy expanse of meadow beyond the church house. As the afternoon light found him, Eileen noticed that his pale skin was slightly flushed, glowing with perspiration. He rubbed his lips tentatively along the knuckles of his right hand. His gaze was distant.

She had lost control. She had become something else with him, something she did not recognize now, though at the time, at that moment, she felt she had become something better than herself. She wrapped her arms tightly around her torso, shaking her head slightly. A sourness developed in the pit of her stomach. She had become as wanton as any crib worker on State Street. She had become the thing she had guarded against for so long. And she winced when she considered that she had become such a thing while a married woman. *Oh, how could I?*

She rose in a panic, almost toppling the wooden chair. "I must be going now," she whispered, and she retrieved her hat and coat from a nail upon the wall. Her hands shook as she endeavored to tie the hat's velvet bow beneath her chin. She gave up on making a bow, allowing the strands to dangle haphazardly. She had one arm through a coat sleeve when he finally turned away from the window to look at her.

"Eileen," he said in little more than a whisper, "we must not see each other like this again. It just won't do."

Although his voice held no condemnation, she felt like someone caught stealing. She bit her lip to prevent herself from crying in her shame and chagrin.

He took a few steps closer to her, but she moved away from him.

"I take full responsibility for this," he said, holding his hands before him, palms upward. He inspected them as though they held material evidence. He looked to her again. "Please forgive me for insulting you."

Insult? What did he mean? How had he insulted her? *She* had allowed this to transpire, had encouraged it. He was now being a gentleman, claiming responsibility so that her guilt would be eased. But it wasn't.

"But I—"

"Eileen, don't," he stopped her. "This was my fault, and I ask that you will find it in yourself to someday forgive me. But in the meantime, we really must not see each other alone, like this. I fear it would not be wise . . ."

She was touched that he should be so gallant as to try to shoulder the blame. She again wanted to place her hand upon his cheek. She lingered for a moment, deliberating whether to do so.

"I value your friendship so greatly," he continued. "You will never know how dear you are to me." He paused, looking round the room, then at her again. "Perhaps, after some time, we might find that this has become a distant memory and we can continue as friends. But for now, I think it wise that we not meet like this. I could never face your husband—"

"Don't mention him," she interrupted. The thought of Laurie weighed heavy, increased her guilt.

They stared at each other in silence. He simply nodded.

"When can we see each other again?" she asked.

He sighed. "I don't think it wise to meet alone like this again for some time—"

"But how long?" she demanded, the force of her voice surprising even herself.

"Until springtime," he stated quickly, as though it were decided upon, unchangeable.

"Springtime?" she asked. Why, it was only late December. Spring was an eternity away in frozen Leadville. Her heart turned and tears came to her before she could stop them.

He nodded. "Springtime. Perhaps, by then, you and I will be more in control of ourselves."

"And what if we are not?" she asked.

He stared at her. "We will not think about that just now. Go now, Eileen. Here, here is a handkerchief." He drew one from his trouser pocket, handing it to her. "Dry your face now, and compose yourself before you head back home."

She took it from him, doing as told. "Home," she said, letting out a cynical guffaw.

"You must try to make it your home. You must pray and ask the Lord for guidance in finding happiness in your home and with your husband. Do what you know will make him happy."

Again, she laughed. "Do *you* know what makes him happy? Because I do not."

Stanley put his hands in his pockets as he looked down at the floor, then back at her. "Pray for guidance, Eileen. The Lord will grant you what you need."

"Aye, I suppose," Eileen said with resignation as she made her way to the door that led back through the church house.

Stanley led her through the church and to the front doors. "Godspeed, Eileen. Godspeed."

CHAPTER TWENTY-THREE

He viewed his return home at the end of each day as a tedious chore. It was most tiresome to put on a pleasant expression and make small talk with his wife, who had become increasingly distant, agitated, cold. He would pass supper with her by talking about the day's business, which he was certain she did not fully understand, or was not interested in understanding. By the time they went to the parlor to take their evening brandy and port, he would then, finally, ask her about her day. And it was this particular task that had become something even more than tedious, almost abhorrent. Usually she worked away upon some lace, and had recently taken up what she called "bobbin work." Intrigued, one evening he had stood over her shoulder and watched her work away upon the pillow, her fingers deftly pinning and weaving the bobbins. He had thought it charming, until he took a closer look at the bobbins themselves.

"Good heavens! Are those bones?" he asked, for the realization hit him as very macabre.

"Aye, bog heron bones, from back home."

He cringed at the thought. "Could you not get yourself a more suitable, finer set of bobbins? Surely we could have some sent up from Denver, perhaps?" He still stared at the bones dancing beneath her fingers, upon the pillow. There was something almost voodoo-like about it, he thought, recalling the voodoo priests and priestesses he had seen years before, hawking their wares and services in Jackson Square of New Orleans.

"And why should I?" she asked, looking up at him, pausing in her work. "These are very dear to me, given to me by the nun who taught me to make lace. They have served me well. I've no need for different bobbins."

Oh, yes, nuns and Ireland and all that primitive nonsense. No wonder that island could not pick itself up and bring itself into modernity, he thought. He shook his head in disgust and took his seat by the hearth.

"And how was your day, wife?" he asked, after taking a long sip of his brandy, allowing the warmth to spread down into his belly in order to steel him for her answer.

Often she would respond with a penetrating stare and something like "The same as always," or "Oh, nothing as exciting as yours," and these answers exasperated him, but no more than that scathing stare. That was the worst part. He loathed how she studied his face, awaiting some sign, some reaction from him. It was as though she were trying to impart something far more meaningful—vengeful—than her mere trifling words. And he refused, adamantly, to allow himself to be affected by this. Why, he had done nothing at all to deserve such unfair accusation.

But on this night, she did not respond right away to his usual question, nor did she turn that probing gaze upon him. Instead, she stared at the hearth, then down at her lacework.

"One thousand, seven hundred seventy-six," she stated.

"Pardon?"

"I said, one thousand, seven hundred seventy-six." Still, her eyes did not meet his.

Utterly perplexed, he chuckled nervously. "What are you talking about?"

Finally, her eyes met his, and there was no accusation, no vengeance, but rather a softness, a watery despair. His heart ached at the sight.

"That's how many snowflakes I counted today."

"How do you mean?"

She cleared her throat. "I sat at my bedroom window and counted them as they fell, until my vision began to blur."

He was speechless. How could a person do such a thing, sit and stare and count snowflakes? Was it madness? Melancholy? He took another sip of brandy. Could she have a fever? Or, could it be what he dreaded to think, that she was truly so very lonely and unhappy? This would not do. He was alternately angry at her for wallowing in some sort of self-pity or hysterical mood and concerned for her well-being. He felt a pang of guilt, but chased this away with judgments of what he considered to be her selfishness. Had he not given her everything a wife could require? Had he not raised her from the most meager of life's stations?

"You sat and counted that many snowflakes?" he asked, trying to think of how he might respond.

She nodded, took another sip of her port.

"Why would you do such a silly thing?"

She shrugged. "I suppose I am a silly girl, then." Her eyes met his again.

"Did you have one of your eye aches again?" he asked, hoping to perhaps assign blame to something as mundane as a physical ailment.

For a moment she only looked at him, but then gave a nod. "Yes, that was it."

"The eye ache?"

"Yes, of course, the eye ache."

Now the accusatory look returned. *Damn her, selfish chit.* Perhaps this had all been a mistake on his part, thinking that he could take one whom he had assumed was his wild Boadicea and raise her to the comfort and luxury of a life only he could offer. It would never do. He thought of how she had proudly shown him the fruits of a shopping excursion at May's. The kerchiefs and hosiery, various feminine accessories, and those fur-lined slippers in four different hues. Why, it was all cheaply made frivolity, the sort of thing you'd expect to see being hawked to rough, working frontier women as the finest of finery, for they were gullible and wouldn't be able to distinguish a diamond from cut glass, now, would they? And this was the sort of woman his wife was. She had been so glad of her purchases—gleeful, in fact, to the point of it seeming almost as though she were trying to one-up him by spending his money so freely. As though he could be bothered by such a thing! Why, the Avalon was hauling up over $2,500 a day in silver. *A day!* And this, on top of his already vast personal fortune, well, the little fool had absolutely no idea whatsoever how wealthy he was. She could never begin to comprehend such wealth. And so, later that evening, after she had shown him all her purchases with almost a fevered, triumphant, even wild look, he had to wait until he was alone in his bedroom to have a good, hard laugh about the absurdity of it all.

But on this night, he sensed a deep despondency in her. How could one count snowflakes for so very long? It troubled him, despite his annoyance with her. Had Stanley not bade him to be kind to her? What could he do to ease her loneliness? Damn that trashy sister of hers; if only she could have behaved with some couth, she could now be living a comfortable life, married to some honest, successful man who would be proud and honored to have as a wife the sister-in-law of Lawrence Barnard. Did conceit cause him to think such things? It was not conceit, Laurie reasoned, when it was truth.

Eileen took a last sip of her port, and Laurie noticed how the hearth light glimmered on her moist lips. He wanted to kiss her. He wanted to remind her she was his wife, and that she should not feel lonely when she was his wife.

But after they had made love, and after he had left her bedroom and returned to his, he could not shake the image of her watery, despondent eyes. She had been so complacent, as usual. She was much like a deer resigned to the fate at the end of a rifle. How he hated that! How he hated a woman who acted the passive victim. Victim, indeed! His anger, though, could not erase her despair. And so he rose from his bed and went to his wardrobe, where he withdrew a small bottle filled with an amber liquid. He took two sips, replaced the cork, slipped it back into the wardrobe, and returned to the comfort of his bed. He forgot her despair, her self-imposed victimization. He felt blissfully at ease. Soon it was springtime—no, summertime—and he was walking in a thick wood, following a figure. The figure turned round and smiled. And the smile was like the sun.

"Stanley?"

He nodded. "I promised you, remember?"

"I saw Dr. Spencer today," Laurie said to Eileen as Seamus helped him out of his snowy overcoat in the foyer.

"Oh?"

"Yes," he said, trying to come up with a reason why he would have seen the doctor. "One of the workers dislocated his shoulder, you see, and so we called the doctor up to reset it." In reality, he had called the doctor to his office at the Avalon to discuss his wife's melancholia and moodiness.

"Nothing better to remedy a woman's proclivity toward moodiness than a small dose of laudanum, Mr. Barnard," the doctor had assured him, producing a new bottle from his leather satchel.

It was the answer for which Laurie had hoped.

Husband and wife made their way to the dining room.

"I took the liberty of telling Dr. Spencer about your eye aches."

Her eyes grew wide with question. "Did you?"

"Well, yes. I do hope you don't mind."

"No, of course not," she replied, though she looked afraid.

"Are you scared of doctors?" he asked.

Her brows drew together. "No."

"You're not convincing me."

"Well, I don't think I've ever, actually, been seen by a doctor."

The enormity of what she'd just shared with him left him speechless for a moment. *My word, could it possibly be true?*

She glanced down at the parcel he held in his hands as she took her seat at the table. "Well, no matter. What did he have to say about my eye aches?"

"Right. Well, he surmises it has something to do with the altitude, the different, thin air, of course. He suggested you take two teaspoons of this tincture when the symptoms arise." He unwrapped the bottle from the parcel, placing it on the table between them.

She reached for the bottle and studied it. "Laudanum?"

"Yes. Have you used it before?"

She shook her head. "No. I have heard it is dangerous."

"Only if abused. When used medicinally, it is most beneficial."

"Have you yourself used it?"

He cleared his throat, endeavoring to act casual. "Oh, of course, when I was ill."

She placed the bottle gingerly back upon the table.

"The doctor highly recommends it for your complaint."

"Well, then, I will be sure to do as he directs."

"Very good, then."

Harry the cook entered with a steaming tureen of soup, placing it on the table between them. He gave a curt nod, then returned to the kitchen.

"And how was your day?" Eileen asked in her usual manner, rising to serve Laurie his supper.

The following evening, Laurie was surprised to be met in the foyer by only Seamus. "Where is Eileen?" he asked.

"Mrs. Barnard has been asleep in the sitting room for most of the afternoon and evening, Mr. Barnard."

Laurie had to stifle the smile that came to his face.

"I worry that she is unwell," Seamus said.

"Nonsense," Laurie dismissed.

"Shall I have Florence wake her for supper, sir?"

"No, no, let her sleep if she is tired."

"Very well, sir."

And so Laurie, for the first time since marriage, ate supper alone. And he was very glad, indeed.

CHAPTER TWENTY-FOUR

She gazed out the window at the dreary gray sky of an early March day in a high mountain town. She pulled her velvet wrapper closer over her neck, then finished the rest of the coffee in her cup—her third. Sighing in frustration, she wondered just how much coffee it would take to wake her, to disperse the fogginess from her head. She rang for Florence and requested another pot of coffee. As Florence gathered up the tray and exited, Eileen leaned against the cold window, rubbing her eyes, which ached mightily on this inclement day.

The laudanum, she knew, would ease the pain—not just the eye ache—and make everything more bearable.

"No," she said aloud to the room. She wrung her hands, pacing away from the window. She had been relying on or, rather, indulging far too much in the tincture these past few weeks. She shook her head, thinking of how she had shared only three meals with Laurie since he had procured the laudanum for her. Three meals! The rest of the time she had been in deep sleep, unable to rouse herself. She knew this must stop. She was becoming the caricature of the feeble, doped-up wife.

Florence returned with the tray and Eileen hurriedly downed another cup of hot coffee with an extra helping of sugar this time, in hopes that it would finally do the trick and clear the fog from her mind. But alas, she found it did not, and only increased her eye ache. She sat upon the chaise, elbows upon knees, cradling her aching head in her hands. She wept a little, said a Hail Mary, asked the Blessed Mother to deliver her, deliver her. And then she laughed at herself; the Blessed Mother had far more urgent beseechings to answer than those of a wealthy man's wife.

She sighed again and flopped back against the chaise. She stared at the ceiling. And just then she recalled the dream she had not wanted to wake from earlier. Oh! It brought a smile to her lips, and her heart beat faster. She had been back in New York City, in her tiny, shabby room atop Mrs. Brown's boardinghouse. But in the dream, the room was neither tiny nor shabby, but rather spacious, comfortable, well appointed, and warm, filled with sunlight from not only the tiny window but another source within the room.

He awaited her with arms spread wide, and it was his smile, his presence, that was the sunlight in the room.

"Stanley!" She had thrown herself into his embrace, and his arms round her were as delicious, soothing, and transporting as when the laudanum took hold of her.

Eileen closed her eyes and recalled the rest of the beautiful dream: his kiss upon her lips, her neck, his caresses, his arms carrying her to the bed, where he had made love to her, and when he had finished, she realized that she was no longer a woman but a butterfly, with gossamer wings that shone every color of the rainbow. He had transformed her with nothing but his touch, his love.

She had not wanted to wake from the dream, but the laudanum had worn off and the wind—the ceaseless, damn mountain wind—had howled round the house and woke her. What day was it? What time? She had no sense of it until Florence had brought her breakfast, coffee, and the morning newspaper. It was a Wednesday. And Eileen laughed aloud at herself for calling the meal breakfast, for once she finally focused on the mantel clock, she saw it was two in the afternoon.

But oh, the dream had been so very real! How happy her dreams often were, how different from her days in this house. Mrs. Landry had been turned away each day since Eileen had begun taking the laudanum. Florence had told the governess that her mistress was not well, and then carried back to Eileen messages of Mrs. Landry's great concern. The last thing that Eileen wanted to do was work on grammar, but she convinced herself that she ought to take advantage of this, for it would only further educate her and expand her knowledge—certainly a far nobler pursuit than abusing laudanum. She made up her mind to dress for the day and summon Mrs. Landry, even if only for one hour of her tutoring. She also vowed to sup with her husband this evening. But he must think her a silly fool by now! Well, she would no longer play the fool.

And she would not take the laudanum, she swore, except to help her sleep at night, and only then just half the dose that Laurie had said Dr. Spencer recommended.

She rang for Florence.

"Send Jacob to Mrs. Landry with word that I would like to continue my lessons today."

Florence's eyes went to the clock. "Today, ma'am?"

Eileen huffed. "Yes, that's exactly what I said, was it not?"

The maid blushed, her gaze going to the floor. Eileen realized it was the first time she had ever chastised someone in her—or rather her husband's—employment. But it could not be helped. Her eyes ached something horrid and she was impatient to get on with the day, to evade the lure of laudanum's escape.

Laurie's wide-eyed pause in the foyer when he saw her was almost enough to make Eileen laugh aloud, but she did not.

"You seem surprised to see me," she commented as he ushered her into the dining room.

"I did not know if you would be well enough to dine this evening, Wife, that's all," he replied in a pleasant tone.

He helped her into her chair before taking his own.

"Well, here I am," she said, not sure of how else to benignly respond.

He gave a nervous smile. "Indeed! And how are you feeling today?"

"Better," she lied, "though I still have something of an eye ache."

Harry entered, bringing a platter of baked ham, followed by buttered potatoes and roasted beets. After placing the plates upon the table, Harry straightened and loudly cleared his throat. "Sir, I regret to inform you that I'll be leaving your employment."

Laurie nodded. "Oh yes? I suppose we knew you would be leaving our service, though not quite as soon as this."

"And when will your last day of employment be with us?" asked Eileen.

"Today, ma'am."

Eileen was surprised by his answer. "So soon?"

"Indeed," said Laurie, seeming to share her sentiment. "I expected some notice from you so that we might find a replacement cook, Harry."

Harry only shrugged, then untied his apron. "I'll be headed out on the Fairplay sleigh tomorrow morning."

"Well, now," Laurie said, looking flustered. "You can forget about claiming me as a work reference, what with no notice of leave being given."

Harry, holding his apron before him, dropped it on the floor. "Nice knowing you!" he said before quickly exiting the room. Eileen heard the front door of the home open and slam closed.

"Well, I say, I never . . ." Laurie's bewildered look scanned the room before falling on Eileen. "I'll leave it to you to find a replacement cook, Wife. Make inquiries tomorrow in town, perhaps with other wives with households of substance."

Eileen nodded, though she had a growing sense of unease over the task. She hated speaking with the other ladies in town—her great discomfort was debilitating. She would perhaps, instead, inquire for a cook in one of the bakeries or grocers.

"Beets," Laurie said, ruefully eyeing the bowl of bright-scarlet root vegetables.

"Yes," Eileen responded. The grocers of Leadville had been flooded with beets from the Colorado plains for a month now.

Eileen served her husband, then herself, and the two ate in silence for a few moments.

"Have you found the laudanum to help with your eye aches?" Laurie asked.

Eileen debated how to answer. Indeed the laudanum helped, if one wanted to call opiate-induced slumber "help." "It helps somewhat. But you see that it was an inclement day, which always exacerbates the ailment." Eileen was quite proud of her use of such a large verb.

Laurie seemed pleased as well. He nodded. "Yes, the weather does make it worse for you, I know."

They ate on again in silence.

Eileen began to ask him about his day. "And how was—"

"I've a surprise for you. Oh, pardon, I interrupted you."

"Oh no, it wasn't important. What surprise?"

Laurie looked pleased with himself as he wiped his mouth with his linen napkin. "I've procured us tickets for this Friday evening's performance at the Tabor Opera House. What say you to that?"

It was the last thing that Eileen expected him to say, honestly. "Why, that's lovely."

"I thought it was about time that I and my wife went out for a proper night on the town, don't you?"

She was surprised by his sudden interest in her, in being seen with her. "Well, if you should like that . . ."

He cocked his head to the side, looking bewildered by her comment. "Why wouldn't I like that?"

Was he trying to trick her into saying something incriminating? She chided herself for being so wary and suspicious of him, endeavored to change the subject. "What is the performance?"

He smiled—his genuine, boyish grin—and looked thoughtful as he replied, "I believe it is Mozart, *Don Giovanni*."

She did not know anything about it, though she was aware of the fact that Mozart was a well-known composer. "Oh, that should be enjoyable."

"Indeed," he said, rising and helping her out of her seat, escorting her to the parlor. "And of course, Wife, you should wear your green velvet gown."

"I should?" she asked, surprised.

"Why, yes. It suits your figure well, and the color is perfect for an evening event."

She accepted the glass of port he offered her and took her seat before the hearth. "Oh yes, of course," she replied.

"You'll look just lovely," he said before taking a sip of his brandy. "And I've purchased the left-hand opera box, just above the orchestra."

Eileen had never been in a theater, so she had no idea what Laurie meant. She merely nodded and smiled.

"So does this cheer you, Wife?"

She was warmed by his sudden concern. *I have been an ingrate, a malcontent. He aims to please me with this gesture.* Giving him a warm smile, she replied, "Yes, of course this cheers me."

"Good," he replied, taking another sip of his brandy. "I never realized that winter could be so abysmal in a place such as this."

Ah, so he thought her melancholy was because of the weather. Well, let him. It was probably for the best.

The following day, Eileen forwent laudanum once again, despite the throbbing pain in her head. She had a task before her—to locate another cook. She dressed and had Jacob bring her down to town in the sleigh.

She noticed that, though it was still quite chilly, the air had warmed. The sun shone, melting much of the snow and ice. There were growing pockets of mud in the streets. Her heart beat faster and her mood improved with the sudden thought that spring might perhaps come soon to the mountains. Spring's arrival would bring warmth and an end to snowstorms. It would also, perhaps, bring her a reunion with Stanley, as he had promised . . .

"Where to, ma'am?" Jacob asked once they reached the bustle and clamor of downtown.

Eileen had Jacob bring her to the bakery behind May's, the one owned by the Creole woman from New Orleans who created the most beautiful pastries and breads Eileen had ever tasted. Jacob assisted her out of the sleigh and to the boardwalk, skillfully helping her to lift her skirts over a slushy puddle of mud. Eileen thanked him with a smile, and the boy blushed. She entered the little bakery, bemused that she had caused a boy to blush.

The baker and owner greeted her with a grin. "Mrs. Barnard, you look right happy today, like you up to some mischief."

Eileen was surprised by her forwardness, but did not mind. In fact, she found it refreshing, for it made her feel like her old New York self.

"Oh, I wish I were!" she replied with a laugh.

The baker nodded, laughing with her.

"I don't believe I know your name," Eileen said with a touch of embarrassment, for she had often frequented the bakery.

"Paulette's my name."

"Paulette," Eileen said, extending her hand over the counter, "please call me Eileen."

The baker shook her hand. "*C'est bon*, Miss Eileen."

"What's that mean?"

"Very good, Miss Eileen, very good," she replied, smiling.

"Ah! I like that." Eileen enjoyed the sound of the woman's Creole accent.

"What can I get for you today? I just took some croissants from the oven, piping hot, as they say."

"Oh, excellent, I'll take four of those."

Eileen watched Paulette package up the croissants. "Paulette, I've a question for you."

Paulette turned and nodded.

"Do you know of any cooks who might be looking for work?"

Paulette laughed. "I'm sure, Miss Eileen, that there are many cooks in this town looking for work, or cooks who are working in the mines who would much rather be cooking, no?"

"True," Eileen replied, "but you see, our cook abruptly left our service, and I'm afraid that I've got to find a replacement."

"How soon you need someone?"

"Today, if possible."

"Today? Oh, you really do need a cook, and badly! Well," Paulette said, leaning against the counter and toward Eileen. "Today be your lucky day, Miss Eileen, because my niece just arrived from New Orleans three weeks ago, and she's the best cook there is, I tell you."

"Is she looking for work?" Eileen eagerly asked.

Paulette shrugged. "She wants to help me bake here, but I honestly don't need the help. I'd rather see her making a living doing some real cooking, not just baking. Her talent shouldn't go to waste here."

"When could she begin?"

"Today, I suppose, if she accepts. To be honest"—Paulette lowered her voice—"she needs good, wholesome work to occupy her. She left New Orleans mighty hastily, and without much of a plan."

"Is she in trouble?" Eileen asked before thinking. It was the sort of question she would have asked when she was back in New York if she had heard a woman had left somewhere hastily. She regretted asking the question as soon as it had come from her. "I'm sorry, I don't mean to be nosy."

"No need to apologize, Miss Eileen. But no, she ain't in *that* kind of trouble, if that's what you mean."

"Oh, that's a relief."

Paulette laughed and handed the parcel of croissants to Eileen. "No truer words ever spoken! Tell you what, I'll ask my niece if she's interested and I'll send her up to yours this afternoon if she is. Will you be home?"

"Oh, yes."

"You talk to her, work it out with her, have her cook you something. You like spice?"

Eileen wasn't sure if she'd ever had "spice." "I don't know, I suppose I do."

Paulette smiled. "Well, you decide for yourself this afternoon."

"What's your niece's name?"

"Oh, I didn't tell you that, did I? Justine Boisvert. Nice girl, she is, my niece. I send her up to yours, don't you worry, Miss Eileen."

Eileen bade Paulette a cheerful good day. She was relieved to have so easily located a cook, and looked forward to meeting Justine that afternoon.

Laurie will be pleased with me. I just hope she is good, though it won't be difficult to outperform Harry.

"Mrs. Barnard," Florence said, entering the sitting room, "there's a woman at the door asking for you. Do you want me to tell her to leave?"

Eileen looked up from her grammar ledger. "Is her name Justine Boisvert?"

"Yes, ma'am."

"I'm expecting her, Florence."

Florence made a nervous, awkward curtsy. "Then I'll show her in."

A moment later Florence returned to the sitting room, followed by a young woman with a very pronounced limp.

Eileen rose from her seat, approaching the young woman, hand extended. "You must be Miss Boisvert."

She smiled, shaking Eileen's hand. "I am, but you can call me Justine, Mrs. Barnard," she replied in a low voice thickly tinged with a Creole accent.

Eileen liked the sound of it instantly.

Florence looked on, staring at the two clasped hands with wide eyes.

"That will be all for now, Florence," Eileen said.

Florence quickly made her exit.

Eileen gestured to a chair across from her settee. "Please, have a seat, Justine."

Justine awkwardly limped over to the offered seat and took it gingerly.

Once both were seated, Eileen studied Justine. She was beautiful, that was apparent. Her eyes were clear and hazel, fringed with long lashes, which gave her a languid, sultry appearance. Her smile was serene, her skin a tanned olive. Her dark hair—wisps curling around her face—was arranged very fashionably beneath a brown felt bonnet, which she was presently removing. She wore a simple brown wool dress, yet Eileen noted how fine the cut of it was. Justine's posture in the seat was upright and graceful; she was svelte and petite. Such a shame, Eileen thought, that this beautiful young woman was a cripple.

"I hear you are looking for a cook, yes?" Justine asked. "My auntie tells me this today, said I should come directly to your home."

Eileen found she could sit there all day and listen to the dancing lilt of Justine's accent, for it was so pretty and soothing. "Yes, I am looking for someone, as our previous cook unfortunately left us in a lurch."

"Must have been a man, no?" Justine smiled knowingly.

Eileen could not help but laugh. "Of course."

The two shared a good laugh, as though they had some amusing secret. Eileen knew she liked Justine and wanted nothing more than to open her home to her.

"So have you worked as a cook before?"

"I like your Irish accent, Mrs. Barnard," Justine said, relaxing further into the chair. "Like the sound of it. But to answer your question honestly, no, Mrs. Barnard, I have never worked as a cook before."

"Oh?" Eileen was confused.

"Not officially. But I love to cook, and my mama taught me well, you see."

"What sort of work have you done?" asked Eileen.

"I was a bookkeeper, you could say," Justine said.

"Ah, in a shop in New Orleans?"

Justine laughed a little to herself, looking down at her bonnet perched upon her lap before returning her gaze to Eileen. "I suppose you might say a shop, yes."

Eileen waited, hoping Justine might continue, but she did not. She was curious. "A dry goods shop, perhaps?"

Justine considered Eileen for a moment. "I'll be honest and direct with you, Mrs. Barnard, because I sense you are 'real people,' so to speak. I kept the books at a prestigious brothel on Rue Dauphine."

This admission put Eileen further at ease. "You don't say! I once rented a room on the top floor of a brothel, back in New York City."

Justine raised her brows.

Eileen immediately regretted letting this information slip. *What if she should think that I was a whore?* "I worked as a lacemaker in a milliner's factory," Eileen quickly blurted out. "I wasn't one of the brothel workers."

Justine shrugged and tilted her head to the side. "Well, I *was* one of the brothel workers, until a patron beat me with a cane and threw me down a flight of stairs. That's how I got this limp, you see. Doctor didn't set the bone right. But the madam was nice enough to let me stay on as her bookkeeper."

"Oh," Eileen said, surprised by Justine's frankness. She felt a sudden desire to take Justine's hand in hers—irrational, yes, Eileen knew, but Justine's admission ignited a sisterly bond within her.

"My auntie told me not to tell you anything of my past, but I don't have anything to hide, Mrs. Barnard. I know you're a sensible woman, and here we are in Leadville, on top of the whole wide world. Don't it feel that way to you? All kinds of crazy men and women up here, the thin air making them even crazier, I reckon."

Eileen laughed. "It's true, though I never thought about it like that."

"Maybe I speak too much out of turn, Mrs. Barnard."

Eileen emphatically shook her head. "You don't need to worry about that with me, Justine."

"So, you want me to cook you something, yes?"

"Yes, I would like you to prepare supper, if you have the time, that is."

"I got all the time in the world, Mrs. Barnard, now that I'm here in Leadville."

Eileen rose and led Justine to the kitchen. She walked at a slower pace, hoping she wasn't too deliberate. The sound of Justine's uneven hobble upon the polished wood floor followed her.

"I took the liberty of taking some things with me—ingredients and such—to cook with."

"Oh?" Eileen entered the kitchen.

Justine, somewhat breathless, took a look around the room. "Still getting used to this thin air. Just can't seem to catch my breath ever."

Eileen had thought that Justine would be impressed with what she considered a most modern, well-appointed kitchen (she had never seen one like it, and Laurie had told her it was so). But Justine only glanced around with one brow raised—an amazing affect, Eileen thought, attempting to do so herself with little success while Justine's gaze went about the room.

"Hmm," Justine muttered as she limped about the kitchen, studying the cast iron and metal pots and pans hanging from the rack, the utensils, the stove, the knives, the contents of the larder, the icebox, the spice cabinet. She glanced again up at the pots and pans. "No copper?"

Eileen followed her gaze to the rack. "I don't believe so."

"Hmm. Well," Justine said with a dismissive shrug, "I suppose it will have to do."

"Is it not a good kitchen?" Eileen asked, seeing it all anew.

"It will do," Justine said to her in a tone that sounded as though she were the mistress of the house and Eileen the servant. "I'm sure there's none better in Leadville, that's for sure."

Eileen cheered somewhat at this. "No, I imagine not, though I am no expert on such things."

"Mrs. Barnard, you like trout?"

Harry had cooked trout on a couple of occasions. It had tasted of lard and flour, but Eileen had thought it satisfactory. "I like it fine, Justine."

"*Bon*, that is what I brought with me. I left my things in the foyer. Where's your girl?"

"Florence?"

"Oui." Justine limped to the doorway. "Florence!" she yelled out.

Eileen stood by, allowing Justine's forceful personality to take over the kitchen.

Florence arrived, looking thoroughly surprised that she had been summoned in such a fashion.

"Florence," Eileen said, "Justine is going to cook supper this evening. She has applied for the cook's position Harry vacated."

"I see," Florence said warily.

"Girl, go fetch me that box I left in the foyer," Justine said.

Florence was clearly taken aback by Justine's order. She looked to Eileen.

"Do as she asks, Florence," Eileen said, nodding.

Florence's eyes narrowed when she glanced at Justine, who levelly returned her gaze while effortlessly sharpening a very large chef's knife. She tested the edge against her thumb, then worked the blade again in a swishing motion against the sharpener, all the while not removing her eyes from Florence.

Florence returned with the box and roughly dropped it upon the worktable. "Mrs. Barnard, is there anything else?"

"No, Florence. Thank you."

Justine watched Florence go as she again tested the knife's edge upon her thumb. "You can observe me if you like, Mrs. Barnard, I don't mind at all."

"Well," Eileen considered, "I suppose I will. I've nothing else to do." In fact, Eileen was thoroughly intrigued to witness Justine at her task.

Justine, looking at the contents of her wooden box as she unloaded it, only raised her brows at this, but did not comment.

Eileen spent the next two hours seated on a wooden stool in the kitchen, watching Justine prepare supper. She did not ask questions, only watched the performance of chopping, sautéing, and stirring, reveling in the savory, somewhat foreign aromas that soon filled the kitchen.

Justine was at one with her work, it seemed, not bothering to chat with Eileen but only muttering occasionally to herself as she looked for ingredients or tasted her cooking. She hummed a little tune when she seemed pleased with her results.

"Mrs. Barnard," Florence said, poking her head in the kitchen, "Mr. Barnard is home."

"Thank you, Florence," Eileen said, waking from her trance, rising from the wooden stool and smoothing her skirts.

"You go see to your husband, Mrs. Barnard," Justine said as she stirred the contents of a large pot. "I'll have supper ready in just a few minutes."

"Very good, Justine," Eileen said. She went to the foyer, so very pleased with herself for having found Justine on such short notice.

She greeted Laurie and led him to the dining room, where delicious aromas floated in from the kitchen.

"Have you found another cook already, Wife?" he asked, lifting his nose to breathe in the scent as he helped Eileen into her seat.

"I believe I have."

He took his seat and said, "It certainly smells interesting."

Just after he finished speaking, Justine entered the dining room with a bang of the door. Despite her limp, Eileen thought Justine's posture and carriage so elegant as she placed a tureen of soup before the couple.

Laurie stared at Justine, wide-eyed, his mouth slightly open as though he'd been about to speak but forgotten the words.

"Laurie," Eileen said, "this is Justine Boisvert. She has applied for the cook's position. I've had her cook supper this evening so that you might decide if you find her skills suitable enough."

Justine dropped into a most graceful curtsy, despite her disability. "A pleasure to meet you, Mr. Barnard, and more of a pleasure to cook for you this evening."

"Yes," Laurie replied, as though he still hadn't found those words he'd lost earlier.

Eileen wondered if Laurie was flabbergasted that she had allowed a Creole to cook for them in their own home, or perhaps if he found Justine beautiful. The former assumption, oddly enough, caused her more upset than the latter.

"Here," Justine said, gesturing with her hands, "we have my Leadville gumbo."

"Leadville gumbo?" Laurie asked with a chuckle. "Why, I didn't know there was such a thing."

"You ever have gumbo before, Mr. Barnard?"

"In fact I have, Justine, when I visited New Orleans two years ago."

"Ah," she replied, smiling wide and looking thoroughly pleased, "then you know how it should *really* be served." She began to serve the two of them, ladling the steaming, aromatic, dark soup into china bowls. "You see, there isn't any good andouille to be had in Leadville, of course. So I replace that with some nice smoked elk jerky I find yesterday in town. And I use pheasant instead of chicken. No chicken to be had in town at the moment."

She waited at the table. Eileen and Laurie looked at her like they thought she might continue.

"Go on then, taste my gumbo!"

Like two children, they readily did as told. Eileen's mouth was filled first with a smoky richness, then a savory delightfulness. She relished the unctuous piece of pheasant meat that was in her spoonful of the soup.

Laurie's eyes closed as he mulled over his mouthful. As he swallowed, he opened his eyes and smiled. "Beautiful!"

"Yes!" was all Eileen was able to say about her sensory experience. She noticed that the spicy warmth had spread from her mouth and into her nose. She had to pull her kerchief from her pocket and dab at her nose, but she did not mind this.

"The spices and filé—or as some folks call it, sassafras—are all mine, very special, you see."

The two nodded and took more spoonfuls.

"Well, I leave you both to your meal," Justine said, smiling proudly as she surveyed the table before her. "You just ring for me when you're ready for the main course, *oui*?"

"Merci, mademoiselle," Laurie replied between spoonfuls.

Laurie and Eileen remained speechless as they finished their gumbo. Eileen knew that, obviously, Laurie was pleased with the soup, but she wondered if his silence was a sign that he did not approve of her choice of cook.

After they rang, Justine entered with a platter. "Trout in *beurre blanc*," she declared.

This course was met with equal silence, but for the sighs of satisfaction. Eileen thought to herself that this could not be the same fish that Harry had floured and fried for them. This trout was like buttery silk, light and sweet and savory all at once. Eileen had never tasted anything so divine. And though it seemed dramatic to think so, she suddenly realized that she had never *loved* food until that very moment.

Laurie finished his meal, sighing. He leaned back in his chair and wiped his mouth with his napkin. "I am utterly *undone* by this meal."

"How do you mean? Did you not enjoy it?"

Laurie chuckled a little. "Oh, silly Eileen," he said, shaking his head and looking very bemused at her expense.

Eileen hated when he did that.

"What I mean is that I am overwhelmed, amazed, stunned!"

"Oh . . . good."

"Dear Wife, you have done very well! I am so pleased with your choice! You are more discriminating than I had surmised."

Eileen was unsure what Laurie meant by "discriminating," but she sensed that, once again, he was belittling her somehow.

"Shall we call Justine from the kitchen and offer her the position?"

"Indeed!" Laurie exclaimed before downing the rest of his wine and ringing the service bell.

Justine hobbled out of the kitchen. "You ready for dessert?"

"Oh, yes, Justine," said Laurie. "But before you do so, I would like to offer you the position of cook in our home. Will you accept?"

"How much you pay me?" Justine asked, standing tall before the table.

"Room and board, fifteen dollars a week."

She planted her hands upon her hips. "Room and board, twenty dollars a week."

Eileen was thoroughly entertained with the exchange between Laurie and Justine. She looked to Laurie to see how he would react.

He rubbed his chin as he mulled over Justine's counteroffer. "I'm not feeling very argumentative today, Justine." He offered her his hand. "Agreed. Room and board, and twenty dollars a week."

Justine glanced down at his offered hand. "Room and board, twenty dollars, and copper in the kitchen."

"Copper?"

She nodded. "I will not continue to cook on cast iron like some frontier camp woman."

Laurie smiled, looking very amused. "Very well."

"And I'll bring my cat with me, sir."

"Your cat?"

"Oui. Her name is Zoe, and she is the only family I have here in Leadville, aside from my Auntie Paulette." Justine nodded, as though to assert the claim.

"Of course you can bring your kitty-cat. Don't you agree, Laurie?" Eileen asked, not hiding her delight at the idea of having a cat in the house. "My mother always said every house needs a good cat."

"She was a wise woman, your mother," added Justine.

"Why, I haven't any qualm about having a cat in the house, not in the least bit. I wasn't allowed pets as a child, so I welcome the idea," said Laurie. He extended his hand again. "You shall have your copper as soon as I can get it from Denver."

She nodded and smiled, shaking Laurie's hand. "You have yourself a proper chef, Monsieur Barnard."

"I don't doubt that for a moment, Justine." He looked to Eileen. "Many thanks to my dear wife for making such a discovery."

Eileen was brimming with pride and happiness at her husband's words. She smiled back at him.

"Next course, Monsieur and Madame, *tarte tatin*."

CHAPTER TWENTY-FIVE

"Are you warm enough?" Laurie asked Eileen, tucking the buffalo furs around her in the sleigh.

"Yes, thank you," she replied. "Besides, it won't take us too long to get to the opera house."

She smiled as she looked at him, her words materializing and then dissipating in the chill of the night. There was an almost full moon and it illuminated her, highlighting her delicate features, her green eyes, the gloss of her auburn hair. She was beautiful, this wife of his. He only wished she did not bore him so. He told himself that he must be patient with her. How odd it was, he contemplated, how his sentiment wavered from fond kindness to annoyance when it came to his wife.

They soon turned onto Harrison Avenue and joined in the traffic filing toward the opera house. Laurie and Eileen watched the sleighs unload patrons onto the boardwalk. In hushed voices, they exchanged comments on the attire and appearance of these, sometimes laughing at each other's observations. *This will be a pleasant evening, I'm certain.*

"Come on, make way for Mr. and Mrs. Barnard!" shouted Jacob as he jostled the sleigh closer to the Tabor.

At this announcement, it was as though the Red Sea parted. Other sleigh drivers showed instant deference, allowing Jacob a swift arrival before the Tabor. Opera patrons stopped and stared while Jacob and

Laurie assisted Eileen out of the buffalo furs and onto the boardwalk. Eileen blushed as her husband and her driver helped to arrange the skirts of her green velvet gown. Laurie wished she wouldn't. Was she not yet used to the attention she would receive as his wife? Could she not have the grace and poise of other wealthy wives?

Nonetheless, he was proud of her, for she was a vision, her green gown and white rabbit fur wrap glowing in the light of the moon and the gas lanterns that illuminated the Tabor's entrance. He heard the admiring whispers of other patrons as they stared at her. For a moment his heart thrilled at the sight of his Boadicea, his bride, his own. He forgot momentarily her embarrassment, her ignorance, her uninspiring embrace, her passive, virginal bed. He took her arm through his, tipping his hat and exchanging good-evenings with various businessmen and wives, entrepreneurs, philanderers, thieves, and corrupt officials who were the beating heart of this town at the very top of the world.

The orchestra noisily tuned up in the pit below them. Laurie and Eileen took their seats in the first opera box above the left-hand side of the stage.

"Your hair is so very fashionably arranged this evening," he said to her.

She smiled and gently brought her fingers to her coiffure. "Justine arranged it."

"Justine? I wasn't aware that she was a hairdresser as well as a cook."

Eileen laughed, the sound of it warming Laurie. "Well, at first Florence dressed it. But when I came downstairs, Justine happened to be on her way to the kitchen. She took one look at my arrangement and told me to go back upstairs. She followed me up and quickly reworked my hair."

"And what did Florence think of this?" Laurie asked.

"She was furious," Eileen said, laughing more. "She told Justine that there was nothing wrong with her style of arranging, and Justine told her to stick to pressing my linens."

"No!" Laurie said, sharing in her laughter.

Eileen nodded. "Florence stormed out of my bedroom. I'm afraid we're going to have to keep an eye on those two."

"Indeed. I trust that you can take the matter in hand, Wife. If you need to dismiss Florence, then do so if you wish."

"Of course," Eileen replied, then took in her surroundings eagerly. Laurie was amused as he followed her gaze to the lengths of the red velvet curtains hiding the stage, the gilded seats, the sparkle and glow of gaslit chandeliers, the finely painted ceiling murals, the other patrons dressed in their finest. She commented on all this to Laurie, who was bemused and charmed, thinking how poorly it all stood up to the likes of the Academy of Music in New York. But he did not mention this to Eileen; he rather enjoyed her admiration and awe and how it lit her up.

But no sooner had he thought this than her expression changed, her smile fading, her forehead creasing. He followed her gaze over the railing to the box of honor, to the right of the stage just above the orchestra pit. There was Pickering, settling his heavyset frame into a gilded chair. Beside him was that saucy tart he so adored these days, Dolly McGraw, and her constant companion, Mary. Laurie let out a slight groan.

"Why, why must she be here tonight?" Eileen muttered, sinking into her chair, hunching over, perhaps hoping to remain out of Mary's view.

Laurie, in order to avoid any unpleasant conflict between the sisters, thought to do the same, but did not act quickly enough.

"Mr. Barnard!" Pickering called out, waving.

Laurie noted Pickering's ruddy face, knowing that he was well on his way to inebriation, a chilled bottle of champagne arriving in the box just as he thought this.

What could he do? He gave a quick, polite wave back. The two wealthiest men in Leadville were now the center of the opera house's attention, despite the fact that the lights had dimmed and the orchestra had begun the overture. Both Dolly and Mary looked in his direction. Dolly giggled her little girl's giggle, her ringlets bouncing, while Mary gave him a cynical smile, her eyes finding Eileen, who, if it were possible, slumped further in her chair.

"Sit up, Eileen," Laurie whispered to her peevishly. Why did she act the guilty one in this ridiculous drama? "You've nothing to be ashamed of."

"She will surely ruin my evening," she whispered back.

"Yes, that's right, she will, if you let her," Laurie said back, losing patience with her.

Don Giovanni began, the familiar melodies filling Laurie's ears. He thought how inferior the performance was compared to when he had seen it less than a year before at the Academy of Music. His mind drifted away from the Tabor House in reminiscence, recalling that night at the opera with James, the ensuing trip to Hattie McFee's brothel, and his lack of enthusiasm. He remembered his eventual stroll down Broadway, all the way to the Bowery, where he had stumbled into that rough Irish pub and beheld Eileen for the first time—a songbird trapped in a nasty watering hole. How enchanted he had been! He glanced at her now in the darkness of the theater, noticed how her fingers ceaselessly and nervously toyed with the fabric of her gown. *Boadicea—what a farce!*

He resumed his reminiscing, picturing the stroll up the dark alleyway to the opium den, where he had experienced the bliss found smoldering inside a hollow bamboo pipe. His mind hurriedly skipped over his drug-addled coupling with the den mistress to when he had spied an angel, an angel sent specifically to save him from the depths of darkness. He vividly pictured the light blond hair and pale skin, the chiseled face like some Viking god come to life from a saga. He could recall every beautiful detail of Stanley's visage in the hired coach, the harsh winter's early-morning light discovering each and every angle of him.

Laurie shivered slightly in his chair. What he would give to go back in time, return to that musty hired coach. He would shake himself free of his illness and timidity. He would find the boldness to take hold of Stanley and kiss him, press his lips to every aspect of his face until he was sated.

Would he—could he—ever be sated when it came to Stanley?

Could springtime come soon enough?

He realized that the curtain was closing on act 1. The gas in the chandeliers was turned up, illuminating the opera house.

"Will you excuse me?" Eileen woke him from his contemplations. "I must go to the ladies' lounge."

"Of course," he replied absently, standing as she quickly left the box.

He resumed his seat, glancing over the railing and down to Pickering's box. Shrills of giggles and laughter emanated from there as Pickering opened yet another bottle of champagne with much flourish. *The man makes an utter fool of himself. Could he not act out his proclivities in private, like most respectable businessmen of wealth?* Laurie thought how very differently things would be if Mrs. Pickering had not gone to Denver for the winter. He laughed a little, considering what might ensue once the matron returned to Leadville.

Soon the audience filed back to their seats.

"Sorry." Eileen returned to the opera box, arranging her skirts before resuming her seat.

Why she apologized, Laurie wasn't sure.

And then there was no mistaking Mary's boisterous brogue.

"Well, well, well!"

Laurie groaned. The tart was yelling to them across the theater.

"There's my sister, Mrs. Barnard, too high and mighty to speak to the likes of her own sister!"

The audience hushed to a sensational murmur, turning its collective gaze to Eileen.

Dolly's idiotic, shrill giggle sounded out.

Laurie took Eileen's hand in his, squeezing it, hoping that she'd find the composure and strength to either ignore her sister and appear unbothered or, better yet, say something very witty and cutting back to her sister.

She removed her hand from his. "I must go home. I'm not feeling well," she said, quickly rising from her seat and nearly stumbling over his feet to be free of the opera box. He sighed, exasperated. He thought to say something nasty back to Mary, disgusted as he was with her, but knew better. He should not get involved in his wife's drama, nor should he call out the guest of his fellow businessman, Pickering.

"Now, now, Mary, compose yourself, girl!" slurred Pickering. He looked over at Laurie and waved unsteadily. "She means no harm, Mr. Barnard."

Laurie did the only thing he should do. He stood and tipped his hat to the audience before making his quick exit out of the opera box in pursuit of his wife.

He found her outside the Tabor, on the boardwalk. The rough-and-tumble throngs of a Friday night in Leadville still had the wherewithal to allow space for the wife of the wealthiest man in Leadville, keeping their distance as they made their way around her, gawking as they did so.

She shivered in the chill of a winter night in the highest town in the country. She hailed Jacob, who was doing his best to maneuver the sleigh to the front of the Tabor.

"Wait for me, Wife," Laurie said, taking her elbow in his hand.

She glanced up at him. "Oh, I thought you would stay for the rest of the opera."

He shook his head in exasperation. "How could I do that? That would not have been proper, Wife, would it have?" He sounded as though he were speaking to a child. But, in all honesty, she acted as ignorant as one.

"I've ruined your evening," she said as she stepped, with Jacob's assistance, into the sleigh.

Once he settled by her side, Laurie noticed that she was crying. He scoffed.

Jacob artfully wove his way into the Harrison Avenue traffic before heading east, toward their home.

"Stop acting like a child, Eileen."

"I am no good at this." She cried into her gloved hands.

"If you don't stop your self-pity, I'll head out to find some other diversion," he said, growing further agitated with her. Why, he had planned this night to be an enjoyable occasion for her, and she was such an utter ingrate. Why were these Catholic girls such martyrs?

"Go on, then. I wouldn't want to ruin your evening," she said between sniffles.

"No one likes a martyr, Eileen," he said after taking a long drink from his silver flask of whisky, which he'd procured from his overcoat pocket.

"Leave me be!" she shouted at him. It was the first time she had ever spoken in such a tone to him. Her wrath utterly stunned him. *How? How could she turn like this?* She was nothing but a malcontented ingrate, more concerned with her sister's love than her own husband's happiness. Damn shrew.

"Jacob, turn round and drop me off on State."

Jacob glanced over his shoulder at Laurie with a look of surprise. "You and Mrs. Barnard?"

Laurie took another swig from his flask. "No, you fool, just me!"

Jacob turned the sleigh around and brought Laurie to the raucous corner of Spruce and State. Laurie hopped out onto the boardwalk without even a glance back at Eileen. He knew he would be causing a spectacle, that his every action would be the talk of the town the next day, but he didn't care.

As he made his way through the throngs and down the boardwalk, he came to the realization that no action of his here would tarnish him. Why, look at Pickering, carrying on with a whore from Central City! This was not New York. There was no proud tradition of some 250 years of Dutch and English ancestry lurking in every corner, on every street, and in every charitably endowed Anglican church. None of that existed here. It could not traverse the Hudson, the Appalachians, the Mississippi, the Great Plains, never mind Mosquito Pass.

Soon he had become one of the throng making his way through the night, searching for something—drink, drug, high stakes, or whore—to forget that they were in this hackneyed, haphazard town with too-thin air and too much cold, too much sulfur and too little decency.

At the corner of State and a nameless alley, he detected an eerily familiar scent—heady, earthy and foreign. He paused, glancing down the alley. A few stray drunkards stumbled along, one singing as he pissed on a pile of rubbish. A skinny dog searched for something to eat. A paper lantern, hanging over a nondescript door, glowed soft red and swung in the chilly breeze. Laurie headed down the alley and paused before the door. It opened, revealing an elderly East Asian woman, dressed in a fashionable gown of dark red.

"Good evening, sir," she said with a warm smile and with very little Oriental accent. "Do come inside, out of the cold."

Again his nose was overwhelmed by the aroma so very familiar to him. He removed his hat and, without another thought, stepped inside.

A rooster called in the distance, waking him from slumber. He lay upon his stomach, his fingers flexing against cool, liquid-like fabric—silk satin. One eye opened to study the fabric, which was crimson. Dazed, he tried to sort his opium-addled thoughts to get his bearings. He slowly lifted his head from the pillow, and this triggered movement beside him. He looked down to see her stirring, unfurling her arm from his bare waist, her long, sharp, painted nails skimming his skin as she did so. He shivered at the sensation as he turned onto his side. He looked down at her naked form—so lithe, tiny, *young*. Before he could consider just how young she might be, he felt fingers and lips upon the back of his thighs. *What?* He looked over his shoulder to see another naked waif slowly, silently trailing her tongue up his buttocks and to his hip.

She smiled at him. "What's your pleasure?" She pressed her body against his back.

He now recalled where he was, how he had come to be there, and how he had passed the prior evening. He shut his eyes against the quick pang of instinctive guilt that came over him. He did not utter a word but only let it happen, for it was happening and why not let it?

"Oh god," he uttered. It seemed over before it had begun. *But these are skilled whores.*

One woman remained, busily preparing the resin for the pipe. The earthy scent filled his nose as she took the first drag before handing it to him.

This was familiar. The silks, the pillows, the whore, the smell of sex, the smoldering resin. His mind's eye recalled the scene in the opium den in New York City, and the angel who had saved him and brought him back to the light.

"Stanley," he said in a breath.

The woman tilted her head to the side in question, the bamboo pipe still awaiting him in her hands.

"No," he said, pushing the pipe aside, raising himself from the bed. *Stanley, oh god, Stanley.* Stanley would be so very upset with him. But the scent of the pipe's resin brought back memories of Stanley's head upon his chest, Stanley's perfect visage in the harsh morning light, Stanley's lips upon his . . .

"Oh, I shall please you again," she said with a giggle as her hand went to his aroused state.

Good god. Only the thought of Stanley could arouse him and bring him back from the dead so quickly. Only Stanley.

With a frustrated groan, he pushed the whore away, searching for his clothes. He found them upon a nearby settee and cringed in disgust as he brushed aside a large brown wolf spider from his underpants.

"Let me assist you," came a voice from behind him.

He turned to see the portly East Asian madam, attired in red and gold silks, her hair artfully arranged atop her head.

Before he could stop her, she was dressing him. She eyed his waning erection. "There is no need to leave us yet, Mr. Barnard. We can find a way to satisfy your *impressive* needs." She gave him a smile.

Of course she knew who he was. Everyone in this town knew who he was. "I must be going." He wanted nothing more than to be free of the confines of the brothel and in a different realm—the realm of men and work and business, where perhaps he could free himself from Stanley's hold upon his heart and libido.

"Very well," she replied and assisted him into his garments. He sighed as he realized he was again donning his evening attire. Certainly he could not arrive at the Avalon mine office in the prior evening's clothes. It would be most unseemly. He must go home and change into proper day fashion, and of course this would mean that he might have to encounter his wife . . .

He settled his debts with the madam, rather surprised by how little he owed, thinking in passing that such skilled, exotic whores would fetch a fortune back in New York City.

"Mr. Barnard," said the madam, "I will be more than happy to have my establishment see to your needs whenever you so desire. And of course," she said, leaning closer to him and lowering her voice, despite the fact they were alone, "you can rely on my *full* discretion."

He was surprised at both her mastery of English as well as her professionalism. "Thank you. I'm not sure when I shall return," he replied vaguely. He wanted to tell her emphatically that he would no longer need her establishment's services, but as he thought of the sharp fingernails trailing up his thighs, he could not be certain how honest such words would be.

As he exited the brothel and entered the alleyway, early dawn light startled him. He squinted as he quickly made his way—head down—back to State Street. Lord, how would he avoid the eyes of Leadville? Luckily, he noted with a sigh of relief, there were only stumbling drunkards too overwhelmed with their own unfortunate states to notice anyone else.

"Sir?" Jacob startled him with his hand held out, gesturing with a nod toward the sleigh, which sat awaiting him about a block up State Street.

Laurie was surprised by this. "How long have you been waiting for me here?" He worried now that Jacob and, more importantly in his mind, the sleigh with the Barnard crest painted upon it, had been sitting on State Street the whole night through.

"Mrs. Barnard sent me out just before sunrise to await you, sir."

Laurie grunted as he climbed into the sleigh. "Is Mrs. Barnard awaiting me?"

"No, sir. I—I believe," he stammered, "she returned to her bedchamber . . . not that it is any of my business, sir."

Laurie was bemused by Jacob's discomfort. He smiled for the first time since the prior evening. "Why, Jacob, if I didn't know any better, boy, I'd think you were trying to hide your dalliance with my wife."

The boy gasped, turned upon his perch, and stared at Laurie, mouth agape. "Sir! Absolutely not, sir!" He turned three shades of red as his mouth opened and closed a number of times, like a fish out of water.

Laurie shook his head, chuckling. "Of course not, Jacob. You're a good lad," he said and reached over to slap the boy's shoulder.

Jacob blinked quickly, looking both insulted and horrified.

"Go on then, Jacob, bring me back to purgatory."

"Sir?"

"Home, boy."

CHAPTER TWENTY-SIX

Eileen rubbed her forehead vigorously, trying to alleviate the fog in her mind, the familiar ache. She sat at her writing desk in her bedchamber, absently reviewing Justine's weekly list of purchases for the kitchen and pantry. She went to file it away in one of the desk's cubbyholes, but Zoe the cat sat in the way of them. "Zoe! You sweet pussycat! I won't disturb you now." Justine's cat was a fluffy, regal feline with bright-green eyes and silky black fur. Zoe was in the habit of responding to humans, so she gave a sweet meow back to Eileen, then allowed her to stroke her fur and kiss her mane. "I love you, you beautiful thing!" Eileen took such delight in Justine's furry friend, and she did not endeavor to hide this one bit.

As she stroked Zoe, Eileen sighed, thinking about how things had greatly changed over the past few weeks, since that unfortunate evening at the opera house. Laurie never missed supper—he was always home on time and took great pleasure in every delicious meal Justine presented. But he no longer retired with Eileen to the parlor for a nightcap. He would quickly make his exit, saying he had business partners to meet, things to attend to. She went to bed alone, woke up alone.

Just then, Eileen's attention was drawn to the hallway outside her bedroom. Seamus carried a basket of used linens and laundry out of her husband's bedchamber, down the hall. Justine had just reached the top of the stairs and entered the hallway. Without a word, she stopped Seamus, reached into the laundry basket, pulling out what looked to be one of Laurie's white evening shirts. She brought the linen to her nose and inhaled. She then dropped it back in the basket, giving Seamus that penetrating look that Eileen had become so familiar with—the look that said, "I know *exactly* what's going on here."

Seamus, just then, caught Eileen's gaze upon them. He cleared his throat and said, "Sorry, Madam." He quickly made his way past Justine and down the stairway.

Justine remained in the hallway, her eyes meeting Eileen's. A moment of silence passed. Eileen wanted to know the meaning behind Justine's odd behavior. Did Justine know something about her husband that she did not? She and everyone else in the house knew, of course, that Laurie spent many evenings out on the town and did not arrive home until well into the night or even early in the morning, only to change his clothes and head out once again to his office at the mine.

It had been this way ever since their quarrel after leaving the Tabor Opera House. Despite Laurie's paltry excuses, Eileen assumed he was busy at gambling, drinking, or perhaps he had a mistress he kept housed at the Clarendon . . . She accepted this; theirs was a marriage of misfits. She knew that this was how it was in such marriages—why, just look at Pickering, Tabor, even. She accepted this, yes, but not without a pang of hurt, accompanied with guilt. Could she have somehow prevented this?

"Madame?" Justine asked. "Do you need something?"

Eileen opened her mouth to ask Justine why she had sniffed her husband's used linen shirt. But then she closed it, for did she really want to know why, or what Justine might know that she did not? Eileen rose from her chair at the desk, silent with the struggle going on within her.

Justine came to the door of the bedchamber. "Madame, may I?" She gestured into the room.

Eileen nodded.

Justine entered quickly, shutting the door behind herself. "Madame Eileen," she said, taking hold of Eileen's arm and leading her to the small settee by one of the bedroom windows, "you look pale. Please sit."

Eileen did so, then patted the settee, inviting Justine to join her.

Justine sat, her full attention directed to Eileen. Zoe quickly joined, sitting between the two of them and purring.

"Why did you do that?"

"Sniff Monsieur Barnard's used shirt?" Justine readily replied, as though she knew the reason for the pending interrogation.

Eileen nodded.

Justine licked her lips, sighing through her nose. "I must be frank with you, Madame Eileen."

"Of course."

"I am worried that Monsieur Barnard is, well . . ."

"Go on, Justine. Don't play me for a simpering fool."

Justine shook her head. "I never do, and you know that."

Of course Justine was right. She had never minced words when speaking with Eileen, and it was just that straightforward way about her that Eileen so appreciated, and what had formed an unspoken bond of trust between them. She had never acknowledged this in any outright manner, and decided to change that at this very moment—perhaps out of anxiety over what Justine might be about to impart to her. Whatever the reason, Eileen followed her heart and gently took Justine's hand in hers and held it firmly. With a sudden rush of sensation, Eileen realized that it had been a very long time since she had held another woman's hand. Her thoughts went to Mary and she closed her eyes.

Justine allowed Eileen to hold her hand. "You are no simpering fool," Justine continued, "but there's a lot of things you don't see, or perhaps you refuse to see, Madame Eileen. I'm not sure which."

Eileen met Justine's gaze again. "So, what do you detect upon my husband's used linen?"

"Opium smoke," she replied directly, as if she had been longing to say it.

Eileen gasped. No, she had not expected *this*. The idea of her husband in an opium den had not been one of the possible scenarios that she had envisioned. She felt the whole of herself sinking, not so much from the particular news but because she had not readied herself for such news. "Are you certain of that?"

Justine shifted slightly upon the settee, her hand still in Eileen's, her other hand absently stroking Zoe. "Yes, indeed. I'm familiar with the odor that comes from the pipes." She paused, her gaze going down to her hands upon her lap. "I had a brother who got lost to opium, in New Orleans."

Eileen stared intently. "Lost?"

Justine nodded, looking into her eyes. "Those who can't quit it, they get lost, like they don't want to be in this life, this world anymore." Justine took a deep breath through her nose, composing herself. "You did not know, then. I see this now."

"No, I had not suspected."

"Ah, I am sorry to tell you." Justine slid her hand out of Eileen's.

A pang of sadness filled Eileen, not so much because of Justine's news but because Justine's hand was no longer in hers. She felt alone again. Alone, with a husband lost to a smoky evil.

"No, I change my mind," Justine said, taking hold of Eileen's hand. "I'm not sorry to tell you this, because you ought to know."

Eileen could only stare into Justine's eyes, awaiting more from her.

"Madame Eileen, you are a good woman, though very naive, if you don't mind me saying."

"I don't mind," Eileen replied, wanting Justine to continue.

"I know you don't. And there's a lot of things I'd like to say. But I don't know if I should say them all because my mama always told me I didn't know when to bite my tongue, and you white people have an invisible line between what you consider permissible and what you consider unacceptable, and oftentimes I don't know where that might be—"

"Enough, Justine. I have no 'invisible line,' as you say. I am no hothouse orchid."

Justine nodded, smiling. "I like that. It's true. You're more like a wild honeysuckle vine, but you just haven't come into full bloom yet." Zoe moved to sit upon Justine's lap, loudly purring.

Eileen drew herself closer. "Tell me what you've been wanting to tell me."

"You've trapped yourself in this place—his place," Justine continued at a rapid pace. "You never leave. You need to stop acting like the hothouse orchid and be that wild honeysuckle vine."

"My sister is that wild honeysuckle vine," Eileen said, shaking her head.

"Your sister's no honeysuckle vine. She's more like a burning bush, and she will burn her own self alive soon, but I don't want to talk about your sister. Now listen," Justine ordered. "If your husband be such a fool that he want to destroy himself with opium and Chinese whores, well then, let him. He has all the money in the world, yet he's still searching for something more. God himself only knows what that might be, and maybe He don't know either!" Justine took a deep breath, shaking her head. "You're no fool, I know that. But I see you sleeping through the morning until noon, drinking coffee after coffee, trying to fight that thing that's eating you. You say it be the eye aches, and I don't doubt that. But I know what it looks like when someone has the shakes because they be needing more of something that's eating them away."

Eileen felt a rush of guilt. Justine knew.

Justine nodded. "I know about your bottles of laudanum, Madame Eileen. I'm no fool, either. Those little bottles are no better than the opium your husband smokes. It puts you in a stupor and eats away your brain. You use it as a way to stop thinking, to get away from thinking, from seeing what's staring you in the face. I know, I've been there myself, after my injury, to help with the pain, both the pain in my body and in my heart." She nodded slowly.

"Is that why you left New Orleans?" asked Eileen, wanting to deflect away from her own embarrassment.

"Mostly I didn't want to get trapped. I knew I had to spread my wings and get away quick, like my auntie Paulette did. There's a great big world out there, Eileen, you know it. And you gotta leave home to see it. Just like you did, leaving Ireland, right?"

Eileen nodded. "Mary and I knew there had to be something better, and Ma told us to go and find it."

Justine laughed a little. "My mama did, too. She told me to go see Auntie Paulette and stay with her until I figured out God's plan for me."

"God's plan," Eileen repeated. "Mary and I had a plan once." The familiar flood of guilt came over her.

"I have a plan for myself now, and I think it's God's plan, too," Justine said, a smile coming to her lips.

Suddenly Eileen's insides filled with gladness and hope. "You've found your calling, to be a chef here, in Leadville, to me, and to be my friend?"

Justine's smile changed to something of a smirk, and she tilted her head to the side, scrutinizing Eileen. "No, Madame, that's not my plan. Though gaining your friendship has been a nice development along the road to making my plan come to fruition. But I got a whole lot more planned for me than staying up here in this crazy town, that's for sure. I've got a mind to head to California with Mademoiselle Zoe here, set up shop somewhere, a nice bistro where people will be glad to get a table and dinner. And maybe I'll get lucky in love, have a family of my own."

Eileen let go of her hand, crestfallen. "I'll be so lonely without you, Justine. And I will greatly miss Zoe."

"Well, I didn't say we are leaving yet. I'd like to save a bit more before I move ahead with the plan."

Eileen smiled and breathed a sigh of relief.

"But I'm not done saying what I would like to say to you, Madame. I suspect what's staring you in the face is that you've become someone you don't know. You've lost your way. I don't know what your plan was, but you married a man who ignores you, and you lost the only family you got left in this world because you're stubborn and she be crazy."

Eileen alternately wanted to embrace Justine and strike her, for her words cut through her to that place of truth within herself where she did not want to tarry, never mind visit. "Your mother was right—you don't know when to bite your tongue."

"You want me to stop?" Justine rose from the settee, Zoe in her arms.

"No," Eileen said, coaxing Justine back down beside her. "It just hurts to hear the truth."

"I know. Most people don't like hearing the truth, ain't *that* the truth! And I know something more about you that I don't think you've even let yourself know. And it's another reason to put aside the laudanum."

Eileen could not guess at what Justine was referring to now. What did she mean?

"I suspect you be about two months gone."

"Gone?" Eileen's heart raced. She rose from the settee, going to the calendar at her desk. She counted days and weeks. How had she not noticed? How had she not realized that she had missed two menses? She gasped, bringing her hand to her mouth, sinking to the floor.

Justine placed Zoe down and went to Eileen's side, putting her arm around her shoulders. "You probably didn't notice because you been taking so much of that laudanum lately. I only know because no one can get any wood wool diapers in this damn town, and I see your laundry hanging to dry, and there haven't been any linen diapers."

"You're right. My god, you're right."

"Come now, Madame Eileen, get yourself off the floor," she said, and she coaxed Eileen back to the settee.

A jolting ripple went through the whole of Eileen, from the roots of her hair to her toes. How had she not noticed? How had she not realized? Her mouth went dry as she tried to make sense of it all. She was pregnant. She should be happy. She always saw herself a mother someday. She was married and wealthy, secure. She searched for a fluttering, warming sense of happiness within the house of her heart, but all she found were empty rooms, empty rooms and wallpaper not of her choosing.

"What shall I do?" she asked, as though in a maze and unable to discern her way out. She was in a maze—how had she gotten herself into such a place? Her eyes darted round her bedchamber—not her bedchamber. This home was like the house of her heart—unfamiliar, lacking. She hadn't chosen this mauve wallpaper, either. She hadn't ever chosen any wallpaper in her life. She was not of a world where one chooses wallpaper. Her world was a place where one thanked the Lord when there was a warm hearth and a roof above one's head to call one's own.

Justine raised one brow quizzically. "How you mean, what shall you do?"

Eileen could only stare at her, feeling as if she were waking from a disturbing dream and trying to get her bearings again.

"You don't want the baby, you mean?" Justine asked in little more than a whisper. "Only you can make that decision, Madame. There are ways—"

A baby, a baby swaddled, a baby's fist, a baby's whimper—all these formed something tangible in Eileen's mind. They still seemed separate from her, but she was beginning to have some understanding. "No," she said, shaking her head. "No, I could never live with that. It's a sin."

Justine shrugged indifferently. "So they say."

Eileen absently rubbed one shoulder as she stared off to the corner of the room. "But there is so little love."

"Hmph! That ain't never stopped a baby from coming into the world, that's for sure."

Eileen turned her gaze back to Justine. "But now I'm really trapped. There's no getting out now."

Justine's eyes widened a little. "You're beginning to see that you done trapped yourself."

"And what good is it to see that now?" Eileen jumped from the settee and began to pace to and fro. "Now, now with *this* news, there is nothing to be done. I must accept this."

"You can do that, Madame, or you can try to change it."

"I wish I could just close my eyes and wake up to find it's all a dream, and that I'm back in New York City—"

"You hear yourself?" Justine asked. "You're saying that you would have been happier back in New York City, working in a factory and your sister whoring herself out?" Justine rose from the settee. "I knew you were unhappy, Madame, but never knew you were that unhappy."

"Why wouldn't I be?" The floodgates opened on the dam that had held all Eileen's unspoken sentiments, unshed tears, sharp truths made dull by sips of laudanum. Tears spilled down her cheeks. "I have lost my sister, and I can't remember how it all happened or even why it happened. And my husband dislikes me so much he smokes opium. How am I to find happiness in any of this?"

Justine quickly glanced around the room.

"What? You think that I'm the sort of woman who can just forget all of this in the face of material luxury, a fine home?"

"No, Madame. I—"

"Do you know what?" Eileen interrupted. "This is all my fault, all my doing. I never was able to please my husband. No one ever taught me the art of lovemaking."

Justine laughed aloud.

This outraged Eileen. "How dare you laugh at me!"

"Oh, I'm not laughing at you, Madame. I'm laughing at the idea of you blaming yourself for your husband's unhappiness. I don't think the most skilled whore from Babylon could please that man. There's no pleasing him. He's an odd kind. I been around enough to know an odd one when I see one."

Eileen felt constricted by her corset, her bedroom walls. She threw her arms out, exasperated. "What am I to do?" A sob shook the whole of her. "Justine, what am I to do?"

"Oh no, I'm not here to be your mama and tell you what to do. Only your own heart can tell you what to do. If I tell you what I think you ought to do and then you go do it, and something goes wrong, you'll blame me and then blame yourself for not listening to your heart."

"My heart is silent, it has no voice."

Justine leveled a steady gaze at her. "You know that ain't the truth. That simply ain't true. What I see before me is a woman whose heart is screaming out to be heard." She shook her head. "Your heart is silent—like hell! You know what you gotta do. You don't need me or Mary or anyone else to tell you."

Eileen knew Justine was right. She had to take charge of her path forward. "I shall tell Laurie, and tell him that things must change."

"That seems a wise place to start," Justine encouraged.

Eileen nodded slowly. "What about Mary?"

"What of her?"

"Do you think that, maybe I should, say, reach out to her?"

Justine shrugged. "No way to tell what you'll get back from her. You realize that, right? She might take your hand or she might spit on it. There's no telling with your crazy sister."

CHAPTER TWENTY-SEVEN

"Good evening, Laurie."

Startled to hear Eileen's voice, Laurie quickly turned round just as Seamus removed his overcoat. "Good evening, Eileen."

The two stood in the foyer, staring at each other. Laurie realized that it was the first time he had used her first name in a very long time. It sounded foreign, like it belonged to a stranger. Perhaps it did.

As he took her arm in his and led the way to the dining room, she said, "I like it when you call me by my name."

"Very well, then, Eileen."

They dined quietly, but for small conversation about the weather, Leadville news. Laurie noted, though, how Eileen's pale hand shook slightly as she served him his dinner. He assumed it was the laudanum's hold. A pang of sadness filled him before it quickly subsided. *Such is the way of it—better medicated than melancholy.* He abhorred the idea of her melancholy.

He was jolted out of his contemplations by the crash of her drinking glass, toppling over upon the table.

"Oh, forgive me!" she gasped, rising from her chair to mop up the mess with her napkin.

No, he realized just then, this was more than the jitters of weaning from laudanum. She was plainly agitated. Perhaps, he decided, he could spend a little time with her after dinner and try to discern why she was so fretful.

When Laurie and Eileen retired to the parlor, he noted how her hand quaked as she took the offered glass of port from him. He sat in his great chair beside her, and Justine's cat quickly took over his lap, making herself at home while kneading his thighs. He stroked her thoughtfully. He had grown fonder of Justine's cat than he would admit. He took a long sip of his brandy before addressing his wife.

"Eileen, what is troubling you this evening? You seem to be nervous about something."

Her eyes went to the fire burning in the hearth. She took a very large swig of her port. It was now he who was nervous, for he sensed that she was preparing herself to impart something of import to him. Good lord, what could it possibly be? That she had bought every pair of shoes for offer in May's? He hid his smirk behind his hand.

"Laurie, I've news," she finally said in a shaking voice.

"What is it, Wife?"

Her eyes went to the port glass in her hand, upon her lap. He spied that shy smile once again playing upon her lips. It both charmed and annoyed him.

"We are expecting."

The words hung in the air. He frowned, puzzling. Surely she couldn't mean . . . "Have you ordered a parcel from Denver?" The question sounded absurd as soon as it left his lips. It was a feeble attempt to deflect the looming truth.

She giggled, bringing her hand to her mouth. She shook her head. She uncovered her mouth, revealing a breathtaking smile. "No, Husband. We are expecting a baby."

He was truly surprised. He rose from his chair, and Zoe quickly jumped away with a meow of protest. He raked his hand through his hair. He made his way to the mantel and placed his brandy upon it. He stared into the fire as he tried to recall when he had last visited her in her bedchamber. Had it been two, three months?

From the corner of his eye, he saw her rise from her chair, looking to him. "Laurie?" she asked, her voice filled with uncertainty.

He turned to face her, his thoughts a riot within his mind. "How far along are you?" was all he could muster.

She blinked. "About two months, I'd say."

He stared at her, then turned his gaze back to the hearth. A baby, a child—his child. "My!" The wonder within him found shape and came from him. "Well, I . . . my!"

He realized that he sounded like an imbecile, but could not find a way to make up for his shortcoming.

She came toward him, before the hearth. "Are you pleased?"

A child, his child. A boy to inherit all that he had inherited. A boy, a Barnard. He had never contemplated such a thing, a Barnard beyond himself. He had, quite frankly, never humored himself with the fancy of being a father. He never envisioned holding a little hand in his. At this mere thought, he laughed, placing his hand over his face, only to realize there were tears on his cheeks.

"You are crying," Eileen whispered and drew closer. "So you are pleased?"

Were they tears of joy? Perhaps, but more so tears of utter bewilderment. How in the world would he begin to be a father? He recalled so little of his own father. What sort of change must he make of his person to fulfill this new role? How would his life alter?

Little, he reasoned, trying to assuage his building sense of panic. *Little,* he repeated to himself again as he took Eileen in an embrace, for wasn't that what one did when he learned of such news from his wife?

She seemed to relax within his embrace. "Tell me you are happy," came her muffled voice from against his chest.

"Of course, dear Wife," he obediently replied.

He scanned the study. Soon there would be not two but three. Soon he would be further bonded to her, his wife.

Little shall change, came the voice within him once again. He saw in his mind's eye dozens of established, distinguished men of his acquaintance, all with wives and children, all with mistresses, favored gentlemen's clubs, and brothels.

"Are you surprised?" she asked.

He chuckled, for surprise was only the tip of the thing overwhelming him. "Yes, I am!"

"Shall we tell anyone yet?" she asked. "I'm not sure of how such things are broached in polite circles."

Ah, there she was, his little, mousy, ignorant Irish lass. A wry grin crossed his lips, marveling over how he had ever thought her his Boadicea.

Boadicea—how had he ever considered her so? He recalled the time when she had sat before him in his parlor in Manhattan. He remembered his excited, elevated spirits and then realized why, just why: Stanley.

"I'll tell Stanley Jones," he said. "He will be most glad to hear the news, don't you think?"

An odd, puzzled look crossed over her face. "I had not thought about it," she said quickly, but then smiled. "Yes, we should share the news with him."

The thoughts swimming through his mind made him feel as though he would burst unless he were able to sit alone, uninterrupted . . . "I think it wise if we retire now, dear Wife. You realize that you are in a very fragile state now, and you must take utmost care of your health, yes?"

She nodded. "Yes, of course, Husband. But . . ."

"Yes?" he asked, annoyed that she did not immediately leave him to his thoughts.

"What of Mary?"

"Your sister? What of her?"

"Shall I tell her?"

He was taken aback by such an idea. "Why on earth would you tell her of our personal affairs now, after all this time? She has never even apologized to you for her scandalous—"

"Yes, I know that." Eileen looked down at her skirts, then returned her gaze to him. He was surprised by the determination in it. "But she is all the family that I have."

His temper flared and he fought to keep it in check. After all the public spectacles, all he had given her, all to which he had elevated her, why must she defy him in this, the matter of her lowly sister? "You shall have no contact with your sister, and that is my final word upon the matter, do you hear?"

Her eyes grew wide.

Even Laurie was surprised at the force of his words.

"But I find that I need her now, more than ever," she said, her voice cracking with emotion. "I can overlook . . . forgive—"

"It greatly vexes me, dear wife, that you would let the matter of your sister upset you to this degree. You've the child to consider now."

Her mouth moved to form words, but none came.

"You must calm yourself."

"What would you have me do?" she whimpered like a lost pup.

He firmly took her arm in his and ushered her out of the study, up the stairs to her bedchamber. When they were at the doorway, he said, "You must do what Dr. Spencer has prescribed."

"Laudanum?" she whispered.

"Yes, of course," Laurie replied, though not without acknowledging the latent guilt from which he could not free himself. "You must rest, for the child, Wife." He kissed her firmly upon the forehead, longing to lock her in her room so that he might find the solitude for which he so longed.

She nodded with a sad resignation. "Yes, Husband," she whispered before entering her bedchamber.

He breathed a sigh of relief as he made his way to his own bedchamber. Now, now he could be alone with the thoughts crowding his mind. But there awaited Seamus, ready to help him undress for the evening.

"Quickly, Seamus." He removed his sleeve buttons and placed them in the Irish manservant's large paw of a hand.

"Sir, if you don't mind my asking, is there a matter I should know about?"

Laurie paused at Seamus's concern. "Why do you ask?"

Seamus's gaze faltered. "The cook—"

"What of Justine?" Laurie asked, growing annoyed at the mention of the Creole, who seemed to have the disconcerting ability to see through a man. He had tried to ignore this aspect of her, dismiss it as nothing but an off-putting vestige of voodoo culture. Those Creoles were such a superstitious, pagan lot.

"Sir, she tells me there will be much change soon under this roof. Is there something I should know of, being your manservant?" Seamus probed.

Laurie slumped down onto the settee at the foot of his bed. Seamus quickly descended to remove his shoes. "Seamus, I shall be a father."

Seamus's hands paused. He looked up, a genuine smile lighting the whole of his ruddy face, making him appear a jolly leprechaun, Laurie mused.

"Oh, sir!" He grabbed hold of Laurie's arms. "This is surely wonderful news!"

Laurie looked at the hands upon his arms in surprise. "News, it is indeed."

Seamus removed his hands. "I mean no disrespect, sir, but I am mightily glad to hear of it. Miss Eileen is a fine lass—lady, sir."

Laurie considered him. How had he come to surround himself with so many Hibernians? It was his foolish doing, and he wished nothing more than to be rid of them all at this moment.

"Then pour yourself a hearty dose of whisky tonight, in celebration, Seamus," Laurie said with a cynical laugh.

"Are you not happy, sir? Are you not eager to become a father?"

"I know nothing of it, so how can I look forward to it?"

Seamus's white brows drew together. "But a child, sir . . ."

Laurie, in his agitation, rose and paced away, only to realize that he had one shoe on and one off. He violently kicked the other shoe free. "I'm not like you Catholics!"

Seamus was still upon his knees by the settee, his mouth agape.

"I need time to think, time to consider," said Laurie as he rubbed his forehead.

"There's nothing to consider, sir. A child is coming and you best be ready."

Laurie dropped his hand and stared at Seamus in disbelief. "What did you say?"

Seamus rose from his knees slowly, and when he stood, he raised his chin much like a prizefighter. "I said you must be ready to be a father. You must change your ways and take control of your life."

"How dare you!" Laurie lashed out, for he was so surprised by his manservant's insolent words he felt winded. "What 'ways' do you speak of, man?"

Seamus looked him squarely in the eye. "Oh, aye, Mr. Barnard, you know what I speak of. I'm no fool. I launder your linens. There's no mistaking the stench of opium smoke."

Never in his life had Laurie been scolded, accused. And now his manservant, of all people, would dare to do so? "And who are you to speak to me about what I should and should not do?" This was what he reaped for employing an Irish gasworker. Perhaps his mother had been right . . .

"You've no father to give you a thrashing, so I suppose it's got to be me to tell you what's what."

Laurie had the sudden sensation that all this was some macabre dream, ever since he'd entered his home this evening: news of impending fatherhood and now his own manservant becoming an insubordinate lout! The roots of his hair grew hot as he pointed to the door of his bedchamber.

"You shall leave my home this instant, and never come back. You are fired."

Seamus showed no surprise, but only gave Laurie a knowing smile. "One day, lad, you'll regret this." He turned and made his way to the door, at which Laurie still pointed. He paused at the threshold, looking thoughtful. "I thought you were different, that day when you approached me at the grave of my wife—God rest her soul." Seamus made a quick sign of the cross.

Laurie scoffed.

"I thought that maybe you were of a new, enlightened generation of the moneyed lot." Seamus shook his head, never removing his gaze from Laurie. "A fool I was to think so. You're no different from the rest. You were just an idealistic youth when I met you. Now you're as jaded and entitled as the rest of the gents."

"Get out!" Laurie boomed, as infuriated as he had never been the whole of his life.

"Oh, I gladly will," said Seamus with a wry, crooked grin. "But just remember that there's an innocent lass across the way that comes from my world, and now you've brought her to yours, and she's like a baby in limbo, and it's all your doing."

"'Limbo'? What in the hell is 'limbo'?"

Seamus opened the bedchamber door, offering Laurie a view down the hall, to where Eileen's door stood open, and to where Eileen, clad in her dressing gown, gripped the doorway, her face pale, her mouth taut.

"Purgatory. Limbo is purgatory." And with that, Seamus made his way down the hall. Before descending the stairs, he bowed to Eileen.

Eileen started after him, then turned her attention to Laurie. "What did you do?"

Laurie felt the tingling desire to strike the accusatory look from her face. Instead, he slammed his door shut, closing her off from him, his thoughts, his world.

It was a harsh reality that confronted him after a night at Miss Leung's brothel. In the ink blackness of early morning, Jacob drove him home so that he might change into his work attire and go to the Avalon office. He entered the silent house, surprised not to find Seamus awaiting him to take his hat and coat, see to his needs. Sighing, he absently tapped his forehead, and he recalled just why he had been inclined to seek refuge at Miss Leung's for the night. He had dismissed his manservant.

And when he entered his bedchamber, he cursed himself. Folly of all follies, to dismiss a manservant before finding a replacement. Like a fumbling child, he searched his wardrobe and drawers to find suitable work clothing. Was this drawer the one that housed his socks? Laurie paused in his search, shaking his head. He had wanted to go west so that he could become a different sort of man, one not hindered by the trappings of New York society and money. He had married an immigrant, turned his back on the world of his blood. But, he realized, chuckling, when he had imagined himself in a secluded log cabin at the edge of the desert, had he also considered how he might dress himself? Or had he assumed that Seamus—much like any good, trusty manservant—would dwell with him in a one-room cabin?

"Fool," Laurie said aloud.

But as he located the drawer that housed his socks, he felt as proud as a child who had just solved a math problem with no help at all from his tutor.

Dawn's first rays made it appear as though Fryer Hill had a heavenly halo. Laurie thought to himself of the even greater, heavenly glow that was found within its depths. The veins of silver that pulsed through these mountains were a wonder, indeed. As Laurie's sleigh made its way up to the Avalon office, he thought to himself how he had at least fulfilled one of his ambitions since coming to Leadville—he had become a Barnard in his own right, adding a staggering fortune to an already vast one, which could follow its roots back to the Dutch trading companies of New Amsterdam.

He had become a Barnard in his own right, just as Stanley had urged him to do on a day, long ago, in his study. A searing vision of Stanley's lips upon his flashed through his mind, as quick and startling as lightning. Laurie brought his gloved fingers to his lips, trembling slightly. He gazed out, noting the downy piles of snow upon the roadside. *Damn it all, when will spring arrive to this wasteland?*

He remembered that he had reason to call upon Stanley, or request Stanley call upon him. Yes, he would do the latter. Why must it always be he who paid the visits? Let Stanley come to the Avalon office and see what he had created from a mere hole in the ground. Let Stanley behold how he had fulfilled his ambition—one of his ambitions.

And now there was to be a child, perhaps a boy to pass on all this great legacy. For a brief moment Laurie had pity for the boy, just as he pitied himself for being weighed down by the great responsibility of such a legacy. But this pity faded to disbelief, that he might actually soon become a father.

And the mother? "Purgatory," he heard Seamus's deep voice level at him in his memory. Laurie grimaced. Purgatory, indeed—these ridiculous, superstitious Catholics. Martyrs, the whole lot of them, and if the Vatican were to give out awards for such things, surely his wife would be first in the queue. Why should she suffer? The thought made his temper flare—god, how he wanted to throttle her for all her "suffering." Perhaps it was true, that if you give too much charity to the poor, then they will become dependent upon it and ask for more, that the more you gave, the more they'd take. Look at Eileen, put upon a pedestal of comfort and luxury, and it was not enough to make her happy, to tease a smile to her lips.

"Damn shrew," he said under his breath as the sleigh approached the Avalon office.

Once inside, early-morning light coming through the east-facing windows assisted him to his great chair behind his large desk. While he made himself comfortable, the office boy hurriedly illuminated the gas lamps and got a good fire going in the stone hearth. Soon the mine came to life. The night shift miners emerged from the earth to be replaced by a fresh lot of workers. Tradesmen came and went from the office—all dealt with by various assistants and overseers hired by Laurie's investment company. Laurie, uninterrupted by all this hustle and bustle, enjoyed his morning coffee as he looked over the account ledgers for perhaps the hundredth time. The marvel of the sums of money being produced underground would never grow dull for him, no matter how many times he stared at the figures.

"Your personal correspondence, sir." The office boy placed some mail upon the corner of Laurie's desk.

Laurie put aside the account ledgers and took up the first envelope. He recognized his mother's handwriting. He sighed, debating whether to open the letter or leave it for later, but decided to get the ordeal over with. His mother scathingly remarked that there must be something perverse in the nature of her child that he must be so rash and lacking in judgment in his romantic dealings, this ridiculous folly with this Irish girl. Her final words, though, beseeched Laurie to return to New York, to let others oversee the mine.

> *Return to your place, with your family in New York. And leave behind that Irish strumpet you must insist on calling your wife.*

A sudden protectiveness, which had lain dormant, flared within him. How dare his mother label his wife a "strumpet"? In his mind's eye came one of the most intimate, honest moments in his life, when he had withdrawn from his bride and spied the blood upon his loins, the smears of crimson upon the insides of her ivory thighs, upon the bedsheets, like a wax seal, making the act official. He quickly rose from his chair, agitatedly pacing to and fro behind his desk as he chewed upon a knuckle.

"Sir? May I assist you?" asked an assistant who was very eager to please.

Laurie said nothing, just waved him off dismissively.

Eileen was his wife. She was his. And now she carried his child. He grinned, considering how this news would most certainly induce a case of the vapors for his mother. Ah, so there was *something*, at least, from which to derive happiness in this situation. That was a good start.

Laurie returned to his desk, taking his mother's letter and tossing it to the flames in the hearth. He left the office, taking a turn outdoors in the cold morning air. The eager office boy chased after him with his overcoat and hat in hand, but Laurie waved him off and strode away. The grinding, whining sound of metal cables straining and turning with each load of silver filled his ears. He tried to escape it by walking farther north, to the edge of the clearing, until the sound of his leather boots crunching upon the snow was all he could hear. The chill of the mountain air became suddenly apparent to him. He turned and made his way back to the office. If he contemplated the matter of his mother further, he would grow more irate, he knew. Best to concentrate on business.

"Sir, can I be of any assistance?" asked the office boy, a look of concern upon his face. "Might I deliver any correspondence for you?"

He was a little too eager for Laurie's liking, though Laurie could not deny that he was a good, industrious boy. At the reminder of correspondence, Laurie remembered that there was one very important letter he had intended to write that day.

"Yes, I'd like you to deliver a letter to Stanley Jones, the pastor." Laurie took up a fresh sheet of letterhead as he quickly dabbed his pen in the inkwell. "I'll be just a moment as I write it up."

Stanley dismounted from his horse effortlessly before tying the reins to a hitching post in front of the Avalon office. The sunlight shone upon his golden-blond hair, bound in an old-fashioned queue at the nape of his neck, and upon his head sat his usual stovepipe hat, revealing the worn patches of felt and the fraying satin band.

Laurie's heart soared, for Stanley appeared to him like some paragon of manhood. My, but it was so very good to behold him.

Stanley extended his hand to Laurie as he made his way up the front steps of the Avalon office. "Good day to you, old friend!"

The feel of Stanley's hand in his was like a bolt of lightning. He found it difficult to speak, for his throat was choked with gladness.

"Do come in," he was finally able to muster as he gestured to the office door.

"I say"—Stanley stopped, and looked toward the massive pull house, where the metal cables moaned and whined as they hauled load after load of fortune from the mine's depths—"I would very much like to tour the mine. I've never been able to see its workings before."

Laurie was caught by surprise by Stanley's request, but was then glad of it. Perhaps they would be able to speak more privately whilst outside the confines of the office. "But of course. Just allow me to fetch my coat and hat."

Laurie then proudly guided Stanley on a tour of the pull house, explaining all its mechanisms as best he could, allowing the workers to offer further detail when he was at a loss.

"What time does the mine operate until?" Stanley asked as the two made their way out of the pull house and to the mine shaft's opening.

"Why, it operates twenty-four hours a day, six days a week."

"Such industry is admirable," said Stanley. "But I should very much like to see the inside of a mine. Is this possible?" he asked, turning to Laurie.

Laurie's breath caught in his throat, for Stanley's expression held such boyish hope and eagerness. Though Laurie was usually reticent to descend into the mine—it was somewhat unnerving, he found, and, honestly, frightful in its darkness—he had done so on a few occasions, usually with one of the overseers or with fellow businessmen like Pickering or Tabor.

"I suppose we could do so, if you like."

"I would like to very much," replied Stanley. He stepped closer to Laurie and placed his hand gently upon his shoulder.

Laurie gripped the side of the cart tightly as it jolted in descent. The groan of metal cables did not allow for conversation as he, Stanley, and one of the overseers were lowered farther and farther into the mine shaft.

Stanley reassuringly patted his hand upon the cart's edge.

Laurie wiped a bead of sweat from his brow, embarrassed that his fear was so apparent.

Soon they were inside the mine. This first area was well lit with gas lanterns. Miners—dark with dirt and damp with perspiration—shot curious glances at Laurie and Stanley, yet still tipped their hats to them in deference, knowing that Laurie was the man who controlled their fates and fortunes.

But Laurie paid no heed to the workers, for he was so consumed by the presence of Stanley by his side in this otherworldly place within the earth.

The overseer then guided them farther along in a mule-drawn cart. Laurie pitied the beasts that worked in the mine, unable to glimpse the sun and breathe the air above the earth. He always felt the loss of a beast more profoundly than that of one of the workers, and saw nothing odd in this. A man, he reasoned, could choose whether to work underground. A mule had no such freedom of choice.

"And here to the right," said the overseer as he gestured down a dark tunnel, "you'll see a shaft we've abandoned, for now, as the vein wasn't as pronounced as elsewhere down here."

"We may revisit it eventually," commented Laurie to Stanley.

Finally, they reached the extent of the shaft's tracks. Ahead of them, in the dim light of oil lanterns, they beheld workers striking away with pickaxes at the surrounding dirt and rock. The farther one was able to glance down the shaft, one could make out workers on their hands and knees and, in the deepest depths, upon their bellies, working away with hammers and chisels.

The smell of burning lamp oil, acrid dirt, mule dung, and unwashed male bodies permeated. Beneath the loud echo of tool against dirt and rock, one could hear the men's grunts and labored breathing.

With Stanley so close beside him, Laurie found all these things—melded with the knowledge that it was all under his control and ownership—had a somewhat arousing effect on him. He knew it to be perverse.

"My," said Stanley, "it's like Sodom and Gomorrah after being dealt God's wrath and vengeance." He muttered this in an awed voice as he surveyed the scene before him.

This comment further aroused Laurie. "That's an interesting idea. I've often thought it like what I envision Dante's *Inferno* to be."

"Which stage of Hell?" asked Stanley.

Despite the dimness, Laurie could still see the intensity of Stanley's gaze. If this were Dante's Hell, then let it be the second stage of Lust, and let him at least experience Stanley's forbidden touch before the winds of the melancholy storm tossed them to and fro for all eternity. He dared not answer.

In his mind's eye, he envisioned Stanley's mouth claiming his, followed by the press of his bare skin against his, within the walls of this underworld. It seemed the perfect, most fitting place to consummate a love, such a forbidden love.

The temperature rose so that Laurie felt his breath quicken. "Let's be on our way. The dust is causing me to feel ill." He turned to face the entrance of the shaft.

"Very well, sir," said the overseer as he led the soot-covered mule round to the other side of the cart and hitched him to it.

"Are you unwell?" Stanley asked, looking down at Laurie with concern.

"Yes. I apologize for rendering our tour short."

"Not to worry," Stanley said, patting Laurie's shoulder. "I've seen all that I wanted to see."

As the cart jolted and made its course back to the shaft's entrance, Stanley bent his head low and whispered in Laurie's ear, "I would like to return again, with you and only you."

It was all Laurie could do to not visibly tremble and sigh aloud. It took every ounce of self-control not to grab hold of Stanley's hands in his, and kiss them over and over, to cry in joy and delight, for he was so elated that Stanley shared his beautiful fantasy of the second stage of Hell.

"When?" Laurie asked as they ascended back to the light, back to where each had his place, his role, his daily routine.

"It's your time to name. But spring has arrived, my friend," said Stanley, and Laurie could have sworn he spied the briefest of winks.

"Saturday night," Laurie whispered. "That is when the mine closes for Sunday."

"Then Saturday night it is. I promised you, Laurie, remember?"

How on earth could he have ever forgotten? How many times had he dreamed of what it might be like, this spring that Stanley had promised over and over.

Yes, it was a promise of awakening, life springing from what appeared to be death, a symphony of heady color and scent and warmth. And now he had it within his grasp, and it came in the form of the darkest, most secret, deepest depths of the underworld. He shuddered in delight.

When the two came to the surface, Stanley bade Laurie goodbye as he mounted his horse and headed back down Fryer Hill and toward town. Laurie watched his form disappear down the road from the front steps of the Avalon office.

It wasn't until he returned to his desk and his account ledgers that he remembered why he had originally summoned Stanley to the mine: to tell him the news of Eileen's pregnancy. He would not tell Stanley now, not until after Saturday evening.

Nothing—not impending fatherhood, not the thought of his wife's dreary melancholy and laudanum shakes, not the lecture of a letter from his mother—could faze him, could steal away his utter ecstasy at the thought of this Saturday evening. His imagination ran wild. *Let it,* he thought, for soon enough those melancholy torrents of wind of the second stage of Hell would steal it all away. Pleasure was fleeting, this he knew, and he would make the most of it any way he could.

CHAPTER TWENTY-EIGHT

Eileen winced after taking a sip of coffee. Its strong bitterness caught her by surprise.

"What on earth are you brewing?" she asked Justine as she rubbed the sleep from her eyes. Glancing at the mantel clock in her bedroom, she was surprised to see it was after two o'clock in the afternoon. Had she really slept so long?

"That's proper coffee, from New Orleans," said Justine. "It finally arrived at Aunt Paulette's bakery. Chicory coffee. Should shake the slumber and drink from anyone's system." She gave Eileen a sharp glance from the corner of her eye.

Eileen could recognize that accusatory look anywhere, now that she was so familiar with Justine. "This baby has me so very tired. I feel I could sleep the whole day through."

"Is it the baby or something else?"

Eileen sighed. "Justine, please, no more of your lecturing. Dr. Spencer says that I need rest, and that laudanum would not harm the child."

"Mm-hmm. Well, I ain't a doctor, but I've seen some pretty doped-up babies come out of women who were told the same thing. And that's all I'll say on that."

Eileen neither wanted to hear nor believe such tales. "Very well, Justine. We'll just have to agree to disagree."

"I suppose so, Madame Eileen. I suppose so." And with that Justine made her way to the bedchamber door, but paused. "Oh, I forgot to tell you that you had a caller while you were sleeping."

"A caller?" Eileen never had callers. "Who?"

"Mr. Stanley Jones came to call on you."

"Stanley?" Eileen gasped, sitting up straight in her bed. Her heart began to race as it hadn't for some time, and the sensation was so pleasing, as though her heart were shaking free from a cocoon of cobwebs.

"Mm-hmm." Justine's mouth spread into a sly smile. "But you were right, Madame Eileen—that man is a looker. Like someone come walkin' out of a fairy tale."

Eileen nodded, sighing. "It's true." Once, Eileen had told Justine all about how she'd come to be in Leadville, and of course had described Stanley Jones in vivid detail. "What did he say?"

"Said he just wanted to say hello to a 'dear friend.' I told him you were sleeping. He actually waited around in the sitting room for an hour, but I told him that the doctor had you on some medicine that made you sleep the whole day through, almost."

Eileen was outraged. "You did not! How could you tell him that?"

"He's your friend, ain't he? He's the reason you're here in Leadville."

Eileen could not respond. Justine was right, but oh, it was so embarrassing for Stanley to know her business.

"He didn't like the sound of you taking such medicine, asked me what it was, and I told him I didn't know." She gave Eileen an accusatory look. "He left, said he would come callin' another day."

"I'm so sorry that I missed him," Eileen said, growing despondent. Her life was running like a river, right before her, and each day more of it washed away. She placed a hand upon her belly, upon the life she knew was held within. "I think I'll lie down again." She wished she could pull the fine sheets and covers over her head and escape to a warm and cozy place where time stood still. She wished she could become a part of the pillow, burrow inside the mattress, for there was such solace within her bed.

"You go on then, go on and feel sorry for yourself. Ain't no one else gonna do it for you because they don't see what you got to feel sorry for."

If Eileen had had the will and strength, she would have thrown something at Justine. But instead she wept. Justine was right, she knew it. But she didn't care. Didn't have the ability to care. Yet she must have, because she could not stop crying.

She felt the mattress shift under the weight of Justine, who had sat by her side. "You listen to me, Madame Eileen. You got to get a hold of yourself. You got to stop taking the laudanum, you hear? Your husband just wants you sedate, Lord only knows why. You got to take back your life. You got a little one inside of you. Now, how do you want me to help?"

Eileen turned onto her back and Justine placed her cool hand upon her forehead. It was so soothing, the feel of it. She pushed her head into Justine's hand so that she would pat her. She was like a cat, starved for attention. "I don't know. I want to see Stanley."

Justine nodded. "You want me to send for him?"

"Yes."

The two stared at each other.

"Is that bad?"

"Is what bad?" Justine asked.

"To summon a man who isn't my husband."

"You're asking the wrong woman. Your husband ain't much of a husband. He's neglectful. And a neglectful husband reaps what he sow."

Eileen loved it when Justine spoke so honestly with her. She reminded her of Mary.

"Go send for Stanley." Eileen rose from the bed, donning her dressing robe. "I'm going to write a letter."

"To whom?"

Eileen closed her eyes as she sat at her writing desk. In her mind's eye she saw Mary, lying upon her old bed on the fifth floor of Mrs. Brown's. Her golden curls were strewn about her and she appeared like an angel. It was one of their last days in New York. Eileen had caressed her sister's cheek. She now ran her finger gingerly over her palm. She could still feel the curve of her sister's soft, warm cheek.

It hurt so much to think of how much she missed Mary. It was a physical pain in the pit of her stomach. It was one of the reasons she needed the laudanum, and it had taken Justine's frank words to remind her of this.

"I'm writing my sister at the Clarendon, to tell her my news."

When Justine returned later that afternoon with word that Stanley was not at his church, Eileen's spirits sank. And when she did not receive word back from her sister the following morning, nor see her arrive to call and embrace her at her news, her sprits sank further. And when the weather turned violently rainy, her eye aches began again, and she opted, once more, for the companionship of the little amber bottle.

At one point she awoke to the sound of her husband arriving home. It was then she had the briefest moment of clarity, though she wasn't sure if it were that or just momentary hysteria; she hated him.

She wept, blew her nose, then took more medicine from the amber bottle.

She was wading in the sea. The water was cool yet not so cold as she remembered from her childhood in Ireland. She looked out to the sea, and there was only water and horizon and light—what light! The ocean was a living thing, dazzling and bejeweled with diamonds. It was overwhelming to her eyes. She looked down at her feet in the water again, noticed that the hem of her fine red taffeta gown was soaked. Another pair of feet stood beside hers—they belonged to a man. He stationed himself beside her in this place of utter contentment, serenity, but the sun's light blinded her. Struggle as she might, she could not make out who he was.

A voice said softly, "Eileen . . . Eileen."

She gasped and raised her head from her pillow. The room was stifling hot; she wiped a bead of sweat rolling down the side of her neck with a trembling hand. Oh, how her head ached.

"Eileen."

It was the same voice again. Her eyes darted across the room, and there sat Stanley upon her small, flowered settee. She stared, wondering if she were still caught in a dream. She even pinched her arm. No, it was no dream.

"Stanley?"

He smiled. "I'm glad to see you are awake, finally."

Sudden modesty took hold, and she pulled the bedcovers up to her chin. "How on earth did you get in here?"

"Your servant, Justine, sent for me and told me to wait in here for you."

"What?" Eileen was flabbergasted by Justine's presumptiveness. She would have to have a word with her. Why, she did not know how things were done in the fine homes of New Orleans, but certainly this went far beyond propriety.

"Do not be cross with her, Eileen," Stanley said, rising and slowly making his way to the bed. He sat his large frame by her feet.

She had forgotten just how very large he was. She felt herself warm beneath his gaze. She had not been this close to him since . . . since that day in winter, in his tiny chamber in the back of the church. Embarrassed, she closed her eyes. "I would ask you to leave, Stanley, while I make myself decent."

"Of course. I shall be right outside your door."

"I shall have to have a word with Justine. This isn't proper. I'm a married woman, you know."

He chuckled, and the sound was melodious. "Indeed I am well aware. Justine was worried about your state. She says you have slept for two days now." He opened the bedchamber door. "Shall I summon her?"

"Yes, please."

After he had shut the door, Eileen jumped from the bed and wrapped herself in her best, most fetching dressing gown of emerald velvet. She sat before her vanity and stared at her complexion. My, but she was pale, and look how her cheeks burned red! She removed her nightcap, and her auburn curls were a mess. How could she ever look presentable in so little time?

Justine arrived in the bedchamber with a sly grin upon her face.

Eileen pointed at her. "How *could you* let him in my bedchamber?" she said in a hissing whisper so that Stanley could not overhear her. "What on earth were you thinking?"

Justine made her way to Eileen, taking up the wide-toothed ivory hair comb from the vanity. "I was thinking just this, Madame Eileen. Look, you are fully awake now, and alive and well." She let out a triumphant chuckle as she began to work her magic upon Eileen's curls. "Don't you worry, I'll have you looking lovely in no time."

Eileen stared at Justine's reflection in the mirror, still in disbelief. "Have I really slept for two whole days?"

Justine only nodded as she removed a hairpin from between her lips and placed it in Eileen's hair.

"Did my husband come to check upon me?"

Justine's eyes met hers in the mirror. "What do you think?"

Eileen sighed, shaking her head.

"Don't move," Justine scolded through pursed lips holding hairpins.

"Did my sister call?" Eileen asked. She suddenly remembered her letter from two days prior. "Did she write?" Her spirits lifted with the possibility.

This time, Justine looked a little more sympathetic as she met her gaze in the mirror. Justine shook her head. "No, Madame."

Eileen's bottom lip begin to tremble.

Justine removed the pins from her mouth and bent her head down to Eileen's ear. "Don't you go crying now," she hissed in a whisper. "You'll ruin your pretty face."

Her words snapped Eileen out of her reverie. She must look her best. Justine was right. But sudden guilt walked into the room. "He isn't my lover, Justine. You know that."

Justine jabbed another pin into what was becoming a beautiful hair arrangement. "I know that, Madame Eileen," she replied without meeting her gaze. "He's just a dear friend, isn't that it?"

Justine could be infuriating, in that same blunt way that Mary was. "Yes, that's it."

"Mighty handsome friend, he is. And Zoe is wild for him. She keeps weaving between his legs and purring like she's in heat!"

The two laughed. "Aye, he is handsome." Eileen had no desire to fight for propriety's sake. The last time she had been this happy was when she realized she was pregnant.

She was pregnant. Good God. At moments it seemed unreal, to think that there was a tiny being inside her womb. She did not feel it move yet, for she was so early on in her pregnancy. When would she begin to feel him stir? She did not know. But funny, she realized, she somehow knew it was *he*, a boy.

"Does he know?" she asked Justine.

"Know?" Justine's expression then softened as she nodded. "Ah, about the baby. I don't know, Madame Eileen. Not unless Mr. Barnard has told him."

Eileen rolled her eyes. "I doubt that."

When Justine completed Eileen's hair arrangement, she sprayed a bit of rose water upon it. Eileen admired Justine's dexterity with her hair.

"Shall I send him in now?" Justine asked, a smile playing upon her lips.

"You look as though you're reading one of those dime-novel romances."

"Oh, but you'd be surprised." Justine winked at her before opening the bedchamber door. "You may come in, Mr. Jones."

Eileen quickly sat herself down upon the settee by the hearth, arranging the folds of her dressing gown as Stanley slowly entered, a smile playing upon his lips. Zoe followed him, seeming entranced as she gazed up at him.

"I do apologize if I offended you."

Eileen waved her hand. "I was more surprised than anything, really." She gestured to the great chair across from the settee. "Please have a seat."

She noticed that he was not dressed in his usual, worn black wool ensemble. Today he wore brown tweed trousers and a brown wool jacket over a simple, collarless linen shirt. Brown suited him, made him appear more healthy, golden. His blond hair was swept back into its usual queue. Would he ever update his appearance? If he had a wife, she would persuade him, of course.

He paused by the great chair, seeming to consider it. He then looked at her and made his way to the settee, sitting beside her. Zoe quickly followed and made herself at home upon his lap.

Surprised, she shifted slightly to face him. She could feel the telltale blush spreading over her chest, on full display in the generous cut of her dressing gown. "How have you been, Stanley?" she asked quickly to hide her embarrassment.

"The better question, dear friend, is how have *you* been?"

She glanced down at her fingers, toying with the velvet fabric of her dressing gown. "I've been very tired of late."

"So I've been told."

There was silence. She glanced her bedside table, fretful that Stanley would see the laudanum bottle.

His keen gaze followed hers. The realization dawned on his face.

"Is that medicine?"

"Yes," she answered in a meek voice.

"Who gave it to you?"

"Dr. Spencer."

Gingerly he lifted Zoe from his lap and put her upon the settee with a caress. He went to the bedside table, took hold of the amber bottle, uncorked it, and sniffed the contents. "Laudanum."

She felt like she had been caught in a lie by a priest.

He placed the bottle down, made his way back to the settee.

Eileen flinched slightly when he resumed his seat beside her, awaiting his scolding. Instead, she was surprised to find him taking her hands in his. Intoxicating warmth spread through her, like when she drank her port too quickly.

"Why are you taking laudanum? For what reason did the doctor prescribe it?"

"I have terrible eye aches, ever since arriving in Leadville."

"Yes, I remember that."

There was silence again. Stanley's beautiful eyes searched her face. "There's something else you're not telling me."

"It's also for my nerves. You see . . . Laurie, he wants me to remain calm and get plenty of rest."

He gripped her hands a little tighter.

She felt small and unsure. She should not whilst close to Stanley. She looked at him squarely. The moment was palpable and she held it tenderly, like a . . .

"You're pregnant," he declared.

She could not contain the joyous grin that spread over her lips.

Stanley gasped, and a look of wonder, or even something like sudden reverence came over him. But then his brow creased, puzzled.

"You are taking laudanum while with child?"

"Yes. Laurie says that Dr. Spencer recommends it so that I get rest, for the child's sake—"

Before she could finish her thought, he let go of her hands, rose from the settee, and paced before the hearth. He passed a hand quickly over his hair, tugged at his queue. He stared into the flames, and his jaw flexed.

"Stanley?"

"You must stop this, Eileen," he said as he faced her, his breathtaking eyes locked upon hers. "Promise me, you'll stop taking the laudanum, no matter what Laurie or Dr. Spencer tells you, understand?"

She wanted to tell him that yes, yes, she would do as he bade. But she thought of the pain, the days, the clock ticking upon the wall, the sound of the door clicking shut as Laurie made his way out into the evening, into the arms of Lord knew who. "I . . . I . . ." Her lips trembled as she searched for a way to convey this to him, for the words were just out of reach, or too painful to reach toward.

He sat beside her again, very close, and put his hand to her cheek.

The words were gone. She had no words. She was no words and all skin, all alive yet dying for this, his touch.

"You must, Eileen," he whispered.

He was so close now she could feel the breath of his words upon her lips.

"What must I do, Eileen? Where is the girl I met on the top floor of Mrs. Brown's boardinghouse? Where has that spirited, idealistic lass gone?" His thumb stroked her cheek, his eyes searched hers.

Her lashes fluttered shut as she gave in to his touch. "She is here, but she sleeps."

His thumb continued to caress her face, his other arm wrapped around her waist. "Then I must awaken her."

Her breath came from her in a shudder. She could not open her eyes, for fear the moment would disappear and she'd be alone again, again.

"Speak to me, Eileen," he ordered.

"Once I dreamt that we were back in Mrs. Brown's boardinghouse," she whispered, then gave a breathy laugh as she recalled how very sweet the dream had been. "You turned me into a butterfly." She wanted to tell him all her dreams, the desires that haunted her when she woke in a sweat with a racing heart.

"Eileen, look at me."

She let her eyelids unfurl like her wings in the dream. She saw before her a man with purpose and something wild in his gaze. No one had ever looked upon her in such a way, and she was both frightened and glad.

"How did I turn you into a butterfly?"

She moved her lips closer to his. "We were one, and I was complete."

He claimed her mouth, stealing the gentle kiss she had intended to bestow upon him.

It was the darkness she preferred, because in the late afternoon light, she had to remember who she was. In the darkness she could become anything and anyone and she did not have to think or consider. In the darkness she was beautiful and something new. She burrowed deeper into the darkness beneath the covers and listened, listened to their breathing and the sound of her heart beating a frantic, wild rhythm within her ears.

"Imagine," Stanley breathed, his lips brushing her earlobe, "if this were my home and you were my wife."

She gave herself to it, his pretend world, because it was so very satisfying to feign that, yes, she was his wife and all this was his. She yielded to his commanding hands and hungry mouth. She unfurled for him, arching against him like a graceful cat, deliberate and enticing in her every movement.

He was forceful, yet his touch was gentle, and this contrast made her thirst for more. There had always been that precipice, that wondering what was beyond, that desire to step closer and to know that, yes, this is what exists and can be yours to claim. As his mouth descended below her navel and his tongue tasted her, it was like the breathless, startling sunlight and wondrous view from atop the Continental Divide. She gasped, pulling the sheets taut above her head, her fingernails threatening to break through fine Egyptian cotton and pierce the flesh upon her palms.

"Give me this." His low voice strained as his hips pressed between her thighs. They emerged from the darkness of the covers and his chest, his shoulders like marble imbued with life.

She had no need for words. Her body answered as she instinctively tilted and pressed him to her, embracing him with her limbs. And as he submerged himself within her, she let herself descend and drown, drown in his scent, the burn like hot bathwater, the burn, the burn that spread ever so quickly, the exquisite burn, her eyes shut so tightly, her breath like steam, flashes of color behind her eyelids igniting like dry pine boughs, her body like smote sagebrush, crumbling slowly, slowly to ashes, soon lithe and airborne, scattering and free, carried by the wind.

Eileen watched Stanley dress himself. She envied how the linen of his drawers caressed him ever so closely. She would like to linger upon his skin, too.

His eyes met hers, and again the blood rushed and crashed within her ears like waves upon the Cliffs of Moher, which had so frightened her as a child.

He smiled. "Beautiful."

"I'm frightened."

"No. You are indomitable."

She did not know that word, but gleaned its meaning. "Indomitable," she said, liking the feel of it on her tongue. She embraced the word and smiled back at him. Yes, she was indomitable, and he had made her see this. It was as though she were drawn anew. There was no going back to her old skin.

He made his way toward the bed, toward her. She boldly stroked his hip, his thigh, quickly racing her hand up and down the wool of his trousers, rough against her fingertips.

He looked down at her, an amused smile playing upon his lips.

She dug her fingertips hard into the muscle beneath the wool.

He tensed, his eyes fluttering closed, a sigh escaping his sweet, sweet lips.

"Indomitable," she said with determination.

He moved from her hold, toward the bedside table. Swiftly he took the amber bottle in his hand. "If you are indomitable, then what shall you do with this?" His eyes searched hers.

The bottle within his large hand appeared so tiny and trivial. How had something so insignificant held such sway over her? She narrowed her eyes with sudden jealousy, wanting nothing else within Stanley's hand but her. "Toss it into the fireplace."

He walked toward the mantel, then threw the amber bottle, which smashed with a startling pop against the fireplace's back wall. The liquid within burst into a blue flame—vibrant yet fleeting.

A joyous laugh rose from the depths of her, escaping from her uncontrollably. She fell back upon the bed, succumbing to her fit of happiness. Soon she felt the bed shift beneath his weight, heard his low chuckle. She watched through tears of laughter as he quickly unfastened his pants and then hiked up the skirt of her dressing gown.

"This is mine," he hissed.

"Yours," she answered, spiraling, escaping to a place where no little amber bottle had ever been able to ensconce her.

CHAPTER TWENTY-NINE

It was Saturday, finally! The minutes seemed to drag the whole week, especially now that all the miners in Leadville had collectively walked off the job in solidarity, demanding that the mine owners increase their pay and meet various other labor-related demands. Fools, the lot of them, Laurie thought, and all easily and readily replaceable. And damn those owners of the Chrysolite mine—they had stirred the bees' nest, insisting that miners couldn't smoke or talk while working the mines. Ridiculously draconian. Now the whole of Leadville was in a state, with the merchants in an uproar over how much their businesses suffered with the loss of miners' patronage. It was all so absurd.

That morning dragged, for Laurie must wait another fifteen hours before meeting Stanley at the appointed time at the Avalon. Laurie's nerves were a shambles; every tick of the mantel clock in the study was an annoyance, each newspaper page numbing in its mundane reporting of nonsensical minutiae. Honestly, did it really matter whether Chester Arthur was born in Vermont or Ireland or Canada? If the Democrats had to resort to such tactics to besmirch a vice-presidential candidate, then perhaps their own candidate was sorely lacking. Politics, Laurie judged, was the realm of failed actors and circus performers.

A sudden tinkle of joyous giggling interrupted him from his contemplations. He had not seen Eileen for some days. This did not upset him, of course, but he did find himself rather curious, especially with the oddly stirring sound of her gaiety. He allowed his curiosity to lead him out of the study and to follow her laughter up the stairs. The door to her bedchamber was open, and Justine leaned casually in the doorway. She had become more than just the cook of the house. She was also now Eileen's hairdresser, much to the chagrin of Florence, who seemed to have been demoted to the inferior tasks of housekeeping and laundry. But even more than that, Laurie suspected that Justine had become Eileen's confidante. With one hand upon her hip, the other caressing the doorjamb, Justine's stance was as brazen as a whore's on State Street.

Perhaps his distrust of her was palpable, for she met his stare boldly, knowingly. There was no surprise in her hazel eyes, and a sly, sensuous smile spread upon her full lips. She did not say a word to him as she gestured into Eileen's bedchamber, as though proudly presenting a work of art of her own creation for his viewing pleasure.

Silently Laurie moved forward and Justine moved away, humming a melody as she limped down the hallway and left the husband and wife alone.

He peered into Eileen's bedchamber. She sat at her dressing table, clad in a green velvet robe, admiring her reflection in the mirror. She tilted her chin up, elongating her pale neck, and proceeded to perfume herself. He watched as she languidly glided the frosted glass dabber down her neck to the hollow of her throat, and then farther down her cleavage. Her eyelids fluttered, then closed as she smiled. "Mmmm," she uttered, giving herself to the pleasurable sensation.

He was a spy, a boy taken by surprise at the sight of a woman in private bliss. He blinked, still somewhat disbelieving that this creature was his wife. How could this sensuous thing be the same who refused to respond to his touch? Where had his wife gone?

Realization registered upon her face as she spotted his reflection in her mirror. She turned quickly, rising from her bench. The glass dabber was still in her fingertips, frozen in movement like a lover caught in the act. But her wide eyes softened, narrowed as she met his gaze. She raised her chin, challenging him in some way, daring him to accuse her of something. She tossed her mane of auburn curls back from her shoulders—a graceful yet feral and equine gesture he had never witnessed from her before.

He was speechless, stirred. She was a hothouse orchid finally come to bloom. Better yet, she was the vibrant, heady, feathery mimosa blossom, which he had watched unfurl before his eyes one early morning in a courtyard in New Orleans. He longed to touch her. He stepped over the threshold and into her bedchamber, which smelled of talcum powder and rose water. A dizziness came over him; what had awoken her?

Oh yes, he realized just then with a burst of pride and gladness in his heart. "Motherhood becomes you."

A giggle escaped her lips—a giggle that rang cynical in his ears. Could it be?

"Aye, motherhood," she replied, her fingers absently stroking the front of her dressing robe. The smile faded from her lips. "Are you heading to the mine today?"

He shook himself free of her spell. "Not today."

"Ah," she said. She cocked her head to the side, inquisitively.

He was not wanted in her realm. He knew this. He hated this. She would be nothing without him. She would still be in a factory in New York, slowly losing her sight to lacemaking. She would be pregnant, indeed, with the whelp of some filthy Irish gasworks toiler. He wanted to say all this to her, but to what end? This creature that stood before him was not the creature he had wed months before. She was something new and proud, and he did not think mere insults could take this new woman down from her lofty place.

But he had Stanley. The thought filled him with a delicious eagerness and pride. "But I shall be at the mine later this evening . . . to give a personal tour to a foreign dignitary—"

"Very well," she said dismissively before he had finished, and seated herself again before her mirror. "I'll tell Justine not to prepare dinner for you."

"Good day," he muttered through clenched teeth. He exited her room, descending the stairway. The coolness of the polished wooden banister gliding beneath his hand did nothing to relieve the fire that brewed within him. He alternately wanted to strike her face and make love to her. What was this madness? He glanced up at the grandfather clock in the main hallway. Ten o'clock a.m. Good Christ, he longed to throw something at it, but uttered a curse instead.

He made his way to the kitchen, where he saw Jacob seated upon an empty milk crate, captivated by Justine as he devoured one of her croissants. She was polishing a copper pot rigorously upon the worktable, her breasts swaying to and fro above her corset, within her chintz dress, with the rhythm of her labor. That knowing smile playing upon her lips told Laurie that she was keenly aware of the spell she had cast upon the young lad and was thoroughly enjoying herself.

Laurie cleared his throat and Jacob jumped up, brushing the croissant crumbs from his hands and trousers.

"What can I do for you, Monsieur?" Justine asked.

"Nothing," he said, realizing that his voice sounded angrier than he had intended. "Jacob, I need you to take me to the mine. I've some urgent business to attend to."

Laurie almost cried out with joy when the sun had finally set, casting Fryer Hill and the Avalon's office, pull house, and iron-framed lever in a rust-red glow. The quiet surrounding him was eerie. It was strange to sit in the office and not hear the cacophony of sound from the pull house, the incessant groan and whine of hauling fortune from the mountain's depths. It was unsettling, both the silence as well as the interruption of the flow of money.

But this sudden change of fortune was, he realized, two-sided, for now he and Stanley might finally have the moment he had long desired. Solitude and secrecy could prevail in the midst of this labor dispute.

Laurie endeavored to appear occupied with accounting matters in his office, but soon grew frustrated with this folly. He grabbed a random tome off the bookshelf behind his grand mahogany desk. He licked his index finger and flipped to the title page. He let out a low chuckle, amused by what fate had placed in his hands. It had been quite some time since he had read Voltaire's *Candide*. Reading the opening lines, he was reminded of his days at Cambridge, when he had derived such pleasure from Voltaire's sarcasm.

God, but that seemed like ages ago. And what an entirely different person he had become since then. Never had he envisioned himself a mining baron in the Rocky Mountains. Never had he thought that he would have a lowly Irishwoman for a wife. And never had he imagined that he would one day eagerly await the embrace of a lover like Stanley.

He shuddered at the thought and closed *Candide* with a thud, throwing it down upon his desk. He rose from his chair and made his way to the window. Absently he stared at the still pull house, vacant of workers aside from the few guards watching over the orifice of his fortune. Was he mad? How had all this transpired? Had he been blinded by lust, lust for a man, no less? The thought of Stanley's touch aroused him, yet the hairs on the back of his neck stood and his stomach seemed to do an ungraceful flip. He ran his hand through his hair, reminding himself to breathe, reminding himself that he was the master of his own destiny, the ruler of all this before him, the lord of immense wealth and clout. He had always and would continue to do as he damn well pleased.

As he absently traced his bottom lip with his thumb, he recalled an image—a fresco—he had beheld in Italy whilst on his grand tour. He had stepped inside a tiny, cluttered shop of antiques and souvenirs in Naples to escape the suffocating heat, stench, and sun of the city. An old man with a cane had audaciously taken hold of his arm and guided him farther into the shop, to an alcove displaying various ancient frescoes stolen from the walls of Herculaneum and Pompeii. Many depicted portraits, others nature scenes, but some were most indecent and erotic. All were for sale, and at surprisingly low prices, or at least in Laurie's opinion.

One fresco had captivated him. It left him shaken, yet aroused. There were three lovers; she was being taken from behind, and so was he. The first aspect was nothing new, but the second was something he had never actually seen depicted. He could not tear his eyes away until the obnoxious old man tugged at his sleeve and barked out prices in Neapolitan. Laurie looked down into the dark, leathery face of the Italian and was assaulted by breath tinged with garlic, grappa, and rotting teeth. He shook himself free and hastily departed the shop before retching up his breakfast.

Satisfy your undying curiosity. Just do it once and be done with it all, be done with Stanley.

Laurie thought that, with the crisp glow of moonlight, the hills and mountains surrounding the Avalon appeared desert like. This land had been stripped of its trees and brush years before in order to feed the appetite of an ever-growing Leadville. All that remained were undulating, heaving, and falling slopes and ridges, which appeared as smooth and supple as skin in the bluish-silver moon glow.

The rider approached, made his way up the hillside. The horse kept a quick pace, gliding toward the Avalon office.

Laurie's breath caught in his chest as he awaited Stanley.

The horse reared before the steps of the office. Stanley wore no hat; his long hair was disheveled, loosened from its queue. Had it not been for his contemporary attire, Laurie thought that Stanley could have passed for a timeless knight, warrior, highwayman—any and all brave and masculine figures that had always been the makings of fiction and lore.

"We ought not stay here," said Stanley in a low tone. He cast a furtive glance toward the guards by the pull house. "Saddle up and follow me."

Laurie, glad that at least one of the two of them had the gumption to think of such practicalities, untied the reins from the iron hitching post and mounted his horse.

Stanley led Laurie on a tiny path, heading southward toward the abandoned mines just west of Stumptown. When they arrived at the opening of a nondescript mine shaft, they dismounted and tethered their horses' reins to the trunk of a stripped pine.

Stanley lit a match and ignited a torch, which he then dropped down the mine shaft. The flame descended and landed with a thud in the rocky bowels of the mine. The light illuminated a fairly sturdy-looking ladder as it fell.

Without a word, the two climbed down. The only sound was their boots upon the rungs, their breathing, and the crackle of the torch.

Once within the mine, Laurie looked up into Stanley's face, which had taken on the appearance of a chiaroscuro portrait. He trembled, his mouth dry in nervousness and anticipation.

"How did you find this place?" he managed to ask.

Stanley shrugged before pulling his sweater up over his head, casting it aside. "I've had many hours alone to reflect, to explore, to plan." He placed his hands upon his hips. "Take off your coat."

Laurie did as he bade, feeling the cool, musty air of the mine shaft through his shirtsleeves.

"Now the rest of it," Stanley ordered with a curt nod.

Laurie removed his waistcoat, collar, shirt, and trousers as ordered. He did not want to have to think anymore. He wanted Stanley to tell him what he desired. He wanted to submit to his every whim.

As Stanley slowly walked around him, inspecting his nakedness, Laurie felt he might die in his eagerness to be touched.

Stanley stood before him and unbuttoned his simple linen shirt.

Laurie's breath came quickly as the torchlight revealed the muscular planes and ridges of Stanley's torso.

Stanley removed his shirt, then hooked his thumbs in his suspenders. He slid them back over his bare shoulders and chest, staring down his nose at Laurie. "How could you fail your wife so?"

Laurie was surprised by the question, by the mention of Eileen. "How's that? Do you mean by my meeting you here?"

"No. You have gotten her with child, yet you push her to drink laudanum. How could you do such a disgusting thing?"

Laurie took a step back, unprepared for this verbal assault. "Look here, she is following the orders of Dr.—"

"Shut your mouth!" Stanley sneered at him. "You paid that doctor handsomely to tell you exactly what you desired."

"What are you insinuating?"

"She was nothing but a girl, an innocent girl, and you took her just for the sake of taking her, and you were too selfish—too lazy—to bother to make her happy as a husband should."

Stanley had hit a nerve. Laurie returned, "Who are you to say such things so authoritatively? Do you see inside my wife's heart?" He scoffed at the absurdity of the idea. "Are you so omnipotent?"

But at this, Laurie lost his will to combat, to argue. He could answer his own question—Stanley had seen inside his heart the moment they had met that fateful evening in New York.

"You wanted to be with me? Here we are," said Stanley, gesturing around the mine shaft. "But I am not the lover you imagined. I am something from the Hell you've longed for. You're nothing but a selfish beast, Laurie, and I shall rein you in, treat you like the dog you are."

Before Laurie could respond, before he could even contemplate Stanley's words, Stanley's mouth was harshly claiming his, devouring him. The roughness of Stanley's stubble chafed his chin. Stanley licked the inside of his cheeks, his tongue thrusting against his.

Laurie lost all ability to think, to reason. He was governed by passion, by his body, by his instincts. Stanley was right—he was nothing but a selfish dog.

Stanley broke the kiss. He rounded Laurie and, with sudden gentleness, slid his roughened fingertips down Laurie's back, then kissed his shoulder blades.

Laurie sighed, trembling with the sweetness of Stanley's touch. But abruptly it ended, replaced by the feel of Stanley's hand taking a tight grip of the back of his neck.

Stanley shoved him forward, as though he were livestock.

"Goddamn you," Stanley hissed before the two became one.

And through the night, by the light of a single torch, in the belly of the earth, Laurie was reduced to a mindless beast, utterly mastered and controlled by Stanley. And he desired only to please, to do as he was bidden, to somehow bring back the Stanley he loved by giving in to his every desire. In this world of their making, in this dank cave created by desperate, driven men, in the glimpses of damp flesh and glassy eyes, he was born anew.

The sun rose over Fryer Hill as Laurie watched from the porch of the Avalon office. He saw dawn with new eyes. He had never noticed how soft and velvety it could be, as ethereal and pink as that mimosa blossom in New Orleans. He then recalled thinking just the previous day that his wife was also like that mimosa blossom. But oh, how very wrong he was. He could not even think of her at this moment. It seemed blasphemous to think of her at such a sweet, untouchable time as this—much like thinking an impure thought whilst in church.

He placed his hand over his chest to try to calm the ferocious rhythm of his heart. He ran his tongue over his lips, which still felt bruised, which still tasted of Stanley. How delicious the taste, like ocean water and honey and flesh—*his* flesh.

His stomach churned and he squinted his eyes shut. Stanley had made him feel like an animal, a horse prized yet ruthlessly ridden to the grand finish of a high-stakes race. He knew he should feel disgust with himself, with what they had done. But he did not and could not. He would do it all again, indeed, without hesitation. Sinking to the porch steps, his body ached in the descent. He relished the pain, trembled as he began to relive the last few hours in his mind.

The thought of it all so overwhelmed him that he rose from the porch step, quickly slammed the office door open, made his way into his own office, where he retrieved a silver flask of Highland Park whisky. He drank until the tremors disappeared, until his heart slowed, so that it did not pound in his ears like some tribal drum.

Stanley had drawn him apart, yet hewn him anew.

CHAPTER THIRTY

Everything became amusing. Eileen peered through new eyes. There was a crispness to her worldview. Snow was brighter—yes, she'd learned after a full year that it was common to have snow in Leadville in spring, well into May—the sky more azure, the black of a raven's wing more nuanced in hues of glistening, inky blue. Her lungs tingled with each breath. Men were less anonymous, more individual, and there was something interesting—sometimes beautiful—in each of their faces. Sometimes she would stare too long from the safety of her carriage, and they might stare back. It became a game that she would play until the waves upon the Cliffs of Moher would crash within her ears and she would look away, an elated smile teasing her lips.

Women became windows—transparent, their inner workings on full display, for Eileen had knowledge now, she fancied. She was once that woman there, with the sad eyes and drawn cheeks, wondering when her prince might arrive to this mountain town and take her away, away, to a place where she might breathe easy once again.

Eileen had found her prince. He was foremost in her thoughts. Her every gesture, movement, task took on new meaning, for he was with her in each. Just the manner in which she stepped out of the carriage, descended the staircase, signed her signature—all these took on more poignancy.

The air! What was that scent, so sweet yet indecipherable? It was there, more heady than a flower, more like honey, a scent like the feel of rabbit fur. Was such a thing possible? Eileen would giggle at such whimsical thoughts.

This was love. She knew it to be true. She knew love could be a transformational thing, and behold how she had burst into life! She longed to tell Mary, for Mary would understand. And it was only the thought of her missing sister that could sober her, but she did not want to be sober, so she replaced her sister with Justine.

She could not eat. Sleep evaded her. She would not allow her bedsheets to be washed, for she could still smell him upon them. She was feverish in that manner that her skin was so much more sensitive; the feel of the bathtub's copper faucet against her bare, wet foot was electrifying. The sensation of Zoe's whiskers on her face when she would kiss the lovely little panther would make her laugh in delight. The scratch of her hairbrush upon the nape of her neck charmed a sigh from her lips.

There were moments of uncontrollable shaking, chills, aching to the bone. Her head would throb in pain, and her throat seemed always parched, no matter how much she drank. Not wanting to admit that this was her body yearning for the opium she had denied it, she reasoned it was her longing for Stanley's touch—a new addiction far more pleasing.

And yet, there was her husband. But no matter, she could avoid him just as she had while in the stupor of laudanum. For she ate little now, despite Justine's scolding.

"Chérie!" Justine would exclaim. The useless impediment of employer/servant boundary had disintegrated some time ago. "Chérie, you must eat! A real man likes a woman with something to hold on to, not skin and bones."

She was right, Eileen knew, so she would quickly eat the little pastries and delicacies Justine prepared just for her.

"And the baby, too, chérie, don't forget . . ."

And that was when she would lose her appetite, but not because of the lovesickness.

"The baby . . ." She would stroke her small belly.

Justine would shake her head. "Don't think on that now, chérie. It is still a long way off."

But Eileen was keen, and she saw Justine's worry.

"A long way off, yes," she would repeat to assuage herself.

Three days had passed. She could not wait. She thirsted for him. She could think of nothing else. She waited until she heard the sound of her husband leave for the mine in the early-morning hours, and she bounded out of bed. Justine helped dress her and arrange her hair. Florence had been relegated to laundry duty. Eileen was ready in the foyer, clad in her fox-fur cape and muff, breathlessly awaiting Jacob's arrival back from the Avalon. Before he could disembark from the carriage, she was outside, holding out her hand for his assistance in. The boy looked utterly surprised when she asked to be taken to the little chapel on the south edge of town.

"What is it? I simply want to pray with a friend," she tossed at him.

That place where the chapel sat had always been so picturesque, but now, as she stood before the chapel doors, she could hear in the distance the sound of the little silver streams coming to life in the field beyond, dancing free from the ice and melding together to become that big river—which one? Oh yes, the Arkansas River. This place was magical, like something out of a tale with knights and princes and princesses.

And there was her prince, answering the chapel door. He had known she would come. She could see it in his smile, the way his eyes drank her in as though dying for her. The chapel doors slammed shut and she was within his embrace, devouring his lips.

"I could not wait," she said between kisses.

"Don't speak," he responded, before scooping her up in his arms like an ancient man claiming his woman, draping her over his shoulder.

She went limp, her pregnancy completely forgotten, letting her head and arms dangle from his height, laughing aloud in elation and at this silly thought, the sound echoing through the empty chapel. His swift movement stirred the pages of a Bible left open upon a wooden pew. She saw this upside down. How absurd! She laughed harder.

When they reached the confines of his tiny living quarters, Stanley tossed her from over his shoulder, flinging her down upon his small spartan bed. The springs shouted in protest—or delight? He struggled with her skirts, impatiently tore at her pantaloons. She ripped his shirt open. A button fell from it and into her mouth. She spit it out and bit at his neck. If she could eat—devour—him, she would. She stretched her arms above her head upon the bed. She felt like the waxen ballerina she had once seen spinning within a music box in a shop window in New York City. She was spinning, frozen in perpetual grace and perfect form.

But no, she was that butterfly in her opium-laced dream from long ago. He had carried her from the bed to the wooden table. She felt gossamer wings unfurl from her back as he tilted his hips just so and quickened his pace. She was transformed to a winged creature as he took her to climax.

"This is all mine," he gasped before finding his own release. He laid his head upon her shoulder, his breath hot upon her neck.

"I love you," she whispered.

He raised his head from her shoulder and looked into her eyes. "No, I love you."

There was such fierceness in his gaze that she could only nod. The whole of her body felt basked in an unspeakably beautiful light. Her every desire had come to fruition with his utterance of those three simple words.

She was complete, yet she needed more. She knew the amber bottle of his love must never run dry.

Eileen desired to be with Stanley more than anything or anyone else. But there was a nagging, a pulling within her that she could no longer deny. How she longed to confide in Mary! The past two weeks with Stanley had erased from her mind all anger toward her sister. She wanted nothing more than to impart every detail of her meetings with him, see how her sister would react, watch her light up, and her big, beautiful grin break into the howls of high-pitched laughter Eileen so dearly adored and missed. Mary would understand her fevered state, racing mind and heart. Mary would hold her hands and say in that singsong voice, "My, Eileen, but it sounds like love!"

Her husband did not want her to speak to her sister. She scoffed, thinking of how little she considered, or even cared about, her husband's wishes. He did not love her. He did not treasure her. He did not bring her to life like Stanley.

She should be Stanley's wife. She knew this now, now that she was better acquainted with the ways of love, marriage, and her own heart's wishes. What a little fool she had been, a year and some months before, when Stanley had knelt at her feet and kissed her hem in the confines of his tiny room on the fifth floor of Mrs. Brown's. She should have taken his face in her hands and looked into his sky-blue eyes and professed her love for him. Perhaps now she would be his wife rather than Laurie's. She would be scrubbing his floors and cooking his meals and not living in such finery as she did now. She laughed aloud; she would trade all this comfort and luxury if it meant she could mend Stanley's clothes and then dress him in them, and undress him, and have him hold her each night. She would give all her wardrobe and perfumes and jewels away if it meant she could be his, open herself to him whenever he so desired, be wrapped in his scent and warmth, have his tongue upon her skin and wake each day sore and satisfied.

She slid her hands to her belly and thrilled at the thought of conceiving Stanley's baby, one she could give to him. What beautiful babies they could make: chubby, cherublike, with Stanley's golden hair and blue eyes, her curls, and the dimple on her right cheek that only appeared when she smiled in earnest.

But this baby was not his, and she pictured within her a dark-haired, green-eyed selfish creature much like Laurie. But, also, much like herself.

Shaking her head and rising from bed, she knew a task would usurp any further dark thoughts. She dressed and had Jacob ready the carriage, and summoned Justine. They would go to town and find her sister. She would end this stupidity, this feud over what? Her mind was so brimming with ecstatic happiness that she couldn't even recall why she had scorned her only sister.

"I could have done this errand for you, chérie," scolded Justine as their carriage joined the incessant traffic of Harrison Avenue. Striking miners stood on the boardwalks, many holding signs demanding workers' rights. There was a restless, wary energy about Leadville with all these angry, out-of-work men milling about, with no money to pursue their usual pastimes of drinking and debauchery on State Street.

"What if she should cause a scene and upset you?" demanded Justine. "Why must you tempt fate, as they say?"

Eileen patted Justine's knee with her white-gloved hand. "You must stop fretting over me. I am not some simpering wallflower."

"And where do you plan to go?"

"The Clarendon, of course."

It took time and shrewd maneuvering, but Jacob was eventually able to bring the carriage before the hotel, assisting Eileen and Justine out onto the boardwalk and stopping the pedestrian traffic with a few harsh words so that the two women could make their way to the door. Eileen looked over her shoulder.

Justine smiled and gave Jacob a gentle pat on his cheek. The young man blushed red and cleared his throat in embarrassment, though Eileen could see that he fought a grin.

"You are relentless with Jacob," Eileen whispered to Justine as she nodded to various gentlemen who wished the wife of the wealthy Mr. Barnard a very pleasant day. "He's just a boy, after all."

They approached the front desk, greeted by a hotel clerk. "How might I be of service to you today, Mrs. Barnard?"

"I've come to call on my sister, Mary. Might she be taking her breakfast now?" Eileen asked, glancing down the hall toward the dining room, where breakfast was served until eleven.

"Oh, but I'm sorry, Mrs. Barnard," replied the clerk. "Miss Mary left her rooms at the Clarendon almost a month ago."

"Certainly not?" Eileen said in her bewilderment.

He nodded. "I am quite sorry, madam. I would have thought that Mr. Barnard would have told you—"

"Have you a forwarding address for her?" Justine asked him as she worriedly eyed Eileen.

"Let me check, ma'am." The clerk seemed happy to have a task to take him away from an uncomfortable situation, and he examined record books behind the desk.

"How could he have not told me this?" Eileen asked Justine, fighting the angry tears that threatened to spill.

Justine shrugged and shook her head. "I couldn't tell you why, chérie. That man has always confused me."

The clerk soon returned. "I am terribly sorry, Mrs. Barnard, but we've been given no forwarding address here. I do apologize—"

"You've been so kind to check. Thank you for your time."

"But of course. My pleasure, Mrs. Barnard." The clerk gave a slight bow.

The two women made their way to the front door, where Jacob awaited. He ushered the two back into the carriage.

"That sister of yours." Justine paused, shaking her head and searching Harrison Avenue. "She is trouble. Where could she have gotten herself off to?" She took hold of Eileen's hand. "Do you reckon she's shacking up with that Stinson trash?"

Eileen turned her gaze to her hand in Justine's. "It's possible, I suppose. But it doesn't seem like Mary, to put all her eggs in one man's basket, so to speak."

"Should we head home, ma'am?" asked Jacob over his shoulder.

Eileen deliberated for a moment. "Head to State Street, Jacob."

Jacob's shoulders heaved with a sigh. "Very well," he muttered as he snapped the reins.

"What are you going to do on State?" asked Justine. "Inquire in every saloon and barroom? You're being mighty foolish. Be like finding a needle in a haystack, what with all the saloon girls and whores down there."

"If it's meant to be, Justine, I shall find her," Eileen said with mock conviction. In truth, she had no idea what she might do once they got to State Street.

Once Jacob was able to bring the carriage east, round the corner, they became entangled in the ever-present traffic of State Street. Eileen scanned the boardwalk and was startled to hear someone call her name.

"Mrs. Barnard, yoooooo-hooooo! Over here!" called an unmistakable girlish voice.

Eileen saw Dolly McGraw in the adjacent carriage, just to their right. She was, as usual, as resplendent as a porcelain doll, wearing a garish bonnet, decorated with fake red geraniums and stuffed cardinals. Her pert lips were painted an identical shade of red. She waved a lace kerchief to hail Eileen.

Eileen never thought she would feel such gladness at the sight of Dolly, but she did, as though Dolly were a sign from the Almighty that she would soon find her sister. "Hello there, Miss McGraw. You are just the person I was hoping to see!"

Dolly gasped in delight as she scooted over to the left in the carriage, her hand and kerchief dangling over the side, seeming to caress the Pickering coat of arms.

It took much to shock Eileen, but she found herself slightly scandalized by just how brazenly Mr. Pickering carried on with his mistress. "Dolly, I am seeking my sister, Mary. I was just informed at the Clarendon that she no longer resides there. Do you know where she might be?"

Dolly's lashes fluttered as she bit her lip. "You didn't know?"

"Know what?" asked Eileen.

"Mary off and went to Deadwood about a month ago. I thought your husband would have told you, honestly." Dolly put a hand to her bonnet, touching one of the cardinals.

Eileen had the sudden sensation of falling down a flight of stairs. It took her a moment to respond. "Deadwood? Why?"

Dolly shrugged and toyed with one of her perfectly coiffed curls. "Don't know. I wish she hadn't, since she was such a good chum. She just said that she was tired of this tiny town and wanted to get rolling before her wheels got stuck in the mud."

The two carriages jolted into movement, only to stop again—typical State Street impasse. Eileen felt the guilt and remorse that always came when she remembered their original plan, the splendid dream of San Francisco.

"What about that Stinson fella?" Justine asked.

"Yes, did he go to Deadwood, as well?" asked Eileen.

Dolly shook her head. "Oh gosh, no. Beau won't ever leave Leadville and his gang of fellas. They had quite a row over it all. Beau doesn't take too kindly to rejection."

Justine chuckled.

"Has she written you? Given you any forwarding information?" Eileen was struggling to keep the trail to her sister going.

"I'm so sorry, Mrs. Barnard, but no. I really wish she'd write me . . . and I daresay she'd be mighty pleased to know you were looking for her. Don't know why you two couldn't ever sort things out, if you don't mind me saying. Lands, but I wish I had a sister."

Just then Jacob was able to maneuver around some traffic, bringing the conversation to a close.

"If you hear from her, do let me know!" called Dolly, waving her kerchief in farewell. "I miss her sorely!"

"Where to, ma'am?" asked Jacob.

"Home, I suppose," Eileen replied forlornly.

Eileen and Justine sat in silence as Jacob slowly made progress east on State. Eileen fought the tears that threatened to overflow by studying the rosebud pattern on the lap of her chintz dress.

"Speak of the devil himself," muttered Justine in a low voice.

"What?" Eileen said, scanning the boardwalk.

Beau Stinson and gang were lolling about on the boardwalk in front of Shay's.

Her eyes locked with his pretty baby blues.

He gave her his lazy, slanted grin, but there was nothing warm in it, Eileen could tell. He leaned against a hitching post, chewing tobacco and picking at his fingernail with a hunting knife. "Why if it isn't the high-and-mighty Mrs. Barnard."

Eileen would not—could not—be threatened by the likes of him. She had known much worse than him in the Bowery. He had obviously forgotten where she'd come from. Had she risen so high in the world that he could forget? No matter—she put the thought out of her mind. "Mr. Stinson, have you had word from my sister?"

"Oh, you're looking for your sister, are you?" He returned his gaze to his knife and fingernails. "Well, ain't that sweet." He spat a wad of tobacco toward her carriage, then wiped his mouth upon his black linen sleeve. "Say," he said, craning his neck to get a look at Justine, and then hailed her with a slur, a slur that, despite the countless times Eileen had heard it tossed around among white men, never lost its palpable hatred.

Eileen's hand instinctively clasped Justine's.

"Ma'am, I'm going to move along now," announced Jacob, a strain of anger in his voice.

"No, Jacob, I'm still speaking with Mr. Stinson here, who seems to lack manners."

He chuckled, tossing his knife in the air and catching it by the handle. "Y'all know, when I was a young lad on my daddy's plantation, my daddy kept a sweet thing like that locked up in a shed, for his and my personal entertainment."

The gang around him laughed approvingly.

"Well, now, is that so?" said Justine in a saccharine tone. "Too bad Abe Lincoln and his men came down and shit all over your good time."

The smirk disappeared from Beau's face. "You better watch yourself, bitch, or I'll get you and lock you up in a new shed."

"And my husband will alert the constable and you will be arrested, Mr. Stinson," replied Eileen, quaking in anger. "Now, I'll ask you again: Have you had word from my sister?"

"I ain't had word from your damn sister. And good riddance!" His friends whooped in approval. "But if I see that bitch again, you can be sure she'll be sorry she ever took off." He flung his knife into the hitching post with such force that the knife handle vibrated.

"Move along, Jacob," Eileen said, choking on the oaths and obscenities she longed to hurl, like a knife, at Beau Stinson.

CHAPTER THIRTY-ONE

Could this continue?

The question, like a guilty conscience, came to haunt Laurie throughout his days. It had continued into the summer; after their first rendezvous in the abandoned mine shaft, he and Stanley had many more times descended the ladder into their own secret world. Each time, Laurie reveled in his humiliation, his subjugation at Stanley's hands. Every bruising grip and harsh word was like a divine blessing, for Stanley was the god of his world. He could admit this to himself—he would craft no pretense otherwise.

Whilst at his desk, Laurie listened to the loud sounds of the pull house and miners, who had resumed work back in mid-June, thankfully. It was August now. Laurie longed to be away, in the bowels of the earth, watching the shadows of their silhouettes play upon the mine wall in the flickering torchlight. In daydream, Laurie would bring his fingers to the nape of his neck, slide them upward into his hair. He would coil the waves round his fingers and then form a fist and tug. The sensation instantly brought him to arousal, for this was what Stanley would do to him as he took him.

The orchestration of their meetings was a simple task. Laurie would write one word upon his embossed stationery: *Tonight?* He would instruct the messenger to await Stanley's response and return it immediately. In handwriting somewhat foreign in style—much like the handwriting of the German tutor who had instructed Laurie as a boy—Stanley would respond: *Yes. At Dusk.*

Laurie delighted so much in the details of each encounter that he decided to begin keeping a journal for his own personal remembrance. This he locked away in the top drawer of his mahogany desk.

He had received word that they would meet that night. Dusk seemed an eternity away. He knew he was abrupt and acerbic with his foremen, accountants, and various tradesmen, but it could not be helped. If he could single-handedly force the sun beneath the horizon, he would.

When dusk finally arrived, he mounted his horse and headed southward down the route that he could now navigate blindfolded. *Blindfold—there's an intriguing idea.* He smiled, pleased with his whimsical concept. He would propose it to Stanley.

And Stanley readily accepted, fishing out of his saddlebag a red cotton handkerchief.

"Have you another?" asked Laurie.

"Are you afraid you'll rip this one?" Stanley joked in a whisper as he retrieved a second handkerchief.

"No. For you."

Stanley paused, looking him in the eyes. "Why?"

"Why not?"

"It's not what we do," said Stanley, his fine jaw tightening in that cruel manner with which Laurie had become so well acquainted.

"Let's try it once."

Their fingers became their eyes. At first Stanley's touch was forceful and angry, as usual. But Laurie decided to use the power of persuasion—his lips—to stay his eager lover, so that this night together might last longer. So that he could postpone his return to reality—a place of no meaning or color without Stanley's touch and taste in his immediate grasp.

He traced the contours of Stanley's powerful arms with his tongue. He lingered upon Stanley's chest, feeling the strong, steady rhythm of his heart through his lips. He sensed Stanley's body tensing with the unknown of it all. Laurie needed no bidding; he undressed himself. Tenuously, in his self-imposed darkness, Laurie dared to let his fingers find Stanley's face, which he pulled down toward him to meet his kiss.

It was the kind of gentle kiss that one, with much trepidation, bestows upon a lover in the wonder and ambiguity of adolescence. It wasn't like them to meet so tenderly. The novelty of it emboldened Laurie to allow his lips to linger upon Stanley's. He continued in this way until Stanley pulled away with a shudder and choking sound.

What was this? Laurie removed his blindfold to see that Stanley had done the same, yet now covered his face with his hands.

"Don't look at me, please," Stanley said, and Laurie could tell by the tremble in his voice that Stanley struggled against tears.

"Why not?"

"I can't bear to have you see me like this."

"What have I done?" Had he, perhaps, crossed some intangible line with Stanley?

"Nothing. It's just me. I'm all a shambles."

"Why?"

Stanley shook his head, still covering his face. "I don't know how much longer I can go on like this."

It was as though Stanley had ripped his heart out of his chest and ground it with his heel into the earth of the mine shaft. "What do you mean? Don't do this to us so soon."

Stanley turned away. "I feel spent and filthy. You've no idea. I'm drowning in my own sins."

Laurie had to stifle his groan. He'd known this would come, sooner or later. "There's no such thing as sin. It's preposterous." He had wondered how Stanley could reconcile this secret, carnal side of himself with his fervent faith.

"Indeed there is!" replied Stanley. He uncovered his face, which was damp with tears yet devoid of emotion.

"It's a ridiculous concept invented by paranoid Catholics."

"And I was raised a Catholic."

Laurie could not choke back his laughter at the absurdity of it. How could one man be so duplicitous with his own self?

"Now is not the time to ridicule my religion." Stanley's jaw set and his eyes narrowed.

Laurie's annoyance was stoked by his arousal, the need to proceed. "Very well, then. So you cry because you are a sinner. Then go to the church tomorrow and confess your transgressions against your god. In the meantime, let me pleasure you." He went to his knees before Stanley, unfastening his trousers.

Stanley's hands threaded into his hair. "God forgive me."

But Laurie stopped suddenly, as the scent of a floral feminine perfume wafted from the wool trousers. He pulled away and stood up. "Have you been with a woman?" Rage flooded him.

Stanley stared levelly into Laurie's eyes. "What do you take me for?"

"Answer me. Have you been with a woman?"

Stanley struck him hard across the mouth.

Laurie turned his back to him, brought his hand to his lips, felt and tasted his blood. His fury seeped away.

And now it was Laurie who spilled tears silently. All the while, he found his own release in the pain so sweet that only Stanley could dispense.

How could he ever have doubted his one true love?

But the doubt crept back and followed him like a shadow. Laurie endeavored to ignore his suspicions and imaginative incriminations. But could Stanley love another—and a woman, at that? *I, myself, have enjoyed the company of both sexes now. Could he be like me?*

Stanley had left him and headed back to town two hours before. Laurie still sat by the entrance of the abandoned mine, sipping scotch from his flask, contemplating the night sky above. The idea that Stanley might even possibly love another consumed him, devoured any other notion. No, he could not go home. He must have some resolution, some answer to this nagging anxiety that harangued him unabated.

With the waning moonlight above and the twinkling gaslights of downtown below, Laurie headed west, down Fryer Hill, toward the little chapel on the south edge of Leadville, where the streams melded and became one river.

He rapped upon the door to Stanley's living quarters and heard a shuffling within.

Stanley opened the door, squinting into the darkness of the night. He gasped when he saw Laurie. "What are you doing here?"

"Please, allow me inside." Laurie did not await his answer but pushed his way past, into Stanley's dwelling.

An oil lamp burned upon the table, beside which a Bible lay open.

"You should not have come," Stanley said as he closed the door and walked toward him. "What if someone should see?"

"I don't care. I am past caring, don't you understand?"

Stanley placed his hands upon his hips and silently regarded Laurie.

Laurie trembled. How beautiful he was! How beautiful, yet fearful.

"What is it you want?" Stanley asked in a low voice.

"What do you think I want!" In his rage, Laurie kicked at one of the chairs. "I must have something more!"

"What more?" Stanley shouted, holding his hands out before him. "Did you not get your fill this night?"

"No!" Laurie smarted at Stanley's blunt words. "I shall never have enough!"

Stanley paced the room, tugging at his gathered hair. He stopped short and turned toward Laurie. "I don't know what more I can give you. I . . . I'm worn thin."

"How do you mean?" There it was again, this hint at his feeling of fatigue. "Do you grow weary of us?"

Stanley shook his head. "No. No, that's not it. I'm worn thin. I feel like one of those horses you see coming down the other side of Mosquito Pass, dripping sweat and foaming at the mouth from the effort of it all."

"The effort of what?" Laurie went to him and grabbed hold of his arms. "There should be no trying! Do I exhaust you somehow? Do you not take pleasure in this? Tell me, damn you!"

"Selfish thing, you!" Stanley shouted, shaking himself free of Laurie's grip. "You'll never understand."

"Let me try to understand! Explain yourself!"

"I can't ever begin. I can't . . ."

"Yes, yes you can. Please."

Stanley sat. He put his elbows upon the table, rested his forehead in his hands.

Laurie took the chair across from him, waiting for some revelation he both desired and dreaded.

"I am plagued by compulsions. My compulsions rule me, make me into a man I despise."

Does this all go back to religion once again? "I do not want to hear your religious lamentations."

Stanley dropped his hands and studied Laurie, a sad smile lifting his lips. "And so you do not want to understand me, then, despite your pleadings."

"I want to understand *you,* not your religion and your guilt."

"These are all a part of me. We all have our edifice, and when you remove one aspect or another, the edifice crumbles."

"An edifice is a physical structure and speaks nothing of the world within."

"Ah, you are a Romantic," Stanley said, chuckling, "through and through. Go and build your tiny hut upon the shores of Walden Pond.

Better yet, go and dress yourself in blue and buff and roam the streets of Wetzlar, pining away for your own selfish desires."

A sudden anger flared within Laurie. He gripped the corners of the table and leaned forward. "If I am Goethe's Werther, then it was you who made me so."

"Oh, it was I? Did you blame poor, guileless Lotte for Werther's demise?"

"You, sir, are no guileless Lotte."

Stanley sat back, regarding Laurie. "True. But I fear I am more like Dr. Frankenstein and you are the monster of my creation."

"Monster? Or the lonely, misunderstood creature who read and loved Goethe's Werther?"

"You are a clever student of literature, Laurie."

"And I grow weary of discussing it. Let's stop speaking of ourselves through literary metaphors. Speak to me of you, Stanley," Laurie pleaded, reaching past the gas lantern and taking hold of Stanley's hand. "Do you love me?"

Stanley's eyes narrowed as he removed his hand from beneath Laurie's. "In one breath you ask me to speak of myself, then, in the next, ask me to speak of you."

"Love is selfish."

"'Love is patient, love is kind. It does not envy, it does not boast, it is not proud.'" Stanley leaned forward, bracing the table, focusing his gaze upon Laurie. "'It does not dishonor others, it is not self-seeking, it is not easily angered, it keeps no record of wrongs. Love does not delight in evil but rejoices with the truth.'"

"That is a Bible verse, I take it."

"Yes, Corinthians thirteen."

"There are different kinds of love," Laurie argued. "This love—the love in the Bible—is the kind of love between family."

"It is *love*. There exists no other kind. What you call love is nothing but lust. You don't care about me, the inner workings of my heart. If you loved me you would embrace the religion and guilt that is so essential to the edifice of me." Stanley placed his hands over his chest.

Laurie drummed his fingers upon the table. Why speak of religion and guilt when one could speak instead of desire, when one could act upon desire? He realized that, for the first time, he wanted to dominate Stanley, to take and not be taken.

"I see desire in your eyes," said Stanley.

"How can you know?" Laurie asked.

"Don't play the skeptic now, Werther. I know you well enough, to see how your eyes narrow and glisten, to note the flush that creeps over those high cheekbones and the parting of your lips." He chuckled. "I speak of love, you think of lust."

"And do you feel that sort of pure love for me?" Laurie's insides tightened, and he steeled himself for the answer he feared.

"I love you in the way you want to be loved, in the way you desire to be loved." Stanley's gaze went to Laurie's lips, down his throat, to his chest.

He was succumbing, again. He was drowning in his desire. But before he let himself be fully submerged, he allowed himself to ask the question that had haunted him the whole way there. "Do you love anyone in the way it was written in Corinthians?"

Stanley abruptly rose from his chair and walked to a shelf that contained sundry pantry items. He busied himself with repositioning a can of coffee, a jar of preserves, a tin of soda crackers. "Yes."

"Who?" Laurie demanded, jealousy raising him out of the chair. "Look at me, Stanley!"

Stanley turned, but his gaze was upon the floorboards. "My family, of course." He rubbed at his forehead as though endeavoring to massage away a headache. "And my parishioners, my flock."

Yes, of course. Stanley was a good and dutiful man, and he would dearly love his own mother and father, brothers and sisters in this way. "But not another . . ."

"No, Laurie."

He smiled, but to Laurie it seemed artificial.

Stanley approached Laurie and embraced him. "Come now, my lover," he whispered down into his ear. "I'm weary of all this talk." He moved away, sliding his suspenders over his shoulders and unbuttoning his shirt. "I know what you want, Laurie. I know that you won't rest easy until you have it." He cast his shirt aside, then took Laurie's face in his hands and kissed him softly, gently.

Before he could stifle it, a moan of satisfaction escaped from Laurie's lips. He kissed Stanley back with the hunger he had been suppressing.

Stanley moved away from the kiss and began to unbutton Laurie's shirt. "Let's pretend we are not who we are. You be Werther, and you finally get to have your Lotte."

The sunlight found them. It worked its fingers round the flimsy white paper curtain that covered the window over Stanley's bed.

When Laurie's sleepy eyes adjusted, he saw Stanley leaning over him, studying him. When their eyes met, Stanley smiled, then trailed his finger gently along Laurie's cheek, down to his chin.

Peace filled Laurie's chest, cleared his mind, made him feel as though nothing else existed but this bed, the early-morning sun, and Stanley. He relived in his mind the prior hours, how he had made love to Stanley, how finally they had become one and there had been no pain, no subjugation nor humiliation. They had become one and no words had been said because none were needed. He laughed, unable to confine his joy. He felt beautiful and noble. He was the Lancelot to Stanley's King Arthur.

"What is it?" Stanley asked.

"You," Laurie whispered, reaching up to caress Stanley's face. "You love me."

The smile left Stanley's face as he moved from Laurie's caress and left the bed. He retrieved his drawers from the floor and donned them quickly. "You must leave now, Laurie. Ruth will be here soon enough to do the washing, and I must ready my sermon."

Laurie had just been cast out of heaven. He felt as though he were falling and falling and his heart remained above him, and he struggled to gain hold of it again and put it back into his chest.

"Come now, Laurie," Stanley said, tossing Laurie's clothes onto the bed. "Do you really want Ruth to find you here?"

Suddenly the tenderness of their prior meeting became a trivial memory. Perhaps it had meant nothing at all. Perhaps he had dreamed it.

Laurie sat up in the bed and stared down at his hands upon his lap.

"Laurie! Quickly!"

Now Laurie knew how it felt to be a loyal dog chastised by its master. Oh yes, the tender lovemaking? It had to have been a dream, for there they were, back to their old roles once again.

Laurie left the bed and dressed himself, numbing himself emotionally, for he realized he must go through town to head home and surely people would know his face. And his face could not betray any of this, oh god, no, or it would be his ruin.

But he turned at the door, looking at Stanley, who busied himself with the crank of a coffee grinder. "Goodbye, Stanley," Laurie muttered, not sure if Stanley heard him over the din of the grinder.

Stanley stopped and looked up at Laurie. The sunlight caught in his hair, highlighted the planes of his strong face. Laurie's breath caught in his throat as he recalled seeing Stanley illuminated just so, nearly a year and a half prior, in a dirty, hired coach in the Bowery.

"Go, Laurie. Leave me now."

Leadville had returned to its bustling beehive self once again, ever since the resolution of the mining strike. He knew he ought to go to his office at the Avalon that morning, but instead he lingered at home and wrote in his leather-bound journal, transcribing the prior evening and early morning's events well into the afternoon. He had kept a journal whilst at Cambridge, to chronicle all his exploits, and he had recently resumed this habit. It was a way to relive and revel in the pleasure, a second go-around.

"Oh!" Eileen stood in the doorway of the study with a book between her hands.

He raised his head, interrupted from his daydream. "Yes?"

"I was going to put this back and find another." She focused on his face—his mouth—and she gasped. "What happened to you?"

The swollen lip. He was prepared for the question and had formulated what he conceived was a good answer. "Lack of grace got the best of me. I stumbled up the stairs of the Avalon yesterday, just as Pickering had come for a chat."

Quizzically, she tilted her head to the side, seeming to ponder him. He could not say if she had bought his lie.

"You ought to ice that. I'll have Justine bring some."

"Nonsense, I don't require it," he replied, but she had gone before receiving his response. He sighed and resumed his journaling. He should feel some remorse—*look how she cares for me and my well-being.* But alas, he did not.

Laurie did not realize Justine was before him until she cleared her throat. He jumped and shut his journal with a resounding thud. "You ought to knock and make yourself known before entering a room. Didn't they teach you that in New Orleans?"

She regarded him with cool eyes and a slightly amused curl of the lip. "*They* didn't teach me that. *They* just taught me every other way imaginable how to please a white man. I suppose they must have forgotten that particular lesson."

Laurie was struck dumb.

She extended a wrapped ice chunk toward him. "Madame Eileen said you might need this for that bruise you got there on your mouth. Better ice it up good if you want to look presentable."

He took the proffered pack. "You certainly have a lot to say, don't you?"

She sauntered away, pausing in the doorway. "I guess I didn't get a lesson on when to shut my mouth in front of a white man, either."

"You're lucky my wife dotes on you so, and that you're such an extraordinary cook."

"Very lucky, indeed. Good day, Monsieur."

He shook his head at her audacity, then placed the ice pack upon his lower lip, which smarted mightily from the cold. He felt like a stranger in his own house. Had Justine spied his writing in the journal? He shook away this sudden anxious thought; certainly the chit was illiterate.

But the anxiety would not let go. He must get out of the house, he must see Stanley. Quickly he took a piece of stationery and wrote his usual request to meet. Within moments, Jacob was on his way to deliver it, with the instruction to await and return with the response.

Laurie paced the carpet before the study's hearth, a glass of brandy in hand. He swore an oath each time the clock chimed the hour. Two had passed with no word. What could that boy be up to? Could he have detoured to get into some mischief? It didn't seem like Jacob to do so.

Another half hour passed, and by now, Laurie had downed four glasses of brandy. His impatience flourished into anger. Slamming the empty crystal glass upon his desk, he exited the study and went to the foyer, to the base of the staircase.

"Eileen!" He waited exactly ten seconds before calling louder. "Eileen!"

"Yes, yes, I'm here." She stood at the top of the staircase, hands resting atop her growing belly. "What on earth is the trouble?"

He had to vent his frustration to someone. "I sent Jacob out with a letter over two and a half hours ago and told him to bring the response immediately. Where the devil could the boy be?"

Eileen slowly made her way down the stairs. "I haven't any idea. Where was he going?"

"One of my accountants."

"In town?"

"Yes, on Harrison."

"Do you think there could have been an accident?"

"I thought the same. Should I ride down and see for myself?"

"I suppose. It's not like Jacob to be late."

"I didn't think so, either."

She paused on the bottom step, before him. "It's a pity Seamus isn't here. You could have sent him."

It was just the sort of comment she would make, right when his temper was at its shortest. "Must you really—"

The front door burst open and Jacob stood at the threshold, breathless. "Sir, sir, you won't believe what happened! The streets are humming with the news. Pastor Jones has been shot dead!"

Silence descended upon the foyer.

"What did you say?" Eileen asked in a meek voice.

"Stanley Jones! He's been shot dead, right in his chapel!"

"Where did you hear this?" Laurie advanced upon Jacob and grabbed the lapels of his ill-fitting waistcoat. Laurie was in no mood for cruel jokes or unfounded, sensational gossip. "Tell me where you heard this!" he demanded through clenched teeth.

Jacob paled. "Sir, I heard it from one of the constables in front of the chapel. I went there with your letter, just as you told me, and when I got there, there was a small crowd gathered in front and about four constables blocking the chapel door—"

"Stanley?" Eileen gasped as she seated herself with a thud upon the bottom stair.

This must be a nightmare. Or the brandy was laced with laudanum. Laurie did not let go of Jacob's lapels. "When? How?"

Jacob breathed heavier, shaking his head frantically. "I don't know when. The constable said Mr. Jones was discovered by one of his Finnish parishioners this morning, before service. I don't know anything else."

A sound like the bugle of an elk filled the room. It was lonely and mournful and inhuman. It grew in volume, in its desperation. It came to a crescendo before capitulating into howls that tore from his wife. "No! Oh god, no!"

Laurie let go of Jacob and stared at her. She gulped for air, tearing at the high neck of her gown. Had such a terrible sound come from her?

"Eileen?"

She howled again, her face red, her fingers fighting with the chintz fabric of her neckline.

The dining room door opened with a crash as Justine rushed out. "What was that?" Her wide eyes took in the scene, finally settling upon Eileen. Justine went to her and deftly unfastened the tiny buttons at her neckline. "What's wrong, chérie?" She stood and rounded upon Laurie. "What have you done?"

The world—his world—was turning into liquid. Everything was running together so that he could not decipher the boundaries, the reality. Stanley was dead. What now? How could he swim in a liquid world?

"Answer me!" Justine shouted above Eileen's heaving, wild sobs.

"The Pastor Stanley Jones has been shot dead," Jacob said.

Justine gasped, stepping back. "Oh, Lord, no." She sat beside Eileen and held her like one might hold an injured child. "Come now, chérie, come now, breathe for me. Just breathe." She rocked Eileen against her.

"Not Stanley," Eileen cried. "No. Please, God, not him."

Eileen's beseechings mirrored Laurie's own inner voice, he now realized. Disbelieving her sentiment, finding it rang hollow and disingenuous, he wanted her silent. How dare she? "Compose yourself, Eileen. You are overreacting. This display is absurd."

Justine coaxed Eileen to rise and pressed her to go upstairs. "Go on, chérie, go on up, please. Chérie, please, for your own good . . ."

Laurie watched as Justine practically dragged his incoherent wife to the top of the stairway. Why was she so insistent in her desire to have Eileen away?

His feet followed them up the stairs on their own accord, as though his body knew what was transpiring before his mind comprehended. But halfway up the stairway, the realization hit him as quickly and powerfully as lightning. "You whore!"

Eileen fell to her knees before her bedchamber door. Justine, perspiring and breathing heavily, swore as she struggled to pull her off the floor.

"It was you!" he boomed in a low, feral voice foreign to his own ears. "It was *you* I smelled upon him!"

"Stop, please, Monsieur!" Justine pleaded in a shriek, holding her hands up to protect Eileen from any blow he might strike.

Jacob made his way up the stairs. "Sir, please, don't—"

Laurie shoved Justine aside, grabbed Eileen's wrists, and pulled his wife to her feet. If he could have, he would have crushed her bones within his hands. He pulsed with a hatred he had never experienced. He screamed into her face, "You took him from *me*! I gave you *everything*! I raised you from *nothing*! But it wasn't enough for you, you Irish slut!"

He shoved her into her bedchamber with all his might, ignoring the shrieks and protests of Justine and Jacob. The cat, who had been sunning herself on the settee at the window, shrieked and hissed, then bolted out of the room. He pushed with all his disgust, and she landed against her dressing table with a force that sent the bottles, brushes, and boxes flying and the mirror shattering down upon her. It was not enough. He pulled her slumped form up by the neck and wrapped his hands around it as tightly as he could. "You damned whore! How dare you betray me this way!"

She wheezed and gagged against his grip, clawing with bloody fingertips against his hands. Her eyes were as wide as he had ever seen them.

Jacob grappled at Laurie's arms and tried to force his hands away from Eileen. But it was the thump and crack of an object, wielded by Justine, against his head that defeated him and smote his murderous rage.

CHAPTER THIRTY-TWO

Eileen drifted, floated in a sea, the ebb and flow of which was between pain and a numbness more excruciating than the pain. All the while she skimmed, submerged her fingers in the liquid making her buoyant; it felt of fresh milk, of soapy laundry water, of hot, metallic-smelling blood soaking her nightdress between her thighs.

Her mother had lost three babes from her womb. Eileen, but a child, had not understood. She knew only that Ma, who was usually up before dawn and at her daily toil, had remained, moaning and pale, in her bed. The village midwife hummed a comforting melody whilst she flushed and washed Ma's insides with a tincture that smelled of pennyroyal and chamomile. Mary had whispered in Eileen's ear, "Ma lost the babe," and Eileen had fought back tears of bewilderment, not having known there was a babe—a sister or brother that might have been—to begin with.

Had she become her mother? Their moans were the same. She could only assume that the cramping, the strain beneath her navel, like a clock clanging every three minutes, was the same as her mother's pains. But, unlike her mother, she was confined to a bed made of fine goose down rather than straw, and there was no patient, wise, weathered midwife humming a sweet lullaby. Instead, there was Dr. Spencer, Dr. Spencer and his rueful eyes, and cold, dry fingers endlessly violating her until they struck her womb and he would mutter, "The uterus is slowly closing." And she did not know what this meant. Each time his fingers reached her womb, she would cry out at the intense cramping that seemed to reach her throat. She clawed at the bedsheets and writhed. She would have given the whole of her life to be a man at that moment, rather than a vessel, open, exposed, and vulnerable.

Minutes and days became interchangeable. What did it matter? She believed she was dying. Yet somehow her heart was more alive, more vigorous than ever. She knew this because never, never had she felt such an overwhelming ache. How could the rest of her be dying, how could her heart be rent in two yet larger, stronger than ever? Is the heart like a base yet tenacious worm, severed in half only to live on as two? Did she now have two hearts, two hearts to go on throbbing, hurting endlessly whilst the rest of her perished?

When her aching eyes scanned the bedchamber, she swore she saw an ethereal creature floating by the window. It had wings and was like a butterfly, yet when she stared harder, she saw that the body was that of a newborn.

"Was he baptized? I would not want him to linger here, in purgatory."

"That would be the laudanum talking," said Dr. Spencer, who never addressed her directly.

"Hush, chérie," whispered Justine. "I blessed the baby. He's in heaven now."

"Justine, will you hum me a song like the midwife did for my mama?"

"Yes, gladly." Justine hummed a melody foreign to Eileen, but ever so soothing.

Eileen drifted on the sea toward the place of numbness, only to have a wave crash against her and bring her back to pain.

"Doctor," she heard Justine say in a low tone, "you stick your fingers inside her one more time and I swear I'll cut them off, you hear? You let nature do its thing. She knows better than your man hands ever will 'bout how to heal herself."

"I'll see to it that you lose your job over such insubordination," Dr. Spencer snapped. But he, thankfully, removed his fingers from within her.

Abruptly the wave dissipated and Eileen wept in gratitude. "I love you, Justine."

The heart is a base creature. Eileen acknowledged this as the laudanum's blanketing refuge retreated from her, and her womb's fiery anger slowly smote and burned itself out.

The heart thinks only of itself, its desires and longings. And is it ever satisfied? Unlike a beast, it is never appeased with indulgent caresses, sweet words, hearty sustenance, unencumbered sleep. No, the heart is constantly in pursuit, furious in its selfishness.

She wanted not to suffer anymore. She wanted to be free of past folly—how had she ever? Her mind endeavored to force the heart into a crate, thrusting self-deprecating words like metal bull hooks between the wooden slats. She had seen a bear-baiting in her village when she was five, had winced each time the wretched beast was jabbed within the crate when the entertainment was finished. She recalled how she had longed to take the bull hook from the baiter's grimy hands and prod him in the arse. Her hatred had been palpable—she could barely contain her fast breathing.

See? See how the heart cannot be contained?

Hatred? Perhaps, but there would be more of that later. For now, the heart, like some foreign thing from the depths of the ocean washed ashore, throbbed and writhed in a sadness that was infinite. "Infinite"—she had learned this word from Laurie early in their courtship, when he quite possibly had loved her? She could never know for certain. The past year of her life was like a play in three parts performed in a round theater—there was no place to hide, no place unseen, all corners exposed, her heart as open and vulnerable to leers and ridicule as her womb had been to Dr. Spencer's unyielding fingers.

If she could have ripped her heart from her chest, she would have—to be done with her inconsolable heart just as her womb had furiously expelled an unloved, unwanted babe. Poor, poor sweet babe! No, no, no, no, she did not mean those things, her poor sweet babe. At moments she would have torn down Mount Elbert with her bare hands so that she could hold the baby, the dulcet, innocent, vulnerable baby! Stop, stop the pain, sweet Mary, Mother of God.

How can one love a thing that did not fully exist in the world? Eileen asked herself this as she sat up in bed and took her first sip of tea in an eternity. *It's not the thing, but the idea of the thing and the dreams and hopes pinned upon the thing, is it not?*

She gasped, spilling some of the tea out of the cup and into the saucer she held in her hands. The thing was like Stanley. Had Stanley—*her* Stanley—ever really existed? Or had she pinned her ultimate desire upon a man who was nothing but enslaved to his own proclivities and desires?

No, no, no, she would not let her mind go to that place, for when it did, her heart became a pot boiled over, sizzling upon the flame. But it mattered not how much she might scold herself. The tears came in a torrent, her chest heaving with the weight of it. She clasped her hands over her nightdress and wondered: Would her eyes ever again be unswollen? Would this ever end?

He was gone. Taken from her.

Her husband had come to her bedside on many occasions.

"Hello, Eileen. How are you feeling today?"

She had peered over the covers to get a look at him. His eyes were wide, like a frightened boy's. What did he want from her? Not love, certainly. Some kind words to appease his guilt? Never. Did he seek companionship in the wake of his own shattered heart? Then there was never a greater fool than he.

Justine had told her of the journal and its contents. There was no lock on this earth that Justine couldn't undo with a hairpin, her keen ear, and nimble fingers. It had been quick work for her.

When Eileen had first learned of Laurie's affair, her stomach had turned over and she'd retched into the chamber pot.

The second time she contemplated it, she was flooded with an anger unlike any she had ever known.

The third time she wept, for she had been deceived twice over.

The fourth time she damned herself, for letting herself be deceived twice over.

The fifth time she tried to imagine Stanley and Laurie together and found it instantly beautiful. Yet then she broke into tears again that someone had taken her lover from her.

Who had taken her lover from this world?

CHAPTER THIRTY-THREE

For two days Laurie had not slept.

His throat ached from the silent sobbing, and each time he swallowed, he was reminded of his grief. Who had taken his lover from this world? He must know.

He rode into town to see the constable, to ascertain whether the man had yet discovered who had murdered Stanley Jones. The newspapers proclaimed it a mystery. But surely, the constable must know something more.

He would have come sooner but had remained at home during his wife's trials, had witnessed the lifeless bundle wrapped in linen spirited away in Dr. Spencer's hands. Laurie's mind puzzled over how he had become a father and was no longer a father and how it had all been his doing. He wept over this, for truly he was guilty of this crime. He kept vigil at his wife's side, wiping her brow and dispensing laudanum between the sweet, sweet lips he had always admired.

It was not love but tenderness he felt for her. He could not love her, he thought, with that burning feeling in his gut that he knew was the remains of his initial inferno of anger. She had deceived him with the man he loved. But he soon realized, as he stroked her fine auburn curls away from her face and studied her creamy skin, that he admired her like one admires a fine piece of art, and he felt kindred to her, for they had loved the same man. It was as though she were a living aspect of Stanley, for she had known him so very intimately, too.

He must make it up to her, somehow, for all this pain he had brought upon her. He was not a violent man, he reasoned. It had been temporary madness incited by jealousy. Many men have devolved to such base actions in the heat of emotion, of course. Why would he be any different from his fellow man? Oh, but he was very different, he knew. Men schemed, vied, injured, and even killed to possess the women of their desires. But he had desired a man. Did this make him unnatural and perverse? Again, how could a love so strong be wrong or flawed?

"I'm sorry, Mr. Barnard," Constable Harris said with a sigh as he plopped down in a chair on the opposite side of his desk. "We've reached a dead end, so to speak. My men and I have nothing to work with. No evidence, no witnesses, nothing. Unless someone should pass along some incriminating information to someone else and that person relays this to us, I'm afraid the murderer shall remain at large."

Laurie gripped the wooden chair arms. "Have you not sent investigators out into the city, to question or eavesdrop?"

Constable Harris chuckled as he stroked his bearded chin. "Mr. Barnard, I am compelled to say that our victim was a clergyman, not some gambler, politician, or nefarious posse member. Now, had he been any of those, I'd know just where and to whom to send my investigators for questioning. I have not an inkling of an idea of who might have it out for a man of the cloth."

Laurie rose from his chair and paced the unpolished pine floorboards of the office as he ran his hands through his hair. It was maddening to him that there was no resolution to this matter and that there may never be. "I find this terribly unacceptable, Constable Harris. What is it that you might require to properly and effectively discharge your duty as a keeper of the peace in this city?"

Constable Harris grimaced, tilting his head and regarding Laurie for a moment. "With all due respect, Mr. Barnard, I do my best to keep the peace in this city. I do not require any pecuniary incentive, if that is what you are so mistakenly implying."

Laurie sniffed at this.

"Might I be so bold to ask, why do you take such an interest in this case? By my knowledge, you were not a regular parishioner in the Reverend Jones's church."

"I and my wife were married by him," Laurie tossed out quickly. He hoped that the heat rising to his cheeks was not visible to the constable.

Constable Harris slowly nodded, still studying him. "Ah, yes, I do recall that."

This was followed by silence. Laurie sat down in the chair again, folding his hands before him. "It seems to me, Constable Harris, that we should be concerned not only with the murders of prominent gamblers in this town, but perhaps also with the murders of upstanding, righteous citizens such as Mr. Jones."

"Of course, Mr. Barnard, I heartily concur."

There was a loud knock upon the constable's office door.

"What is it?" called Constable Harris.

A breathless officer quickly entered. "Sir, we've apprehended a murderer and have her in custody."

"*Her?* A woman? Who is the victim? One of her johns?"

"No, sir. The victim is Bill Denahy, the wheelwright, and the murderer is his wife, Ruth."

Laurie started at the news. "Ruth Denahy? She has killed her husband?"

"Details, Officer James," barked Constable Harris.

"Shot him in the face with a shotgun, just this morning, sir. Neighbors said he had been out on a drinking binge the past two days. Wasn't like him to do so. The wife had been beside herself. Again, wasn't like her to be in such a state, either, as they say she was as quiet and sullen as a mouse. But she ain't no mouse now that we have her in custody. She bit one of the officer's hands right through the skin while they were apprehending her."

The constable rose from his chair, muttering, "What in damnation could all this be about? Seems things are even more topsy-turvy around here than usual." He followed the officer out of the room and down the hall to the stairway.

Laurie joined the men, only to have Constable Harris turn around at the top of the stairway. "Mr. Barnard, you need not concern yourself with such sordid business as this."

"Nonsense," Laurie replied, gesturing toward the stairway, for he, too, was curious to learn the details.

The constable sighed, shaking his head. "Very well, sir, but don't say I didn't warn you."

Ruth Denahy, a murderer? As he followed behind the constable and the officers, he remembered the last time he had seen Ruth. It had been during winter, that day long ago when he had visited Stanley, who had been ice fishing out in the streams beyond the chapel. Laurie stopped dead in his pace down the hall. Bill Denahy had been drinking for two days and Ruth had been "inconsolable." His heart and mind began to race. He recalled the last time he had seen plain, dour Ruth. She had finished her chores tending house for Stanley Jones, and she had looked upon Stanley with such unbridled adoration.

Two days. For two days she had been inconsolable and her husband had been drinking, until today, when she had shot him dead. Two days had lapsed since Stanley Jones's murder. "My god."

Laurie raced down the stairs, after the constable and officer.

The din of rowdy, angry prisoners in holding cells of the female wing of the jail filled Laurie's ears. The scantily clad women in ragged, filthy chemises and petticoats, scratching at themselves and their lice-ridden hair, reminded Laurie of depictions of the old Newgate Prison by the likes of Defoe and Dickens. Some laughed and hollered and banged tin cups against the cell bars. Laurie mused that perhaps a prison was a prison, no matter where in the world it might be—Old World or new frontier.

Officers were gathered before the last cell, struggling to subdue the prisoner. He quickly made his way, not bothering to cover his nose against the reek of unwashed bodies and human filth.

He witnessed her, Ruth Denahy, as she struggled against the shackles newly clasped to her wrists. Her usually tightly bound brown hair was like a bird's tangled nest round her face, which was ruddy, sweating. Her nose was swollen and profusely bleeding into her gaping mouth and down her chin and the front of her ripped, disheveled dress. Never could he have imagined her so wild and alive. Her pupils were dilated as she caught sight of Laurie. She paused in her screaming and struggling. She stared at him as though pleading for something—he knew not what. And then she broke down into sobs, crumpling to the hay-strewn floor of the cell, forming herself into a tight, quaking ball.

The crowd of officers was silenced, the shouts of the female prisoners abated, yet still they clattered upon the cell bars with their tin cups. The clamor was an eerie, off-key symphony to the drama unfolding before Laurie. He stepped closer to Ruth's cell.

"Mr. Barnard, sir!" shouted Constable Harris over the din. "I must urge you not to interfere in this matter—"

He did not heed the warning. "Ruth, I beg you, tell me who killed Stanley Jones."

Slowly she raised her head from her arms and knees. Those wild, black eyes searched his. "My husband killed Stanley Jones," she said in a low, calm voice, "and so I have killed him."

A murmur ran through the officers. The prisoners resumed their shouts and catcalls, adding insults and slurs against their new fellow prisoner.

"Why did your husband kill Stanley Jones?" asked Laurie, his voice trembling with a sudden fear of what she might reveal.

She began to weep again.

"Ruth, look at me," ordered Laurie in a stronger voice. "Tell me why."

"You knew him!" she shouted.

Laurie's heart raced. What did this woman know? Was it something to do with him? Did he stand, before these officers and the constable, on the precipice of his own ruining?

"You knew Stanley Jones, Mr. Barnard. You knew his power, his ability to persuade." Ruth shook her shackles as she unfurled herself to a seated position upon the cell floor. "He was my lover. Yes, I was an unfaithful wife!" she confessed. "I was a sinner! I was the preacher's lover!"

Laurie stepped back from the cell as though he had touched a flame. "You?" Did she jest?

"Yes, me! What?" she asked, rising to her feet. "Do you think me too plain to be a man's mistress? Stanley Jones loved me. He *loved* me!"

The prisoners jeered loudly.

"Nearly ten months I was Stanley Jones's mistress and my husband never knew. The fool!" She cackled, and the sound was haunting.

"And how did he learn of your transgressions?" asked Constable Harris.

"He finally discovered us. And I was glad of it! He came round to the church early to take me home, and he found us together in the reverend's living quarters." She broke into fits of wild laughter. "But you should have seen the look on his face!"

"And then what?" barked the constable.

"And then he went back to his wagon and got his shotgun . . . shot my sweet love in the face. I returned the favor this morning . . ." Her laughter resumed, but it sounded forced.

Laurie could not listen to any more. It was like a nightmare. He swiftly made his way down the hall of cells, past the shouting prisoners, up the stairs, and out through the constable's headquarters. He was flooded with panic, shocked by this sudden, unexpected development. When he reached the boardwalk of Harrison Avenue, he retched bile, garnering a few complaints and oaths from passersby, who stepped quickly out of the way. An approaching officer recognized him, likely as the richest man in town, and solicitously offered assistance, which Laurie dismissed as he reached the hitching post and untied the reins of his horse.

As he rode back to his home, Laurie felt as though a curtain had been lifted, revealing a reality quite changed from the one he had originally perceived. When he had learned of Eileen's transgression, it had shocked him to the core, yet because Stanley's deceit had been with his own wife, it somehow, strangely, felt as though their affair were an aspect of his own life—a part of him. Now, to learn of this other deceit, it seemed as though he were reading a salacious novel, only to surprisingly find that he'd been one of the players in it and that it had been no fiction at all.

He must tell Eileen. She would want to know. She must desire to know who killed her lover, as had he.

When he arrived home he went straight to Eileen's bedchamber. She was sitting up in bed, holding a cup and saucer, a blank look upon her pale face. He was surprised not to see her lying prone, as she had the past two days. He stood by her bed, staring at her, wringing his brown leather riding gloves in his hands.

"Have you some news?" she asked calmly, as though reading his thoughts. Her green eyes met his, but he did not see eagerness in their depths.

"Do you want to know?"

She placed the cup and saucer down upon her lap, then looked up into his eyes again. "I know you want to tell me something."

"Don't you want to know who did it?"

"I don't know that 'want' is the right word. Perhaps I'm resigned to learn the truth of it."

Laurie took a nearby chair, brought it to Eileen's bedside, and seated himself. "This morning Ruth Denahy was arrested for shooting her husband."

Eileen's brows drew together. She looked down at the cup on her lap, then back to him. "I did not expect this news. What provoked her? Do we know?"

"He found her with Stanley."

He watched her eyes grow wide, heard the slight gasp escape her lips.

He could not wait a moment longer. Now, he thought with odd amusement, now he knew how the Papists felt when they hurried themselves to the confessional to unburden their sins.

"She was Stanley's lover for the past ten months, she claims. Two mornings ago Bill Denahy arrived at the church to find the two of them together. He shot Stanley between the eyes. This morning, he was found in a similar state—"

He was interrupted by the sound of Eileen's cup rattling in its saucer as she quickly raised it toward him to take away. He did so, briefly touching her icy-cold fingers.

"Is it true?" she asked in little more than a whisper.

"She confessed it today to the constable. I was there to hear it."

The two sat in silence.

"We've deceived each other, and now we've been deceived by another," Laurie said.

Eileen shook her head. "Never would I have guessed it of the likes of Ruth Denahy, that sour-faced prude."

Surprised laughter escaped from Laurie. "Indeed!"

Their eyes met. A sudden fear seized Laurie, a fear that, were he to lose Eileen, he would be completely alone. She was his Guinevere. Stanley, he realized, had been Lancelot. Had Laurie been a cuckolded Arthur all along? No, it was not so simple as that, of course. But Eileen, she knew him, understood his heart as no other could because she had loved and lost Stanley, too. He could love her again, yes, he could, because she had lost what he had lost and their hearts had been equally broken. He must not lose her, too. He could not carry on alone. The thought, the vision, was terrifying.

"What is it?" she asked.

Timidly he put his outstretched hand upon the bed, hoping she might take it. But before he could find the words to express the fear in his heart in a way that might persuade her to have him again, there was a knock upon the bedchamber door.

"Yes?" asked Eileen.

"There is a Mr. Rask here to see Monsieur Barnard," said Justine.

Laurie rose from the chair and opened the door. "Who the devil is Mr. Rask? Did you ask for his card?"

Justine held the card before her. "I'm not stupid, Monsieur Barnard."

He took it from her hands, to learn that Mr. Thomas Rask was an attorney, certified by the State of Colorado. "Show him into the study."

The man seated before his desk—the lawyer Thomas Rask—was perhaps approaching middle life yet still youthful in appearance. Small in stature, Mr. Rask had a foreign look to him, rather like a sprite grown up, with unruly brown curls in need of a good trimming. His big brown eyes, peering through small spectacles, darted round the study, as though taking every detail in, yet displayed no reaction to what he observed. When his eyes finally met Laurie's, there was a determined set to them, signaling that he was ready to begin the business at hand.

"Mr. Barnard, I come here, charged with my client's affairs."

The accent was odd. Magyar? But the surname was not Hungarian. "Mr. Rask, I detect an accent."

"I come from Finland, Mr. Barnard. But I am an American now." He showed no surprise at the question.

"Ah, of course. Proceed."

Upon his lap Mr. Rask opened a black leather briefcase, quickly producing a document. He closed the case and put the document atop it, then adjusted his spectacles. "My client has named you the executor of his will and testament."

Laurie started at this. "And who is—or rather, was—your client?"

"Mr. Stanley Jones, sir."

A cold wind's fingers trailed up the nape of Laurie's neck. "Truly?" he muttered before he could check himself.

"Yes, Mr. Barnard. Did my late client not make you aware of this?"

"No, no, he did not."

"Well, I am sorry to inform you so soon after his passing."

"Not at all. Proceed." Laurie was eager to hear his lover's last words, his intentions, his requests. Laurie's heart quickened as though he might receive one last kiss, one last declaration of love.

Mr. Rask cleared his throat as he held the document before him. "'I, Stanislav Jankowski—'"

"Who?" Laurie demanded, his hands pressing down upon the ink blotter.

"Allow me to proceed, Mr. Barnard."

"But you said this was the will of Stanley Jones, did you not?"

"Yes, Mr. Barnard. If you would allow me to proceed, you shall see."

Laurie nodded. "Go on, then."

"'I, Stanislav Jankowski, otherwise known by my Americanized name of Stanley Jones, hereby lay out my will and testament.

"'I name my friend and business associate Mr. Lawrence Barnard, of Leadville, Colorado, the executor of my estate and posthumous wishes.'"

Stanislav Jankowski? Laurie's mind tried to make sense of this new revelation. "I was under the impression that Mr. Jones was an American by birth. Was he not?"

"No, sir," replied Mr. Rask, again appearing unbothered by any question that Laurie might present him. "Mr. Jones, as you knew him, was an immigrant from Poland."

Laurie suddenly remembered the moments when he had detected a slight accent in Stanley's speech yet could not place it. He recalled the foreign style of Stanley's penmanship, much like that of the German tutor of his childhood. He thought of the time when he had asked Stanley where he was from, and Stanley's adamant response that he was born an American. *Fooled, once again. A cuckold I have been, through and through.*

"Shall I proceed?" Mr. Rask regarded him.

"Please."

"'I direct that my body be embalmed by a mortuary of Mr. Barnard's choosing. I then request that my remains be held until they can be claimed by my wife, Mrs. Yvonne Jankowski, of Brooklyn, New York.'"

Laurie bolted out of his chair, the sudden force of his movement knocking it over. His heart raced, and his fingers tingled with the shock of this revelation. "Wife? *Wife?* How . . ."

"You were not aware, Mr. Barnard?"

"Heavens, no!" He laughed nervously, raking his hands through his hair. He laughed again, at himself, at the absurdity of the whole situation. How completely, how wholly, he had been deceived.

"Shall I continue, Mr. Barnard? This news seems to have unsettled you. I can certainly proceed with this business when you are better prepared—"

"I don't believe I can ever be prepared, Mr. Rask."

A wife! A wife in Brooklyn! It was unfathomable. It was as though Mr. Rask had opened a door and a cliff's edge lay beyond it. He looked down at the lawyer, whose hands clasped and unclasped upon the document before him. Finally, the Finn showed a small sign of emotion; Laurie's reaction had unnerved him. Laurie was glad of it. It would be unfair if he were the only person in the room who was unsettled by the ghost of Stanley Jones. He studied the sprite-like lawyer. How had Stanley Jones known him? His suspicions—and jealousy—arose. "How did Stanley Jones come to hire your services as lawyer?"

"I was a member of his parish, Mr. Barnard."

"Was that all you were?" Laurie lashed out.

Mr. Rask seemed to gulp. "How do you mean, sir? I do not understand your question."

Laurie shook his head, trying to banish his irrational anger. "Dare I say, proceed, Mr. Rask."

The lawyer took a breath, returning to the document before him. "'I wish my wife to have my remains interred in the burial ground of my own church, beside the streams that form the Arkansas River. I am not fit to be interred in the sacred ground of our Catholic parish of Saint Casimir, Brooklyn, New York.'"

His church! His wife! Laurie laughed again. "Proceed, Mr. Rask!"

"'I direct that my executor then deliver into my wife's hands the cash money of my savings, which is in the safe keeping of my lawyer, Mr. Thomas Rask, of Finntown, Colorado.'"

"And how much is that?" Laurie shot back.

Patting the briefcase upon his lap, Mr. Rask replied, "Mr. Jones entrusted me with $17,547 in cash, sir."

Laurie pondered this information as he righted his desk chair and resumed it. "That's quite a large sum of cash for a humble preacher."

"I believe that Mr. Jones grubstaked a few prospectors within his parish, some of whom found success in California Gulch."

Yet another revelation. Laurie sighed. "Is there anything else contained in this will?"

"'Lastly, I direct my executor deliver into the hands of his wife, Mrs. Eileen Barnard, my mother's garnet-beaded rosary.'"

Laurie slammed his hand down upon his desk. Deceived to the very end! "Damn it all!" he exclaimed.

"Sir?"

Laurie felt the acerbic smile spread over his lips, the bile percolating in his stomach. Was there not one crumb of kindness left for him? "Continue, Mr. Rask."

"'Let this be my last will and testament, signed this day, May 2, 1880.'"

A silence descended upon the study. In order to hide his struggle with tears, Laurie glanced down at his gold pocket watch, fiddled with the gear. How? How was there nothing more? How could Stanley leave him alone in the world? How could he name him executor to his estate, only to hand out kindness to others and leave nothing for him? What cruel trick was this?

Laurie had never known true hate before. But he recognized it instantly. It was uncannily similar to the bubbling, churning molten lava within the depths of Mount Vesuvius. On his grand tour, he had paid a local to guide him up the steep, rocky, barren slopes of the volcano that loomed over Pompeii. Once they had reached the crater edge, he'd had to cover his nose and mouth with a handkerchief as he peered down into the smoking depths, for the sulfuric steam was putrid and overpowering. But my, such a marvelous yet terrifying thing he had never witnessed in all his life. And now, at this very moment, in his book-lined study, some eleven thousand feet above the sea, he stood witness again, and the marvelous, terrifying thing was inside him, threatening to destroy the civilization within him at any given moment. He felt the hatred like nature waiting at the most inopportune, random moment to unleash her fury on the unsuspecting humanity.

"I am most sorry, Mr. Barnard," the lawyer said, interrupting Laurie's contemplations, "if you expected something different from Mr. Jones's final will. Such an unfortunate tragedy, his passing."

And there it was, like a deluge that smote the volcano: the undying love, the inescapable longing. Just the mere mention of Stanley's death brought forth such a flood that it snuffed the volcano within him as though it were naught but a candle by a windowpane. He must speak. He must speak now or the tears would overcome him, get the best of him. He must speak to save face in front of this Finnish lawyer. He cleared his throat and the pain, the struggle within his throat to form sound, he thought, was like torture. "Has Mr. Jones provided the address of his . . . widow?"

Such things are easily completed when money is of no object. A telegram, along with a wire transfer of funds to provide for travel costs, were dispatched to Mrs. Yvonne Jankowski via Laurie's business agents in New

York City. The body was delivered from the Leadville city morgue to a reputable mortuary. When Laurie exited the mortuary he had to pause upon the boardwalk, breathing slowly, deliberately through his nose until the nausea passed.

And there was the rosary, which he was charged with delivering into the hands of his wife—his lover's lover. One day had passed since the reading of Stanley's will. He had not yet found the strength within himself to tell Eileen all this information, this sudden revelation of yet another aspect of Stanley's secret life. He knew it would come as a shock to her, just as it had to him. But it was the last piece of business to execute before the arrival of Stanley's widow, and he longed to unburden himself of it, like one longs to shake oneself free from a nightmare come morning.

Clutching the worn, flimsy cardboard jewelry box in his palm, Laurie knocked gently upon Eileen's bedchamber door, awaiting her response before entering.

She sat at her dressing table, before the mirror, which was laced with a web of fractures and missing shards as a result of his rage some days before. Her green eyes were reflected a hundred times over in the numerous remaining slivers of glass. And all the eyes were focused upon him, like an audience awaiting the performer, like the gallery of a courtroom expecting the verdict.

His hands perspired, further weakening the worn cardboard box held captive in his hand. He was loath to part with it; he felt this acutely. It was a last physical vestige of Stanley, and an envy welled up inside him before he could even speak.

"Yes?" Still she did not turn away from the broken mirror, allowing her fractured reflections to meet him instead.

He licked his lips before speaking. "I ought to have that repaired, shouldn't I?" He hated that his voice came meekly.

Finally she shifted upon the bench, meeting his gaze. Her eyes went to his hand, which grasped the box. "What have you there?"

He slowly approached, and when he was before her, he knelt, so that their eyes would be level. He noted her slight flinch at his closeness. He longed to both strike her and caress her. She was maddening. Her mere proximity stirred such duplicity within him. He must be away, be done with this deed.

He held the box before her, offering it to her.

"This was left to you by him." His voice cracked.

Her brows drew together. "Him?" She tenuously took the worn box from his hand. "Stanley?"

He could only nod, for if he spoke again, the tears would surely come, unabated.

She removed the lid, a little gasp escaping her as she eyed the contents. Delicately, she lifted a strand of glowing garnet beads, as rich as droplets of blood. She tossed the rest of the box upon the dressing table and held the rosary, suspended between them. The golden crucifix dangled there. "Oh!" she said in a trembling voice. A wry smile crept over her lips. She shook her head, a silent laugh escaping her. "Oh, how could he!"

Instinctively he placed his hands upon her knees. She did not shy from his touch.

"There is something more," he said in a low, trembling voice.

Slowly, she let the rosary cascade into her palm. "Tell me, Laurie. We're beyond secrets now."

The sound of his name from her lips was like a comforting caress. He gave in. He wrapped his arms round her waist and laid his head upon her lap. "He had a wife. She arrives in one week." A sob escaped him. He turned his face into her lap, burying it in the folds of her skirts in shame.

"Oh!" Her body quaked. "How *could* he?" she gasped.

Her hand glided over his hair, down to the nape of his neck. He tightened his grip round her waist. She was the last vestige. "Eileen. Please, don't leave me."

There was a long silence as she continued to stroke his hair as though he were a distraught child.

"Eileen?" He lifted his head from her lap and met her gaze.

She did not cry. She was the picture of composure, her sweet lips slightly parted. "Hush," she said, drawing her thumb over his cheekbone, wiping away fresh tears.

"Don't leave me, Eileen. Not now."

CHAPTER THIRTY-FOUR

"You gonna come on outside and help me hang the laundry."

"What?"

"You heard me," Justine replied as she handed Eileen a cup of the chicory coffee she so loved. "It's Florence's day off, so you gotta get up off that chair, get some fresh air, get moving so your mind stop spinning so much."

When she stepped out the door, Eileen's eyes throbbed painfully in protest of the relentless Leadville sunshine. Her whole body jolted like she had been struck by lightning. This sensation happened often, as she had refused laudanum for the past five days. Despite its frequency, Eileen found she could not get used to it. She quaked and tried to shake herself free from the inevitable numbness that followed the jolt.

Justine plopped a large basket of laundry on the ground. "You know what to do, I expect. I'll be inside starting dinner."

Though the aching of her heart might betray her—*damn heart*—she had begun to persuade herself to loathe the memory of Stanley, to hate the penetrating wound of his deceit.

Soon she completed the task of hanging the wet laundry on the lines behind the house. In the intense sunlight and bone-dry wind, the linens were already almost dry. Just then the wind picked up. The laundry danced gracefully, then jerked with a revivalist's fervor. She watched, noticed how the linens shone so very white in this relentless sunlight.

Her nightdress, though, escaped the clutches of its clothespins. It frantically fled, headed toward the shelter of the meager, gradually deforesting woods beyond.

Eileen swore, hiked up her skirts, and ran uphill after it. The dancing laundry on the line struck her face, her neck, her arms, as though insulting her, taunting her that she'd even think she might be able to catch the runaway dress.

Her boots were unsteady upon the craggy earth, her steps clumsy as she struggled uphill.

The nightdress floated upward, above Eileen, then arched its body, arms spread open, chest heaving toward the sunshine.

Eileen squinted up to the sky as the fabric danced in the sunlight. She jumped, arms above her head, endeavoring to claim the elusive dress, but to no avail. She jumped higher, her body, her breath, straining against her stays. Jolt after jolt of the laudanum shakes raced through her body. She grunted, gasped, as the nightdress escaped her grasp.

The wind whipped at her body, her skirts, her hair. The nightdress swooped close to the ground, like a hawk hunting prairie dogs, then resumed its flight toward the woods uphill.

Eileen gave chase again. She threw her whole body into her long strides. The nightdress was too lithe, too quick, for her to catch. And when she reached the edge of the clearing, where the pathetic stand of woods took over the mountain, she watched helplessly as it fled upward and onward, like a discarded newspaper.

"Like a ghost," Eileen whispered. A little shiver went up her spine when she recalled Mary's tale of the white ghost she claimed to have seen as a child in the churchyard in Limerick.

She then, finally, allowed herself to think of Mary, Mary's big, determined blue eyes, stubborn pout, and joyous smile, generous arms that would be her own undoing. Eileen's insides lurched at the remembrance of her sister. "Mary," she whispered to the nightdress as it moved farther and farther away from her. "Mary, but I miss you. But I miss you so." She was startled to feel a few tears spill down her cheeks because she hadn't blinked, her gaze so intent upon the nightdress that she now believed was a palpable aspect of her missing sister.

"Forgive me, Mary."

And just then, the nightdress dropped, lifeless, to the ground. Like a woman fainting, like a ghost vaporizing, the fabric lost all its humanlike form and collapsed.

Down the mountain, in town, a train whistle blew. Yes, finally, Leadville had gotten her railway, just two weeks prior, to connect her to the rest of the world. The sound echoed, reached, called to Eileen.

She gasped, returning to reality, to the mountainside of Fryer Hill, above Leadville on a sunny, windswept day. She looked down at her boots, then toward the place where Mary's ghost had lingered ever so briefly.

She wiped her cheeks with the back of her hand and reluctantly turned away from Mary's ghost, leaving the nightdress. She made her way back down the mountainside, to where the laundry now hung motionless, like a crowd of onlookers.

By the time she returned inside the house, sat down in the parlor, and caught her breath, Eileen had remembered her dream, the promise she had made to Mary and that Mary had made to her.

"Mrs. Barnard?" Jacob stood in the doorway of the parlor, holding a small piece of paper. "A telegram has come for you."

Never before had Eileen received a telegram. The service had only arrived in Leadville last fall. Curious, she held her hand out for the paper. After Jacob left, she opened it.

> Am in Deadwood, Dakota Territory. Have housing and manage saloon. The Golden Spigot. Gave

> birth two months ago. A boy. Stanley Jones, father. Shall raise myself. Don't tell him. I don't need man.
> Love, Mary

The paper fluttered out of her fingers, down to the carpet. She gulped for air, suddenly realizing she had been holding her breath. First shock, like a tree struck by lightning on the mountainside. How? When? Even her sister had fallen prey? Then elation, that Mary was alive. Happiness, that she had written and told her where she was. Gladness, that she'd spent the extra to say "love." Wonder, that she was an auntie. And then, then, had she read that part right? Eileen retrieved the telegram and ran to the kitchen.

"What's that you've got there?" asked Justine, who was chopping ingredients for dinner.

Eileen tried to speak, but couldn't find words. She waved the telegram before Justine, offering it to her.

Justine quickly wiped her hands on her apron and took the telegram. Her eyes widened and she gasped. She looked to Eileen. "Lord above!" She shook her head. "Lord above . . . Stanley Jones?"

The sudden revelation caused an uncontrollable laughter to bubble out of Eileen, because it didn't even seem real. She put her hand to her mouth to stifle it. Her cheeks were wet.

"That man was something else." Justine studied her. "Are you upset?"

When Eileen had caught her breath, she said, "No. Nothing can surprise me anymore. Nothing at all! He played us all like fiddles, and he was Mozart or somebody! I've seen and heard everything. I'm an auntie. She still loves me." And Eileen broke into laughter again, but it wasn't her normal laughter. It sounded hysterical, slightly mad. She held her arms out to take Justine in an embrace, because she felt unmoored.

Justine held her and rocked to and fro. "My oh my, it's like one of them Italian operas or something. It's crazy!"

"Thank God she isn't in Leadville, for all of this. Thank God in heaven," Eileen said, wondering how Mary might have reacted to all this mess.

"But wait, there was something I was needing to do." Eileen remembered, let go of Justine, and left the kitchen.

She went upstairs to her bedroom and walked to the settee. Bending over, she reached beneath to grab hold of the handles on either side of her travel trunk—the one she had brought with her from New York. She pulled it out, then knelt down before it, unlatched the locks, and lifted the lid. She was met with a musty scent that transported her back to her tiny attic room on the top of Mrs. Brown's. Gingerly she pushed aside her two dresses, old winter coat, and various knitted wool scarves, to reveal what had been theirs. She remembered a brick in a wall in a small, dingy room on the fifth floor of a brothel, her fingers deftly removing the brick and retrieving the rusted tin can. She wrapped her fingers around that same rusted tin can and pulled it out. The worn bills and cool coins saw the light of day in Leadville. She felt again the softened and crumpled paper advert, tenuously unfolding it, and saw the bold print upon it.

San Francisco.

The morning arrived. August 10, 1880. The hour was the pinnacle, not unlike Leadville itself, perched high atop the world. Soon she would descend from such an unnatural place and breathe easily once again.

Jacob had completed the last task she would ever ask of him. In the early-morning hours, he had brought her trunks to the new railway station, just above Annunciation Church. She had secured a private compartment aboard the Rio Grande for herself and Justine.

How could she have ever done without Justine? Not a day passed, in the wake of Stanley's murder, that Eileen did not ask herself this question. She had told Justine of her intention to leave Laurie and head west. She had not assumed anything of headstrong Justine, but said that, if she wanted to accompany her, Eileen would pay her passage.

Justine had regarded her long and hard with those dark-fringed, hazel eyes of hers. She nodded. "I told you my dream, remember? I mean to go to California and finally have my bistro." She smiled and patted Eileen's shoulder. "I'll go along with you. It's more fun to travel with a friend than to travel alone. But what are you gonna do in California, Eileen? Are you sure you're ready to make your own way, and leave this place of comfort and privilege behind? Do you really want to work again?"

"You think I'm a fool, don't you, for walking away from this?"

Justine shook her head. "I don't think you're a fool. But I know it's hard to start over unless you're chasing a dream. I'm lucky in that I have a dream driving me, and I don't plan on letting go of it." She smoothed the front of her dress and stood a bit taller. "I hope you figure out what your dream might be." She leaned closer to Eileen and said in a low voice, "And I know you're no fool."

But was she? What sort of woman walked away from the man who had raised her out of poverty and put her atop the world? What sort of woman left her husband? Surely it was always the other way around, was it not? Only low, sinful women left their men. What did the Lord think of her now? But then she laughed at herself. She had not been so concerned with the Lord's opinion of her when she was Stanley's lover. Why worry about standing at heaven's gate now? *Little fool.*

Laurie had no idea of her plan, she was certain. He had spent the last week locked in his study. She had seen Jacob knocking lightly upon his door, holding an amber bottle freshly procured from the chemist's. That amber bottle was like a siren, a gem of unspeakable beauty, a baby calling out to her. Her heart ached to hold it. Every inch of her skin cried out for just a taste, a taste. Her head ached, her stomach turned. She had to quickly run to the toilet and relieve herself again, again, the cramping of her insides doubling her over in pain. "I must go away," she whispered to herself over and over, and it became a novena. "I must go away."

There was no turning back. Like Justine, there was nothing here in this mountain town to restrain her, nothing to stop her from taking hold of a dream she'd once had and could have again.

Despite it being August, a chill in the morning air rattled her bones, and she wished that Jacob had put the buffalo fur in the carriage.

Laurie must have noticed her shivering, for he put his arm round her shoulders just as the carriage turned north toward the depot. Despite the early hour, the station was bustling with passengers, hired drivers, solicitors holding signs for boardinghouses, lodging, pubs, taverns, brothels.

"You can remain in the carriage, if you like. You need not stand on the platform," said Laurie.

"Nonsense. I'll go with you."

Through the depot entrance they went, followed by Jacob and Justine. Numerous people greeted them, knowing them to be the wealthiest couple in Leadville, if not Colorado, if not west of the Mississippi. Eileen laughed to herself; would she miss such attention? But she had never wanted it. The staring, manufactured smiles, and contrived kindnesses had always made her feel like a nervous child with a fistful of candy stolen from the sweet shop.

They found a place upon the train platform. All faces looked southward, the direction the Rio Grande train would come from. Soon enough, a steam whistle sounded in the distance, floating to their ears like a friendly greeting. This was followed by the audible, ceaseless chug of the locomotive, which grew louder.

The huffing black engine came into view. Soon she would be climbing aboard the train, but not just yet. First, there was a matter to attend to; she would meet Stanley's widow, look her in the eye, to be certain that all this was not some macabre dreamworld. And then she would give to her the cardboard box she held in the pocket of her burgundy velvet cape.

And then she would turn to her husband and say farewell. She would thank him for all he had done for her, but she would ask for nothing more. If he should protest, she would take him aside and reason with him. Surely he did not love her. He thought he needed her because his grief was so overwhelming. But he did not need her. He would find another. He could have any other, any other but her.

She broke her gaze away from the slowly approaching train and looked beyond the platform. Her breath came rushing out. The vista reminded her of some grand landscape painting. The snow-dotted mountains—yes, some snow lingered year round at the highest peaks—shone, the sunlight like heaven fawning over such beauty. Beneath such majesty, Leadville stirred like a frantic beehive. Smoke snaked and danced upward from the smelters and refineries. The spire of Annunciation Catholic Church, only nine months old, stood starkly against the scene before her. The cross reaching heavenward seemed to strain, to grow, longing to fly away, away.

As the train pulled up to the platform, Laurie suddenly grabbed hold of her hand, crushing it between his. She winced, but did not protest. She would allow him this.

They watched in a daze as passengers of all kinds disembarked, stumbling onto the platform as though stepping off a ship and onto dry land, squinting against the relentless sunshine. Finally, they saw a tall man with a blond mustache helping a woman out of the train. Beneath her simple black bonnet cascaded loosely curled flaxen locks. And when she raised her head, there was no mistaking that she was Mrs. Jankowski. The skin was pale, and her high cheekbones, blue eyes, and pert lips were like something out of an old fairy tale. Her gaze fell upon them. Dressed in a widow's weeds, she gave a slight curtsy. Eileen turned round to see that the platform had emptied. So that was how the widow knew they waited for her. Or perhaps she knew them better than they knew her.

Behind her, the man with the blond mustache assisted three children down to the platform. All were girls, perhaps between the ages of eight and three, dressed in black mourning. All clung to their mother's skirts, staring up at Laurie and Eileen.

Eileen heard Laurie's audible gasp as she stifled her own. The three little faces were beautiful and unmistakable. They were doll-like, feminine miniatures of their father, Stanislav Jankowski, Stanley Jones.

Eileen brought her hand to her cheek as a sudden dizziness came over her. Those girls, those three children, in a photograph, on a makeshift bookshelf, in Stanley's tiny loft room in the boardinghouse—oh god, she had glimpsed them before. A surprised laugh escaped her lips. *Fool I have been!*

The tall man came forward, shaking hands with Laurie, removing his hat and bowing to Eileen. He introduced himself in heavily accented English as Jonas Michelowizc, the elder brother of Yvonne Jankowski, the widow of Stanislav Jankowski. He explained that his sister and the children spoke little English, and he had traveled with her and the children as both chaperone and interpreter.

In an awkward moment of silence, Eileen, Laurie, the widow, and the children exchanged glances. Finally, Eileen longed for time to move forward, away from this scene, away from this place. She stepped toward the family, producing the cardboard jewel box from her pocket, and with a trembling hand, she offered it to the widow. "This is for you. Your husband desired you to keep it and remember him always."

As the widow gingerly took the box from Eileen's hand, Jonas translated Eileen's words into his Slavic tongue. The widow opened the box, inspecting the contents. She began to weep as she closed the box, bowing her head, saying something between sobs.

"She says that she is grateful to you for keeping this treasure safe, and for being a friend to her husband."

"Why have you done that?"

Eileen was surprised by the loudness of Laurie's voice. She faced him.

His eyes narrowed, his cheeks burned red, and she swore his nostrils flared. He looked as though he might strike her.

"It was mine to give," she said levelly.

"How could you?" he spat.

"Laurie, compose yourself. You are in the presence of a family in mourning. You are better than this."

She watched the struggle upon his face, but her words seemed to win the battle, for the tenseness soon faded. "Yes, of course. You're right, Wife." He turned to the family, who appeared wide-eyed and nervous. "Come, let us go to the carriage. Jacob will have your trunks brought to the Clarendon, where you will be lodging."

"We have no trunks, sir, just these bags," said the brother, gesturing to three worn carpetbags upon the platform.

Before Laurie could summon him, Jacob retrieved the bags and headed through the depot. Wordlessly, the group followed him to the carriage outside the depot.

It had to be done. She had to do it now. The train would depart in thirty minutes. Perhaps this was cruel, to surprise him so and to sever the tie with no warning, no preparation. He was volatile. She could see this in the way he clenched and unclenched his hands and pursed his lips. What might he do? Would he cause a scene? But she didn't care, she found, if he did so. It was all in the past already: him, their home, their marriage, Leadville, and its sulfur stench and streets teeming with desperate souls. So what if he were to make a scene? She could easily walk away, walk away, walk on.

The beautiful widow and angelic daughters silently filed into the carriage. Justine's gaze was upon Eileen, questioning, awaiting, eager to be away from the uncomfortable situation.

Eileen walked away from the carriage, toward a little stand of aspen trees. She stared at her tooled black boots upon the dirt and a few early fallen leaves like golden coins spilled from a treasure chest. Taking hold of the slender white trunk of one of the trees, she braced herself for the inevitable moment. Part of her longed to just run away like a child who knows she shall receive a thrashing. She took deep breaths, the cool morning air filling her lungs, which strained against her stays.

Storm clouds cannot be dissuaded from their path. The air becomes heavy with expectancy, the electricity as palpable as an animal in heat, the scent so heady one can taste it upon one's tongue. It is unavoidable, it is inevitable, it will come.

And like the march of time, it shall pass. But what it leaves in its wake, what change it shall wreak upon the landscape, is unknown. Eventually, the full scale and gravity may be comprehended.

Eventually, this would be a memory.

"Eileen?" She heard the pleading, obscured by the folds of amicable curiosity, yet still there, still real. "Why does Justine have her cat with her, in a basket? Is . . . is there something I should know?"

She let go of the aspen, slowly turning round to meet his gaze. She attempted to smile, but it was like offering encouragement to a child abandoned.

"I am sorry, Laurie. But it is time now."

He took a step toward her, gently shaking his head. "No."

A storm eventually passes. The fearful entity will fade, someday, to memory.

"Yes." She walked past him, toward the depot. Her steps seemed leaden, like when, as a child in Ireland, she had stumbled and struggled against the chill and pull of the sea, her progress marked by an oddly amusing sloshing sound against her cramping thighs. But then not her thighs but her knees, but not her knees but her calves, but not her calves but her ankles. Her steps were no longer hindered.

She had emerged.

AUTHOR'S NOTE

Twenty-three years ago, I moved west, from Boston to Denver. Aside from a semester abroad in London as an undergrad and my postgrad studies in Cambridge, UK, I had only lived in the Boston area. I was a newlywed, and my husband was born and raised in Colorado, so we were returning to his home state. It was nine months after 9/11, and the two of us found ourselves victims of the economic fallout, both laid off, with a mortgage. My husband had been offered a job in Denver, and I was ready for a new adventure, so we sold the condo, packed up a moving truck, and set off for the Rocky Mountains.

Like most kids who grow up in New England, I had this idealistic image in my mind of the West: desert plains, rolling hills and sharp mountains, sagebrush bushes, lots of cows, and the occasional dude in a cowboy hat. But the move was jarring, and I found I longed for crooked, potholed streets and grimy alleyways, three-hundred-year-old houses next to corner liquor stores and Dunkin' Donuts, good pizza, and just the proximity of many other humans. It was isolating in a way, especially as a woman in her mid-twenties who was looking for a job. I can recall the loneliness, listening to the ceaseless wind howling around our condo at the base of the foothills, and I began to think: What must it have been like to be a woman from the East Coast coming to settle in the West in the nineteenth century, alone in a small cabin with the wind howling and no way to escape the sound of it?

That thought got the creative wheels turning, and though I'd already begun what would be my first novel, I swore I'd circle back to this lonely theme—and I did, many years later. But in between the idea and the writing, I came across a little story in the most unlikely of places that further stoked the idea. My husband's great-grandmother, who had lived in the North Fork Valley of Western Colorado the whole of her life, had dedicated her elderly years to writing down all the history she knew of that lovely corner of the world. Her stories are filled with memories, delightful vignettes, and oral histories handed down through generations. One of these stories involved one of the first settlers of Crawford, Colorado, a man by the name of "Larry Barnard." She had heard told that Mr. Barnard had come from New York and had grown up very wealthy in style and luxury, but he was enraptured with the idea of the West, and so he gave all that up to pursue his dream of a life on the frontier. All she knew of him was that he had built a cabin at the base of Needle Rock, an imposing rock formation in Crawford, and that it was filled to the brim with all kinds of books. He was called "the Scholar of Needle Rock" and became a reclusive old man who kept mostly to himself. When he died, his body was shipped back to New York for burial. And that was about all the story she had.

In typical Boston fashion, my immediate reaction was, "Who the hell was *that* guy?" I mused over what would bring a son of New York fortune to become an old recluse in a cabin filled with books at the base of Needle Rock. Of course Laurie Barnard is fictional, of my own making, sparked by this little piece of folklore. That's all I needed to get running. Combining that with the original inspiration, of a woman from the East moving west in the nineteenth century, alone and isolated from everything she'd known, I had the spark for a novel. Obviously, my story found its own trajectory and concludes long before my characters are in their elder years. Novels often have a funny way of doing that, becoming their own little creatures that pleasantly surprise you.

All the characters in this novel are fictional. There is a brief mention of Horace Tabor, the mining entrepreneur and owner of the Matchless

Mine, as well as his infamous mistress and eventual second wife, Baby Doe. They were very real and very much a part of the rich Leadville history and legend. Mr. Pickering and his mistress, Dolly McGraw, are fictional but heavily based on the scandalous relationship of the Tabors. May's Dry Goods in Leadville was real, the very first incarnation of what we know today to be the May Department Store Company, which was acquired by Macy's in 2005. Mr. David May founded the shop along with his future brother-in-law in 1877. The Avalon mine is fictional, as are both Shay's Pub and Shay's Saloon—in New York and Leadville. The Clarendon Hotel did exist, though it has since been torn down and replaced by a gas station. The Leadville Opera House is real and still exists today, on once-bustling Harrison Avenue.

At the heart of this novel is an immigrant's journey. Eileen Maguire, like countless others before and after her, sought a better life and future in the United States. She followed opportunity as well as her own heart. In my mind, her story is the story of most of our ancestors who chose to take the huge risk of leaving home for the great unknown. Some of our ancestors did not make the choice themselves, but were inhumanely forced to emigrate for the enterprise of others. What binds all of us together, as Americans, is the desire and drive to pursue our dreams, and if we have children, to provide them the same opportunity. It is that intrepid ambition that still drives people this very day. Though some might vilify this drive for political purposes, it is truly our common bond.

ACKNOWLEDGMENTS

This novel followed a long and twisting path from birth to print. My thanks and gratitude go out to my Lake Union editor, Marilyn Brigham, who has steadfastly seen to it that this book becomes its very best. To my developmental editor, Tegan Tigani, I'm so thankful for all of your keen input and support, as well as our nerdy discussions of etymology. Your encouragement through the editorial process was very much appreciated. And as always, the Lake Union editorial team is top notch and they each deserve a raise immediately.

My literary agent, Danielle Egan-Miller of Browne & Miller, is The World's Best Literary Agent, second book in a row. I'm forever grateful for all of your wisdom and guidance. Mariana Fisher, foreign rights manager at Browne & Miller—I appreciate all of your thoughtful insights and advice.

To the Rocky Mountain Fiction Writers SW Denver critique group, I'm always and forever grateful that I found you all: Ed Hickok, Mindy McIntyre, Kathy Reynolds, Kathy House, John Turley, Liesa Malik, Joy Jarret-Meredith, Kevin Wolf. You saw this book in its newborn stages and you motivated me to keep at it.

Heartfelt thanks goes out to all of my author friends: Aimie Runyan, Heather Webb, Olivia Hawker, Kris Waldherr, Nancy Bilyeau, Piper Huguley, Paulette Kennedy, Michelle Tea, Zenobia Neil, Shawntelle Madison, Gwen Florio, Kate Moretti, Kate Quinn, Eliza Knight, Gill Paul, Karleen Koen, Megan Chance, Elizabeth Blackwell, Finola Austin,

Kimberly Brock, Margaret George, Lauren Willig, Jason Evans, and Donna Thorland. Now that's one impressively talented list of friends, I must say.

The world is a better place because of amazing librarians like Sue Nakanishi of Langley-Adams Library in Groveland, Massachusetts. It's also a better place because of wonderful independent booksellers. Many thanks to Amy and Randi at Brazos Books, Houston, Texas; Andrea at Molly's Bookstore, Melrose, Massachusetts; Sue and Harrison at Jabberwocky Books, Newburyport, Massachusetts; and Barbara and John at the Poisoned Pen Bookstore, Scottsdale, Arizona.

I would also like to thank the singer and songwriter Grant Lee Philips. For years I have enjoyed his beautiful voice and music, and found his songs to be a constant source of inspiration while writing this novel.

A special thank-you to Brian W Bartlett, friend and sensitivity reader very early on in the creation of this novel. And much gratitude to my most recent sensitivity reader and close friend, Josh Frey—your friendship is invaluable to me.

I am rich in friends who have always supported me and believed in me as I endeavored to make my writing dreams come true: Jamie Cole, Elizabeth Wallace, Erin McLaughlin, Sommer Louis, Jennifer and Kyle Solak, Stephanie Crochet, Joan Dwyer, Helen Read, Melana Ligertwood, Andrea Hindi, Betsey Denson, Alex Talbot, Lisa Beauchamp, Annie Couch, Marianne Huerter, Meg and Brett Randall, Margaret Ferenz, Leanne Dishion, Jane Kelly, Jennifer Evans, Jeanie Michele, Beth Caldwell, Katie Kassab, Brittany Clark, and Shantal Formia. I'm so grateful to you all for your friendship and support.

A very special thank-you to Lisa Polcaro, who has always been my champion. Together, as young teens, we would create fictional worlds together. You taught me to drive in your white 1978 Pontiac Grand Prix with a boom box on the front seat between us. You have always encouraged my creativity, no matter how wild it might be. You have read myriad novel beginnings and synopses and told me what worked and what didn't. You have celebrated even my smallest accomplishments. A few years ago, when I told you I needed to write about thirty thousand more words for a manuscript and I didn't know if I had it in me, you sent me a card that said, "You can do this!" along with a shoebox filled with tiny shreds of paper with printed words—literally thirty thousand words. You are just as crazy as me, and I love you.

To my readers: You have amazed me with your outpouring of praise and support. I cherish your kind words. Some of you even share your beautiful cat photos with me. My readers rock.

Speaking of cats, I would like to express my gratitude to my two fluffy guys: Kodi (Other Husband and Editorial Assistant) and Gus Gus, who, at less than a year old, is still quite kitten-like and full of energy, joy, and very loud purrs. And especially Princess Zora, who was the inspiration for Justine's cat, Zoe. I miss her sweet meows and fluffy black mane. She left us too soon—just as I began edits on this novel—and my heart still aches for her.

I am grateful for my family. Many thanks to my mother-in-law, Charline, who cheers me on and helps with the kids when I have to leave home for research, conferences, and now book signings. To my parents, Ann and John, who have always supported me in all of my intrepid endeavors, thank you and love to you. To my kids, Theo and Gigi, I am so blessed to be yours and you, mine, and I love you. And last but never, ever least, to my husband, Robert, whose unfaltering optimism and faith in my dream have carried me through many years and brought me to this stage in the game where I can say with complete conviction, follow your dreams and true love is very real. Thank you and I love you.

ABOUT THE AUTHOR

Photo © 2024 Jennifer Evans

Andrea Catalano is the author of the Amazon bestseller *The First Witch of Boston*, which was a 2025 Goodreads Choice Awards Best Historical Fiction Nominee. A historical novelist, Andrea holds a master of philosophy in historical studies degree from University of Cambridge, UK. Originally from the Boston area, she currently lives in Texas, with her husband, children, two fluffy cats, and many, many books. Find her online at www.andreacatalanoauthor.com.